— A
Magical Creatu...

Gruhits
H PE

DARREN FINK

Printed in the United States of America.
Published by Transfiguring Adoption, Orlando, Florida
Copyright © 2021 Darren Fink

Paperback: ISBN **978-0-578-88972-6**

First paperback edition: July 2021
Printed in the United States of America
Consultations provided by Felecia Neil
Cover art by Alexandra Brodt

Published by
Transfiguring Adoption
P.O. Box 782347
Orlando, FL 32878
http://www.transfiguringadoption.com

Contents

Chapter 1
Hope Lost

A door slowly creaked open to allow the entrance of a short fellow with a long tail into his dimly lit home. Another figure jumped up where she had anxiously been sitting by candlelight at a kitchen table. The little woman's two curly antennae poked out of her tightly pulled back hair, as she ran over to her husband.

"Oh, for Heaven's sake, Mrs. Snickelfritz! I thought you would be asleep..."

"Asleep?" she cried. "Mr. Snickelfritz, how could anyone sleep at times like these? This is not the evening for sleep. Not when there's news to be heard. I'll put on the kettle, and you can tell me all about your conversation over a cup of tea."

Mrs. Snickelfritz turned from the door and scurried to the cupboard for the tea kettle - or at least her version of a tea kettle. The five-inch tall woman began collecting various herbs and the kettle, which appeared to be made from a discarded piece of metal that had been refashioned into a tool for boiling water. Mr. Snickelfritz, standing at only seven inches tall, hung up his jacket on a nail head poking out of the wall. It wasn't a fancy way to hang up a coat, but it got the job done. Mr. Snickelfritz slowly walked over to a little chair by the kitchen table. Anyone watching him walk across the room could see that this little person was wrestling with stress and anxiety. He rested his weight upon the sturdy small chair. Even though it was fashioned out of pencils for the legs, it offered Mr. Snickelfritz the rest he needed.

Mrs. Snickelfritz skillfully pulled the boiling kettle off the stove and hurried to pour the hot water with sweet smelling herbs into tiny mugs. The mugs were made from thimbles which had the holes plugged up. She sat down at the table with her husband and studied his face by the candlelight. She had so many questions for him, but she wasn't sure where to begin. He had been meeting with the Master of the house and the Council for nearly four hours now. She was actually a bit nervous to hear of the evening's discussion.

As she thought, she noticed that her husband's face seemed to be less jolly. "You best take a nice long sip of tea, Mr. Snickelfritz," she said in her most soothing voice. "It's my special blend. It will calm your nerves in no time."

Mr. Snickelfritz complied and took a long sip from his mug. He carefully set the cup down while continuing to warm his hands with the mug. He wasn't sure if it was the warm tea entering his body, or the warmth from the cup that alerted him to the fact that he had been absolutely icy cold a moment before, possibly from the fear he felt. He looked into his wife's eyes and could see that she was expecting to hear him talk. She wanted news. Maybe if he kept quiet this moment would go on forever, and they would never have to think of anything—neither good nor unpleasant. It was useless. After years of living with his dear wife, he knew she would expect to know what was happening. He opened his mouth to make sure it was still even functioning. Mrs. Snickelfritz leaned forward to hear.

"They have decided to proceed as planned," he stated carefully. The color could be seen draining from Mrs. Snickelfritz's small face, and her long mousey tail fell so quickly that the bow affixed to decorate the end made an audible 'thud' as it hit the floor.

"This is it then. Is this really happening? Don't they think it is unwise?" she questioned her husband, full of anxiety. "We've already lost so much. Why can't they see that?"

"The Master and Mistress believe this will bring about hope," Mr. Snickelfritz reported with a monotone voice, which would lead anyone to believe that he merely was giving an account of what he had experienced and didn't believe in the feelings behind the words. "The Master and Mistress say this can be overcome. They say that hope is worth the risk."

"Yes. Yes. Yes. I surely believe that we all need hope at a time like this but… but… will we be safe enough? What if everything goes wrong?" she asked her husband as she could see his tail droop and sway back and forth with a nervous energy. She could be wrong, but she was sure she could see the stress and grief entering the wrinkles on her husband's face. She looked down at the table with sadness. At the same time, she reminded herself to put more wood on the fire to warm the house before they slept.

"STOP! WE MUST TRUST THE MASTER!" Mr. Snickelfritz abruptly snapped. Shocked, Mrs. Snickelfritz jumped back in her chair and knocked over her mug. The clanking of the metal against the floor seemed to break the small man out of his angered trance. He jumped down from his chair to begin dabbing up the spilled tea with this vest coat. "I'm… I'm so sorry, Mrs. Snickelfritz."

He stopped cleaning as he felt the small and tender hand of his wife touch his back. He looked up into her face as his wife gently pulled him to his feet.

"Here now. Here now. It's just a little water and herbs. We're both a nervous wreck, and we must get some sleep. Yes, we must," the little woman said, consoling her husband as he wearily stood on his exhausted legs.

"I'm… I'm sorry Mrs. Snickelfritz," her husband said with defeat in his voice. "You're right, of course. More sleep is needed for both of us. And of course you're right to question the Master of the house."

Mrs. Snickelfritz helped her dear husband make a few weary steps as he spoke. It was odd to hear him speak about questioning the Master. Mr. Snickelfritz was so loyal to him and not without reason. The Master and Mistress of the house had always cared for all within the walls and parameters of their property. They were lovely and beloved humans.

Mr. Snickelfritz stopped moving. Almost simultaneously, Mrs. Snickelfritz swore that she felt a brisk breeze enter in from underneath the door. Perhaps the cool fall air was settling in early this year. She would definitely need to put another log on the fire after getting her husband to bed.

"Listen to me, Mrs. Snickelfritz. I'm doubting the Master, yet he is so good to us and offers so much hope. And yet, I'm yelling at my wife. I'm apologizing for making messes I've caused from a tantrum. This isn't me."

"Now Mr. Snickelfritz, silence yourself. You know that all of us have been on edge and getting little sleep. It was different when we heard of the disappearances of folks in distant places, but with the disappearance of Mr. and Mrs. Schwartz from our own household… It's naturally too much."

Mr. Snickelfritz let out a sad sigh at remembering the account of the Schwartz family. There were once three families living in the walls of the Master's house, and now only the Dickelbuttons survived besides him and his wife. The two Schwartz children were taken into the home of the Dickelbuttons and seemed to be adjusting the best they could.

Mr. Snickelfritz let out a larger sigh of grief. Mrs. Snickelfritz noticed the lighting in the kitchen grow dimmer. It was a reflex to see if the candle was going out, but the candle likely had several more hours left before it would extinguish. She was definitely as tired as her husband. The chill of the night air had intensified for some reason. This made her begin to direct her husband toward their warm bed once more.

However, she paused as Mr. Snickelfritz said, "Those poor children. No one should ever have to suffer like that. None of us should have to fear for our safety. How can we stop this?"

"Now, now, quit despairing. We need rest. You know that anyone's hope is most vulnerable when they are tired. I should have made you take a nap earlier."

"I fear that a nap will not fix this situation, Mrs. Snickelfritz. I fear that it will come for all of us, no matter how much rest we have been given."

There was no mistaking it now. The room was dimmer and colder. Mrs. Snickelfritz quickly glanced around with a nervousness that she had never known. She could tell that something was in the house—their house. Then she noticed it: her breath was white in the ice cold air.

"This is the end I fear, Mrs. Snickelfritz. It will come for us. We will disappear. This world has no need for magical folks anymore…" Mr. Snickelfritz continued to despair in light breathy tones. He seemed almost to be in a trance. Mrs. Snickelfritz gasped as she saw the eerie darkness of the room center around her husband. First, she noticed that his feet seemed to be harder to see, then his legs, until his middle section was almost gone. It wasn't just darkness that surrounded him. The tiny woman could begin to see through her husband and looked upon the pictures on the wall that were behind him. Not only had It come to their home, but It was taking her husband.

"MR. SNICKELFRITZ! SNAP OUT OF IT! This isn't you!" she pleaded with her husband, hoping that he would listen to reason. But she could see he was already lost in his head as he listed all the unhappy events that happened over the past month. "PLEASE! Just let me get you to bed, and I promise things will look better when you awake! PLEASE! SLEEP DARLING! SLEEP…"

Sleep. That was the answer. Mrs. Snickelfritz grabbed the lukewarm kettle from the kitchen table and quickly snatched a handful of a different herb. She added the contents to her special calming tea as she rushed back to her husband. She hastily poured the contents down his throat. She held his mouth shut so that he could not spit out the tea, but there was barely a mouth to hold anymore. He was becoming more transparent and was barely in existence. She looked at his eyes for signs that the mixture was working.

"Please. Just give into the herbs. Let them do their job. Listen to my voice. You're fine. I'm here. It's your Mrs. Snickelfritz," she said in the most soothing voice she could as she fought back fear. Her husband's eyes looked panicked, wide, and crazed all at the same time. Mrs. Snickelfritz could actually feel the darkness fighting to take her husband. Both of Mr. Snickelfrtiz's eyes began to droop in a sleepy state. His breathing became more relaxed, and Mrs. Snickelfritz guided his body to the ground as his legs buckled. The mixture was working. Sleep was taking over.

Before he fell asleep, Mr. Snickelfritz's eyes showed that he was returning to his right mind.

"My clever dear. My clever Mrs. Snickelfritz. You were right. Don't despair. Trust the Master and Mistress. I was wrong to doubt… there is always risk," he said with a yawn. "But there is always hope. Hope will bring me back to you."

With these final words, the tiny man fell into a deep sleep. The room immediately lightened and warmed. Under normal circumstances, Mrs. Snickelfritz would be jubilant that the danger had left. However, her husband still lay on the floor of their kitchen, half vanished and half in the present. He hadn't ceased to exist like the others, but she didn't know what would happen when the effects of the tea left him.

She leaned over her husband and let the sadness of the situation take over and she cried alone.

Chapter 2
Journey To A New Home

Gruhit Brown looked out the car window. He watched as the city began to give way to corn and bean fields. Gruhit didn't much care for the country, but here he was driving out of the city to who knows where.

At only seven-years-old, Gruhit and his older brother and sister had lived in over seven homes in the last five years. There were years that Gruhit lived in one home to celebrate Easter, but spent Thanksgiving and Christmas in a new home.

He didn't remember all the reasons that caused them to have to leave. House Number 4 wanted to put his sister, Amarie, on medication to "help her focus." That's what they said anyways. Amarie was a ball of energy - all the time. When she wasn't swinging, swaying, or dancing, she was chattering about anything that popped into her head. When she wasn't moving or non-stop talking, she was humming a song. When she wasn't doing any of those, she was asleep. (House Number 6 used to joke that she had two modes: on and off.) Even now in the backseat, eight-year-old Amarie was tapping the armrest to the beat of some song that she was happily humming while looking out the window. Gruhit thought that both their caseworker, Constance, and their doctor had a suspicion that the household just wanted Amarie to be quiet. The medicine wasn't prescribed, and they were told to pack their bags.

House Number 7 asked them to leave after Gruhit's now 11-year-old brother, Chardy, kissed his foster parents' birth daughter. They were caught by the foster mom in the kitchen. The whole incident lasted only a few seconds, but it cost them a home. Gruhit thought that it was unfair, especially since the birth daughter had dared Chardy to kiss her. Chardy didn't even want to but told Gruhit he wasn't a chicken. Since that house, Chardy hadn't hugged his brother or sister.

There were so many questions going through Gruhit's mind as they drove. Would he be able to celebrate Halloween and Christmas in the same home this year? Did those other families ever miss him? Would he be living on a farm? Do they go to school, or do they just do things like milking cows all day?

Gruhit looked up at his caseworker, Constance, who was frantically speaking to her boss on speaker phone while she drove. Her boss sounded angry. Gruhit liked Constance, but thought that she was awfully fast. She walked fast. She talked fast. It seemed that to her there never was enough time. Her favorite phrases seemed to be, "Hurry up! I'm running behind," or "Let's hurry! We're going to be late."

"Constance? Do they milk cows all day on a farm?" he asked.

"Gruhit, I'm on the phone darling."

She went back to her conversation. It sounded like Constance forgot to meet with another child before picking Gruhit and his siblings up. Gruhit could hear her boss telling her she needed to report to the meeting location in fifteen minutes. Constance was begging for more time when her GPS suddenly spoke. "Rerouting!", it said. This was the fourth time it had done that. Beside her, Chardy rolled his eyes. He put in his earbuds and turned up his music—Chardy's way of not having to deal with anything.

Gruhit thought of more questions as the countryside gave way to a small rural town with a small square. Were they going to live in one of the apartments above the little shops? Do the shops decorate for Christmas? Do the people in this town know the Christmas songs he learned at his last school? Do the kids here even speak English?

"Constance? Do people speak English here?"

"Yes, Gruhit. They know English," she said with a tinge of frustration. Amarie began humming louder. She was able to sense when someone was getting frustrated or angry, and would try to cover up the frustration by being louder or happier. It's like she believed that her happiness and peppy tunes could fight against any negativity.

"Constance? Do people sleep on beds here?"

Constance was fidgeting with the GPS on the touchscreen of her car as it was rerouting them for the fifth time. Constance looked absolutely frazzled.

"Constance? Do people have the Internet out here? Is that why the GPS won't work?

Constance continued to drive slowly to an area with rows of houses. Gruhit tried to figure out what kind of house they were going to live in. Would it be a mansion or trailer? He was pretty good at guessing. However, this town was difficult to read. They just drove by an old and stately looking home. It was three stories tall and looked like it could fit four families inside. The house next to it was very small and looked like it needed a lot of repairs. In fact, Gruhit wondered if anyone lived in the home at all. The next house was a simple one-story that wasn't too fancy or too worn. It felt like he was experiencing the story of the three bears with houses that were too big, too small, or just right.

"Constance? Are there bears nearby?"

"GRUHIT! Now no more questions. I promise we are almost there, and this GPS is giving me trouble. I need to concentrate."

Amarie began to hum a little louder, and her song seemed to get a little peppier. Chardy simply pulled the hood of his hoodie over his head and stared out the window.

"We're almost there," thought Gruhit. It was becoming real now. He was nervous. It was like when an adult told you that you had to go to the doctor or the dentist. When the appointment is a week away, you're not that nervous, and it doesn't seem like a big deal. But when you get into the parking lot, you begin to wonder if you'll have to get a shot, or if they'll do surgery on you right away.

Constance turned left down a road. Again, Gruhit could see block after block of nice homes beside ones that looked in disrepair, or large and fancy homes next to simple and adequate homes. Gruhit's heart pounded as he wondered if the next home they passed would be theirs. He almost threw up when the car slowed in front of a small, bright pink home with several bird baths in the front yard. But the car had only slowed because Constance was consulting the map. This wasn't the house, but they must have been getting closer.

Suddenly the car began to shake slightly as the asphalt changed to brick. The sound of the car tires rumbling over bricks was enough to make the three children look up in attention. Even Amarie was quiet for a few seconds. The car pulled over to the side of the road. All Gruhit could see out the window was a humongous old factory which had been closed for years. It seemed to be caving in on itself. Vines were growing around the whole structure as if nature was claiming back its property.

"BLUE!! Blue, blue, bright blue. I LOVE blue," Amarie sang out in a silly little tune with over-the-top happiness.

Gruhit turned from his window and looked out Amarie's. There stood a large home with two shades of bright blue on the corner of a small street.

Chapter 3
Neighborhood At A Glance

Before Constance could urge the children out of the car, Amarie was already over the sidewalk of the corner lot and up to the dark blue stairs of the home.

"Blue! Dark blue stairs and a light blue door! Weee!" sang Amarie loudly. "Are the bedrooms upstairs? I want a window!"

Gruhit crawled over the seat Amarie had been sitting in so he wouldn't get out in the middle of the brick road. He didn't know why he was being so cautious. It didn't look like much traffic ever came through this way.

After closing the door Gruhit turned and stared up, up, and up some more at the tall house. Well, it really wasn't that tall; it just happened to be on the top of a small hill which made the house look taller and grander than it actually was. Although the house had two doors, they were both on the side of the house. Gruhit thought that was odd. Stairs lead up to both doors, but naturally the first door was more decorated and was bright blue.

"Amarie! Gruhit! Get over here and help me get this stuff out of the trunk,"

Constance said in a direct and frustrated manner. You could tell she was out of time and needed to get the children moved into the house. Amarie ran back down the stairs to the trunk of the car. Chardy was already pulling out the first of his big suitcases. One was full of toys and school supplies, and the other was clothes. Gruhit slowly moved to the trunk to collect his own suitcases.

Naturally, Amarie was the last to collect her things but would probably be the first to bound back up the stairs to the front door. Gruhit had no desire to meet his new foster parents before the others. While Amarie struggled to get her first suitcase out of the trunk, Gruhit paused to look at the street sign at the corner of the lot.

"Constance, why do they call this street 'Brown Place?'" asked Gruhit.

"What?" Constance exclaimed. "Gruhit, dear, I'm trying to help your sister get her things. You'll have to ask Mr. and Mrs. Wunder." Constance was doing her best to maintain a professional and caring tone while feeling the pressure of time.

So Gruhit was going to live on a short street named Brown Place. He actually lived on 19th Street and Brown Place because the house was on the corner. Gruhit looked down the small Brown Place street. It was interesting that the street names sort of matched the look of the area. The homes along 19th Street were nice, but ordinary in appearance. As for Brown Place, things got a little more interesting. For starters, there was the blue house he and his siblings were moving into. Then there were five houses down either side of Brown Place.

The blue house, which Gruhit had already nicknamed, "Big Blue," was on the left side of the street. There was a nice, but smaller home, next to his. It would have looked ordinary enough except for the gigantic fort in the backyard and the enormous amount of flowers that grew around the home. The fort was falling apart and rotting, so Gruhit guessed that the home hadn't had children in it for many years. It looked like it had been amazing at one time with its slides, climbing areas, and a large clubhouse on top. The whole yard of this home was full of the biggest and most beautiful flowers Gruhit had ever seen. Gruhit quickly decided that he would call this home "Fort Flowers."

Gruhit's eyes quickly skipped the ordinary and small white home next to Fort Flowers and began to focus on the fourth home. It was the same one-story style home as Fort Flowers. Although it had no flowers, it had strawberry plants all along both sides of the sidewalk. This house might not have seemed odd to Gruhit, except for the sculptures that were scattered throughout the front yard and backyard. Some of the sculptures were rock, but most were metal. There were small metal birds which hung from a tree. There were metal squirrels which were fashioned to look like they were climbing around the small front porch. There was one large sculpture in the front yard fashioned from a large rock of some sort. It was very shiny. Gruhit wasn't sure what it was supposed to be, but it looked like the flame of a candle that might be burning on top of a birthday cake. It appeared to be completely smooth with different metal panels fixed on it. The base of the sculpture was very wide and grew narrower as you looked up toward the sky. The whole art piece was taller than the house. The shiny metal reflected the sun and seemed to make the sunlight dance as it bounced off it. Gruhit decided he would nickname this home "The Lighthouse."

As Gruhit's eyes followed Brown Place past The Lighthouse, they came to an alley and then one last home. It was difficult to see. The trees, bushes, and other plants had almost completely taken over the property. There was a very small concrete path leading from the sidewalk up to the dark home. Because of all the plants blocking the sunlight, Gruhit couldn't tell if the house was blue or simply painted black. It definitely seemed to have the opposite feeling compared to Big Blue. Gruhit could see just enough though to be able to tell that this was the back of the home facing Brown Place. It was as though the house was upset with the rest of the neighborhood and decided to turn its back on the others. Gruhit couldn't figure out a nickname for this home. He decided on "Dark Meadows" for now until he had a chance to explore a bit more.

"GRUHIT! Quit daydreaming and get over here!" Constance's voice stole him from analyzing the neighborhood. "Amarie! Get your finger away from that doorbell! Wait for all of us to get up there!"

"I was BORN to push buttons, Constance," Amarie said as she danced in front of the bright blue door, knocking one of her suitcases over.

"I know, you do like to push buttons," Constance growled softly. She noticed that Chardy must have heard her, as he fought chuckling about the comment.

Chardy was just pulling his suitcases up the stairs when Constance closed the trunk and picked up a small plastic container of toys. Gruhit followed behind her and was staring up at the windows of Big Blue. The sidewalk was at the bottom of the small hill, which made him the perfect height to look into the small windows of the basement. Unfortunately, the glare of the sun made it impossible for him to see into the windows.

His eyes rose upward to the windows of the main floor. He noticed that they seemed to be taller than the windows in the other homes they lived in. All of them were tall except for one, which was sideways and looked like stained glass, though it was clear and didn't have any special colors. Gruhit noticed the silhouette of a woman pacing back and forth in front of this window. Gruhit began to think about his new foster parents.

"Amarie! Get your hand out of there!" Constance said with great force. She was somewhat out of breath as she ascended the stairs with the container in hand.

Gruhit instinctively looked over to see Amarie with her hand stuck in the dark blue mailslot to the right of the front door.

"Can I press the doorbell now?" Amarie said in a singing voice, with a bit of a whine.

"Yes. Yes. Yes! Press the button already. Gruhit, are you up here?"

"I'm right behind you, Constance," he said.

Amarie promptly pushed the doorbell button. Her face lit up as she could faintly hear the impressive *DONG* go throughout the inside of home.

"Ding dong goes the bell of my new foster home!" Amarie was obviously inspired to make up a song. Chardy rolled his eyes and silently wished his sister wouldn't push *his* buttons so much.

Gruhit looked to the left of the door and could see the silhouette of a man standing up from a couch. The silhouette of the woman could be seen rushing to his side through the other windows. Gruhit was beginning to get nervous. He always did at this point. There was no way of telling if these people were going to be kind or mean, strange or normal. By the looks of this odd neighborhood, Gruhit had a lot to be worried about.

As Gruhit was lost in his thoughts, he thought he noticed some movement out of the corner of his eyes. Several of the curtains from the main floor were swaying. A cat, at least he thought it was a cat, stuck its head into view and peered out the window. The cat seemed to be staring out at them as if it knew that the house had visitors. Gruhit looked at the small basement windows and thought he saw the blinds moving. Mr. and Mrs. Wunder must have had several cats. He rolled his eyes as he realized they would have to listen to Amarie sing about all the new cats for at least a month.

Suddenly, a cold crisp wind made the hairs on his neck raise up. He absentmindedly turned around and his eyes once again looked upon the dark, abandoned factory.

"Gruhit… Gruhit… come, child…"

Did he just hear a faint voice in the wind? He squinted and stared harder at a dark window of the factory. Did he just hear his name? Did he see movement at the factory?

The doorknob to the front door of Big Blue was turning. Gruhit quickly spun around to get his first glimpse of Mr. and Mrs. Wunder.

Chapter 4
Awaiting The Children

A man sat on an overstuffed couch in his living room, tapping his socked foot on the hardwood flooring. He glanced down at the floor and took note of all the knots and designs that had been in the grain. The man thought about how many generations of his family had lived in this home and had used this very living room to entertain guests and raise their families.

Mr. Wunder hadn't always liked this home, but he was thinking about its history a lot recently. The home was built in 1901 and had been updated often over the years. However, many of its original aspects, such as the hardwood floors and twenty foot tall ceilings, remained.

Suddenly, a woman with lightly tanned skin rushed into the room.

"Do I look like a mom in this outfit?" the woman asked, standing in front of him.

Mr. Wunder was a little taken aback. His wife didn't normally pay attention to such things. He could appreciate that she wanted everything to be just right when the children arrived. They had never had children in the home. To say that both of them were nervous would be an understatement.

"You look beautiful as always, Malda. But I don't think they're going to worry about the color of your dress or earrings."

Mr. Wunder usually called his wife by the nickname, "Mal," but during times like this he called her by her full name. He wanted to impress that he was serious about his words.

"I know. I know. I just... well... if we're really doing this, I want everything to be done right. I hope that we're making the right decision here," she said with both excitement and heightened nervousness.

Samme Wunder watched as his wife continued to look over her outfit. She wore a green dress with stars all over it. Her blond hair was done up with flowers and had a faint glitter about it. He never quite understood how she was able to execute a new hairstyle seemingly every day. She seemed to have a knack for it.

"Do we have lunch ready?" Samme asked Mal.

"I have everything out to make macaroni and cheese with hot dogs. I also have sliced carrots ready to throw on the stove. I thought we would keep things easy today," Malda stated as she looked up from her dress.

The large dining room and living room were connected. The only separation that existed between the two great rooms were two white marble columns on the exterior walls of the room. These two rooms had originally been built by Samme's family to hold extravagant parties. Samme's great, great grandfather was the owner of the factory across the street, which had once made shoes. It had been the most successful factory in the area. Samme's grandfather would hold expensive parties in his living room for famous guests and sometimes key employees of the Wunder Shoe Factory.

When Malda married into the family, she and Samme changed the inside of the home to display a more cozy atmosphere. She didn't want to scare visitors off with the formalness of the house. While guests often still congregated in the living room, the comfort of the overstuffed chairs and couches were known for their pleasantness and were usually able to relax someone to the point of almost making them fall asleep.

The dining room housed remnants of its stately past merely from the size and height of the room. However, Maldra had replaced the dark-stained furniture with brighter wood. All eight chairs that sat around the edge of the table were absolutely comfortable. There were short tables for food around the perimeter of the room. There was also a doorway from the dining room into the kitchen. As Samme sat in the living room, he could see the pot of carrots on the stove in the kitchen.

Although the dining room had plenty of natural light, Samme chose to strip the stained glass window of its paint to allow for even more light. He never understood the idea of painting the glass anyways. Samme had decided if he and his wife ever wanted a stained glass window, they would acquire colored glass and do the job properly. Still, the whole notion of painting the glass seemed so strange to Samme. Everything in the Wunder home had been planned carefully and executed with a sense of "doing the job right." Painting glass was out of character.

Samme watched Mal rush over to one of the tables along the dining room wall and pull dishes from the cabinet. She meticulously placed items around the table. It was early to be setting out plates, but Samme knew that Maldra was nervous. Working on little projects and making things look perfect gave her something to do. She didn't want to think about the nervousness of taking three children into her home.

Samme was nervous, too. They knew very little about the children arriving today. They knew that finding a home for them was an emergency. Samme and Malda had *just* finished their foster parent training classes a few days ago and didn't have an official license yet. The agency was unable to locate a home in the area that would take in three children together and were planning to place them in different homes. That's what made Malda and Samme agree to take them.

Once they had, Constance told Samme only the names of the children, their ages, and that they were in the foster care system due to severe neglect. He tried to press Constance for more information but quickly realized the caseworker knew little else about the case. She had seen the children in the agency office frequently over the years but didn't manage the children's case until a month ago.

Samme unconsciously tapped his foot faster as he became more nervous. They really knew little about the whole situation. The household believed in giving hope to all creatures when they could provide it, that hope was a powerful weapon that could change lives and transform people and whole communities. The Wunders would give these children hope if they were able to. But Samme had to admit, he was uncharacteristically worried about the area lately. There seemed to be an unnatural coldness surrounding their town. Then there were the disappearances. Could they be putting the children or their whole household in danger?

As Samme troubled himself with these thoughts, what appeared to be a large cat leapt onto the couch. The animal was larger than the average cat. Almost all of its fur was gray except its belly and paws, and also the fur under its chin that almost formed a small bowtie, which were white. The markings often made Samme think the animal was wearing a tuxedo.

"You always know when I need to calm down. Don't you, Kieffer?"

The animal didn't reply. It merely laid next to Samme. Mr. Wunder instinctively petted Kieffer's soft fur and felt the butterflies in his stomach come to a stop. Samme noticed that his leg had also begun to calm its tapping. He looked into Kieffer's eyes. Even though this situation might be difficult, he was reminded that providing hope was always worth the effort.

DONG!

The doorbell rang throughout the house. Malda gasped. Samme shot out of the couch. Both looked at each other. It was as though time had frozen and they were glued to the floor. Finally, Samme came to his senses and extended his arm to his wife.

"Let's get the door together," he said as he grasped his wife's hand. "For hope's sake?"

A nervous Malda looked into Samme's eyes and found the breath to exclaim, "For hope's sake. Let's go meet the children."

Chapter 5
First Impressions

Gruhit held his breath as the door to Big Blue swung inward to reveal a man and a woman smiling warmly.

There was a brief, awkward pause. This always happened when they went to a new home. No one ever knew what to say at this moment. The foster dad (if there was one) would usually speak first. While Gruhit waited, he began to size up his new foster parents.

Both were of average height for parents and appeared to be in pretty good shape. Gruhit wondered if that meant that they liked to play a lot or if they liked to work a lot. He hoped it wasn't the latter.

Gruhit couldn't tell if Mrs. Wunder's skin was normally a light tan color or if it was from time spent in the sun. It was definitely different from his and Amarie's dark skin, or Chardy's, which was a shade darker. Her hair was colored, so he couldn't tell what it was originally. At the moment it appeared to be blond with brown streaks and hues of purple - yes, purple - mixed throughout. She had flowers in her hair and a brightly colored dress on. Mrs. Wunder's eyes were as bright as the blue on the door of the house, and she smelled like baked cookies and treats. She didn't have on any makeup. Gruhit wasn't sure how someone could look so pleasant, but still have an expression that said, "I mean business."

As for Mr. Wunder, he was dressed in jeans and a t-shirt. He wore green socks with stars on them that matched his wife's dress. Gruhit inwardly groaned and hoped this wasn't a family that would buy them all matching outfits. House Number 5 had made them do that from time to time, and it was embarrassing. Mr. Wunder's green eyes looked kind but a bit more weary than Mrs. Wunder's, as if he was often up late worrying. There was a dark brown goatee beneath Mr. Wunder's soft smile. He had a full head of hair with gray stripes running around the lower half of his head. His skin was definitely paler than his wife's, and instead of smelling like cookies, he smelled of old paper and paint.

"Welcome to the Wunder house," exclaimed Mr. Wunder. "We're so happy to have you here as our..."

"Great! Fantastic!" their caseworker quickly interrupted. She knew her job depended on getting to her next appointment. "The kids are excited! I'm Constance. We spoke on the phone."

"The kids all have their things with them. Here." Constance abruptly shoved the container of toys and belongings she had into Mr. Wunder's arms. She continued to talk briskly while moving down the stairs toward her car. "I'll let you all settle in and get acquainted. I'm late for a visit. I'll call later."

Constance quickly stepped off of the stairs and stopped in the middle of the sidewalk as though she remembered something important.

"Children, try to help Mr. and Mrs. Wunder get to know you. Don't forget: I gave Chardy my number so you can call me any—..."

BAM!

At that moment, Constance was knocked down by a boy of about twelve running up the sidewalk. All three children's eyes were wide as they saw Constance fall in the grass. The boy didn't stop, but kept running down the street.

"Oh my goodness! Are you alright?" Mrs. Wunder hurried down to Constance. "I'm fine. I'm fine," Constance said briskly as she got back to her feet and sped to her car, "I didn't see him coming."

"Sorry about that. I didn't notice that it was 8:15 already," Mr. Wunder stated as he glanced at his watch.

Gruhit thought that was an odd response. Constance had just been knocked over, but Mr. Wunder didn't comment on that at all. They now watched together as Constance waved goodbye and drove away.

The moment was very real now. Here he was, Gruhit Brown, alone with his siblings getting ready to yet again begin the awkward process of moving into a stranger's home. He turned from watching Constance's car drive away to look at Mr. and Mrs. Wunder, hoping for guidance on what to do next. But the Wunders were too shocked at the speed of events and simply looked at the children like deer in the headlights.

Chapter 6
A New Room

"**M**r. Wunder?" Chardy's voice broke his new foster dad out of a small trance.

"Yes...yes... um... What is your name?" Mr. Wunder stammered as he was pulled from his thoughts.

"I'm Chardy," Chardy stated matter of factly, "S'pose we should go inside now and maybe find our bedrooms. At least that's what we do all the other times."

"Yes.. yes… inside… of course… let's show you to the bedrooms," Mr. Wunder gave another soft smile to the children as he stood sideways to allow his wife and the children to pass into his home.

The doorway actually led them onto a rather large glassed-in front porch. A ceiling fan was blowing down on them. Gruhit saw a long porch swing. He had seen swings like this in many yards, but never inside a room before.

The children passed through a large and ornate door frame. It was lined with carvings of small animals eating fruits and dancing together. Gruhit was only allowed a short time to examine these fascinating carvings. He noticed a carving of a squirrel climbing the trunk of a tree. The tree was full of acorns and the trunk had a huge knot in its center. Gruhit did a double take; he thought he saw the knot move. He quickly concluded that he must have seen the carvings' shadows move oddly.

They all stopped in the middle of the Wunders' living room.

"Go ahead and leave your suitcases here on the floor," instructed Mrs. Wunder. "I think it's best if we show you all the bedrooms, and we'll let you choose who is sleeping where."

Amarie caught a glimpse of Kieffer running out of a window ledge and toward the kitchen. "Kitty!" she squealed, then began to run after the cat. Mrs. Wunder stepped into her path.

"What is your name honey?" asked Mrs. Wunder. She squatted down to be at Amarie's eye level.

"My name's Amarie. I'm eight-years-old. I like the color pink and can sing any song that pops into my head. Watch this…"

"I would love to hear you sing later, Amarie. However, we are going to look at bedrooms right now," Mrs. Wunder said. Her tone was pleasant, but again, there was a firmness to it that conveyed she meant business.

"You'll notice that there are many creatures in our home," Mr. Wunder interjected. "If you hope to make friends with any of them, you must remember not to touch or grab them. Let them come to you."

"Okay, okay," Mrs. Wunder stepped in. "Let's get them used to the house before you tell them how to interact with the cat."

"You all have more than a cat, then?" Chardy asked. He was half-interested and half-confused that someone would have to explain to him how to handle a dog or a cat.

Mrs. Wunder ignored Chardy's question. Instead, she quickly stood up and looked at Gruhit. "Would you like to open the door to the first bedroom… uh… what is your name, honey?"

"Gruhit."

"Well Gruhit, let's take a peek at the first bedroom," Mrs. Wunder said softly and directed his gaze to the door off the living room.

Gruhit walked up to it and gave the handle a strong turn and push. He entered into a large room with high ceilings and a ceiling fan blowing gently down on him. The room had a second door which gave access into a small hallway. There was a closet along the wall to the left with a nice oak dresser built into it. Gruhit gazed around the soft pale green walls in the room. In House Number 4 the foster dad liked guacamole dip; Gruhit felt like he was surrounded by that guacamole dip which reminded him of the past home. There were two big windows on one wall with curtains on either side. Gruhit saw more carvings of strange animals playing with leaves and plants around the window frame. The room was simple, with a green rug on the hardwood floor. However, the bed looked slightly bigger than he was used to and very comfortable.

"We haven't decorated the rooms because we weren't sure what you liked," Mrs. Wunder stated. She was a bit worried the children might be disappointed with such plain bedrooms.

Gruhit really didn't care about the decorations. History had taught him that he wouldn't be staying in this home for very long anyway. However, he was very interested in the carvings on the window frame. He noticed that a large frog sitting under a flower beside a pond was carved into the wood. Gruhit walked slowly across the room to examine it better, and he could barely hear Mrs. Wunder as she continued to speak.

"This room is right across the hall from our bedroom," Mrs. Wunder explained. Gruhit ran his finger across the carved pond water, the frog, and up the stem of the flower.

SNICK!

Gruhit quickly pulled his finger back and stared at the center of the carved flower. This wasn't a shadow moving. He saw the circular shape in the flower close like a door, and he even heard it shut. He ran his finger over it once more and attempted to push the shape open, but it seemed solid.

"I see that Gruhit has found the toad carving," Mrs. Wunder said. "This is the best bedroom in the house to hear the toads sing at night." She walked to the bedroom window and peered out. "Our neighbor has the most beautiful little pond, and the toads just love to sing under the flowers."

Gruhit looked out the window and spotted a pond with a fountain that trickled happily over a few stones. He could see flowers of all shapes and sizes planted around the pond and dancing in the wind. He kept looking for the toads but didn't see anything. He did notice a rather large pink flower. It seemed to move around a bit more wildly than the other flowers. Gruhit's gaze grew more intense as the flower moved around so violently that it seemed like it might explode. Suddenly, a small creature burst out of the petals and hovered just above the flower. It looked like a small girl with wings and long hair.

"LA! LA! LA! Singing 'La!' like a frog at night!" Amarie randomly half-yelled and half-sang, jerking Gruhit's attention from the window. "I just made that song up. Can you believe it? Does it sound like your frogs? Maybe I can teach them to dance…"

Amarie continued her random chatter with Mr. Wunder. Gruhit turned back just in time to see a large butterfly fluttering around the pink flower. He noticed Mrs. Wunder kneeling beside him.

"Would you like this bedroom while you stay with us, Gruhit?" she smiled and peered into his eyes. "I could be wrong, but I think you might like the singing of the frogs."

Mrs. Wunder stood and walked back to the door. Amarie was still chattering about frogs, singing, and talking about anything that popped into her head.

"I think Gruhit is going to take this bedroom, if no one else wants it," Mrs. Wunder declared. Since there were no objections from the others, she moved on. "Well, let's continue to the rest of the house."

Everyone walked out of the room, except for Gruhit.

Amarie had grabbed Mr. and Mrs. Wunder's hands and was continuing her non-stop chatter. "These ceilings sure are high. Can I call you mom and dad? You're my mom and dad. I'll call you mom and dad. Let's go, Mom and Dad!"

Chardy was the last to turn and leave the bedroom. As he left, he made sure Gruhit heard him say, "Yeah. You can have this room. Wouldn't catch me taking the room right next to the fosters' bedroom."

Gruhit stayed in his room and looked out the window. He wasn't sure if he had seen a flying little girl outside, but he knew he saw the carving on the window close. At least he thought he did. He was pretty tired, and he had been told that he saw things when he was sleepy.

He remembered that his fosters in House Number 2 would tell his caseworker that. He was pretty sure that was because they were not supposed to be throwing the toys he got from his mom away. The toys were always a bit dirty though. Gruhit simply thought that maybe the toy cow and pig liked playing in the mud. He loved them, but his fosters were always upset and would take the new toy away before bedtime. He would never see it again. When he told his caseworker, his foster parents would always say, "Oh, Gruhit. You must have been too sleepy last night. We only took the toys to wash them." All the adults would then agree. Gruhit was willing to admit that he was seeing things incorrectly, but he never saw the toys from his mom again.

Thinking about his mom brought on a wave of emotions. Gruhit didn't want to be around anyone, and he stayed in his new bedroom. He looked out the window to look for the mysterious creatures. When he was sure he heard everyone walking up the stairs to the second floor, he allowed himself to cry softly.

Chapter 7
First Meal & House Rules

Gruhit slowly opened his eyes and peaked at his surroundings. It took him a few moments to remember that he was in House Number 8, which he had named "Big Blue." He must have fallen asleep by the window because he was now curled up on top of the big bed in his new room. The bed comforter was a darker shade of green than the paint on the walls. The bed was soft and comfy. One of the better beds he had ever had. Anything was better than House Number 1's bed—it smelled like several children had wet it.

Gruhit slowly sat up. He felt like he was waking from the deepest sleep he had experienced in a long time. He noticed that the Wunder's cat, Kieffer, was lying next to him and was also just waking up.

"Hello. I'm Gruhit. You're Kieffer?" Gruhit said. It was strange, but it seemed like the cat wanted to say something back.

Gruhit looked out the window. He could see the sky was a shade of pink and orange. He had slept through most of the day.

"Where is everyone now?" he asked Kieffer. He didn't really expect the cat to answer, but he honestly didn't know what he should do now.

Gruhit was surprised when the cat sat up and pawed at his leg. He watched as the cat went out the half-opened door into the hall. As he did so, Kieffer turned around and looked at Gruhit. It was strange, but Gruhit wondered if Kieffer wanted him to follow him.

Gruhit slowly climbed out of bed and went into the lit up dining room and living room. Amarie was dancing around the dining room table. She had found a pair of fairy wings from last year's Halloween costume and was setting the table while she sang.

"Hey, sleepyhead! You were sleeping for a loooooong time. You missed lunch. We had mac and cheese with hot dogs and carrots. I'm helping Mrs. Wunder right now. I'm setting the table. Only I'm not setting the table. I'm flying around the table. Do you want to fly around with me?" Amarie, as usual, had a lot to say.

"Where is everyone?" Gruhit asked. He realized that he was still a bit groggy.

Mrs. Wunder appeared from the kitchen carrying a giant cheese pizza. "Chardy is still downstairs in his bedroom, and Mr. Wunder is in his study. Amarie, please set cups around the table for all of us, and I'll go check on the rest of dinner."

Mrs. Wunder set the pizza down on the wall table by the pass through. She ran back to the kitchen to get pitchers of water and juice and check on the garlic bread. Amarie went over to a cabinet door in a table below the stained glass window and pulled out five blue plastic cups.

"Chardy is downstairs? So there's a basement?" Gruhit asked.

"Yup. Chardy wanted the bedroom downstairs, even though there are two bedrooms upstairs," Amarie started to explain. Her usual fashion was to keep talking until she was all talked out. "I don't think Mrs. Wunder wanted him down there, but Mr. Wunder said it would be fine. I thought it was strange too because the upstairs is so beautiful, and the bedrooms upstairs are right across from each other. I love my bedroom. You can see the treetops and roofs of the other houses and birds. That's why I need to have my wings on now, because I'm going to be a bird and fly like the birds that fly by my windows."

"Why didn't Mrs. Wunder want Chardy to have a bedroom downstairs?"

"Don't know. I mean maybe she thought I would get scared upstairs by myself or maybe she thinks that Chardy is scared of the dark. But she doesn't know Chardy likes to pretend that he likes dark and scary things even though the dark kinda scares him. He'll never tell a foster that he's scared of the dark though. I think that's strange. Do you think it's strange?"

"Is your bedroom like mine? What is the second floor like?" Gruhit took a seat at the table and hoped for a short response.

Amarie told Gruhit about the second floor. It was accessible by the stairs in the kitchen. At the top, Amarie was immediately met by a good-sized playroom that had a few toys and scads of books next to two bean bag chairs. On either side of the play room were two doors leading to two more bedrooms. One bedroom had blue, pale yellow, and brown walls, while the other had owls all over the comforter and sheet. Amarie told her brother she had chosen the room with the owls because they looked so cute, and there was a little white desk by one of the windows that would be perfect for drawing. The room was also right above Gruhit's, and she hoped she would be able to hear the frogs at night, too.

Mr. Wunder had pointed out there were vents near the ceiling on the wall above Amarie's bed. He told her that the air conditioner and heater were not hooked up to the vents, but a whole little world existed behind them. If she got scared or worried at night, she could whisper her fears into the vents, and they would be heard. Amarie wasn't sure if Mrs. Wunder liked him telling her this story because the foster mom changed the subject quickly. Mrs. Wunder began showing Amarie how to turn the ceiling fan on, as well as where she could put her clothes in the closet.

"I'm pretty sure I can see all the way into the next state because my windows are so high above the other houses," stated Amarie.

"Hmm. Probably not the next state but maybe the end of the neighborhood for sure," added Mrs. Wunder as she came back into the room with a basket of garlic bread and a parmesan cheese container. "Well, there we go now. I think we just need the water and juice pitchers, and then we'll be ready to eat dinner."

"Dinner time!" sang Mrs. Wunder loudly.

With Amarie and Gruhit already seated, Mr. Wunder soon appeared from the basement stairs in the kitchen to join them. After a short delay, Chardy came up the same stairs. Once everyone sat down at the table Mr. Wunder said a short prayer before they all began to eat.

Chardy barely said a word throughout the entire dinner. He slowly ate two slices of pizza and sipped juice from his plastic cup. He softly complained that the cups were plastic and not glass. He also judged the Wunders for serving them juice instead of soda, because "everybody knows you have soda with pizza."

"I'm sorry," said Mr. Wunder. "You're sure to see that things are different in this house than what you might be used to."

Amarie ate four slices of pizza and two pieces of garlic bread before stopping herself from eating anymore. Gruhit had a couple slices himself and was surprised he wasn't more hungry since he had slept through lunch.

After everyone was done, Mrs. Wunder went to get bowls of chocolate fudge sundaes from the kitchen

"This would be a good time to go over the house rules," stated Mr. Wunder cheerfully after his wife had stepped out. Chardy rolled his eyes. "We don't expect you to remember all the rules. It's going to take a bit of time for us to all get used to each other, but these rules will help."

"The first is that Wunders watch out for each other. We make sure everyone is safe and healthy. When we go out to stores and restaurants, we don't go off with other people, because if we don't stay together we can't keep each other safe and healthy."

"Rule number two," Mr. Wunder went on. "We don't hurt each other. Not just physically, like when someone hits you, but emotionally, like when someone calls you a name or bullies you. Wunders do not purposefully hurt each other."

"Rule number three. Wunders work hard and then they play hard. We are all responsible for helping get certain tasks done so that our family can function well. That's also a part of rule number one, we watch out for each other. However, once we work hard, it's just as important that we have fun."

"Those are the big rules in the house. What does everyone think?"

"What kind of work are we going to do?" Chardy asked without looking up from his plate.

"There are only two more days before the weekend. You won't even have your first day of school until next Monday," explained Mrs. Wunder. "So there won't be chores until next week, but everyone will be responsible for doing a couple of tasks every day."

"I could be in charge of singing people to sleep," Amarie interjected. "I could also take care of the cat, or I could walk all of the dogs in the neighborhood. Could I do babysitting for people to earn money? I could also…"

"Thanks, Amarie," Mr. Wunder said to stop Amarie from rambling on. "I'll remember those suggestions, but we will all figure out chores together as a family because…"

"We stick together. Ya, ya, we got it," said Gruhit with a half-smile and an eye roll. "What do we call you anyways? Do we call you 'dad'?"

"That's completely up to all of you," explained Mr. Wunder in a kind tone. "You can call me, 'dad,' or 'Samme,' or even 'Mr. Wunder.' It's really up to you."

"What's her name?" Amarie asked Mr. Wunder while pointing at Malda.

"My name is Malda," she stated. "Like Samme said, you can call me 'mom,' but I want to be clear that I… we do *not* think that we are replacing your parents. For Samme and I, being part of watching out for each other and not hurting each other means being truthful. We will always tell you what we know about your case, and we want to do anything we can to try and get you back home to your birth mother."

"Hmph. We'll see," Chardy said. He played with a piece of pizza crust on his plate.

Gruhit didn't like that Chardy sounded so mean, but he completely understood his brother's attitude. It seemed like every foster had a reason for taking care of them. Some couldn't have children of their own. Some wanted to feel good about themselves by loving kids. Some were trying to get closer to God. None of the fosters wanted him and his siblings to go back home to momma.

"Well, hopefully you will all give us a chance to prove ourselves," stated Mr. Wunder hopefully.

"Are those all the rules then?" Chardy asked in a slightly mocking tone.

"Like I've mentioned before, this is an unusual house, so I'm sure that as we all get to know each other better," Samme paused shortly to make sure he was choosing the right words, "we will need to introduce you to some of the other rules of the house."

Gruhit didn't know what Samme was talking about but didn't really care at the moment anyway. Malda had just passed around big bowls of chocolate ice cream with tons of fudge drizzled over the top. The three children had but one goal at that moment and that was to conquer the mountain of chocolate in front of their eyes. Even Chardy looked wide-eyed and amazed. It was the closest thing to a compliment that he had paid his new foster parents all day. Malda noticed that and considered it a major victory for the day.

Chapter 8
Bubbles In The Water Before Bedtime

Time seemed to blur for the children while they ate their sundaes. They were surely going to have to stay at the table all night to eat all of this. However, as Gruhit scooped the last melted bit of ice cream and fudge, only a few minutes had passed by.

"I'm so full!" announced Amarie in a deep voice. She stood up next to her chair and puffed out her stomach, "Look at my big ol' belly right now."

Samme looked up at the clock. It was nearly 9 o'clock.

"It looks like it is well past bedtime for two children," he said looking at Amarie and Gruhit. "It's time to get these dishes rinsed and get ready for bed."

"Do I have to? What time's bedtime?" Chardy curiously asked, hoping that he didn't have a bedtime.

"Children are allowed to stay up until 9 o'clock in our house…" started Malda. Amarie and Gruhit's eyes both filled with joy—it was later than their usual bedtime "... when they turn ten years old."

Chardy tried to stifle a little snicker as he watched his siblings' moods deflate.

"Children under ten have an 8 o'clock bedtime," Malda said matter-of-factly in her pleasant tone.

"Since it's 9 now though, I declare it bedtime for all," Samme said like a game show host.

Everyone got up from the table and placed their dirty bowls in the sink.

"Gruhit, we set up your toothpaste and lotion in the bathroom on the main floor," explained Samme. "Chardy, I know you're already set up downstairs. Do you need any help?"

"I ain't needed any help in the last four homes, so I don't need nothin' now," Chardy growled. He didn't care if anyone actually heard him. He slowly chugged down the stairs to the basement without looking back. Gruhit was a little hurt that his older brother didn't say goodnight. Actually, Gruhit just realized that he didn't really know where his brother was going because he hadn't seen the basement yet.

"I'll be down to check on you in a bit," Samme called after him.

"Amarie, there is a small half-bath on the second floor," Malda said in a soft voice to the little girl. She held out her hand. "Let's go upstairs and get you ready for bed."

Amarie gave a little squeal as she grabbed Malda's hand and dragged her foster mom up the stairs behind her.

Samme turned to face Gruhit. "Well, I guess that just leaves the two of us," he said.

Samme led Gruhit to a small bathroom with a shower, toilet, and sink. The bathroom was colored in varying shades of blue, and there were small figurines of dolphins around the room. There was even a towel with dolphins playing on it. Gruhit could see his toothbrush and toothpaste by the sink. He could also see his pick, brush, and lotion.

"Alright, Mr. Gruhit. Let's say we start by washing those hands and then move on to brushing your teeth," stated Mr. Wunder cheerfully.

Gruhit grabbed the blue-green bar of soap and washed his hands in cold water. He couldn't stand to wash his hands in anything warmer than cold water. Gruhit dried his hands on a dolphin that looked like it was having fun jumping out of the ocean water.

He then grabbed his toothbrush, which Mr. Wunder had already put a dab of toothpaste on while Gruhit was drying his hands.

"I'm going to run quickly to your bedroom and get your pajamas out of the closet. There is a glass of water to your right for you to rinse," Samme instructed as he stepped out.

Gruhit heard the faint *SNICK* of the light switch in his bedroom being flipped up, and he could see the light fall into the hallway. He knew that Samme was still close by, so he didn't need to be scared.

Gruhit brushed up and down and back and forth. He knew this was important, but he could not imagine a more boring task before bedtime. He turned the faucet water on and spit the toothpaste out into the stream. He then set his brush next to the cup of water and used his shirt sleeve to wipe off the toothpaste left around his mouth. Gruhit moved his hand to pick up the cup of water.

GURGLE!

A few bubbles suddenly formed in the cup of water. It reminded Gruhit a bit like water that is just beginning to boil in a pot on a stove. He carefully stuck a finger into it to check the temperature. It was cool. He looked a bit puzzled at the cup. He moved his hand to pick up the cup again.

GURGLE! GURGLE!

A few more bubbles spontaneously formed on the surface of the water. It was almost like the water was laughing at him. Gruhit withdrew his hand and stared at the water for several seconds. He inwardly kept telling himself that it was silly to be scared of a glass of water. Before he could think about the situation any further, he grabbed the cup with his hand and took a big gulp. He swished the water around his mouth quickly and spit into the sink. He looked in the mirror and saw the front of his shirt was all wet.

The water must have dribbled down my chin, thought Gruhit, as he also noticed that there were several small puddles of water on the floor.

Gruhit grabbed the hand towel from the wall and was about to clean up the mess when Mr. Wunder returned to the bathroom.

"Hey, looks like there's some water on the floor, huh?" Mr. Wunder said as Gruhit jumped up. "How did that get there?"

Gruhit could have been wrong, but it seemed like Mr. Wunder was more concerned about the water than he should be.

"I'm sorry. Some dribbled out of the cup. I was just going to clean it up," Gruhit explained. He didn't know how to feel. He was going to clean up his mess, so why was Mr. Wunder so concerned? Gruhit was getting worried when Mr. Wunder gave a small smile.

"No, no, I'm not upset, Gruhit. Don't apologize. I'm glad you were going to clean up your mess, but..." Samme paused before going on, seemingly searching for the right words. "When we spill water in the bathrooms, it's important that you just leave it... to clean up itself."

Samme watched Gruhit, hoping there wouldn't be any more questions from the boy. Gruhit just gave him a confused look.

"Oh... okay... um... so... I should just leave the water on the floor so that... it cleans up... itself?"

"Well, it... uh... will evaporate mostly."

"Okay..." Gruhit wasn't really sure what to say next so he just stared at Mr. Wunder. Samme stared at Gruhit. Gruhit stared at Mr. Wunder some more.

"Can I put my pajamas on while we wait for the water to 'clean' itself?" Gruhit asked, trying his best to not sound sarcastic and still be respectful. "Oh, I need to put my lotion on my arms and legs. I'm getting a bit ashey."

"Yes. Of course. Get your lotion on and then your pajamas. I'll be sitting in the dining room. Call me when you're ready for me to come back and tuck you in. And I have a special bedtime lotion that we use here. It's an old family remedy that helps you to sleep. Some swear it gives you the best dreams."

Samme withdrew to the dining room and sat at the table, hoping that their conversation wasn't too odd for Gruhit. As he sat there thinking, Mal descended from the second floor and sat next to him.

"Well, I got Amarie tucked into bed. How are you doing with Gruhit and Chardy?" She had a tone of accomplishment with a hint of exhaustion.

"I'm waiting for him to get his PJs on. We've already done teeth and lotion…"

"His lotion, right? He does need it for his skin."

"I had him use his lotion, but there's nothing wrong with using our lotion to help him sleep. I mean, can you imagine what they've been through today? I just want to help him sleep. Plus, we had an incident spilling water and I'm afraid I was acting a bit weird…"

"What? You didn't try to tell him about…"

"No, no. It's been a big enough day for them as it is. We'll explain things, but just not tonight. Like we agreed. At any rate, I think he deserves a good night's sleep, don't you?" Samme said, looking for agreement.

Malda wearily nodded her head before saying, "Well, I have one better than spilt water. Not only was there water on the floor of the bathroom upstairs, but there were some paper clips next to the sink."

"Paper clips *and* water? Did she say anything? What did you do?"

"I'm glad that Amarie is a chatterbox… At least I was glad during that situation that she didn't stop talking. While she was making a song about the water, I hid the paper clips." Malda uncurled her fisted hand to reveal several ordinary silver paper clips.

Samme let out a small exasperated sigh. "I suppose we can be grateful that the evening was only that eventful. We will have to explain things, Mal."

"I know. I just wish we could give them something that looked normal, you know?"
Just then, they heard Gruhit's door creak open slowly.

"Mr. Wunder? I have my pajamas on now," Gruhit said. He really had no desire to travel into the now darkened home by himself.

After a brief moment, Samme appeared by Gruhit's bedroom door with Mal standing behind him. "Well, let's say that we get you tucked into that big comfy bed," Samme said cheerfully.

Gruhit walked quickly over to his new bed and jumped up on it. Samme went to the head of the bed and pulled back the comforter and sheets as Gruhit jumped over the passing articles of bedding. The sheets were yet another shade of green with patterns of frogs on them. Gruhit lay down as Samme covered him in the frogs and the dark green comforter. Everything felt so soft. The bedding smelled wonderful and clean.

BAM!

Gruhit sat up straight in the bed. Samme quickly turned his gaze to the door as Malda spun around to look out into the dark hall.

"Hello?" Malda said into the darkness. Gruhit thought for a moment that she sounded scared.

There was no answer, but shuffling could be heard from the dining room.

"Hello?" Malda called out a second time.

"Does the house feel cooler?" Samme whispered.

Gruhit barely caught what Mr. Wunder said. It was an odd thing to say at this moment. Malda simply shook her head no. Malda suddenly turned her face toward Gruhit and Samme. She was now smiling.

"Amarie? Is that you out there?"

"Boo!" Amarie yelled as she jumped into view.

"What are you doing out of bed?" Mal asked.

"I… I just…" Amarie stammered. She didn't want to admit she was scared of being in a new bedroom and was trying to come up with a good story for being downstairs. "I wanted to tell everyone 'I love you,' and 'Goodnight.'"

But Malda guessed what was happening. "Amarie, Samme was about to put a special sleepy time lotion on Gruhit and tell a story."

"I was?" Samme looked surprised.

Mal looked at the two children, "Samme has the best stories. What do you say, Amarie? Would you like to hear a story?"

"Only if it can be about a princess and a frog and they learn how to sing together and…" Amarie began one of her nonstop conversations when Malda interrupted.

"Good, let's both sit on the floor together and listen," Malda said. She sat at the foot of Gruhit's bed and patted the floor next to her.

As Amarie sat down, Gruhit lay back down in his bed. Samme dug into his jeans' front pocket and pulled out a small vial full of a purple liquid.

"Remember when I told you that I had a special sleepy time lotion?" Samme asked. "May I put some on your forehead and forearms?"

"What is it? Gruhit asked. "Is it gonna hurt?"

"Absolutely not, it's an old family remedy. It's supposed to help you calm down and have good dreams."

"Really? How's it going to do that? I don't have good dreams. Not usually."

"Well, you really don't have anything to lose, then. If I'm right, you'll have good dreams tonight. If I'm wrong, you'll just still have your typical dreams. Can we try it?"

"I guess so… but if it doesn't work I won't try it again."

"Sounds like a plan," Samme said. "Sometimes progress just takes one decision to try something new and hoping that things will get better." Samme started to gently massage the purple substance into Gruhit's arms and forehead.

"Do you want to try some of Samme's 'family remedy' too, Amarie?" Mal asked Amarie.

"Is he sure it's safe?" whispered Amarie.

Malda's smile widened slightly. "Yes, I use it sometimes myself. It helps me to feel more relaxed when I'm nervous, and I'm sure I've avoided having awful nightmares when I've used it."

Amarie nodded. Samme handed the vial over to Mal. Gruhit and Mal noted that this was the quietest they had seen Amarie all day. They knew it was only because Amarie was nervous.

Malda began dabbing small amounts of the purple lotion on her fingers. "I'm going to start with your forehead, okay?" Mal explained so Amarie would be less frightened. Mal then moved onto her forearms just like Samme did with Gruhit. Amarie thought the lotion was a bit cold, but she grew more comfortable when she could see that it didn't hurt. The massaging motions made her feel better. It felt like her world was slowing down.

"Well, Mr. Wunder, we are all ready for bed. Except I think we were all promised a bedtime story," Mal said.

"Still? I'm not sure I know any... Really."

"Oh, come on now. You have the best stories. Even ones about this area we live in."

"Mr. Wunder, you said that this house was 'unusual' earlier," Gruhit spoke up softly. "Do you have a story about this house? Why did you call it unusual?"

Mr. Wunder gave a small chuckle as though he was keeping something back. "Tell you what. I do have a story for tonight. It's the story of how children began to pretend."

Chapter 9
How Children Learned To Pretend

S amme took a step away from the bed and dimmed the lights a tad.

"Long ago, there lived a powerful entity which people came to call Victus. From him, everything in existence was made. This included all the planets of the universe and all the creatures upon the Earth. Of the many creatures that Victus created, a special group of winged fairies were chosen to be his messengers and to speak on his behalf. Victus loved all of his creatures, but the large winged fairies held a special place within existence. As for his other creations, some we see in zoos, or in our neighborhoods. Other creatures are magical, and people only talk about them in stories."

"But where do the magical creatures live?" interjected Amarie.

"Well, that's the question, isn't it? Where are all of the magical creatures? The answer to that question lies with the making of human beings," Samme continued. "When everything was still young, Victus wanted to create a creature whom he could talk with, form independant ideas, and create like himself. Thus, Victus created the first humans.

"In the early days, humans were very good for all the Earth. They helped to tend the land and animals. Victus would talk daily with his humans and learn about new songs, stories, or inventions they made that day. Victus was impressed with his humans and his fondness and love for these creatures grew more and more. In those days, there was peace and well-being throughout the Earth. Everyone was grateful to Victus for giving them life. Victus expressed his love for his creatures by showering them with a magical dust, which humans called sundust because it traveled to the Earth on the sun's rays. The dust allowed the plants to flourish so that there was always plenty of food and made the waters safe to drink. It also fended off disease and illness so that all creatures could exist and live long lives."

"This can't be a real story. Nothing is that perfect today," Gruhit stated.

"It's true. Unfortunately, like every story, there is always a problem," Samme explained with a more somber tone. "One of the large winged fairies was the most beautiful of all the magical creatures. Her name was Fridgita Mortes, and she was in charge of all the messengers of Victus. When she was first created, she loved Victus and all his creatures. She was well known not just for her beauty but also for her kindness and helpful spirit.

"When humans were created, Fridgita thought the human poems were so clever, but they soon upset her because they discussed their beauty instead of hers. The human songs were quickly sung by many creatures, and they didn't want to hear her voice. The worst of all was that they captured some of the attention of Victus, and Fridgita began to grow jealous of the affection that Victus showed the humans.

"As jealousy grew and contorted her thoughts and being, she began to poison the minds of some of the other fairies. She never meant to create an uprising against Victus, but before she knew it, she was the leader of a rebellion. Over the years people never heard from the famed Fridgita, and her beauty was lost to folktales and stories.

"Fortunately, for the people and creatures of Earth, Fridgita was created to be a messenger and not a warrior. Her power could never overrule Victus. Fridgita knew this and forever sought out ways to undermine her commander. One day, she had a sly idea to hurt Victus by turning his beloved humans against him. She traveled to the Earth and appeared to a young couple who were tending to the creatures living on their land. The couple had never seen a winged fairy as large or as beautiful as Fridgita. They were sure that she must have been a messenger sent from Victus.

"Fridgita was pleased at the respect and power she had over the couple. She slyly told them she meant to help free them from the imprisonment of Victus. The young couple was confused. They knew Victus provided the sundust, which provided the whole Earth with plenty of food and good health.

"Fridgita warned them that Victus kept them imprisoned by their reliance on the sundust. She told the young couple that surely creatures such as they had the power and strength to be as clever and mighty as the great Victus without the aid of this mystical element. So long as the humans relied on Victus, they would never be anything more than his little pets.

"Fridgita left the human couple, having successfully deceived them. The couple began meetings with their neighbors, and soon a large portion of humanity had devised a plan for using Victus' own magical creatures to create a water barrier around the whole Earth which would shield it from the sundust.

"Heartbroken, Victus saw his creation begin to change over time. Illnesses and hunger were introduced to both humans and animals. Plants experienced droughts. People began to know emotions such as anger, greed, jealousy, and fear. Magical creatures, which depend on sundust to exist, began to gradually disappear from the world. The people hated Victus more and more as suffering became known, and thus hunted the magical creatures who reminded humans of him. The creatures were forced to hide in fear. All of this pleased Fridgita as she watched her commander's creation become twisted and deadly.

"However, Victus could never be undone by Fridgita. He was saddened by the aftermath of the deception that had taken place, but he still loved his creation. While looking upon the shield of water surrounding the Earth, Victus brought into being small birds to live on Earth. The Fleet Birds of the Shining Star are special. Victus knew that while his sundust couldn't penetrate the water shield, the sun's rays could. He made his magical birds with the ability to feed on the sun's rays for nourishment instead of berries or seeds. While the birds stay within the sunshine, their luminescent feathers sparkle in the light, producing sundust that falls to the Earth.

"The return of sundust restored some things, but great damage had already been done. Some plants had been completely destroyed, and we will never see their fruits again. Diseases were already thriving throughout the world. People stole from each other, hurt each other, and went to war against each other.

"Thankfully, the creation of the fleet birds provided more than enough sundust to strengthen the remaining magical creatures. They didn't need to fear going out of existence. However, the vile nature of some humans made it necessary for them to stay hidden away.

"But not all humans had become hostile toward Victus and each other. Some remembered the old ways and how the world was before. These people passed stories down to their children, and their children told them to their children and so on. Some people even knew and befriended magical creatures. However, the more people chose to forget about Victus, the more people forgot about magical creatures and the old ways of the world.

"Slowly the stories that were first told to recount history were then told to children at bedtime. Children, however, began to act like the magical creatures in their play. That is how children first began to pretend."

Samme broke out of his trance. He looked around the room to see Amarie leaning against Mal fast asleep. Gruhit was still looking up at Samme, but sleep was heavy in his eyes.

"Samme?" Gruhit really wanted to fall asleep but had a question.

Samme leaned over until his face was hovering a couple of feet above Gruhit's.

"Samme, what happened to Fridgita Mortes?"

"She has nothing to worry about tonight. I'll tell you more about it some other time if you'd like." Samme smiled at Gruhit tenderly. "Right now it is important that we both get some sleep. You are in a home that will keep you safe, Gruhit. Sleep now."

Gruhit didn't want to sleep. He wanted to know more about the story. But sleepiness had already claimed too much of his mind. He saw Mal pick Amarie up and begin carrying her back to the bedroom upstairs. He looked back to see Samme standing next to his bed before he allowed the sleepiness to take him. He was peacefully asleep with the faint sound of toads chirping outside his window.

Chapter 10
Tangled Hair, Marked Faces, & Talking Cats

Gruhit slowly opened his eyes. He could see different shades of green everywhere. He lay perfectly still in his bed. For a brief moment, he didn't remember where he was. This often happened when he first moved to a new home. He hated this feeling, because he didn't know if he was safe or not.

When he remembered he was at the Wunders' house, he sat up in bed and realized he was hungry. He started to swing his legs over the side to go look for food. His whole body felt stiff. He must have slept in the same position most of the night. The lotion Samme used must have worked because Gruhit could never remember sleeping this long or that deep in a new home. He didn't have good dreams last night, but he didn't have bad dreams either. Actually, he really couldn't remember what he dreamed about. This was fine with Gruhit. The first night in a new home he usually had terrifying nightmares. He would settle with not remembering anything.

Gruhit jumped out of the bed and heard his feet hit the hardwood floor. He began walking toward his door. His bedroom door had not been closed all the way, but was open a crack. He thought he heard faint voices whispering to each other.

"I'm just surprised is all," Gruhit thought he heard Samme say.

"Well, believe it. Here I thought I was going to have to guard Gruhit all night, or maybe Amarie. No, it was Chardy I guarded. He had trouble sleeping as soon as you finished checking on him." Gruhit didn't recognize this voice.

"That doesn't surprise me, actually. He refused to put on the dipsy toad salve," Samme explained.

Dipsy toad salve? Was that the stuff Mr. Wunder put on his head last night? Gruhit was kind of grossed out. He made a small gagging noise. He tried to stifle it, but it was loud enough for Samme to hear.

"Gruhit, are you awake?"

Gruhit walked slowly into the dining room. He tried his best to act like he hadn't been listening. He gave a big yawn and rubbed his eyes. Gruhit surveyed the dining room quickly to see Samme sitting there with a sketchbook in his hand. Mal was emerging from the kitchen with a big plate of pancakes. She placed them in the center of the table. A radio was playing softly, and a commercial was just ending. It now gently played jazz music throughout the first floor.

"Good morning, sleepy head," Mal said to Gruhit as she was making her way back to the kitchen. "Samme just made some pancakes. Are you hungry?"

Gruhit nodded and walked over to the table, keeping his eyes on Samme. Had he heard Samme talking with Mal? No, it was definitely another man's voice. Maybe it was just the radio?

"Are you okay, Mr. Gruhit?" Samme asked when Gruhit wouldn't stop looking at him. "Did you sleep okay?"

"Yes," Gruhit stated simply. He tried to think of where the other voice could have come from but got distracted by the smell of pancakes.

Gruhit remembered how hungry he was. He turned to see plates set all around the table with a large plate piled high with large, round, steaming hot pancakes. There was a small tray with butter on it and a few bowls of various fruits like strawberries, blueberries, and raspberries. Mal came back into view with a bottle of syrup and a large bowl full of scrambled eggs. Everything smelled simply delicious.

"Go ahead and take a seat, Gruhit," Mal suggested. He quickly chose a seat across from Samme so that he could keep an eye on him. He passed Kieffer sitting happily on a chair.

"Go ahead and get some pancakes and eggs. You, Mal, and I can start eating together. I want to let your brother and sister sleep in as much as they would like," Samme explained. "So the lotion worked last night, then?"

Gruhit gave a small nod as he concentrated on loading his plate. He really didn't feel like talking right now. Samme began adding eggs and pancakes to his plate as well. Mal sat beside Samme and set down two hot cups of coffee.

"What would you like to drink, Gruhit? There is water, milk, or orange juice," Mal said.

"Orange juice… er… please," Gruhit answered, almost forgetting to say "please." His birth mother had always stressed that he should say, "please," but he still forgot to say it sometimes. He hoped that didn't mean that he was forgetting about his mom.

Samme stood up from his chair. "I'll just get the pitcher and bring it back here for everyone."

Mal got food for her plate and took a long sip of coffee. Gruhit took the syrup and poured a bit on his pancakes. He tried to make sure that the syrup didn't get to his eggs, but he had added too much. Samme returned with a pitcher of orange juice and filled a cup half full for Gruhit. Samme sat back down in his seat and took a shorter sip of his coffee. Gruhit absolutely loved the smells he was experiencing at the moment. He took the fork from beside his plate and used it to cut a small piece of pancake covered in golden syrup.

As the three of them ate, Gruhit felt brave enough to ask, "Mr. Wunder, who were you talking to earlier?"

"I was talking to Mal while we were making breakfast."

"I mean… I heard you talking to another man. I think I heard my name."

"Hmmm. Well, I…"

THUNK!

All three of them heard loud heavy footsteps descend the stairs. The noise stopped and then Amarie's figure came into view. They fought hard not to laugh at what they saw.

"Mrs. Wunder, I think my sleep cap fell off last night." Amarie held up her sleep cap and pointed up to her hair.

It was a tangled mess. Gruhit thought that his sister could be almost a foot taller with her tangled hair. She looked like she had a clown's afro. Gruhit had to put his hand over his mouth to keep from laughing out loud.

"Come over here and sit down," Mal said with a small chuckle in her voice. "We'll have to take care of your hair later. At least it looks like you slept well, right?"

"I must have," Amarie stated softly. She still sounded like she was half asleep. "Someone put paperclips up all over my bedroom, and I didn't hear you do it at all."

Gruhit stopped chuckling and looked at his sister, confused. He looked over at Mr. and Mrs. Wunder to see how they reacted. Both of them looked up at each other.

"Let's finish eating breakfast and get ready for the day," Samme said. "Then I think we better all have a meeting about a few more explanations and rules of the house."

More rules? Gruhit liked his new fosters well enough, but he wasn't a fan of lots of rules. House Number 4 had a lot of rules. They had rules about what clothes could be worn on various days. They had rules about what time breakfast had to be eaten or else you didn't get any that day. They had rules about what time and where you had to wash your hands. They even had rules for which bathroom each child had to use and at what times they had to shower. They might have had their reasons for the rules, but Gruhit simply couldn't remember everything. It was difficult to follow all the rules and not accidentally get into trouble.

Amarie sat on a chair at the table and stared at the food sleepily. She almost appeared to be willing the food onto her plate so that she didn't have to move. Gruhit enjoyed mornings because he was more active than his sister. It took Amarie an hour or so until she started her non-stop chatter and singing.

Gruhit resumed eating his breakfast. Amarie finally gave into her hunger and started putting pancakes on her plate. Mal continued to eat some strawberries on her plate while silently chuckling at the size and look of Amarie's hair.

As Amarie scooped some eggs onto her plate, she saw Gruhit still staring at her. "Whuuuut? You don't have to keep starin'!" Amarie said exasperatedly.

"Sorry, I just never seen your hair so crazy before," Gruhit said.

"Well, I can't help it. I was so tired last night. I think that lotion stuff helped me sleep because I was havin' good dreams about small, cute little fairies all night long."

"So the lotion helped you too, Amarie?" Samme inquired with a smile.

"Alright, alright, it *might* have helped us sleep last night," Gruhit conceded begrudgingly. "But I don't remember any dreams from last night."

"But you don't remember any nightmares either, do you?" Samme quickly asked.

"What was in that stuff, anyways?" Amarie asked as she poured syrup on her pancakes.

"It was toads and stuff," Gruhit interjected.

"That's gross! How do you know anyways?" Amarie shot back at Gruhit.

"I heard him talk to a man about it this morning," Gruhit shot back at Amarie. Then he realized he was betraying himself about having overhead Mr. Wunder.

"You heard me talking?" Samme asked, surprised.

"He was talking about all of us. I heard him," he said.

"Who was he talking to?" Amarie asked.

"I don't know. It sounded like another man. It wasn't her," he looked at Mrs. Wunder, who was surprised by the outbreak of accusations. Gruhit asked again, "Who were you talking to, Mr. Wunder?"

The children looked at Mr. Wunder. He looked uneasy and took a sip of his coffee. Mrs. Wunder looked just as uneasy, but didn't say anything. The silence seemed to last forever. Gruhit continued to stare at his new fosters, waiting for an answer. Amarie chewed on her pancakes while she joined her brother in the stare-off.

"If you must know, he was speaking to me." The children's heads slowly turned to face Kieffer, who was sitting up on a chair next to Gruhit. "But let the record show, I think it is very rude for people to be listening in on others' conversations."

Gruhit and Amarie's mouths dropped open wide in disbelief. The pancakes that Amarie had been chewing fell out of her mouth and onto the table. Mal put her face in her hands with embarrassment. She definitely did not want things to play out this way.

"Excuse me!" Chardy said with a raised voice. In all the commotion, no one had heard him come up the stairs. "Will someone please tell me what is going on here?"

Mal gasped a tiny bit. Chardy's hair was tangled and knotted and stood even taller than Amarie's. The part that caught the most attention was that Chardy was pointing at his face, on which someone had drawn glasses and a mustache with a black marker.

The room was silent. Amarie and Gruhit stared at their older brother in disbelief. Suddenly, Amarie started giggling. Due to the awkwardness in the room, the giggling seemed funny to Gruhit and made him laugh a bit. This only made Amarie laugh harder until Mr. Wunder began to chuckle too.

Mal was the only one who was still feeling deep concern for Chardy. "Oh Chardy, I thought this might happen. This is why I didn't want you sleeping in the basement."

"What does this have to do with being in the basement?" Chardy demanded in a loud voice.

"Watch your tone with the Mistress of the house!" Kieffer shot at Chardy.

Chardy took a half-step backward as his eyes simultaneously grew large with shock.

"Th… the cat just spoke," stammered Chardy.

Mal quickly put her arms around Chardy, who was so confused that he didn't try to stop her. Mal moved Chardy to a chair before he passed out from fright.

"Okay, everyone, let's settle down," Mr. Wunder said to take control of the situation. "Here is what we are going to do. We are going to sit here and finish breakfast, while Mal and I tell you everything you need to know about our 'unusual' house."

Chapter 11
Explanations, Please

Chardy, Amarie, and Gruhit all sat at the table under the clear stained glass window. Chardy didn't make a move to get any food. There was simply too much information to take in right now. He was scared and didn't want anyone to know it. While he was staring across the table at Mr. Wunder, he tried to keep an eye on Kieffer.

Gruhit was sitting between his siblings, not sure how to feel. He was angry that Mr. Wunder would be talking about all of them behind their backs to a strange creature. Then Gruhit realized he was terrified by Kieffer. Why could this cat talk? Was it dangerous? He didn't know why, but he had a desire to call Constance. No, he really wanted to call his mom, but he couldn't. That's when he realized how angry he was with his mom for leaving him in all these homes.

Amarie was sitting closest to Kieffer, and her dreamy gaze stared longingly at the cat-like creature.

"You know," Kieffer stated, so quietly that only Amarie could hear, "It's quite rude to stare at folks."

"I'm gonna braid your hair," Amarie stated simply.

"Amarie!" Gruhit exclaimed.

"What?" Amarie said, suddenly realizing everyone was looking at her. "Well, I've never talked with an animal before. You know how much more fun it would be to play 'hair salon' if they could talk about all the gossip going on around the neighborhood."

"Alright, alright, we must be calm if we're going to talk about all this," Samme stated. "But you're right, Amarie: Kieffer is an excellent conversationalist."

"Thank you, sir…" Kieffer started to say.

"What is it?" Chardy asked, "What is it and why can it talk? Do y'all do scary magical things around here?"

"Great questions, Chardy. Let's start with Kieffer," Samme said calmly. "Kieffer is *not* a cat. Creatures like him are called guardlings."

"Guardlings? That sounds made up," Gruhit interjected. He wasn't buying any of what Mr. Wunder was saying.

"Yes, guardlings," Kieffer stated. "We are absolutely *not* cats. Which reminds me…"

Kieffer pounced off the chair onto the floor. He gave a long forward stretch, which Gruhit thought looked a lot like something a cat would do after waking up from a nap. However, while Kieffer was stretching, his tail seemed to be unraveling into two parts.

"Although guardlings share the same basic structure as a cat, they are quite different," Samme explained. "As you can plainly see, he is double the size of a normal cat, has two tails, and is able to learn and speak human languages."

Kieffer jumped back up on the chair. "Those aren't the most interesting things we can do, though. We can magically calm creatures when we sit on their laps or when they pet us. Guardlings are also fantastic at alerting families to danger. We tend to pick a family of humans or other creatures to protect against mischief or peril. Which is why I was talking about guarding Chardy last night and was so rudely overheard by…"

"Guarding me?" snapped Chardy. "Do you see my face? I don't think you did your job well. Unless… did you do this?"

Chardy felt a tender hand on his forearm. He looked over to see Mal as she said, "Kieffer didn't draw on your face. It was a golem, who somehow took up residence in our basement. That's why I didn't want you picking that bedroom. I thought that…"

"A what?" Chardy shot back. He snatched his arm away from Malda.

"A golem," Samme stated. "They're creatures that are formed from the first mischievous laugh of a baby. The magic in that laugh pulls things like dust bunnies, paper clips, string, or any small bits of discarded items together to form a golem."

"The golem must have come after I came up to talk to the Master," Kieffer stated, embarrassed he had left his post. "They usually only play their tricks when they don't think they'll be seen. I didn't think it would come out in the middle of a bedroom while the sun was up. They have fluff for brains though."

"Literally," chuckled Samme. "They literally have fluff for brains, and they are not dangerous… well… not to people. Their one ambition is to pull practical jokes. They only care if the joke is funny to them and don't understand that it might hurt others. Sometimes their jokes can hurt some of our smaller friends, but again, they are quite harmless to people."

"Well, fluff for brains has never met Chardy Brown. Payback is going to be horrible," Chardy said angrily.

"Sir, I think I might be starting to grow fond of this one," Kieffer whispered toward Samme, as the guardling gave Chardy a small smile.

"How is any of this even real?" Gruhit suddenly blurted out.

Samme looked toward Gruhit, who seemed to be less frustrated and more concerned or worried.

"Remember the story I told you and Amarie last night?" Samme asked. Gruhit and Amarie nodded. "It's a very old story that the Wunder family has passed down from generation to generation. That story has changed in slight variations through the years, but for the most part it stayed true. Magical creatures have always been here—longer than humans actually."

"I've never seen them," Amarie said in a dreamy state. "And I would've loved to be talking to animals."

"Well, most of the magical creatures choose to stay hidden," Samme explained. "Remember, in my story people had forgotten about magical creatures. If they showed themselves now, some people would want to do horrible experiments on them. Also, you three know more than anyone that some people just are not nice, and they would hurt these creatures just for sport. They might hurt them because they don't understand them and don't like things that are different from what they are used to."

"Is this like a secret you're asking us to keep?" Gruhit asked. There were plenty of times with the other fosters that he was asked to keep secrets and not tell a caseworker something.

"It's not a secret," Malda quickly corrected. "We simply have to be careful who we tell so we help protect them. If you met a stranger, you wouldn't tell them your address or when your birthday is or your phone number. What if that stranger turned out to have evil intentions? We only tell people we know we can trust, who we know well, and only after we discuss it as a family."

"Hmph. I won't be telling anyone at school," Chardy grumbled. "Can you imagine how crazy I'd sound?"

"Only a few of our neighbors know there are magical creatures in the area, and some have them living in their homes as well," Samme explained. "I'm sure you'll be meeting them all. They were very excited to have children nearby again."

Gruhit thought about the homes he saw in the neighborhood. He wondered which homes knew that magical creatures existed. He didn't feel angry anymore. He did feel curious about the creatures in this house. His mind flooded with what seemed like a thousand questions. He tried to remember the story Samme told them last night when one question popped into his head with alarm.

"What about Fridgita Mortes?"

Mal and Samme slowly looked at each other as though unsure of what to say. Mal nodded her head and gave a small smile of encouragement as she held Samme's hand. Samme looked down at the cup of coffee in front of him. He took a short sip and placed the cup back on the table.

"Fridgita does exist," Samme said. "She has never stopped trying to destroy the hope and lives of humans and all creatures. You will learn very quickly that hope is a precious commodity in this house. With hope people can do amazing things and survive difficult situations. However, without hope, we make Fridgita more powerful and allow her to work her evil more easily."

Before Samme could continue, a knot in the baseboard by the hall door opened and a tiny little man edged his way out. He was clutching his tail and fidgeting with it. The antennae coming out of his head were drooping as though to match his mood. Gruhit noticed that his clothes were brown trousers, a white shirt with a dark blue vest, and a long brown suit coat. If it wasn't for the tail and antennae, he might have been from the early 1900s.

Kieffer quickly jumped over to the little man to speak with him. The others couldn't make out what was said. Gruhit could see that Samme and Malda looked tense. Suddenly, Kieffer raised his head from the floor as the little man shut the door and ran off.

"Sir, I think that this definitely needs your attention at once," Kieffer stated.

"Fine," Samme stated. He arose from the table. "Children, I'm sorry but I must attend to this right now. Let me say this. First, I know you still have many questions. We will answer them all, and Mal and I will do so truthfully, even if it is hard for us to do so. Next, I want you to know that you are safe here. We all watch out for each other. Even Kieffer is already guarding you because you're a part of our family right now. Remember what the story says about Fridgita. She is not the most powerful being in the universe. There is always hope."

With that, Samme walked at a brisk pace toward the basement stairs with Kieffer closely behind him. Everyone sat silently, looking over to Mal for what they should do next. This was the oddest first breakfast they had ever had in a new home.

Mal finally broke the silence.

"Okay, then. Chardy, I would like you to eat your breakfast. Gruhit and Amarie, let's get some of these dishes picked up and loaded into the dishwasher. Once we all get cleaned up and dressed, we're going to tour the outside of the house."

Chapter 12
Morning With Mrs. Bangs

No one said another word. The children finished eating and began helping to clean up the table. Everyone was definitely in an odd mood. The information they had just learned was overwhelming. Not only was Amarie not talking and singing as usual but Chardy was more helpful than he normally would have been.

Gruhit helped Mal clear food off the table and put it in the refrigerator. He didn't mind this task. He often liked to take food and hide it in his room. Gruhit learned to do this when he lived with his mom. He would sneak food home from school because she often wouldn't have any dinner for them. Gruhit would take extra bread, a carton of milk, a slice of pizza - whatever he could get. Right now he had his eyes on some pancakes. He quickly shoved them under his shirt to hide in his bedroom for later.

As Gruhit got ready to go outside with Malda, he couldn't help but look everywhere for any special creatures. As he was brushing his teeth, he thought about how oddly Mr. Wunder had acted with the water. Gruhit looked at his cup. He moved closer to it and stared down at the water.

"Hello?" Gruhit said to the water.

Nothing. He would have been embarrassed, or even thought he was going crazy, if he hadn't spent the morning talking to a guardling.

Gruhit moved into his bedroom and began to get dressed for the day, after hiding the confiscated pancakes in his closet. Before he unlocked the bedroom doors and went out to meet Mal, he walked over to the knot he had noticed yesterday in the window frame. He knocked on it like anyone would knock on a door.

Nothing.

Again, he would have felt embarrassed about even considering that someone would answer, except he had just seen a little man come out of a knot similar to this one.

Gruhit walked out into the hallway. Malda was also emerging from her bedroom. She was wearing a comfortable pair of capris and a hoodie. The hoodie had flowers all over it, similar to the stars on her dress the day before. Gruhit almost didn't recognize her as her hair was in a different style.

"I see that you're ready to go," Mal stated cheerfully. "Follow me please."

The pair left the hallway and went into the kitchen where Mal called up the stairs. "Amarie, darling, we are getting ready to head outside. Please come down."

Gruhit could hear a door on the second floor open, followed by footsteps quickly descending the stairs. Amarie appeared in a pair of overalls and a long sleeved t-shirt.

"I think someone forgot to tend to their hair," Mal said with a chuckle. "We will have to work on this after we get back."

Mal led the two Browns to the partial set of steps in the kitchen which led to the back door and turned at the landing to lead all the way down to the basement.

Before opening the door, Mal called down the stairs. "Chardy! Please come up. It's time to head outside."

There was no answer.

"Chardy, come please," Mal stated, pleasantly, but more commanding.

Still no response.

"Well, I guess you wish to be left alone," Mal called down. "Just know that Kieffer is with Samme, so be mindful the golem doesn't seem to be concerned with the daylight right now."

"Alright, alright, I'm coming," Chardy said. He appeared at the bottom of the steps with his hair and face freshly cleaned and kept. As he walked up the steps he took his earbuds out of his hoodie pocket and placed them in his ears.

Mal opened the back door and they all stepped out into the crisp, cool fall air. She led them down the steps of the small hill to the sidewalk in front of Big Blue.

"Unfortunately we don't have much of a yard. There is a park just a couple of blocks away that I'll take you to another day," Mal said with a hint of excitement. "The factory across the street is off limits. It used to belong to Samme's family. It was their shoe factory. They made beautiful shoes there until the factory had to close."

"Why did it close?" Amarie wondered.

Mal looked at the factory and sighed, as though reliving a story in her head. "Alas, that's a story for another day."

Gruhit noticed there were a lot of stories that surrounded the Wunders and their house full of strange creatures.

"I thought you might like to walk down by our next door neighbor's house."

"Fort Flowers?" Gruhit exclaimed before he could stop himself.

"I'm sorry, what?" asked Mal, slightly confused.

"Gruhit likes to come up with funny names for all the houses, and sometimes people living around our foster homes," Amarie explained.

"It's just that I saw a big fort in the backyard, and there are all kinds of flowers."

"Oh, Mrs. Bangs will be so happy to hear that you noticed all of her hard work," said Mal joyfully. "Remember the salve that we used last night before bedtime? Her little pond and flowers make the area between our homes perfect for finding dipsy toads."

Amarie gave a quick giggle and sang in a silly fashion, "Dip, dip, dip. Dipsy!"

"Let's head over and see if we can spot one. If Mrs. Bangs is outside, I know that she would like to tell you more about the dipsy toad," said Mrs. Wunder. "Should we head over, Chardy?"

Chardy rolled his eyes as he listened to his music. "Yeah. Whatever. Not like I can go anywhere else."

Mal led the trio down the sidewalk along 19th Street until they reached the corner of the lot. She then took a sharp left turn and followed the sidewalk to the next house. Some of the taller flowers were shaking.

"Mrs. Bangs, is that you?" Mal called up to the flowers.

Suddenly, a woman about sixty years old, and of shorter than average height, walked out of the flowers. She was smiling down at the four visitors. She wore older capris stained with years of soil and earth on them. She had on a simple orange long sleeved t-shirt and her reddish blonde hair was done up in a beehive hairstyle. She was holding a small gardening shovel and a small container with pulled weeds in her other hand.

"Mrs. Wunder, these must be the children!" Mrs. Bangs said with a rosy voice. "Come on up here. I was just tending to a few weeds that were sneaky enough to start growing next to the house."

Mal walked up to Mrs. Bangs to give her a warm and cheerful handshake. Amarie ran up to Mrs. Bangs, getting ready to give her one of her large hugs. Suddenly the woman signaled Amarie to stop with her outstretched hand. Amarie stopped dead in her tracks in confusion. She always hugged adults when she first met them. She learned that a hug from a little girl was seen as cute, and adults wouldn't hurt what they thought was cute.

"I'm sorry dear, but hugs are special," explained Mrs. Bangs kindly. "Hugs are reserved only for family members. We are just meeting, so I think a handshake is appropriate for now."

Mrs. Bangs gave Amarie and Gruhit the same warm handshakes that she had exchanged with Mal.

"I'm Chardy. I don't shake hands or give hugs," Chardy said matter-of-factly.

"Thank you for telling me. I can appreciate that, Mr. Chardy," Mrs. Bangs said with a serious tone. "Well, I'm Mrs. Priscilla Bangs, your next-door neighbor. I'm so glad to meet each of you."

"Mrs. Bangs," Mal stated, "we have been talking this morning about the dipsy toad. I thought it might be good to come over here to see if you might explain them to the children."

"Ah, I see that we already have a little crew who believes in magical creatures," Mrs. Bangs said almost triumphantly.

"I LOVE magical creatures. I'm going to have a whole room full of them when I get older and have my very own guardling that I can…" Amarie started to chatter before being cut short by Mal.

"Now, Amarie, we cannot learn if we are only using our mouths to talk."

"Well, now, what do you know about dipsy toads?" asked Mrs. Bangs. She set her container and shovel down on the ground.

"All we know is that they use it to make this weird family recipe stuff and put it on people to help them sleep," Gruhit said, trying to make it sound like he thought the Wunders were crazy. He was worried Mrs. Bangs would think he sounded stupid.

"Good, so you know about dipsy toad salve," said Mrs. Bangs. "Well, dipsy toads are going to look like any other toad except for a few things. First, they are bigger than the average toad."

"You mean like a guardling is larger than a cat, but they still look alike?" Amarie asked.

"Yes, exactly! A dipsy toad is going to be about the size of both of my hands put together," she stated. "Secondly, they are going to have this shape on their foreheads."

Gruhit watched as Mrs. Bangs used her finger to form the shape of a crescent moon on her forehead, leaving a faint dirt outline on her head.

"Lastly, the dipsy toad is so special because of its magical saliva."

"What's saliva?" asked Gruhit.

Amarie giggled. "She means their spit."

"Yes. For years people have tried to get dipsy toads to 'kiss' them because if you get their saliva on you, you're bound to have good dreams all night long," stated Mrs. Bangs very excitedly.

Gruhit turned to Mal a bit disgusted. "Are you telling me that there was toad spit in that stuff you put on me last night?"

"But did you have a good night's sleep?" asked Mrs. Bangs.

"I don't remember my dreams," Gruhit said. He was unwilling to admit that toad spit helped him last night.

"Ah, but you didn't have bad dreams either," Mrs. Bangs said, impressed. "The Wunder dipsy salve really is remarkable because it is like putting on lotion rather than thinking about, as you say, 'putting on toad spit.'"

"Can we see a dipsy toad? I want to catch one!" Amarie exclaimed.

"Now children, I must be very clear about one thing," Mrs. Bangs suddenly got very serious. "You must never, NEVER, catch one of the creatures out in the wild. Most of them would never survive a night in a house because other creatures could harm them. There are also creatures that a dipsy toad might try to eat inside a house. It's always best to observe them only and leave them be. As long as everyone promises to abide by this, I can show you where some creatures live around my home. Does everyone agree?"

Amarie and Gruhit nodded their heads in agreement earnestly. They were both very curious to see and learn more. Chardy nodded his head also, but it was more about having nothing better to do than curiosity.

"Good!" Mrs. Bangs went back to her joyful voice. "Let me explain what we're going to do. Now, I heard a couple of toads singing today around the pond over here. We are all going to walk over here and stay against my house so that we can crouch down and hide amongst the flowers. Most magical creatures are skittish around people they are unfamiliar with, so it is important that everyone make as little noise as possible."

Everyone looked at Amarie as though to assure she would stay quiet.

"What? Okay, okay, I promise I'll be quiet," Amarie said defensively.

Mrs. Bangs walked Mal and the three children through a path of smaller, colorful flowers. As the group walked toward Mrs. Bang's house, the flowers began to get taller. Gruhit soon noticed that some of the stalks were far above his head and even above Mal's head. It was as though they were in a jungle of flowers. The smell was very sweet. It was like smelling honey and various perfumes all at once. It was difficult at times not to step on flowers, but they all managed to dodge around various stalks and stems until they could make out the white vinyl siding of Fort Flowers.

Mrs. Bangs turned to face the group. "Now, we are going to walk along the side of the house until we can just make out the pond," she whispered. "The waterfall should cover up the noise of our feet."

The group trudged through the beautiful flower jungle as quietly as they could. Gruhit's ears began to pick up the sounds of water dribbling down rocks into a larger body of water. Before long, he could make out the pond in the near distance. Gruhit could see why they had come up from behind the pond. It lay in the open between the two houses; anyone walking beside Big Blue would immediately tip off creatures to their approach.

Mrs. Bangs motioned everyone to crouch down and held her finger to her mouth to remind everyone to be quiet. Gruhit thought it was funny that Amarie looked like she was going to burst from having to stay silent. He could tell she really wanted to see a dipsy toad. However, Gruhit was doubting that they were really going to see anything. Through the silence, he was suddenly able to hear other sounds more clearly, including a toad singing.

"Look over there," Mrs. Bangs said in a hushed voice. "Do you see near the edge of the pond underneath that pink flower?"

Looking at the pond, Gruhit only saw various shades of green stems and leaves. Amarie's eyes were wide with excitement. She placed her hands over her mouth to keep from saying anything. Chardy looked less impressed. This made Gruhit more determined to see it. He scanned the area and sat a little lower. Finally, he spotted a large brownish-green toad who was sitting next to the pond and singing along with the falling water. It was indeed larger than any toad he had seen and there was a crescent moon shape on its forehead.

Gruhit wasn't sure if this toad was magical or not.

"Do you see it eating the flies?" Mrs. Bangs whispered to the children. "The dipsy toad is similar to a toad in almost every other way. It still likes to eat insects. They stay near water, but don't go in: they prefer to stay dry. This side of my house provides them with plenty of heat during the day. The flowers allow them to have shade if they need it. The flowers even attract all the insects they could ever want to eat."

As Gruhit continued to watch the dipsy toad, he noticed the swaying of a pink flower. He could be wrong, but he could swear this was the same large pink flower he noticed swaying out his bedroom window when arrived at Big Blue. He gazed more intently at the flower as the swaying became more fervent. Gruhit tapped Mrs. Bangs' shoulder and pointed at the flower.

"Oh my," Mrs. Bangs said with a quiet gasp. "Children, remain perfectly still and quiet. If I'm correct, you might be seeing a magical creature that even Mrs. Wunder has not seen very much in years."

"Is that…?" Mal began to ask.

"Oh, yes it is," Mrs. Bangs replied.

A little fairy popped out of the flower - the same one Gruhit had seen the day before. This time, he had a closer vantage point. The fairy fluttered her wings so quickly that you could barely see them. Her golden hair hung elegantly all the way past her feet. Gruhit noted that her flowing long dress was made of flower petals, seeds, and leaves. Her dress covered so much of her body that only the head, feet, and hands of the fairy were visible. The sunlight glinted off the fairy's wings as she hovered above her flower. Gruhit would never admit it, but she was absolutely beautiful.

"That's a tangerella," Mal gasped. She looked at Mrs. Bangs for confirmation.

"Yes, I have noticed about eight of them living among my flowers," whispered Mrs. Bangs. "I wonder if we will see more since the children are here."

All of the children looked at Mrs. Bangs, confused.

"Tangerella's are fairies, obviously," explained Mrs. Bangs. "They believe it is their sworn duty to protect their beauty. They hardly ever come out of hiding. They keep their youth and beauty by sleeping in the hair of children at night."

Mrs. Wunder immediately covered her mouth to fight a fit of laughter.

"What?" Gruhit spoke as quietly as he could.

"Don't you see?" Mal said. "The reason Chardy and Amarie's hair was so knotted this morning was because the tangerellas slept in their hair last night."

Chardy looked disturbed, but Amarie was in absolute ecstasy.

"How did they get in the house?" Gruhit asked.

"Tangerella's can phase through the walls," answered Mrs. Bangs with a small smile.

Everyone watched the fairy hover above her flower as the dipsy toad continued to sing. Gruhit thought this whole moment was amazing and unreal. Suddenly, the group felt a breeze blow through the flowers and the fairy, without notice, flew quickly into the flower patch to seek shelter from the wind.

SMACK.

The fairy flew right into Mrs. Bangs' face.

"Hello, Sparkles," Mrs. Bangs stated, speaking as softly and kindly as she could.

The fairy was stunned by the collision. She quickly flew a few feet away before turning to lay her eyes on the group. When she saw that there were people she didn't know, the fairy looked downright terrified.

"It's okay, little one," Mrs. Bangs cooed soothingly. "These are the children who have moved in next door."

"We're friends," Amarie said in an amazingly calm and soft voice for her. "You're beautiful."

Although the fairy was still concerned, she was flattered by Amarie's compliment. Sparkles stared at the group for a short while. Gruhit thought it seemed like she was working out whether to talk with them or to fly away. The fairy continued to slowly back away. Without warning, Sparkles suddenly flew as quick as a lightning shot to Amarie's hair to give it a quick snuggle and then flew away and out of sight.

"Well, I just can't believe that we actually saw a tangerella today," Mal stated excitedly.

"You kids have no idea how lucky you are." stated Mrs. Bangs. "Well, I would love to continue to show you more creatures, but I must get back to tending my garden."

"Of course, we don't want the creatures that call these flowers home to leave the area," Mrs. Wunder stated.

Once the group had climbed out of flowers, Mrs. Bang looked at all of the children with pride. "Well, I'm just so happy to have all of you here," she said. "Be sure to listen to Samme and Malda. They know a thing or two about taking care of folks."

"Oh, good gracious," Mal said while glancing down at her watch. "I didn't realize we missed lunch time. We really have taken up a lot of your time today, Priscilla. I'm so sorry. However, may I have a quick word with you for one moment?"

Mal looked at Priscilla with a serious expression. Gruhit hated it when adults could communicate just by looking at each other because he had no idea what was going on. Those looks were usually followed by a request that he and his siblings wait in a car or...

"Children, can you please wait for me on the sidewalk by the front door please?" Mal instructed.

Chardy walked briskly back to the sidewalk. Amarie skipped along singing some nonsensical song about fairies and singing toads. Gruhit walked more slowly and looked back often at the two ladies. He couldn't read their lips, but the fact that Mrs. Bangs' face now looked concerned made him all the more curious.

Once he got back to front of Big Blue, he sat on one of the steps and looked toward the old factory. Amarie continued to zoom up and down the sidewalk; she was now pretending that she was a fairy and was saying hello to every object that she saw. Chardy leaned against the front door and fiddled with his iPod.

Gruhit pondered what the ladies were talking about. He wondered if it had anything to do with why Samme had to take care of something right after breakfast. There was obviously something happening that concerned the adults. Gruhit remembered how he had thought he heard a voice call his name in the wind. At first he thought it was all in his head, but after everything that happened today, he wondered if it was real. Was it a magical creature? Surely it wasn't Fridgita Mortes.

The new fosters said he was safe, but adults were always telling him he was safe. His mom was supposed to have kept him safe, and he kept being moved from home to home. So far, his time with the Wunders was amazing. He wanted to trust them. Maybe he could trust them more if he had answers to his questions. As soon as they got back into the house, he would find Samme and get answers - especially about Fridgita Mortes.

Chapter 13
The sketchbook

Mal and the kids had a simple lunch of grilled cheese with tomato soup. Gruhit could have done without the soup. He wasn't a huge fan of tomatoes in any shape or form, except sauce on pizza. He didn't even really like ketchup.

Gruhit kept looking out of the corner of his eye to see if Samme was in the house. He wondered where he was and why he wasn't eating lunch with them.

"Since we haven't handed out chores yet," Mal explained, "I'll clean up the dishes, so that you three can rest or hang out in the house."

"Good, because I'm going to my room to stare out the window," Amarie said excitedly, getting up from her chair. "I want to try to see tangerellas flying around the flowers."

With that, Amarie was running up the stairs with her heavy, loud footsteps all the way to the top.

Mal gave a bit of a chuckle. "I'm pretty sure that every tangerella within five blocks of here heard her go up those stairs. There is no way that they were not scared away."

Mal looked over at Chardy, who was getting up out of his chair quietly. "What are you planning on doing for the rest of the afternoon, Chardy?"

Chardy stopped walking and reluctantly looked back at Mal. "I don't know. I might go play video games in the basement. Whatever. It might be fun or sumthin.'"

"Can I play too?" Gruhit asked.

Chardy scowled, turning his face so the others couldn't see. "Yeah, whatever. I don't care."

Gruhit followed his brother to the basement, giving Gruhit his first view.

After coming to the base of the stairs, Gruhit found himself in a small open alcove with a door standing ajar to his left and a very short hallway ahead of him leading to a great room. Gruhit peered into the doorway for a few seconds before observing that this was the laundry room, which held no interest whatsoever to him. However, something which did capture his attention was the vast and multi-level play area spanning the length of the right wall in the large family room ahead of him. When walking into the room, he was able to see that in the middle of the structure there was a small ladder leading from the floor to an elevated level. The second level had a slide to one side of the ladder and a giant ball bit on the other side. Under the structure was a space just tall enough for Gruhit to crouch and play below.

Gruhit tore his attention from the enormous play area to the center of the room where he noticed a big sectional couch—that could easily fit six people—facing a TV hung along the opposite wall from the play area. Underneath the TV was a shelf with a video game system, a few games, and controllers. Past the TV and at the end of the left wall was a closet that Gruhit thought he would have to explore later. Gruhit wasn't normally a fan of basements, but he really wanted to spend more time down here.

Just before the TV on the wall there was another alcove with three doors. The middle door appeared to lead to the basement bathroom.

"My bedroom is the door on the left," Chardy said.

Suddenly Kieffer came out of the door on the right.

"Ah, I see that we're getting ready to play video games, yes?" Kieffer said.

The boys nodded their heads. Chardy walked over to the couch. Gruhit wondered if he would ever get used to a cat-like creature talking to him.

Kieffer hopped up onto the couch and sat down next to Chardy. "I'm a fan of the Soccer World Championship game myself, but I'm not bad at car racing."

When they were set up, Chardy suddenly felt like someone was looking at him. He turned his head slowly to his left and was face to face with Kieffer.

"Listen to me, kid. Guardlings are extremely competitive so consider this a warning," Kieffer said with a serious tone. "I'm going to bring a world of hurt on you. Are you ready to box, lightweight?"

"Oh, you got the smack talk," Chardy said. "But can you handle the hurt I'm about to bring?"

Gruhit was amazed at how good Kieffer played, and was even more amazed at seeing his brother acting like his old self. Chardy used to horse around all the time and was really good at watching out for Gruhit. He used to cheer Gruhit up when he was sad. But at some point in their constant moves, Chardy didn't seem to care anymore. Even though Chardy was here with him, Gruhit felt like he had lost him, just as he had lost his mom. Chardy had been more of a father to him than anyone else. When his mom was doing double shifts, or two jobs in a row, it was Chardy who fed him. It was Chardy who made sure that he went to bed at night. It was Chardy that made the monsters in the darkness go away.

As Gruhit watched his brother and Kieffer play, he overheard a long sigh come from the room next to Chardy's. He walked over to the cracked door and peered in. Samme was sitting at a drafting table holding his head between his hands. Gruhit tried to get a better look when he accidentally nudged the door. It let out a slight creak.

Samme sat up straight and turned around. "Chardy?"

"No sir," Gruhit said sheepishly. "It's Gruhit."

"Come in," Samme said, trying to sound positive. "What can I help you with?"

Gruhit stepped into what he now saw was Samme's office. Three walls were dark chocolate brown, and the far wall was a brighter blue. There was a recessed window to Gruhit's left which let in a fair amount of light and looked upon the dipsy toad pond.

To his right were all sorts of drawers and a short desk. Everything was overflowing with papers containing sketches, drawings, and notes. Gruhit was not a fan of cleaning his room, but even he could tell that Mr. Wunder needed to organize his office.

As he reflected on the mess, Gruhit noticed a framed ad on the wall for lotion scented with lavender. The logo included a toad sitting on a lily pad with a moon in the background. The words "Johnson's Relaxation Lotion" were incorporated into the design.

Gruhit looked at more of the framed ads on the wall. One ad included a beautiful fairy with long and luxurious hair. The hair wound around in wonderful designs and cleverly made the words, "Somber's Detangler." It was undoubtedly a tangerella.

The last ad to catch Gruhit's eye was of a cat with tuxedo markings sitting in front of the words, "Mirium's Formal Wear For Toddlers and Infants." Now no one else would have noticed it in this classy and upscale logo, but the cat definitely had two tails. This design had to be a guardling.

"What is all this?" Gruhit asked.

"I'm a designer. All the logos on the wall are some of my more popular logos. The mess on the desk are my sketches and some of my failures," Samme explained.

"But... there are magical creatures in these drawings," Gruhit observed.

"Well, you might say that they're my inspiration," Samme said. "Normally, someone comes to the company I work for and asks us to create a logo. Myself and another artist will each make one, then we show them to the client. The client chooses which version they like."

Samme watched Gruhit as he carefully flipped through some of the sketches. Gruhit's fascination and curiosity was clear. It reminded Samme of the wonder he felt when he watched his own father draw. Drawing was something that ran in the Wunder family. It was a hobby for his great-grandfather, and his great-great-grand-

74—Gruit's Hope

father was quite accomplished. This passion continued with Samme, who had made art his livelihood.

"I thought you took care of the magical creatures," Gruhit said, a bit confused.

"Well, I do," Samme said with a chuckle. "But somehow other folks don't think taking care of magical creatures is a full-time job. As a graphic designer, I can mostly work from home. Except for presentations."

"How many creatures live around the house?"

"It would be impossible to know. Even though many of them have trusted Mal and I, there are still many that do not. There are also some creatures that are few in number, so the likelihood that we would see them is small. It's quite possible that you might discover new creatures while you're here."

Gruhit's eyes lit up. It was exciting to hear that he might be able to find more creatures. Most adults only told him that he was too little to do anything.

"Me? How do I look for creatures? Do you know how?" Gruhit asked quickly. He only paused when he realized he was about to excitedly fire off tons of questions.

Samme again chuckled. Gruhit's excitement reminded him of himself when he was a boy. "Give it time. Remember, my family has known about these creatures for generations. My father and I would search for creatures and attempt to befriend them. This is how I got into drawing, Gruhit. When I was a little younger than you, my father gave me my own sketchbook like his. He told me it was my job to observe and learn about magical creatures."

Gruhit was listening to Samme's every word. He liked drawing, but never thought of himself as an artist. To him, drawing was something that he could do to escape. There always seemed to be someone nearby with paper or a pencil. If he was sitting in a caseworker's office, there were pencils and paper. In a doctor or counselor's waiting room, the receptionist had pencil and paper. If he was at a fast food restaurant waiting to have a weekly visit with his mom, there were at least crayons and a child's menu.

Samme could see that Gruhit was thinking perhaps a thousand thoughts, and yet stayed silent. Samme wished Gruhit would say more about his thoughts but at the same time understood that they were strangers that had only met yesterday. Trust would be built and earned over time, but it simply didn't exist right now. Samme suddenly had an idea for helping to connect with Gruhit.

Samme slowly walked over to his desk and crouched down to search through one of the drawers. Gruhit watched as Mr. Wunder searched through layer upon layer of sketches. He could smell the scent of musty pages mixed with charcoal and graphite wafting through the air when suddenly Samme yanked on something in the drawer. He pulled out a small paperback book with a black cover. There seemed to be nothing extraordinary about it at all.

Samme stayed crouched down so that he was eye level with Gruhit, and held out the book. "Gruhit, I want you to take this," he said.

Gruhit was hesitant to take the book, but in the end he accepted and opened it. The pages within were completely blank.

"I've had this for years. I have taken out some of the pages that I've used. I would like you to use this as a practice book and see if you would like to apprentice with me," Samme explained, hoping Gruhit would take him up on the offer.

"What does that mean, 'apprentice?'" Gruhit asked. He asked not because he didn't know what an apprentice was, but because he wasn't sure what he was supposed to do.

"Well, you would come along with me when I do observations of magical creatures and you would be in charge of doing your own drawings as well," Samme explained. "If I see that you're interested in this, you'll earn your own official sketchbook. I earned my own sketchbook from my father when I was probably about six years old. Even then I loved drawing."

Gruhit was very excited. In his head he imagined going on adventures with Mr. Wunder and discovering all sorts of magical creatures. He saw himself presenting overelaborate drawings to teams of scientists in big important meetings.

"So all I have to do is draw magical creatures?" Gruhit asked. He was both excited and unsure, thinking there must be a catch somewhere.

"That's all," Samme stated simply with a smile. "But I cannot very well have you recording your observations when you don't have a pencil, can I?"

Samme stood back up and reached for a coffee mug full of pencils. His hand hovered over the bunch of drawing instruments looking for just the right one to give the new artist. Samme plucked out a nice black artist pencil which was long and already sharpened.

"Keep both of these with you at all times," Samme suggested. "You never know when you'll need them. I actually keep several books, pencils, pens, and such in my traveling coat."

Samme gestured to a long brown overcoat, which looked to be from the early 1900s, hanging on the wall by his drafting table. It was made of a thin material and had pockets all over.

Gruhit clutched the book and pencil closer to his body. He was beyond excited about all of this but still wasn't sure what he was supposed to be doing. As if being able to read his thoughts, Samme began to speak.

"Now the first adventure we will go on will be tonight before bedtime. Remember how I told you the water would 'clean itself up'?"

"Yeah. What was that all about?"

"You had a magical creature playing with you last night," Samme explained. "I stopped you from catching it in the towel and tossing it down the drain."

"I knew there was something going on with that," Gruhit exclaimed.

"Well, tonight I'll introduce you to it, and it can be one of your newest sketches," Samme stated. "For now you could sketch Kieffer while he plays video games."

The two stayed there looking at each other. Samme finally broke the silence. "Is there anything else you need, Gruhit?"

"No," Gruhit said instinctively. He was still excited with his new job and responsibilities, but suddenly he remembered why he needed to talk to Samme so badly. "Well, actually… I saw Mrs. Wunder and Mrs. Bangs talking with each other outside. They both looked really scared about something. You didn't tell us a lot about Fridgita Mortes either."

"You're wondering if you're safe here, right?" Samme created Gruhit's question for him. "Yeah. I mean adults hide stuff from us all the time, and you seem to have something you're not telling us."

"Look, Gruhit, I know that you don't know Mal and I very well, but we *will* be honest with you," Samme explained. "It's not that we are hiding anything from you, but all of this is just a lot to take in, you know? I mean, not only are you having to move into yet another stranger's house, but now these new foster parents are introducing you to the world of magical creatures. It can be a bit much."

"So, it's good to *not* tell us about it? We can handle quite a bit. I've been in houses worse than this."

"Look, Gruhit. All you need to do is come to Mal or me with your questions, and we will fill you in on what is happening. Unfortunately, there has been a lot happening around here lately. It would be complicated to catch you up on the lives of all the creatures and neighbors in one afternoon. It will take time to learn all the stories surrounding everyone here." Samme ended his explanation with an emphasis, "Now, let's get back to your concern about your safety."

"We can take care of ourselves," Gruhit instinctively stated forcefully. "I want to know if I need to be worried about Fridgita Mortes."

"Fridgita has always existed and has been a threat to people and creatures for centuries. While the Wunder family has observed, befriended, and protected magical creatures for years, we have also been on alert for ways that Fridgita might be plotting. For generations no one has really had to worry about her. She seems to be lying low. Some of my ancestors thought maybe she had been thwarted but others, myself included, have thought she has been coming up with nastier tricks."

Samme continued, as if he was watching the story play out in his mind.

"About three months ago, Mal and I were getting reports that some creatures in other regions were disappearing. The scary part is that they weren't getting captured, they were ceasing to exist. Those in our neighborhood who swore to protect magical creatures began looking for why these disappearances were happening. After a month, there were rumors of hundreds of vanishings in other cities or states. We started to learn more. Any creature that witnessed a vanishing reported that the area became very cold and somewhat darkened; it was very unnatural. The disappearing creature goes through extreme feelings of fear, anxiety, anger, and hopelessness. The creature begins to go transparent and stops caring or gives up and then… fizzles out of existence."

"What happens to them? How do we get them back?"

"We can't," Samme said sadly. "Some have come to call it, 'fizzling.' A month and a half ago, we learned from an old and very wise tangerella that the essence of the creatures is being taken by Fridgita. This was confirmed by several other creatures who were unlucky enough to get a glimpse of Fridgita ingesting the energy of a creature as it fizzled out. Our best guess is that she is attempting to get enough energy so she can become powerful enough to rule the Earth and all the universe."

Samme paused for a brief moment to collect his thoughts, and saw how frightened Gruhit was.

"Several weeks ago, we shared with our neighbors and local creatures that we were going to begin fostering children. As you can imagine, many were excited, but others were very concerned. We knew that Fridgita may be planning to harm our area since many magical creatures and protectors live here. A few nights later, we learned that a couple of creatures in this home had fizzled out. Unfortunately, their twin children saw the whole thing and not unlike you, live with a new family now.

"Mal and I were unsure whether to foster or not, but one thing that we know is that Fridgita is absolutely powerless against hope. It is our greatest weapon. What better way to introduce hope to our area than to help a family who is having a rough time, right?

"Well, we met with our neighbours again to let everyone know about our plans. While some had hope, others were still concerned. That night, one little creature named Mr. Snickelfritz, who lives with his wife in our walls, went home and his concerns turned to fear and then hopelessness. Fridgita sensed it immediately and tried to take him. Luckily, Mrs. Snickefritz was able to use a sleeping draught on her husband. He is now in a magical sleep; half laying in his bed in the real world and half fizzled out."

"Can he be brought back?"

"We don't know, Gruhit," Samme said, fighting back a tear. "Remember, I'm only telling you this because you asked, and I want to be honest. But I want you to know that you are safe, and there's no evidence Fridgita plans to harm humans. Besides, she can't as long as we have hope. From what I've seen, everyone is happy and hopeful since you three arrived."

Gruhit didn't want to admit it, but he was scared by all of this.

"What if I don't want to live here anymore?" he asked.

"Then you just need to tell us so we can talk with your caseworker," Samme said. "However, this is happening everywhere, whether people believe it or not."

"Can I meet the children who lost their parents?" Gruhit wondered.

"Not tonight," Samme said. "The little folk families are in good spirits, but they are not up for visitors today. I think it would be best to get some drawing practice in before dinner so you're ready to meet your next creature tonight."

Gruhit forgot all about his new job. His face lit up once again as he took off toward the door to find Kieffer and Chardy. He stopped just outside the door and turned.

"Thanks, Mr. Wunder," Gruhit said, not sure what else to say.

"No worries," Samme replied. "Gruhit, if you have more questions, please ask Mal and me, okay?"

And with that, Gruhit ran to begin his first drawing in his new sketchbook.

Chapter 14
Meeting the Drleck

With everything that occurred during the day, it was no surprise that dinner was a little later than Mrs. Wunder would have liked. But the table was still full of good food, and Mr. Wunder filled the conversation with funny stories about moats, and doats, and little folks. Kieffer shared a few tales of bravery about guardlings who lived a long time ago.

It was still odd for the children to hear these stories, and to know they actually happened. Everything just sounded so fantastical.

"Samme," Mal said before he could begin another story about a little folk, "it's getting close to bedtime."

"Really? Yes. Look at the time!" Samme exclaimed. "Tell you what. As a treat for tonight, I'll clear the table and do the dishes."

Chardy and Amarie still had no desire to get ready for bed, but Gruhit couldn't help clapping his hands excitedly. He had been waiting for what seemed like days for the opportunity to draw his first, magical creature in his sketchbook.

"Everyone go to your bathrooms and get ready for bed," Malda announced.

Amarie leaped to her feet and raced up the stairs, calling out, "Last one to get ready for bed is a fat dipsy toad. Weee!"

"Chardy, do you need me to look in on you?" Samme asked again, knowing that Chardy would reject his offer.

"I don't need nuthin' from you. I got it," Chardy said, standing up. He briskly walked down the stairs.

"Shall I go look after him?" Without waiting for an answer, Kieffer jumped from his chair and hurried to the basement.

"I'm going to make sure that Amarie is tucked into bed, and that she actually puts her cap and lotion on tonight," Mal stated.

"And I need a certain young man to get ready for bed as quickly and efficiently as he is able so that we can still have time to observe a creature tonight," Samme said as he smiled at Gruhit.

Gruhit hopped off his chair and made a beeline for the bathroom. He didn't believe he had ever brushed his teeth so well in his life. He even made sure to put lotion on his whole arms and legs instead of just his elbows and knees. He then ran to the bedroom, quickly changed, then grabbed his sketchbook and pencil.

Gruhit found Samme sitting on the edge of the bathtub in his bathroom. Samme had taken Gruhit's cup and filled it with water before filling the sink halfway to the top.

Gruhit walked into the bathroom and waited for instructions.

"Tonight we are going to be talking to little creatures known as drleck." Samme said as he started to rifle through the many pockets in his overcoat.

"The drleck?" Gruhit asked. "That sounds made up."

Samme chuckled. "Right? After everything you have seen today alone, you should know that most things others say are impossible are in fact possible. It shouldn't surprise you that even though the drleck cannot speak English, we will be able to speak with them using a simple ...." Samme paused his sentence. He had finally found what he was looking for and pulled out an aluminum straw from his bottom left coat pocket.

"A straw?" Gruhit said, puzzled.

Samme set the straw in the cup. "I want you to blow air through the straw, while speaking the words, 'Hello, my name is Gruhit Brown. I would like to meet you. I feel calm this evening.'"

"I feel calm?" Gruhit asked, uncertain.

"Yes. It is important that they know that. Drleck are very friendly, but really like to be happy. They might not show themselves if they think you're nervous, scared, or too excited. Which reminds me..." Samme looked Gruhit in the eyes, "let's make sure you're really good and calm. Let's take ten, long deep breaths together."

Gruhit followed Samme as he took ten breaths.

"Good and calm, then? Alright, please talk through the straw and let them know I'm here as well," Samme stated.

Gruhit stepped up. As he was about to begin, he heard a strange scratching noise coming from behind him. Both he and Mr. Wunder turned toward the noise. On the doorframe, at eye level, was a small hole that had been cut. Gruhit heard a knocking noise on the other side of the circle before it opened a crack.

"Hello? Am I alright for visiting?" said a small, but deep voice.

"Please, come in. We were just about to ask our drleck friends to come and join us," Samme said.

Samme leaned toward Gruhit and whispered, "Little folks are very modest. He was probably making sure that he wasn't walking in on someone using the bathroom."

Gruhit continued to watch the hole in the door frame as it opened. A little man with an antenna came out and stepped on a shelf beside the door. He couldn't have been more than eight inches tall.

"Nigil, it's good to see you. I didn't think you were going to make it. Gruhit, this is Mr. Dickelbutton," Samme said.

"Well, I wasn't going to make it, but then we gots to thinking that it's not good to be living in fear. Plus, one does need to meet the new Young Master, yes." said Mr. Dickelbutton.

Mr. Dickelbutton wore a pair of brown coveralls which looked very worn and had patches sewn on here and there. His t-shirt was a simple red cloth. He wore gloves that seemed to be fashioned from a heavier brown material that wasn't leather. Gruhit could also see loops and pockets all over the coveralls which held small little tools like hammers, wrenches, screwdrivers, and so on. All the tools seemed to be made from bits of 'this and that.' For example, his hammer appeared to be made of an eraser from a pencil and a thick paperclip. Mr. Dickelbutton was dressed for work. The only thing out of place was that he was barefoot.

Mr. Dickelbutton gave Gruhit a big smile from underneath the dark brown hairs of his mustache before saying, "Yes, this Young Master seems to be kind and good."

"He's starting his first night of apprenticeship with me, Mr. Dickelbutton," Samme explained. "I wish Mrs. Dickelbutton and the children could have been here. We are all thinking about them."

"Thank you, Master Wunder. The children are doing better, but it's still a bit too early to have them wandering about the house at this hour. The darkness still reminds them of the unnatural and terribly awful event." Mr. Dickelbutton reported.

"Do you mind if we teach Gruhit a bit about little folks?" Samme asked.

"Not at all, Master Wunder. Please do," Mr. Dickelbutton said happily.

As Samme began to talk, Gruhit remembered his sketchbook and thought he was supposed to be drawing something. He opened to one of the beginning pages and began as he looked over at Mr. Dickelbutton.

"Little folks have the same basic anatomy as humans, except they are much smaller," Samme said.

"None of us are taller than eight inches, which is what I am standing at right now," Mr. Dickelbutton said. He made sure to stand with a proud stature and his hands on his hips.

"Yes. Mr. Dickelbutton will most likely be the tallest little folk we will encounter.

In America, little folks often live inside the homes of people. This keeps them safe from the weather and other creatures that might try to hurt or eat them," Samme explained as he watched Gruhit draw. "Because of their short height, it can be difficult for them to get around a human's home. Can you imagine trying to climb huge stairs or open gigantic doors? However, little folk are able to look at physical obstacles and find solutions by making things out of the objects around them."

Gruhit looked puzzled and asked, "So... what if you wanted to go from the shelf over to the sink? I don't see how you could do that. It's impossible."

"Again, Gruhit, don't forget everything you have seen. Just because other people think it is impossible doesn't mean it won't or can't happen," Samme stated kindly.

"Right," Mr. Dickelbutton said.

As Mr. Dickelbutton looked over at the sink, which was about four feet away from the shelf and five feet off the ground, his antennae started to twitch. Suddenly, Mr. Dickelbutton's antennae stood straight out. The little man grabbed a string from the towel and pulled a good long piece out of it. He wrapped it quickly around his shoulder, then quickly ducked into the circular door while mumbling, "I know I saw one here." He reemerged with a tiny nail. Mr. Dickelbutton tied one end of the string to the nail. The little man twirled the nail above his head like a cowboy with a lasso, then released it toward the faucet on the sink. The string got caught on the faucet and swirled around it several times to securely hold the string in place. Before Gruhit could say anything, Mr. Dickelbutton had already secured his end of the string to a nail by the door frame. He jumped off the shelf and slid down the rope like a zipline until he landed safely on the counter.

Gruhit's mouth was open wide in amazement. He wanted to clap or cheer, but he still couldn't believe what just happened. He was amazed Mr. Dickelbutton could do this so quickly.

"Bravo! And this, Mr. Gruhit, is why you will frequently see paperclip ladders and strings around the house," Samme said with a chuckle. "If you don't mind, Mr. Dickelbutton, I'll put you back on the shelf before we ask our other guests to come." After he had done so, Mr. Wunder rewound the string and gave it back to the little folk.

Samme sat back on the edge of the bathtub and said, "Alright, Mr. Gruhit. If you would please tell our little friends to come out and meet us."

Gruhit walked over to the sink, took the straw, and blew while speaking into it. The water in the cup came to life with hundreds of bubbles which garbled his language. It was so funny that a foster had asked him to blow bubbles; usually they said not to do that.

As Gruhit finished speaking, he stepped back, keeping his eyes focussed on the sink. He suddenly realized that he was a little nervous; he didn't know what kind of creature would appear. His mind imagined something with big teeth that liked to scare children at night. Gruhit tried to stay calm, but the longer he waited, the more he didn't want the creature to appear.

Gruhit suddenly noticed the smell of bathroom soap was giving way to a strange flowery scent. He sniffed the air. Yes, definitely flowers. He noticed then that his anxiety was going down.

"They're here," Samme whispered. "Drlecks often give off a lavender scent to calm those who might be nervous. Everything is going to be fine. They're very friendly and fun."

Gruhit sat down next to Samme on the edge of the bathtub. Mr. Dickelbutton stood as close to the edge of the shelf as he could without falling while peering intently into the sink.

Suddenly, Gruhit heard a soft swishing sound in the water. A blob of water jumped out and landed on the counter. The puddle slowly began to expand until it was about three inches in height. Then it collapsed into a puddle. Mr. Dickelbutton seemed to have a warmer and bigger smile, if that were possible, as he watched the blob of water. Quickly the puddle formed a small tower of water before seeming to almost explode into several bubble-like shapes.

Before them stood a little humanoid looking fellow made completely out of bubbles. It looked over at Samme and waved a small little hand of several translucent bubbles.

"*Gur gurbble garble gurdley gargle gubble?*" said the little creature.

"Oh, sorry," Samme quickly went through the pockets in his coat again and took out a small cup. He placed the bottom part over his ear and the open end next to the little bubbled creature. The drleck once again spoke to Samme.

After the drleck finished speaking, Samme went over to the straw and blew more bubbled words. The little drleck immediately turned around and jumped into the sink.

"What just happened?" Gruhit asked Samme.

"Oh, yes, sorry. I'm not explaining things well," Samme said. "Holding the cup over my ear somehow turns their language into something that humans can understand, while blowing the bubbles in the water turns our language into something they can understand."

"But what did it say, and what did you say back?"

"It wanted to know if you were the boy from the other day. I responded that you were and that you were hoping to do some drawings for your new sketchbook."

"Why did they leave, then? Do they not like me? I wasn't calm, was I?"

"Oh, no, no. Gruhit, look." Samme motioned toward the sink as seven little blobs jumped out of the water. "It just went back to get the rest of them."

Gruhit instinctively rubbed his eyes as seven bubbly creatures began to smile and wave at him from the counter. He waved back, smiling. In all the houses he had ever lived, this was the best experience he had ever had after brushing his teeth. Gruhit giggled a little as a couple of them started singing a garbly song together and the other five began making a large pyramid by standing on top of each other.

"Hehehe. Well, are you going to sketch them? They're showing off just for you," Samme said. "It's been a long time since they had someone new to entertain."

Gruhit quickly opened his sketchbook and immediately began scribbling and doodling as much as he could. He got a little flustered at times because he didn't think the drawings looked good.

"Don't worry, you'll get better the more you practice," Samme said. "You just need to draw so you can remember for later."

Before he knew it, he had sketched out a dozen drawings of the drlecks singing songs, playing tag, doing somersaults across the sink, and swimming around so fast that they turned it into a tiny whirlpool. They would cry, "Weee!" like Amarie, only with smaller voices. Gruhit loved it. Mr. Dickelbutton was also enjoying the scene and often exclaimed, "Look at 'em go!" or "Wowza!"

"Alright boys, that's enough for tonight. It's well past bedtime, and Amarie is already asleep," Malda said from the doorway. They were all having so much fun they didn't notice her appearance.

"Mal's right, Gruhit. Please tell the drleck goodnight," Samme kindly instructed.

Gruhit went over to the cup and straw and blew out words, "It was nice to meet you. I have to go to bed. I hope I see you again."

All the little drlecks, except one, ran to huddle with each other. The lone little drleck ran to the bar of soap and quickly created a large bubble, which it skillfully rolled on top of the huddle of drlecks. Now inside, the six drlecks tilted their bubble head upward and blew. The bubble immediately jumped up from the countertop and floated about a foot over the center of the sink. It burst suddenly and fell happily into the water. The last little drleck waved goodbye to the three humans and jumped into the water himself. Samme opened the drain and Gruhit could hear little voices happily saying, "Wee!"

As Gruhit watched the water go down the drain, he thought about something.

"Can I hurt them? What happens if I accidentally flush them down the toilet?"

Samme smiled. "Those are good questions. Drlecks cannot be hurt. They are also too fast to be drank or flushed down the toilet. As far as I understand from them, they have fun going down the drain because they can play in the pipes before coming back up to the surface again."

"Are these your drawings, Gruhit?" Mal asked. "They're quite good for your first observation."

THUNK! CRASH! THUMP!

"HELP! GET AWAY! HELP! MOM! I WANT MY MOM!" Amarie could be heard screaming from her bedroom.

Samme ran up the stairs as quick as a flash.

Mr. Dickelbutton jumped through the circular door as he yelled, "I'll meet you upstairs, Master Wunder!"

This left Malda and Gruhit to wonder what was happening. Gruhit could tell that Malda was slightly tense, which made Gruhit a bit squeamish. When Mrs. Wunder saw Gruhit looking at her, she quickly put on a smile.

"Let's get you into bed, sir," Mrs. Wunder said, taking Gruhit's hand and leading him to his bedroom. "Let's get you tucked in, and you can show me your favorite sketch."

Gruhit got under the covers. He was so excited about the drlecks and meeting Mr. Dickelbutton that he instantly forgot about Amarie's scream.

"I don't have my favorite part drawn, because it was the part where they all got into the bubble and dove into the water. Can I draw it right now?" Gruhit asked.

"Good try, Mr. Gruhit. It will have to be tomorrow because you need to get some sleep. Would you like some dipsy toad salve?"

Gruhit nodded. As Mal applied it, Gruhit swore he could feel it working immediately. He felt calmer and more sleepy.

"Would you like a hug or a kiss goodnight?" Mal asked Gruhit sweetly.

"No," Gruhit answered quickly.

"Alright, Mr. Gruhit. Get some good sleep. Tomorrow is a new day full of new adventures and, most importantly, new hopes," Mal said in a quiet and tender voice. She peered down on him from his bedside.

Mrs. Wunder turned out the lights and closed the door so that it was open just a crack. Gruhit was excited to see what sorts of dreams he would have tonight.

Then he heard the Wunders' voices in the hall.

"Are you sure Amarie was asleep before you came downstairs?"

"Yeah, I'm positive, Samme. After putting the salve on her, she started to fall asleep pretty quick. Why? What happened up there?"

"It's just that it was a mess. I mean colored pencils and toys everywhere."

"But why was she screaming?"

"That's the other thing. It looks like something got into her closet, took out one of the extra blankets, and then dropped it over her while she was sleeping! By the time I got up there, she was completely tangled up. It looked like part of the blanket was trying to attack her. I might have been scared by all that too."

"Oh no. I can't imagine her doing that to herself, and Kieffer would have stopped Chardy from pulling a prank on his sister."

"Right, and there is no way that a tangerella or little folk would have done this. Mal, the only thing that makes sense to me is that the golem did it."

"Oh, geez. You're right. But how did it get upstairs? I can't believe it would scare that poor little girl like that. Sometimes I wonder why we let that thing stay in our house."

"Now, Mal, it's a living thing and deserves the same right to life as we all do. Besides, it's made from a young child's laugh and has the same IQ. It doesn't really know what it is doing."

"I think you better have Kieffer stay with Amarie tonight. Even if the golem isn't upstairs, at least he can use his magic to keep her calm. The poor thing really needs some sleep."

"Agreed. I'll fetch Kieffer from Chardy's room while I check on Chardy. Mr. Dickelbutton said that he would send his wife to check on Amarie later too."

With that, the light in the hallway was turned off, and Gruhit let the dipsy toad salve take him into a deep slumber.

Chapter 15
Cheese Head

The backdoor to Big Blue flew open. Gruhit raced through it, up the short flight of stairs, and to his room. He quickly closed and locked his doors, tossing his backpack on the ground before throwing himself on the bed. He didn't want to cry. The tears came anyway.

There was a knock. He knew it was a foster, but he wanted to be alone. There was another knock.

"Gruhit, are you alright?" Mr. Wunder's voice called softly. "Can you please open the door? I just want to make sure you're okay."

Gruhit weighed his options. He could let Samme in and talk about school, but that would mean reliving all the emotions that he was trying to tame. He knew Mr. Wunder would try to make him feel better about his situation, and there was nothing good about it right now. This was supposed to be his best first day of school ever. He was just so frustrated at how things turned out.

Gruhit had awoken that morning to hear Kieffer telling him to get ready. It was fun having a guardling wake you up for school instead of a foster. Mrs. Wunder had made scrambled eggs and bacon. She even put everyone's apple juice in mugs so that it looked like they were drinking coffee like the adults. Mrs. Wunder called it their "kid coffee." Of course, Chardy thought it was a dumb idea, and Amarie was so excited that she created a song. Gruhit felt like he was a real apprentice for sure.

"Remember, everyone, this is a new day full of new adventures and most of all, new hopes and dreams," Mr. Wunder announced as they finished breakfast. "I want everyone outside the backdoor in twenty minutes dressed, with teeth brushed, and backpacks in hand."

Gruhit had felt so good that he was delighted to take his breakfast dishes to the sink. In the bathroom, Gruhit began to collect his toothpaste and toothbrush. He looked over at the counter to see a watery mess. However, as he flicked the light on he could just make out the words, "Have Fun" in water. This little message from the drleck made him smile.

Then there was the note on his backpack, written on a thin piece of paper about the size of his pinky. It said, "*Have a good day, Young Master. We are all hoping that your head becomes full with lots of learning. - The Dickelbuttons.*" Gruhit had glanced around quickly, but didn't see any little folks. He felt like the whole neighborhood wanted him to have a good day.

Gruhit had been the first person to make it outside by the backdoor to wait for Mr. Wunder to take them to school. The Wunders had even gotten him a new backpack. It had pictures of superheroes all over it. He was glad that the Wunders were younger than his fosters in House Number 5. They didn't know anything about movies or things that kids liked. In that home, he just got a plain, red backpack. He didn't even like that color. He had also hoped that none of the other kids knew he was in foster care.

As he had waited to leave in the Wunders' minivan, he spotted a boy walking on the sidewalk toward Big Blue. He thought he recognized him, but he couldn't figure out how. He had never been to this town before, as far as he knew. Why would this boy look familiar? He had started to think about what he could say. The boy appeared to be about Chardy's age, so Gruhit knew he wouldn't see him at school. However, if he lived nearby, they could hang out.

The boy was two paces away from the corner of Big Blue's yard when several things happened. The backdoor opened and Samme stepped outside. The boy started running along the sidewalk like his life depended on it. Gruhit said, "Hello. My name's Gruhit," to which Mr. Wunder joked, "Hello, Gruhit Brown. I believe we met a few days ago."

Gruhit ignored the joke and just stared in confusion as the boy kept running. He then remembered that this was the same boy that ran into Constance when she dropped them off.

Samme looked down at this watch. "I see it is 8:15 already," he said. "Running boy is right on time, which is more than I can say for your brother and sister. By the way, is it getting cold in your room, Gruhit? I noticed the basement seemed to be a bit chilly."

"Why does the boy run, Mr Wunder?" Gruhit asked. He was still very curious.

"Oh, well, I'm afraid that is Kieffer's doing."

"Kieffer?"

"Yes. It seems that he was having some fun with the boy when he would walk to school every day. Kieffer would sit outside on the top of the steps here in the morning to enjoy the sun warming his fur. When the boy would walk by, Kieffer would call out strange things to him like, 'Your zipper's down,' 'Look out for the snake,' or 'They're all going to laugh at you.' When the boy would look around for the voice, Kieffer would pretend to be an ordinary house cat. It wasn't until I noticed the boy running by every day that I figured out what was going on and put a stop to it."

Shortly after this explanation, Chardy came out of the house wearing a hoodie with the hood up and his earbuds in his ears. He ignored Mr. Wunder's question about the temperature of his room and took the front passenger seat in the minivan. Amarie bounded out the door wearing a brightly colored outfit; Gruhit thought she looked like a living rainbow. Her mood almost seemed to match as she skipped to the van. Her backpack was full to the point of almost bursting. Gruhit knew that she was bringing her toys with her, but not to play with. He knew she always tried to make new friends by giving away her things. The problem Gruhit noticed is that the children might not like her the next day, and some kids only played with her because they thought they would get new toys.

Gruhit and Mr. Wunder were the last to get into the minivan. Gruhit stared out the windows as they passed the homes that he had seen when being brought to the Wunders. It was odd that just a couple days ago he was a complete stranger, and now he was somehow part of this community. The van took a left turn and, after a few blocks, came upon a large middle school which looked like it had been built in the early 1920s. The words "High School" were etched in stone at the top of the building. There were also two prominent doors that said "Boys' Entrance," and "Girls' Entrance."

"Why can boys only go in that door?" asked Gruhit.

"Hmmm? Oh. They don't use those signs anymore," Samme explained. "That's from a long, long time ago when schools used to keep boys and girls separate in classrooms."

The van pulled behind a line of vehicles. When it was Chardy's turn to exit the van, Mr. Wunder called to him, "Remember to go to the office. It will be just to the left of the front doors. The principal is waiting to show you to your new class-room. Are you sure you don't want me to come and…"

Chardy turned around and walked off. He gestured a goodbye with his hand and quickly walked into the crowd.

Mr. Wunder guided the van back to the main road. They drove back to 19th Street, only instead of turning right to head towards Big Blue, they took a left. Gruhit noticed a small little convenience store on the corner. Gruhit wondered if they had candy. It was probably only six blocks away from Big Blue, so he could easily walk there with his allowance money. They passed a large, elaborate church built in the early 1900s. Eventually, they came upon a small elementary school.

Gruhit could feel his anxiety rise when the van pulled into the drop-off line. He didn't know what to expect.

"Alright, you two. Remember that the principal's assistant will be meeting you at the line here and taking you both to your classrooms. There are so many nice people in this town and many great kids. I'm sure you'll have a great first day. Either way, I want to hear all about it when you get home. Ah, it's Mrs. Stevens."

Gruhit saw a short and plump woman walking up to the van.

"Good morning! This must be Gruhit and Amarie. Well, let's get out quickly so we don't hold up the line," Mrs. Stevens said.

"Do either one of you need a hug before going?" Samme asked.

"I'm fine," Gruhit said.

Amarie, however, gave Mr. Wunder a hug. Mrs. Stevens kindly took their hands as they watched Mr. Wunder drive away back to Big Blue.

THUMP. THUMP. THUMP.

Gruhit broke away from his thoughts about the morning to hear Mr. Wunder knocking on the door again.

"Gruhit, I just need you to at least tell me that you're alright, and I'll go away for a bit," Samme said.

Sounds of someone working the lock on the door could be heard. Then slowly the door opened into Gruhit's bedroom. The fall sun was dancing its way into the green bedroom and created a cheerful atmosphere. It was the opposite of how Gruhit felt. He was able to keep the tears from flowing so that he didn't feel embarrassed. Gruhit could feel the mattress move as Mr. Wunder sat next to him. A warm hand began to rub his upper back.

"Gruhit, what happened at school today?" Samme said softly.

Gruhit wasn't sure if he wanted to talk about it. What if Samme thought that there was something wrong with him, and then they all had to move again?

"Would it be helpful for me to ask your teacher?" Samme inquired.

Call the teacher? Hearing that was like an alarm in Gruhit's head. He absolutely did not want Mr. Wunder talking to his teacher. What if the teacher told the other kids that he snitched, and then they all made fun of him? Gruhit let out a sigh.

"Gruhit?" Samme prodded again.

Gruhit turned over and sat up on the edge of the bed next to Samme. He kept his eyes on the ground to keep from crying.

"What do you want to know?" Gruhit asked.

"What happened at school today?" Samme questioned again.

Cautiously and slowly, Gruhit started to recount his day after Samme had dropped them off. Mrs. Stevens had taken Amarie and him to their classrooms, which were right next to each other. Gruhit was introduced to his teacher, Mrs. Snow, who was thin and very friendly. She had short, spiky black hair and talked in soothing tones. Mrs. Snow showed Gruhit to his desk at the front of the room.

Gruhit somewhat liked being at the front of the classroom because he couldn't see if the other kids were looking at him strangely. If he pretended, he could imagine that there were only the two kids on either side of his desk and no one else. It helped to pretend because Gruhit always felt out of place. Not only was he the only student in his class with darker skin, but he was sure no one else was in foster care. What made things worse was that since this was a small town, everyone else knew each other. Mrs. Snow made him stand in front of the class and introduce himself.

He had looked at his feet and didn't know what to say. Was he supposed to talk about his mom? The apartment he came from? Should he tell them about the other homes he lived in? He hadn't wanted anyone to know that he was different, that he lived with fosters. Most of the students snickered and whispered to each other as he softly cracked his voice to say, "I like cheese."

"Did you tell Mrs. Snow that I was in foster care!?" Gruhit angrily demanded through falling tears while looking Mr. Wunder straight in the eyes.

"No, Gruhit, no," Samme said, shocked. "The teachers always ask kids to introduce themselves."

Gruhit stared at Samme until he decided he could trust what he was saying. There was little else to report for the morning. After the class settled down from his embarrassing moment, he sat back at his desk, and they learned English, math, and reading.

Mrs. Snow then instructed the class to line up at the door in single file when called so they could all walk to the cafeteria for lunch. Gruhit got up from his seat to join the line when his name was called. As he walked by the desk of the girl to his left, a foot came out and tripped Gruhit. He stumbled and fell flat on his face. Several students had laughed as he sheepishly got up. The girl smirked at him maliciously, then whispered, "Watch it, Cheesehead. You might trip." Shortly after, Mrs. Snow called for Judy Credulent to join the line.

Things didn't get much better in the cafeteria. Since all of the students knew each other, they sat together. Gruhit went to the end of a long table by himself. He desperately wished someone would join him, but there he sat alone, feeling like everyone knew he was a foster kid and that he was different.

Gruhit put his hamburger down and hung his head. He thought about his mom. He should be able to tell the class about his mom and that she is wonderful. His mom should have been the one to bring him to his first day of school. He was so angry, but at the same time, he desperately wanted his mom to be there. He wanted her to tell them all that he was a great artist and how dare they laugh at and trip a boy of his talent. As Gruhit imagined the different ways his mom could save him, he felt the tears welling up at the lunch table. He desperately held them back. He knew that crying would seal the deal, and everyone would think he was a freak.

As lunchtime ended, Mrs. Snow asked the students to stack their trays at the washing station and line up quietly by the door to the playground. Gruhit was still trying to keep himself from crying when he noticed Amarie's class coming into the lunchroom. Amarie was her overly cheerful self and appeared to have made at least five new friends. Gruhit wondered what toys she had bribed them with. Amarie smiled and waved at her brother while she talked with her friends. Gruhit noticed the girl who tripped him, Judy, stopped to say something to Amarie, as she passed.

Outside, many of the boys were playing soccer. The girls played tag or were on the merry-go-round. A few of the kids were doing various tricks on the monkey bars. Gruhit sat against the school building and watched the other kids play, trying to hold onto his mixed emotions. In front of him, a few girls chased after each other. The last girl stopped in front of him. Since Gruhit was looking downward, he could see the red canvas shoes that had tripped him earlier.

"Hey, look there. It's Cheesehead."

Gruhit stayed silent, hoping she would just go away. Judy knelt down to be eye level with Gruhit.

"You know you don't belong here," Judy said sneeringly. "I thought you looked like you lived in the ghetto. But then I saw your clothes and thought they look too nice, unless your parents sell drugs. Then your sister said something about your foster parents."

Gruhit was shocked that Amarie had told someone. He looked up toward Judy's face.

"Did you have to go into foster care because your parents got busted? Or are they too poor to afford a house in the ghetto? Dad says that the people in the government housing area need to be run out of town because they cause nothing but trouble. Maybe, you're with your foster parents so they can train you to be a decent person."

"Leave him alone, Judy."

Gruhit and Judy hadn't noticed a boy from their class come over. The boy wore jeans and a blue sweatshirt with images of video game controllers on it. He had a stern look, and his hands were on his hips.

"I was leaving anyway," Judy said with an attitude. She stood up and got partly into the boy's face. She stayed there for a moment to show she wasn't scared, then walked away. "I miss seeing your grandma around here, Nathan."

Judy rejoined her game of tag with the other girls. Nathan put his back against the building and slid down to sit next to Gruhit. Both of them sat in silence, staring forward before Nathan finally spoke.

"Is it true that you're in foster care?"

Gruhit eventually nodded. Nathan continued looking out at the playground.

"Look, I came over here because I thought Judy was trying to make friends. I didn't realize that she was... well... her dad's family has been in this town for generations. She says they helped start the town. Anyways, we're not all like her."

The two boys continued sitting on the ground until the silence became awkward. They could see the soccer game in the distance. A boy had just scored a goal. Another called out to Nathan in frustration.

"I need to get back to the game. I'll see you around, Gruhit."

Gruhit couldn't concentrate on his afternoon classes. His only thought was that he didn't belong there. He kept wondering how many people in his class knew he was a freak in a foster home. Gruhit was never so happy for the end of the school day to come.

The students had their backpacks filled and were told to sit at their desk drawing or reading books. Mrs. Snow answered the phone and shortly after announced, "Alice, your ride is here. Walk down the hall to the pick-up line."

Over the next few minutes, several children were called to leave including Judy, Nathan, and several girls.

"Gruhit Brown," Mrs. Snow announced. She motioned for Gruhit to come toward her instead of going directly out the door. "It was good to have you in class. I can't wait to see you tomorrow. I expect you can find the line without causing any trouble. Yes?"

Gruhit nodded. He walked out of the door at the end of the hallway and out into the afternoon sun. He could see the Wunders' minivan toward the end of the line and Amarie already getting into her seat. Gruhit was walking with determination to leave this awful day behind him when he heard a high-pitched voice call his name. He looked back over his shoulder to see Judy and three other girls giggling in his direction.

"On top of spaghetti, all covered with CHEESE," the girls sang. "A Cheesehead TRIPPED on a noodle and fell into disease."

Gruhit quickened his pace as the girls burst into laughter. He hated this place. He hated being in foster care. He hated being away from his mom. He was filled with rage and grief all at once. He could feel the two emotions filling him. He ran to the minivan before he exploded in a volcanic eruption of crying and screaming. He lunged onto the back seat and bit his lip hard to try and stop the tears that were already pooling at the bottom of his eyes.

"Oh, Gruhit, that's terrible," Mr. Wunder said, next to him on the bed. "I hate that you had to go through a day like that."

Gruhit suddenly realized he had leaned over against Samme. It felt good to have

Mr. Wunder's arm around him. It was good to hear someone else say that the day's events were horrible. Above all, he felt safe right now. It was nice to feel safe again.

"You know, I was bullied a lot in school too," Samme said. "It seems that when you're extremely fat and telling other children about magical creatures that live in your home, most kids think you're a freak."

Gruhit looked up toward Samme. He was having a hard time picturing Samme fat.

"I usually spent recess by myself," Samme went on. "There were a few kids who would play with me, but sometimes their families would move away, and I'd be by myself again. I'll tell you what my father always told me. 'Gruhit, tomorrow you will leave this house, and you will meet many people and face many adventures. Sometimes you'll be scared, and sometimes you'll feel alone. However, at the end of the day you will come home, and at home you know we always love you and are always proud of you.'"

They sat in silence for a bit. When Samme could feel that Gruhit was breathing calmly again, he crouched down to look at the boy at eye level.

"I have to get back to work. Are you going to be okay?"

Gruhit slowly nodded.

"Do you need me to talk to your teacher?" Samme asked.

Gruhit shook his head no.

"Your friend, Nathan, was right. The Credulent family has been around this town for many years. They likely did have an ancestor establish this town. They have a lot of connections and seem to get people to do what they want. Do you want me to talk to Judy's parents? I will be happy to do that for you."

Gruhit thought for a second before finally shaking his head no again.

"Alright. Let me know if you want me to do something though, okay? It's okay to ask other people for help," Samme instructed. "I can't keep bad things from happening to you, Gruhit. I can, however, make sure that you have hope for the future and remember that you're special."

With that, Samme stood and left Gruhit by himself. The boy slowly slid off his bed and walked over to his backpack to pull out his sketchbook. He sat on the hard floor and thumbed through the pages. Most were still blank. He passed his sketches of the drleck from the night before and was impressed with them. He stopped as he came across a page with a monster. The name Fridgita Mortes was written under it. Gruhit thought about the winged fairy who was leading a rebellion. He thought about Judy at school and wondered if she would join Fridgita if she was given the chance. Fridgita did anything she could to steal hope away from people, just like Judy had taken away his hope of a wonderful school year. Gruhit decided then that he wouldn't let her do that. Afterall, he did meet Nathan because Judy was being mean to him. Yes, he would concentrate on being friends with Nathan.

Gruhit felt a little better but was still scared. Judy and those other girls would probably still sing their songs and make fun of him. He could always tell Samme to talk to Judy's parents to make her stop. This would be a last resort. There was hope he could do something about the bullying, and that was all he needed at the moment.

Chapter 16
Plotting Against The Golem

Amarie, Chardy, and Gruhit had been living with the Wunders for over a month when Halloween arrived. It was also a Saturday, and when Gruhit woke up, he realized he had survived yet another week at his school.

Despite all the concerns at school he still seemed to sleep well as did Amarie. They seemed to both wake up constantly with a crusty substance underneath their eyes every morning. Gruhit had learned this was more than likely due to a walluping wallop visiting each of them in the night. Wallops were tiny jelly-fish-like creatures with giant eyes. They floated through the air at night. The small delicate creatures move up and down in a bobbing motion with their tentacles dangling below them. When they find a sleeping boy or girl, they insert a tentacle into their ear and feed off their dreams. Gruhit thought the amazing part of the creature was that the dream of the person showed on their giant eyes like a television. The whole process was supposed to be pleasant and actually put boys and girls into a deeper sleep. Mr. Wunder told Gruhit that if the wallop began to feed on a nightmare, they would shoot sundust through their tentacle, and the tentacle would disintegrate before the scary dream had a chance to poison the small creatures. The dust works its way through a child's head and exits through the eyes. Gruhit never dreamed that would be where eye boogers came from.

School had become easier. He and Nathan had become close friends. Malda helped him think of questions to ask Nathan, and now he knew that Nathan's favorite color was blue, his favorite food was cheese pizza (just like him), and he lived with his mom and dad. His birthday was in March.

Gruhit laid in his bed, not quite wanting to start the day. While he was very happy to be staying with the Wunders, he was a bit worried about all the changes in the house. During the first month, it seemed like the new fosters and the kids were getting used to each other and always putting their best foot forward. That was normal for a new house. Gruhit knew that he tried to be more helpful and didn't want a new foster to see his weaknesses the first few weeks. If you were weak or seen as a "bad" kid, then the adults would move you to a different home. But he knew that after a month or so, weaknesses and flaws couldn't be hidden any longer.

For Amarie, this meant that she began to show just how scared of the dark she really was. There were times in their birth home that Amarie, and even Gruhit, could remember that their mom would be gone all night while she worked a double shift. Their apartment building seemed to never sleep. There were always people walking by the front door or laughing or screaming. Sometimes they thought they heard gunshots. Often someone would jiggle the front door knob to see if it was locked. Luckily, they never got in, but the kids were always terrified.

This whole experience affected Amarie the most. She was absolutely terrified of dark areas. For Amarie, chattering kept her mind on other things and away from the scary places.

If it were just constant chatter, most fosters would be able to cope. However, she would sometimes be too afraid to leave her bedroom at night, even though she had to use the bathroom. Gruhit knew that Amarie absolutely adored the Wunders and was embarrassed about wetting the bed. She had been hiding in her bedroom closet to pee and hoping the Wunders wouldn't find out. Of course they did when her bedroom started to smell.

The tangerellas continued to visit Amarie almost every night and slept in her hair. Mrs. Dickelbutton also frequently made trips up to Amarie's room to check on her. It wasn't uncommon for Amarie to wake up to find a paperclip ladder coming out of her air conditioning vent. She often found little notes of encouragement to her saying such things as, "Fear not, Young Mistress, for I check on you at night," or "You are smart, Young Mistress. You are safe in this house," or "I'm sorry you cry when you sleep, Young Mistress. Know that we all care for you deeply." A couple of times Amarie even found Dickelbutton pie, made from raisins and various berries, with a note. They were small, of course, but they tasted absolutely delicious and always made her feel special and happy.

Chardy continued to lose himself in his iPod. He wanted to seclude himself as much as possible. He often barked orders at Gruhit and Amarie. Gruhit didn't like it when Chardy was bossy, but sometimes it was comforting to have a father figure. The last couple of weeks, the Wunders tried to tend to Gruhit's needs and repeatedly told Chardy to stop parenting Gruhit. This happened in all the homes they had lived in. New fosters seemed to hate that Chardy would tell Gruhit when to go to bed, or do his homework, or to try new foods at dinner. Chardy became more frustrated with the fosters. On these days, Chardy seemed to only get along with Kieffer. Maybe it was because they were both annoyed with the golem that lived in the basement.

Gruhit didn't want to bring any issues to the household, but he knew he wasn't making life easy for the Wunders. Just the other day, Mal found his whole underwear drawer full of pancakes, a few chicken strips, crackers, suckers he got from his new teacher for good behavior, and several small cartons of chocolate milk he took from the school lunchroom. Gruhit had to clean up the mess and listen to a lecture about food attracting bugs, which could make the magical creatures ill. Gruhit had heard it all before (except the part about magical creatures, of course) and thought fosters worried about odd things.

While things in the home had become more hectic, Gruhit still liked the Wunders. They were honest, and they didn't pretend to be perfect. Mal had yelled at him when she found the food stuffed in his drawer. However, she came back to Gruhit at bedtime and apologized. He had heard both Wunders apologize to his brother and sister too at other times. This was so different from the other homes. The fosters there expected him to realize that they were right about everything and would not hesitate to call Constance about his poor behavior.

The best thing about the Wunders was that Mal was trying to become friends with their mom. Before the kids would leave for their weekly visit with her, Mal would give them a handwritten letter - all boring adult stuff. They mostly talked about how each child was doing at school and summaries of recent doctor visits. Each note always ended with Mal hoping that Gruhit's mom was doing well and letting her know that Mal was wishing her well. His mom always got really quiet and teary-eyed when she read the letters.

Visits happened like clockwork, every Friday without fail. Constance would pick up all three kids from Big Blue and drive them about 45 minutes to a neighboring town. Their mom would meet them at a fast food restaurant. She never missed a visit and always seemed overjoyed to see them. The visits went somewhat the same each time. Constance would buy everyone a children's meal, and the group would sit at the same large booth next to an indoor play area. Gruhit would sit on one side of his mom and Chardy on the other. Amarie would sit on the end of the bench because she was always interested in eating quickly so she could play. Constance usually watched Amarie so Gruhit and Chardy could have more time with their mom. Sometimes their mom bought all of them ice cream when she had a little extra money.

Gruhit broke from his thoughts to notice new little paper jack-o-lanterns attached near the top of his windows. He sat up in his bed and stared at the handiwork.

Then he jumped out of bed and ran to the dining room hoping for some breakfast. He was awestruck to see pancakes shaped like pumpkins and a thick, sticky topping that smelled like maple and cinnamon. He saw Mal dressed in fancy orange leggings with a pumpkin pattern all over them and a long green shirt with a leaf pattern. Even though his foster mother might be more stressed and getting less sleep with all the challenges in her home, she was still able to perform a new hairstyle every day. Today her hair was braided and rolled into a pumpkin-type shape with a small green leaf poking out to the side.

Gruhit took a seat at the table. He could now see the top of the large windows had the same little paper jack-o-lanterns. There were also pumpkins sitting around all the tables and shelves with scattered candles here and there giving off various fall scents. He looked at the curtains alongside the windows to see them adorned with colored leaves. The whole house from top to bottom was ready for fall. Gruhit didn't know why, but the scents and sights made him happier this morning.

"Good morning, Gruhit," Mal said, both tired and cheerful. "Mrs. Snickelfritz and the Dickelbuttons have finally gotten around to decorating the house. It seems they are starting to feel like their old selves. So I thought we would celebrate with the traditional Wunder fall pancakes. They're pumpkin pancakes with a special maple syrup and to wash them down, we have our own special, sweet pumpkin juice."

Mal began pouring cups of a juice that was a bit darker than apple juice. She then walked over to a side table and filled five tiny mugs, which were fashioned from thimbles. She also partially filled a small bowl, which she placed on the dining room table.

"Wheee!" squealed Amarie, walking into the dining room. "It's all beautiful down here too!"

As Amarie was trying to contain herself, Samme came up the stairs from the basement. He had clearly been working on sketches in his office, because he had pencil and charcoal smudges on his hands and face. Gruhit had noticed that Samme liked to scratch his nose or rub his face when thinking. Samme looked a bit weary when he saw Amarie.

"Amarie," Samme said, crouching down to be at her eye level. "Come here please."

Gruhit knew what this meant. Amarie had an accident again last night and Samme was going to quietly tell her to clean up her mess. His sister and Samme spoke for a minute before she said, "Yes, sir," and ran back up the stairs.

About the same time, Chardy came in listening to his iPod. He passed where Samme was squatting, nearly knocking him over.

"Good morning, sir," Mr. Wunder said half-sincerely and half-sarcastically.

Chardy went directly to the table and took a seat.

"Remember, no headphones at the table," stated Mal. She motioned for Chardy to take them out of his ears.

"Whatever," Chardy muttered, then added, "Because I gotta care what all of you are saying at the table anyways, right?"

Mal bit her lip and forced herself not to respond. She chose instead to go upstairs to check on Amarie.

Kieffer had quietly walked into the room and jumped up onto his seat. He gave a big yawn.

"Wunder pancakes? Pumpkin juice?" Kieffer questioned. "What's the occasion?" Gruhit chuckled. "I thought guardlings were supposed to be observant since you're so good at guarding."

Kieffer looked around the room. He was delighted to see the decorations but felt the need to shoot back at Gruhit, "Young Master, I will have you know that my guarding skills are as good as ever. I mean, have you seen any more faces drawn on your brother?"

Chardy smirked a laugh. "Prolly cause we also set a trap for the thing," he said.

Kieffer tried to keep his normal dignified demeanor, but couldn't hold back a smirk.

"Kieffer," Samme said with a disappointing tone. "I really wish you wouldn't. It just seems cruel. I mean, it only has fluff for brains."

"We haven't done anything to hurt it, sir," Kieffer stated. "Oh, but we must check the heater later. There was no damage to the golem, but I must say that it is a bit chilly in that bedroom."

As he spoke, Gruhit noticed that Kieffer's voice sounded like he was a bit stuffed up. Maybe the chilliness in the basement had given him a cold.

"But we did make fluff-for-brains think about drawing again," Chardy said, then turned to Gruhit. "I set a big black permanent marker on my nightstand to tempt it. What Mr. No-Brains couldn't see was that it was attached to a string and a small net full of markers. It created a big mess."

"The golem isn't hurt sir," Kieffer said to Samme. "However, it did have a lot of obstacles to crawl out of over the course of the night."

Gruhit watched as Chardy and Kieffer looked at each other and laughed. As Chardy gave Kieffer a fist bump, Gruhit thought it felt good to see his older brother making a friend.

Chardy usually kept to himself mostly in foster homes. He would never admit it, but this was the furthest thing from what he actually wanted - to be left alone. However, Chardy found that as the oldest sibling, most fosters expected him to help with the chores, know important things like clothing sizes, and help care for his younger siblings. Fosters never seemed to spend time with him just for fun or to get to know him. Fosters always seemed to want to dote over Gruhit because he was small and cute. Amarie was nearly every foster mom's dream because she liked doing girly things.

Chardy was often left out. Even at his mom's apartment, he was expected to help his siblings get ready for bed, eat dinner, get ready for school, and take care of them when they were sick. He wasn't able to just be himself. Chardy couldn't figure out that he felt several things at once. He knew he loved his brother and sister and would do anything to protect them. But he also felt invisible. He felt like no one noticed him or cared to learn his interests. He had these feelings of being abandoned too. He knew his mom cared for him and he loved her, but she let them get taken away.

Gruhit looked at his brother who was now plotting with Kieffer to thwart the golem again that night. Gruhit knew that Chardy wanted to feel like someone wanted him, someone that would ask about his feelings and not just wait for Chardy to share them.

It reminded Gruhit of a cartoon he saw when someone fell off a boat. The person in the water never expects to find someone on the boat. The people on the boat are supposed to notice them and throw a life preserver. No one had noticed Chardy enough. Chardy had tried several times in other homes, like by starting a fire in a wastebasket in his room. He didn't want to burn the house down. But instead of being noticed, he was yelled at, punished, and forced to start therapy sessions. Then they were all moved to a new foster home.

Gruhit smiled because he could see a guardling connecting with his brother. It was good to see him make a friend. He hadn't completely connected with the Wunders yet, but Gruhit hoped he would soon.

"Mr. Wunder," Gruhit said excitedly as his train of thought made him realize something. "The golem can't be hurt. Remember they are made out of inanimate objects - like dust balls, paperclips, string, and stuff lying around the house."

"Gross!" exclaimed Chardy. "You're telling me that thing is made up of all the trash that collects by the baseboard?"

"Sure. A golem is created when a toddler gives their first mischievous laugh. The laugh collects discarded items all around it to make a golem," Gruhit turned to look at Samme. "That's why they can't get hurt. Even if their arm breaks off, the magic just collects a new item to replace it."

Samme looked over at Gruhit and smiled approvingly.

"It sounds like someone has been doing some research lately," Samme said, retrieving his own sketchbook from his overcoat pocket. "Do you have anything new to show me?"

"Not really," Gruhit said. "I've done a few more drawings of Kieffer, and the drlecks showed themselves to me a few more times. I'm really hoping to see a tangerella or the little folks."

"Mmm-hmmm," Samme agreed. He glanced through his sketchbook. "Tangerellas are extremely difficult to see..."

"Because they feel that it is their sworn duty to guard their beauty and not have it seen by most human eyes," Gruhit interrupted. "Tangerellas, like the one we saw with Mal and Mrs. Bangs, always wear long dresses to hide their bodies. They don't want anyone seeing their beauty."

Samme looked up at Gruhit, much impressed. He thumbed through his sketchbook a bit more before setting it in the middle of the table, just as Mal and Amarie came into the room. Amarie had on play clothes and was holding her bed sheets.

"Go ahead and set the sheets inside the washer, Amarie," Mal stated. She noticed the open sketchbook. "Oh, no! It's the Halloween Party this evening. Are there reports of storms tonight? Is that why you're looking at these creatures?"

"Nah, no storms but," Samme said with a grin, "I think tonight would be a great night to see the dwarves."

"On Halloween night?" Mal said, slightly exasperated. "You know tonight is their festival, right?"

"Of course!" Samme exclaimed. "It will be the best time to see the dwarves having fun. Come on, you know they're usually workaholics."

"Actually, I like to think that they simply like a job well done," Mal smirked. "I kinda really admire them for that reason."

"So we're going on a creature search tonight?" Gruhit said excitedly.

"Well... I guess so," Mal said very thoughtfully. "But we'll do it after the Halloween Party at the school this evening."

Mal sat down in her chair. Gruhit could tell by looking at her face that some sort of plan was being constructed in her head. While Samme might be the creative outward thinker of the house, Mal was a whiz at forming plans and sorting out issues.

"Right, here we go," Mal stated. "After breakfast, we're going to complete all the chores…"

"What? On a Saturday?" Chardy exclaimed with disgust. "Can't you just get some of the drlecks or the Dickelbuttons to do that stuff?"

"That would be dishonest and cruel," Mal said bluntly. "The little folks, while they love hard work, are not our slaves and have their own homes to clean."

"Whatever," Chardy rolled his eyes and sat back in his chair. Gruhit couldn't figure out why, but Chardy really did seem to have a dislike for Mrs. Wunder.

"Here now," Kieffer added, "take some pride in yourself, Young Master. Learning to care for oneself and one's family is very noble. Guardlings have known since the beginning of time that protecting a family means more than merely from large attackers. Sometimes the attacks come from germs and small insects. Very noble indeed is the task of cleaning and keeping a home."

Chardy still looked a bit disgusted at Mal, but his face softened.

"As I was saying, we will complete chores," Mal jumped back on her past train of thought. "Then I think it would be a good idea if we inspected costumes to be sure that nothing needs touching up. We should be done with all of that by lunchtime, and the school event doesn't start until 5 o'clock. That means you should have plenty of time to walk down the street to meet Mr. and Mrs. Lusplendida."

"Yes, yes," stated Samme. "They know more about the dwarves, fleet birds, and charmyrrls than anyone I know. Well… besides Mal and myself."

"That's not saying much," Chardy mumbled, "since there aren't that many folks who know anything about these things."

"It's a great idea Mal," Samme said jubilantly. "We'll head over there after lunch, and maybe you'll learn why Mal thought a rainstorm was coming tonight."

As Amarie stood in the doorway to the kitchen, a knothole door opened up in the trim. A boy about five inches in height, with antennae coming out of his head, stepped out of the hole and onto a side table. He was wearing overalls with patches all over them and a dark orange shirt. He was barefoot with toes which were quite hairy. The hair on his head was a tangled, curly mess. Amarie gasped slightly at the boy's sudden appearance.

The boy looked up to see most of the people staring at him from the breakfast table.

"Um… er… I'm sorry to interrupt," the boy said slowly with notes of embarrassment.

"Not at all. There is no reason to feel bad. This is your house too," Samme said in a calming voice. "Everyone, this is Tad Schwartz. He lives with the Dickelbuttons along with his sister, Emily."

"Would you like to have some Wunder pancakes, Tad?" Mal asked the little folk boy. "Will Mrs. Dickelbutton be joining us this morning, too? I have cups and food ready for all of you."

"No, thank you," Tad stated, still nervous. "I need to speak with Mr. Wunder… the Master… sir."

"Call me whatever you like, Tad," Samme said. Samme had wished they would all just call him and Mal by their first names, but, out of respect, they insisted on Master and Mistress. "What message do you have for me?"

"It's the Snickelfritz's, sir," Tad said, staring at the ground. He couldn't stand that people were looking at him.

Mal and Samme instantly looked concerned when they heard that name. Mal immediately got up and ran to the kitchen.

"Has his condition worsened?" Samme asked Tad.

"We cannot tell, sir, but Mrs. Snickelfritz is much worse," Tad said, fighting back tears. "Mom went to go see her this morning. Mrs. Snickelfritz had stayed up all night in her chair thinking after we finished decorating. Mom said that she would barely speak to her, but kept staring off into the distance. Mom said that the room seemed to be colder than the rest of the house."

"Kieffer!" Samme stated in a slight alarm.

"I'm ready to go when you are, sir."

"Mal!" Samme called into the kitchen, with the same sense of urgency.

"Hold on! I'm hurrying!" Mal came running back into the room with a small cloth sack of Wunder pancakes cut up into tiny portions. "Tad, take these to Mrs. Snickelfritz. They're still warm, and they always seem to lift her spirits."

"Where is everyone at right now, Tad?" Samme asked the little folk.

"When mom felt the coldness, she ran to get me, to fetch you. Mom went back over there, and Dad stayed with Emily at home," Tad said. He clutched the bag of Wunder pancakes and continued to fight his tears.

"Tad, I want you to go back over and stay with your mom. Kieffer and I will get there soon," Samme said.

Tad turned around urgently. He began to walk through the knothole door when Samme added, "Tad, you're doing an excellent job. You got help, and we are on our way. We don't know what's going to happen, but there *is* hope."

Tad disappeared through the doorway. It closed behind him, blending perfectly into the wooden texture of the door's trim again. None of the children knew exactly what to say. They could tell something serious was happening. They weren't sure whether they should be scared or not.

Samme and Kiffer jumped up and started off quickly for the basement steps. Mal stopped Samme to give him a bigger container of Wunder pancakes and a travel pitcher full of pumpkin juice.

"Good food always seems to lift spirits," Mal stated.

"I'll be back as soon as I can, but I'm not sure I can guarantee I'll be back in time to..."
"We'll be fine," Mal interrupted. "You make sure that the little folks are okay."

With that, Samme and Kieffer disappeared. Mal sat back at her seat, still looking concerned. The children and Mrs. Wunder began eating their breakfast in silence.

Gruhit felt like he needed to be on guard for something bad that might happen. Which is also how he felt back in his mom's apartment most nights. He always mentally prepared himself for what he might need to do in case someone broke into the house or his mom never came back home. He hated this feeling. He hated how these scary moments reminded him of the past. He knew that Chardy and Amarie were also reliving their own moments. They all sat at the table trying to concentrate on how delicious the Wunder pancakes tasted. However, all Gruhit could seem to think was whether Fridgita Mortes was planning an attack.

Chapter 17
Sundust and Dragon

Samme was gone for a long time. Malda expected all of them to continue with the day as planned. She explained that what was happening with the little folks was out of their control; there was nothing any of them could do at the moment. However, they *could* still take care of the house and their chores for the day.

"Remember, we work hard and then play hard," Mal said several times throughout the morning.

Each of them was expected to straighten up their rooms and sweep the floor. They were to take their dirty clothes to the laundry room and sort it into piles of whites, light colors, and dark colors. Gruhit had a little trouble with this, but Malda was always happy to answer his questions. Lastly, each of them had a chore they were responsible for daily. Chardy had to empty the trash cans and take everything outside. Amarie was responsible for putting away the clean dishes from the dishwasher before clearing, as well as wiping off, the emptied dining room table after each meal. Gruhit had to sweep the kitchen, dining room, and living room floors. Gruhit thought it was a bit much to have to sweep the floor everyday, but Malda countered that five people created a lot of crumbs and dirt.

He didn't want to admit it, but he did have a lot of waste in the dustpan each time.

Malda walked around the home to survey the children's work.

"Well, it's not completely up to code," Mal stated as she eyed crumbs on the haphazardly wiped table and several dust bunnies in a corner, "but we'll continue to improve with practice."

Halloween costume inspection time was next. Each child's costume seemed to fit well. Malda instructed each of them to go to their rooms and hang their costumes so that they didn't get wrinkled. She also instructed them to put on some warm clothes and report back to the dining room for lunch.

Gruhit rushed to his room and began removing his costume. He fidgeted with the hanger and did the best he could to get his outfit hung up in the closet. It was difficult for Gruhit to get his fingers to do things like other kids, he noticed. When he lived in Houses Number 1 and 2, he visited a therapist who helped him with things like zipping up a zipper, buttoning small buttons, and lacing up shoes. He overheard the therapist tell his fosters that he would have difficulty using his "fine motor skills" because he didn't get practice doing these things when he was smaller. It's true. Chardy had always been there to help him. He never had to tie his shoes, or zip up a hoodie, because Chardy would do it. Even if he wanted to draw with crayons, Amarie would do the drawing for him. In fact, now that Gruhit thought about it, most of his existence in that apartment involved him walking or running from room to room and watching people instead of actually doing things.

Gruhit felt that lunchtime was pretty uneventful. There was still no sign of Samme or Kieffer. Malda made a special pumpkin soup. Gruhit thought it looked really weird, but tasted very delicious. He liked how Malda seemed to know just how warm to make soups, so they made all of your insides feel nice and warm.

"Well, that was just the right thing for lunch on Halloween," Malda stated as she let the spoon down into her empty soup bowl.

She was right. To Gruhit, the Wunders often seemed to know what to do, at least more than the other fosters he had lived with...even though they were the first children to ever be in the home.

"Mrs. Wunder, how do you know what to do all the time?" Gruhit asked.

Mal laughed. "What? Why would you think that?" she asked.

"It's true, Mrs. Wunder. You seem to make all the best foods, and Samme tells all the best stories," Amarie chimed in with a smile.

"Are you sure you haven't had kids before? Are you magic?" Gruhit asked, somewhat hopeful.

"Ya'll are nutty. There ain't nothin magic about these people. They're just your ordinary fosters," Chardy said.

"Says the boy that sleeps with a guardling at night," laughed Amarie.

Chardy shook off the comment. "Okay, well, I'll admit that there's some magic about this place."

"Well, thank you for what I think was a compliment, Gruhit. No, I'm not magic, nor do I know what I'm doing all the time. However, Samme and I have taken care of magical creatures who have been in danger or homeless for years. Actually, Samme was raised around it, so we both know how to help other living things through traumatic times. That's all. I can't tell you how many times I have cried before going to sleep because I know I have messed up. I also don't think I can say it enough: I don't want to replace your mom. My goal with the time you spend with us is to teach you as much as possible about how to live healthy and well. I do it because I would want your mom to teach and care for my children if I weren't able to be with them."

Gruhit recalled the last visit they had with their mom. She was normally so happy to see them. It wasn't that she was unhappy this time, but she seemed a bit more distant than usual, even defeated. She still had not found a safer place for them to live. She also lost one of her jobs because she was taking too much time off work to look for a safe, affordable apartment. To top it all off, her car was making a funny noise and might need repairs. Gruhit wasn't really sure how he could help her, so he just hugged her. When she read the letter Mal had sent with him, his mom just looked up at the ceiling. Her beautiful brown eyes sparkled from the sunlight. Gruhit saw tears forming, and she was biting her lower lip. Chardy scooted closer to her, took her hand and put his head on her shoulder. Constance, who had been watching Amarie in the play area, came over and asked Gruhit to go with Amarie for a bit. Gruhit was glad that his mom knew someone was taking care of her three kids, but who would take care of his mom?

Mrs. Wunder interrupted his thoughts, "Amarie, get the table cleaned while I get your jacket. Boys, be back here with jackets or hoodies in five minutes."

Malda stood up abruptly and walked toward the kitchen door. She stopped in the doorway and turned back quickly with a smile.

"I can't wait for you to meet the Lusplendidas. I think after meeting them you will..." she paused in her sentence with almost a coy grin "...see the world a bit differently."

Gruhit noticed that he wasn't the only one excited. Amarie and Chardy both jumped into action and went about their tasks quickly. Gruhit went to his room and grabbed a yellow zippered hoodie. He didn't bother trying to zip it knowing he couldn't get his hands and fingers to make the motions. If Constance was here, she would be telling him to practice, but he was too excited right now. He paused at the door and ran back to get his sketchbook and pencil off of the nightstand. He couldn't believe that he had almost forgotten them. Samme would no doubt be asking him about his adventures later, and a good apprentice would be able to show off his drawings. At least, that is what Gruhit thought should happen.

Gruhit hurried into the living room. He could see Amarie was almost finished with cleaning off the table. He rolled his eyes when he noticed her knocking food onto the floor. He would have to sweep it up later. Chardy walked into the dining room wearing a brown jacket with his iPod blasting in his ears. Amarie ran to the kitchen and threw the washcloth into the sink just as Malda came down the stairs holding out a cute blue hoodie with a unicorn on the back of it.

"Okay, crew," Mal started, "it's nearly two o'clock. I already texted Cindy, and she knows we're on our way. Now, we won't be staying long because we will be returning to the Lusplendida's home tonight for the Festival of the Dwarves. If I find that you all have been listening well, I'll introduce you to a friend of mine. Has everyone been to the bathroom?"

All the children rolled their eyes and nodded.

Looking pleased and excited for a small adventure, Mal began to sing, "Hey, hey! Ho, ho! This Wunder show is on the road."

Mal walked at a brisk pace out the front door. Gruhit noticed that she stumbled a bit as the cool fall air hit her. Her face looked shocked and concerned. Malda was normally very graceful. Gruhit wondered if the chilled air made her think about Fridgita Mortes. Regardless, Malda quickly recovered heading out the door and made two sharp left turns on the sidewalk to head down Brown Place. They passed Fort Flowers, and then the boring little white house. The next house was...

"The Lighthouse!" Gruhit said instinctively.

"The Lighthouse?" Mal asked. "Is that the name you gave the Luspendida's home? It's very appropriate. Now, Cindy is going to meet us outside, but I want all of you to take a look around before she explains everything."

As Gruhit noted when they first moved into Big Blue, the Lighthouse had all sorts of metal animal sculptures in the trees or attached to different areas of the house. Amarie, especially, was having a grand time looking at a family of small metal squirrels who were playing along the banister of the front porch. One squirrel was even holding a giant flower in both hands. It was filled with water, and real birds were coming to drink from it. Another squirrel, which was made to look as though it was climbing the side of the house, was holding out a windchime. It made the most delightful noises as the wind danced through.

Gruhit was very interested in a large rock sculpture that took up most of the front yard. He could see from up close that the rock was covered in tiny pieces of colored glass. The sunlight glinted off each piece and made colorful sparkles all around the rock. It almost seemed to Gruhit like the sculpture itself was glowing. Not only that, but the colors seemed to change depending on how the sun was interacting with it. At times he thought he saw the deepest reds and oranges, while other times he was confronted with yellows and magentas. It looked like a giant flame in the front yard.

"Isn't it just beautiful? It always makes me feel warm inside," Malda said to Gruhit.

Gruhit didn't know whether to answer her or not. He felt like this flame was something that you looked at in silence. It really was odd to have something as big and majestic as this next to whimsical birds hanging from the nearby trees.

"What is it? Is it important?" Gruhit whispered.

"I don't think I'm the person to answer that question," Malda said quietly. "I think that question is best left to Mrs. Cindy Lusplendida."

Malda directed Gruhit's attention to the sidewalk leading to the Lighthouse. He had been so enamored with the presence of the dancing light that he didn't notice that a woman slightly shorter than Mrs. Wunder was walking out of the house toward them. Amarie and Chardy both stopped looking at the metal animals and shyly stood behind Mrs. Wunder.

Mrs. Lusplendida appeared to be about twenty years older than Mrs. Wunder. However, she still had a youthful energy, more so than other people her age.

"Mal! *Hola!*" Mrs. Lusplendida exclaimed. She took Mal's hand warmly in a greeting. "We haven't seen you enough lately."

Mrs. Lusplendida immediately transferred her gaze from Mrs. Wunder to the three children. Gruhit knew this look. She was looking them over to try and get an idea of them. Gruhit couldn't judge, because he was doing the same thing. While standing next to Malda, the two women looked like opposites. While Malda had a fancy hairstyle, Mrs. Lusplendida kept her hair neatly in a braided ponytail. Malda always seemed to wear colorful clothes with whimsical designs, but Mrs. Lusplendida was wearing a simple long-sleeved, red shirt with dark denim overalls which showed signs of being worn and stained from work. Gruhit also noticed a pair of thick work gloves sticking out her back pocket and a drop leg bag—a bag fastened around both her waist and one leg by two straps.

"Welcome, children, to my home," Mrs. Lusplendida said, satisfied with her inspection. "I hear that you want to know more about the magical creatures who live around our home."

"Do you have tangerellas?" Amarie questioned. She hadn't yet seen another tangerella since their initial meeting with Mrs. Bangs, and that made her sad.

"Tangerellas? Oh, no," said Mrs. Lusplendida with a slight chuckle. "I don't think our metal sculptures and such are what they would think is beautiful."

"I think they're all fantastic," Gruhit announced.

"I'm sure my husband will be happy to hear that you enjoy his work. I can see that you are liking the memorial statue to sundust."

"Sundust? What's that?" Chardy asked in a surprisingly interested tone.

"According to the story, sundust is what Victus created to keep magic and magical creatures in the world," Gruhit said.

"*Si! Perfecto!* All the magical creatures in the world can only exist if there is sundust around," Cindy said as she looked at Gruhit with a happy smile. "The statue tries to mimic the magic and wonder of sundust through the sparkling of the light that is all around it."

"But why does the sculpture look like fire? I mean, does this dust stuff burn you?" Chardy asked. Everyone except Cindy stared at him in wonder since he was showing so much interest in this subject.

"No. Sundust is very, very good and is not harmful to people. In fact, the old stories tell us that it kept the first humans healthy and provided them with special fruits which had all sorts of uses beyond nourishment." Mrs. Lusplendida looked from the children back to the statue and continued. "The reason for the fire shape is…"

"To show the power and life-giving nature of the whole process," said a man walking toward them from the Lighthouse.

"Ah, children, this is my husband, Jon," Cindy stated with a large smile. She put her arm around her husband's waist.

Mr. Lusplendida was very tall, definitely taller than Mr. Wunder. Jon also had broader shoulders and a bigger build. Gruhit looked upon the face of this man who seemed to wear a kind but serious smile under his dark mustache. The graying hair on top of his head was short and curly. Gruhit saw that Mr. Lusplendida wore a simple white undershirt and a pair of jeans. However, just like his wife, Gruhit could tell that months or maybe years of work had left his clothes somewhat worn. Mr. Lusplendida had a thick jacket over his white undershirt and Gruhit could see similar work gloves sticking out of the jacket pockets.

"Fire always has a history of helping us," Jon started to explain. "It gives us warmth, allows us to cook our food, in primitive times it kept predators away…"

"It can burn down a house or hurt a person," Chardy interrupted.

"Yes. YES! This too. It warns us about the power of fire," Jon responded to Chardy in an unexpected excitement. "All of these qualities show us what comes from the sundust and the old stories about Victus. The sundust gives life; it sustains health;

and the dust is provided to us from Victus. The memorial statue reminds us about the past, but also cautions us that we must all protect the present."

"You see children," Malda started, "although Mr. Lusplendida is a sculptor for his work—quite a popular sculptor actually—Mr. and Mrs. Lusplendida have devoted their lives to helping the Sunburst Dwarves and fleet birds."

"Mr. Wunder told us that the fleet birds make sundust," Amarie chimed in.

"*Si*, little one!" Cindy looked happily at Amarie, who seemed to be thrilled that someone was paying attention to her. "So many fleet birds fly over our heads in the sky during the day. They somehow feast on sun rays while in flight. When sunlight sparkles off of their feathers, it falls to the earth as sundust to nourish the magical creatures in the area below."

"Why can't we see them flying if there are so many of them every day?" Chardy asked.

"The coloring," Jon stated in a slightly gruff tone. "Fleet feathers are luminescent and somewhat translucent in places, mimicking the brightness of the sun as they travel along with the daylight. Many of them have colorings of reds, oranges, and yellows on the top of their bodies, and most have white underbellies. Sometimes when you look up, you see the resemblance of a cloud or simply a lighter part of the sky. Most people just don't have the knowledge or good enough eyesight to see them. But that doesn't mean they're not there."

"The birds are very important to magical creatures," Cindy explained, "There are some people who believe the sundust still gives life to the Earth itself. Thus, it is very important that we aid the birds in their task."

"Whee! Are we gonna fly? How do we do that?" Amarie asked in an excited and somewhat sing-song voice.

"No flying!" Jon said forcefully in alarm. Gruhit was unsure how someone could look kind but sound so intimidating. "We must help the dwarves. They are the key to helping the birds."

"Let me tell you," Cindy said, realizing that the children might react better to her softer tone. "The old stories tell us that the fleet birds were created to bring sundust back to the world. The birds must be in the sunlight to make the dust or feed. Unfortunately, none of the birds can live very long without a good meal, so they are almost always flying with their flocks to keep up with the movement of the sun. Sometimes one or two of the birds get too exhausted and drop out of the sky. When a bird falls to the ground, it is not the fall that hurts them. The bird stays asleep for many days, and even just one day will make a fleet bird too weak to survive."

"How come we don't see birds falling out of the sky all the time, then?" Chardy asked.

"This is the amazing part," Cindy explained. "The old stories tell us that just as there are dark creatures, like Fridgita Mortes, there are also very good beings who serve Victus. A special family of dwarves was chosen to help the fleet birds. An ancient being taught the dwarves how to make 'Beam Rockets.' When they explode, they release a bit of sunlight that has been captured and contained inside of it. The explosion wakes the falling birds and gives them enough energy to rejoin their flock."

"We might not be able to see the birds in the sky, but wouldn't we be able to see rockets going off?" Gruhit asked.

"You do notice it, but people have different names for it all," Mr. Lusplendida explained. "The Beam Rockets can quickly create large dark clouds from the burning up of the rocket. When an explosion happens, people think they are looking at lightning. People actually think all of these occurrences are simply storms from nature. They cannot see that it is actually dwarves keeping the Earth healthy and retaining the magic in the world. People miss all the wonder and just see what they can understand. Sometimes a little mystery is good for a person."

"I know your next question, Mr. Smartypants," Mrs. Lusplendida said playfully toward Chardy. "Why don't you see dwarves running around with rockets?"

The children looked amused.

"The old stories tell us that the same ancient being that gave the Sunburst Dwarves the knowledge to make Beam Rockets also gave them the ability to shrink any dwarf-made object along with them. Thus, you see, Mr. Smartypants, they can easily run around without being detected."

"Now, remember children, we will be back here tonight after the Halloween Party to be with the dwarves during their Fall Festival," Mal said.

"We're so happy that you'll be able to come over," Cindy said. "The dwarves work very hard all year round. This is the one time during the year that they allow themselves to have some fun. It's perfect because humans have their own celebrations and tend not to notice them."

"Cindy, Jon, can you talk about another creature that you help?" Mal suggested.

"Ah, *Si*! The charmyrlls!" Mrs. Lusplendida exclaimed. "The charmyrlls have periodically been coming to our home as the city has been growing and taking over more of their natural forest space. Jon has many little metal houses made for them in the backyard. We think we are averaging about eight charmyrlls per night who are sleeping here and eating strawberries."

"Charmyrlls are small animals. They look very cute - very, very cute. They look like a squirrel, chipmunk, and a bunny all in one," Mr. Lusplendida stated.

"Ah, Jon loves the cute little creatures," Cindy said, then looked a bit more serious toward the children. "You must never take one in the house. They are not pets and are too wild with fire. Literally, they will burn the house down."

"Charmyrlls have a special defense mechanism against predators or things they don't trust. They can light their bodies on fire, or at least become superheated," Mrs. Wunder explained further.

"This is why Jon never sculpts anything out of wood anymore. We also have to keep these fireproof gloves with us at all times in case we have to help a new charmyrll that doesn't know us yet." Cindy dug the gloves out of her pocket and tried them on. "Mal, Jon has to get back to work on a sculpting project for a client, but I have time. Can we show the children the homes in the back?"

"I actually promised to show them our friend by our house," Mal stated with a coy smile.

"Ah, I see. Well, let's head over to your house then," said Mrs. Lusplendida.

The children said goodbye to Mr. Lusplendida, then started walking back to Big Blue. Jon and Cindy wanted to speak with Malda for a brief moment before Jon had to leave for work. Gruhit felt frustrated as he walked. Here he was, an apprentice of identifying magical creatures, and the adults always seemed to have things to discuss away from him. What were they talking about? Were they hiding something?

Was it about the three of them? Did the Wunders want to get rid of them?

"Goodbye children! See you tonight!" Jon yelled as he rode quickly by on a blue bicycle.

Gruhit turned to see Mrs. Wunder and Mrs. Lusplendida walking along behind them as they continued talking when Malda began waving at someone. He looked over and saw Mrs. Bangs come out of her home. She was dressed in a fancy shirt depicting autumn leaves and a pair of green jeans. Soon Priscilla joined the other two women in their whispered conversation.

"Children!" Malda shouted as they neared Big Blue. "Go ahead and walk in between the two houses to the end of the house."

Amarie immediately ran ahead of the other two, stopping by the small little pond with the waterfall. Gruhit was sure that she was looking for a tangerella.

Gruhit and Chardy walked past their sister and stopped at the back of Big Blue. Underneath the windows hung small rectangular flower pots which held miniature sunflowers for the fall season. Gruhit's eyes moved to the blue block at the foundation and his gaze was met with a door. This wasn't like doors he normally saw; this was a short rectangular door that went sideways instead of up and down.

"Ah, good," Gruhit heard Malda say as the three women approached. "Do you see the old coal chute door?"

"I wanna see! Where?" Amarie shrieked in a sing-song tone as she ran over to catch up with the others.

"You don't know what a coal chute is, do you?" Mrs. Bangs commented. "Before we had electric heaters in our homes, families had to use coal to keep the fire going in their furnaces. A family had to have a constant supply of coal in their home to keep the furnace lit. Coal is extremely messy, not to mention that carrying heavy bucket loads would be a difficult task. Thus, many homes had a coal room with a coal chute on the outside. A delivery man would back a truck up to the home and shovel coal through the chute. That's how your family got the coal they needed and there was no mess made to your house. Look over there."

Mrs. Bangs pointed toward the back of her home, where there was an almost identical door toward the bottom of the house.

"Now, as I promised, I'll introduce you to my friend, Dragon. However, I first must warn you: he doesn't know you, so any sudden moves or any attempts to touch him will result in him bursting into flames for protection," Mrs. Wunder instructed.

"Charmyrlls do understand human speech, so feel free to talk with him," Mal continued. "Now, I want you all to take a step backwards with Mrs. Bangs. Mrs. Lusplendida and I will ask Dragon to come out." Next to her, Cindy began to put on her gloves.

All three children took a large step back and waited with anticipation. Gruhit got his sketchbook and pencil out of his back pocket in hopes that he would have another creature to draw and show Samme.

When Mrs. Wunder was satisfied with everyone's distance and saw that everyone was calm, she knocked on the door lightly. "Dragon? Are you home?" she called. "I have children here who would like to meet you."

The group waited in silence for something to happen.

"Dragon? Are you alright in there? Should I open the door for you today?" Malda said in a sweet and concerned tone.

Everyone stared at the blue door of the house. For a moment, Gruhit thought this all seemed kind of silly. Just as he was about to chide himself for believing in this crazy stuff, the door jiggled a bit, and there was a faint sound as though something were moving about behind the door. Slowly the metal door cracked open and the nose of the cutest little creature you have ever seen poked out.

"Good afternoon, Mr. Dragon," Mal said with sunshine in her voice. "Dragon, is it alright if Cindy holds you? I would like you to meet the new children living in our home."

Gruhit couldn't see exactly what happened next, since the two women were in front of the door. There did seem to be quite a bit of smoke. Then Gruhit believed he could see the image of a "thumbs up" rise into the air. Shortly after, Mrs. Lusplendida picked the creature up using her gloves and slowly turned around. Gruhit was ready to draw whatever it was he saw.
"Ah! Look at the little darling," Amarie said in almost a baby voice. She took a step closer and instinctively held out her hand.

Mrs. Bangs caught Amarie by the shoulder. "No, Amarie. Remember, the charmyrll will burst into flames if it feels threatened. It has to get to know you first."

Amarie thought for a moment before looking at the creature. Finally she said, "Hello, Dragon. My name is Amarie. It is nice to meet you."

Amarie made an awkward little curtsey as if she was in front of royalty. Gruhit set out examining the charmyrll right away and sketched it. Dragon was adorable with his various shades of orange, red, and brown fur. He was about the size of the average house cat and mostly looked like a rabbit with extra long and floppy ears. He distinctly had a long, bushy tail, similar to a squirrel. His chubby cheeks and other other areas of his body reminded him of a chipmunk. Somehow all three of those animals were rolled into one creature, a very cute and unique creature.

"Thank you, Amarie," Cindy stated. "I could actually feel his body begin to get very hot when you stepped toward him. Now he has gone back to his normal temperature."

Chardy looked unsettled. "If that thing…" he began.

"It's a 'he.' Don't forget that charmyrlls can understand every word you say," corrected Mrs. Wunder.

Chardy rolled his eyes and started again, "If *he* lives under the house and gets too nervous… isn't anyone else worried about him burning the whole place down?"

"That's a valid concern," Mrs. Wunder said. "First off, Dragon doesn't 'live' here. He stays here most of the time, though. He's one of my closest friends in the magical world. I happened upon him during a heavy rain one day. He had gotten so wet and cold that he might not have survived. After nursing him back to health, we set up this spot for him under the house. This way he has a place to go if he can't find shelter from the cold and rain."

"It's getting harder for these animals to live out in the wild because humans are developing more of the forests," added Mrs. Lusplendida.

"As far as being concerned about the house," Mrs. Wunder started again, "the corners of the bottom part of the house are made of concrete blocks. The interior wall is actually at the back of the closet in your bedroom, Chardy. It is also made of concrete block. We don't know the reason, but someone had the old coal room filled part way with dirt. You can see it through the coal door. Samme and I hung a flame retardant material along the ceiling and then put metal over that material. Thus, every part of the area is flame retardant. Lastly, when charmyrlls are by themselves, they usually keep their temperature low."

"However, you must all know that you should never bring a charmyrll into the house," Mrs. Lusplendida reminded. "Some of the younger ones cannot control their body temperature well. And if a charmyrll gets scared because you accidentally make a loud noise like dropping a pan, or something like that, they might accidentally become overheated. Charmyrlls are very cute, but they are not pets. One thing they do like is to talk to kind people and learn more about them."

"How do you know it can understand you?" Amarie said with a quizzical look.

"Charmyrlls have a unique way of speaking. They can heat up some of the water in their bodies to create steam which comes out of their ears. Then they use their floppy ears to form the steam into cloud shapes to communicate with us," Cindy explained.

"Think of it as their way of using emojis without a phone," Mal said with a small giggle.

"Here, we'll show you," Cindy said. "Amarie, tell Dragon about your favorite color and then ask him about his."

"My favorite color is pink. I like it better with glitter because that reminds me of fairies and unicorns," Amarie said in her rapid sing-song voice. "What is your favorite color?"

Gruhit had already half-drawn Dragon in his sketchbook and paused. This seemed like one of those instances that adults set up to impress kids, but it ends up being nothing. Like when his foster dad in House Number 2 told Gruhit he could do magic and pretended to pull a quarter out of Gruhit's ear. Gruhit knew the quarter had been in his hand the whole time; he thought it was a bit lame. Nothing was happening with Dragon either.

"Oh, I can feel him getting much warmer even through the gloves. The answer must be coming," Mrs. Lusplendida said with a hint of excitement.

Suddenly, Gruhit noticed steam coming out of Dragon's ears. Each stream was thick, white, and easy to see. Then without warning, Dragon's ears came to life and almost looked like skillful fingers sculpting something out of clay. The ears turned, bent, and cut through the steam with ease until an image was rising into the air. Did it look like balloons? No, it was a tree branch with many tiny leaves. All over the branch hung the most detailed and delicious looking…

"Oranges!" Amaries said with excitement and a big giggle. "His favorite color is orange!"

"How do you know he isn't lying, or just coming up with a random picture?" Chardy said gruffly.

Dragon looked at Chardy as though he could see right through him. The white steam began coming out of his ears again, and the floppy ears went to work. There was instantly a visual replica of the factory across the street. Everyone seemed to be puzzled by this image, but Chardy's eyes went wide, and he started shaking ever so slightly.

"Hmmmm. Well, I'm not sure what that was," Cindy said, "but I will say it is like talking with a person who speaks a language you don't understand. For example, when my mother comes from Mexico to visit us, she has to use hand gestures and motions. But there are times when someone misunderstands her. It's difficult to know what a charmyrll is saying with their pictures because we don't know exactly what they're thinking."

Cindy slowly turned back around and set Dragon just inside the coal door. She quickly took her gloves off and reached into her drop leg bag to pull out some strawberries. She looked at the children over her shoulder while holding up a big, juicy berry.

"Charmyrlls have to use a lot of their body's water supply to create pictures. They get most of the water they need from fruit, but if they can't find any, they have been known to drink from a mud puddle," Cindy said, then set a handful of bright red strawberries inside Dragon's area. "There you go, little one."

Gruhit couldn't see Dragon as clearly anymore, but he could make out the image of a white heart in steam rising into the air.
"Dragon, I'll check on you again tomorrow," Malda looked at the children. "Maybe some of the children will help look in on you. For right now, we will let you get back to your day. Please say goodbye, children."

All three children and Mrs. Bangs said goodbye in unison. A white fluffy smiley face appeared in the air followed by a waving hand. Malda slowly shut the door as Dragon could be seen munching away on delicious strawberries.

Gruhit looked down and surveyed his two sketches. One was Dragon sitting in Mrs. Lusplendida's hands, while the other was him using his ears to make the factory from across the street. Gruhit's sketches weren't as good as Mr. Wunder's, but he was still happy with them. He decided he would show Mr. Wunder later that day.

Gruhit remembered the day they had arrived at Big Blue and thought he had heard a low and icy voice whisper his name. At the time he thought he was just hearing things, but after all he had learned about magical creatures, he wasn't so sure. He would need to ask Samme. Then another thing came to his mind.

"Mrs. Lusplendida? Mrs. Wunder?" Gruhit called as both women looked his way. "You mentioned that an ancient being gave the dwarves their abilities... And that there are helpers? Servants?"

"It's true," Cindy said. "The old stories tell us this much, *si*."

"If there are messengers for good," Gruhit paused as he calculated, "then there are also messengers and helpers for FrIdgita Mortes?"

"*Si*, the old stories would say that some were jealous of people and followed that awful Fridgita," Cindy explained.

"Stop it!" Chardy unexpectedly yelled. "You're going to scare him with all this talking about evil monsters and stuff."

"I'm not scared!" Gruhit said defensively.

"Chardy, that's no way to speak to Mrs. Lusplendida. I'm sorry if you thought she was trying to scare your brother, but she was simply communicating about the facts of..." Mrs. Wunder started.

"Facts? How do you all know that you have the stories right? How do you know that these 'dark' messengers aren't the victims? How do you know that the squirrel-tailed monster under the house isn't the liar? This is all too weird!" Chardy spouted off. Gruhit could swear that he was looking more anxious. Then Chardy turned to his siblings and shouted, "Get in the house now!"

"But I don't wanna go inside!" Amarie shot back. "I'm meeting new friends, and you can't make me."

"I said get inside!" Chardy yelled again at his siblings.

"Chardy," Mrs. Wunder said in a very firm tone. "I understand that you feel uneasy about something right now. And I know that you had to act like a father to Amarie and Gruhit in the past. However, you are free to be a child in our home and I am the parent on duty right now."

Chardy sent a sharp glare toward Mrs. Wunder. Through gritted teeth, he replied, "Oh! You're on duty? You ain't been nuthin' for us but a place to stay for a few nights. And don't think that showing us a bunch of sideshow freak animals makes you special. You ain't never gonna be my mom!"

Chardy spewed venomous speech like a fighter throwing a punch, then waited to see how his foster would respond. Gruhit had seen this a million times. Chardy would get into a fight with the fosters and then get grounded or have his iPod taken away. Gruhit wasn't sure which "weapon" Mrs. Wunder would go for right now. He watched as Mrs. Wunder kept her poise. She stood straight, tall, and kept her anger in check. He could still see a pleasantness about her eyes. But she kept a firm stare that showed she would not be challenged by Chardy's words.

"Chardy Brown, I hope you are listening quite clearly," Mrs. Wunder said, her stare almost holding Chardy back from speaking anymore. "I am not, nor will I ever be, your mother. I will never claim the rights to that special title or try to replace her. I agree with you, I will never be her."

Mrs. Wunder bent forward so that her eyes came down to be level with Chardy's, "Let me be clear about another thing. Just as I believe you deserve to be respected, my friends deserve the same respect. You can feel that our knowledge and care for magical creatures is ridiculous, that's fine. You will not, however, treat my friends and creature friends as though they are ignorant or less special than you. After all, one day you might hope that other people treat you with the same respect."

Mrs. Wunder stood up straight once again and looked at Chardy with a slightly relaxed glance. "Do we need to take a break to finish this discussion?"

Chardy stood silent for a moment. He had not gotten the rile out of Mrs. Wunder that he was used to with other fosters. He continued to glare at her and fumed.

He said through gritted teeth, "We're done."

"Good. Everyone can have mixed feelings about the situation they're in," Mrs. Wunder said. "It's okay to have fun learning about new magical creatures, and to be upset that you're not home with your mom at the same time. It's okay to be angry that you live in Big Blue while still having fun with Mrs. Bangs and Mrs. Lusplendida. All those emotions mean that you're human. Sometimes humans need help figuring out our lives and emotions. Chardy, I want you to go to your room. Amarie and Gruhit, you are welcome to stay out here for a bit, or you can head inside."

There it was. Gruhit had guessed that Mrs. Wunder would send Chardy to his room, but she didn't yell. The fosters that did just started taking anything they could see away from you.

"Just to be clear, Mr. Chardy," Mrs. Wunder stated. "This is not a grounding or punishment. I just want you to stay in your room long enough to think about how you're feeling. Samme or I will be happy to talk with you after if you need to talk about anything. *Anything.*"

Gruhit could have been knocked over by a feather. This was by far the most un-expected confrontation that Gruhit had ever seen with Chardy. The odd part was that Gruhit had no idea what set his brother off. Chardy didn't like fosters, but the whole situation just didn't make any sense. Gruhit glanced over at his sister, thinking about everything. He could see Amarie fight back tears, then put on a smile. Gruhit knew all the talk about their mom upset her. He missed her so much it hurt. He was definitely having mixed feelings right now. He was angry at himself for having a fun day when he thought he should be sad about being away from his mom.

Mrs. Bangs, who had been the closest to Amarie, asked if she could give her a side hug. Gruhit heard the slight creaking of a door. He turned his head to see that Dragon had been watching the whole situation. Dragon looked into Gruhit's eyes and swiftly set to work making a new stream of steam. It took him much longer than the factory image.

Gruhit continued guessing what the image might be. A circle. No. A piece of swiss cheese. No. A star. No. A snowflake. Yes. A snowflake? What was that supposed to mean? When Dragon finished, he went back under the house and closed the door. As Gruhit turned back to face the group, he saw Mrs. Wunder looking at the little door with wide, shocked eyes. The image seemed to mean something to her.

Gruhit wanted to ask about the image. Before he could get his words out, Mrs. Bangs called, "Mal, if it is okay with you, Amarie and I would like to look for tangerellas for a little bit. I'm going to show her a nice calming place in the flowers by the water."

"That sounds great," Mal said, sounding a little unnerved.

Cindy came over and put her arms around Mal. "Don't let this shake you up. You were right. He has a lot of emotions jumbled up. He needs some time."

"Thanks, Cindy. It's not that... it's not him, well..." Mal trailed off, but Cindy seemed to understand. "I don't know what I think, but we could all use rest before the party and festival tonight."

With that, everyone went their separate ways. Gruhit hoped the Halloween party would be less eventful.

Chapter 18
The School Halloween Party

Late afternoon turned into evening. Mrs. Wunder had asked everyone to stay in their rooms until dinnertime so they could have time to themselves. Gruhit figured it was Malda's adult way of saying that she needed a break. It seemed to work, though. By the time dinnertime came about, everyone was full of excitement for the Halloween Party. Most of the town would be there.

Well, Gruhit noticed that everyone but Kieffer was looking forward to it. Granted, Kieffer seemed to have a certain dignity about him all the time, but he seemed worn out. He was still talking like his nose was stuffed up. It was odd that he was so tired; he had napped in Chardy's room most of the afternoon.

Malda seemed worried about him too. She put a blanket over him at the dinner table. He appeared to be so tired that not even the warm meal could perk him up.

When dinner was over, everyone helped clean up the dishes and wash the table so they could get dressed into their costumes.

"I think I shall go down and turn in early for the night," Kieffer said wearily. "I don't want to get sick."

Before he could disappear into the basement, Amarie ran over to give Kieffer a big hug.

"Are you gonna be alright, Mr. Kieffer?" she asked. "I'm gonna miss you tonight. I thought you would be able to come with us to the party."

"I'll be fine, Ms. Amarie. I just need a good night's sleep. You'll see," Kieffer explained. He slowly made his way down the stairs.

Soon after, the children went to their separate rooms and changed. Malda and Samme waited in the kitchen with large plastic pumpkin containers for candy. Amarie was the first to be ready, racing into the room in a unicorn onesie. When she pulled the hood over her head, she was able to sport a unicorn head with a shiny, silver horn and a rainbow colored mane.

"This costume needs one more thing," Mal took Amarie's hand and guided her to the Wunders' bedroom.

Chardy came up the stairs next wearing tattered clothes and a few fake sores on his neck and face. "Do zombies have hair that is messed up, or not?"

"I'm not sure if I've ever learned about zombies, to be honest. Maybe more messed-up hair," Samme said.

Chardy moved his fingers through his hair and pulled on it to make it look like he just woke up. "Kieffer is already asleep in my room. Do you think he'll be alright?"

Samme was somewhat taken aback. This was the first time Chardy had shown concern for anyone else in the house. Maybe he had a good friend in Kieffer.

"I'm sure he'll be fine. The weather is getting colder, so this is the time that people and even guardlings can come down with a cold or the flu," Samme assured Chardy. "Is he warm enough in your room? I'm afraid I never got around to checking the heater today."

"Never fear! Gruhit is here!" Gruhit said triumphantly as he pretended to fly into the kitchen dressed as his favorite superhero. The costume had a red cape and tall boots. There were even fake muscles sewn into it. If he was going to pretend that he was a superhero, he was going to pretend he was super strong too.

"Look at everyone! You all look great!" Malda said as she returned to the kitchen with Amarie.

Malda put a little makeup on Amarie's eyelids to make them look silvery and sprayed some glitter around her face and hair. Gruhit thought Amarie would probably never stop dancing with excitement.

"Well, hey, hey! Ho, ho!" Mr. Wunder suddenly sang out.

"This Wunder show is on the road!" Malda finished the song as she ushered the children toward the door.

Upon pulling up to the parking lot of the elementary school, they could see that half the town was already there. The outside of the school had been decorated with a plethora of jack-o-lanterns all lit up with various carved-out faces. There were also scarecrows and bales of hay by the door leading to the gym. Plus, there was a gigantic inflatable spider on top of the roof, smiling at everyone that was entering the gym.

"Okay, kids, remember: Wunders stick together, and Wunders have fun," Samme instructed.

Gruhit was amazed by the colorful decorations. He could see pumpkins and scarecrows everywhere which students from other classes had made. There were various stations set up around the gym where you could collect candy or do an activity. There was an apple bobbing station, a table for making your own dancing skeleton with construction paper, a small maze made of cardboard, and even a dunking booth where students could try and dunk their principal.

"Shall we go to the first table and get some candy?" Malda asked. "Oh, and it looks like cupcakes."

They walked over. A teacher offered a large handful of candy to each of the children, and another gave a cupcake with a spider made of icing to the fosters. Gruhit couldn't believe the teacher had given him a whole handful.

On their way to the second table, two girls ran up to Amarie. They were students from her class; they asked if she would go around the room with them.

"I'm fine with that, but you must stay in the gym where Mal and I can see you," Samme instructed.

"I promise, I promise. Thank You! Wee! Let's go!" Amarie sang gleefully and ran off to the apple bobbing station with her friends.

Gruhit received another large handful of candy at the second table. As far as he could tell, there were at least twenty different tables around the gym. He was going to get a lot of candy tonight.

"Are you Mr. and Mrs. Wunder?" a voice behind them said in a friendly tone.

The four of them turned around to see a woman with black and spiky hair dressed all in black with cat ears.

"Hello, Mrs. Snow!" Gruhit yelled out happily. "This is my teacher!"

"Well, hello, Mrs. Snow," Samme said as he shook the teacher's hand. "It is good to meet you."

"It's good to meet you, too. I hate to ask this at a party, but do you think we could talk real quick? This shouldn't take too long," Mrs. Snow suggested.

"Oh, um, sure. Boys, head over to the next candy station and then the dunk tank. We'll meet you there," Mrs. Wunder said.

"Thank you. Like I said, I hate to interrupt a good Halloween party, especially when the boys look like they're having so much fun. I mean, I'm sure with being in foster care they're not used to having things like this," Mrs. Snow continued in a sweet tone and did not know exactly how to stop talking.

Samme jumped in, a little perturbed that their fun evening was being interrupted. "I'm sorry. Should we be concerned about something with Gruhit?"

"Oh, no. No. I just, well, I am concerned about him, of course," Mrs. Snow said.

"Concerned about Gruhit? Why?" Malda asked, a bit shocked.

"Well, I'm not sure he is really used to being in a school with rules," Mrs. Snow started to ramble.

"He's been in school in his past foster homes, and…" Samme started to retort.

"And did they have any problems with him? Was he in any sorts of trouble? Fights? Hurt other children? He seems to be doing well with his homework. However, at recess he doesn't play with the other kids. He just sits on the side of the playground and watches them. That seems like anti-social behavior, right? I mean you hear about that type of behavior on the news, and we don't know what he was exposed to in the other homes or at his parents' home…" Mrs. Snow continued to ramble in her sweet tone.

"His mom's." Malda said flatly.

"What? I'm sorry," Mrs. Snow said.

"Gruhit didn't live with his dad," Malda said firmly, but without losing her cool. "He lived with his mom. I don't know much about her, but I believe she is a darling woman who was working several jobs, trying to pay the rent and put food on the table for her children. She adores them. I choose to believe that she is someone who needs help getting back on her feet after her boyfriend left her with the kids. We're helping these children survive away from a mom who loves them until they can be reunited with her. I believe there is always hope. We will not read into the situation any other way. Will we… Mrs. Snow, was it?"

"Oh, of course. Gruhit is a darling boy, and I only bring up all this because I'm so concerned for him. I want to be able to help keep him on the straight and narrow," Mrs. Snow said, somewhat faltering and embarrassed. "You also have to understand that I have to think of the other children in my class. I mean I'm so thrilled that you are helping Gruhit. God bless you both for helping him and his siblings. You're such special people. Just remember, though, that the other parents in the class might not think it is the best idea for their children to be exposed to a child from a unique background."

"Hmmm. I see," Samme said, calculating something in his head. "Mrs. Snow, I have one major concern with Gruhit that he hasn't shown in other homes."

"Oh, yes. Please. I want to do everything I can to help." Mrs. Snow leaned in closer to listen. Malda looked at her husband. She had no idea what concern he was thinking of. "I'm sure that a woman with your teaching experience and concern for her students must be repulsed by bullying, right?" Samme paused, watching Mrs. Snow's reaction before going on. "In fact, I have been intending to talk with the principal. Gruhit is exhibiting severe anxiety due to the lack of adult support while other children in his class attack him verbally because of his skin color and because he is in foster care."

Gruhit glanced over at the adults while they talked about him. He really had no idea what was going on. He kept to himself mostly at school, except for when he talked periodically with Nathan at lunch. His grades were A's and B's.

Gruhit looked back to the dunk tank. It was Chardy's turn. The principal from Chardy's middle school was getting into place as someone gave Chardy three baseballs to throw at the target. Gruhit had seen a tank like this in cartoons. When someone hit the target on the side, it made the chair drop and the person fall into the water. Gruhit was excited to see how this played out.

"Is Cheesehead wearing a dress?" a high pitched voice said. He turned around to face Judy and three of her friends. "Oh, no, it's a cape."

Judy was dressed up like a pink poodle with sparkly barrettes in the ears. Her face was painted with a black spot over her left eye and a black nose. Her friends were dressed as a fairy, a clown with pink curly hair, and a rock singer.

"It's my favorite superhero," Gruhit said, hoping they would be nice to him. He quickly scanned the crowd. The Wunders were still talking with his teacher, Amarie had her head in a large pan of water trying to get an apple, and Chardy was concentrating on throwing his first ball to hit the bullseye. He, Gruhit, was alone.

"Oh, I saw that movie with my dad," Judy declared. "He took me on a daddy-daughter date. Just me. It was a very special time. I got a soda and anything I wanted from the concession stand. Do you know what a concession stand is?"

"I've been to the movie theater loads of times," Gruhit retorted.

"But did you ever go with your dad? Hmm?" Judy asked.

"I don't know where my dad is. He left after I was born, and I've never seen him except in pictures," Gruhit said in a small voice.

Gruhit didn't know why he shared this information. Maybe he thought if they could hear his situation they would leave him alone. Gruhit could've been mistaken, but for a brief second he thought the other two girls felt sorry for him. Then Judy continued.

"There is one good thing about your situation. At Christmas, the local movie theater puts on a special free movie for all the poor kids in town, so you'll get to go to the movie theater again."

The girls laughed. Gruhit fumed in his skin. Suddenly his brother's hand appeared on his shoulder.

"Hey, Gruhit, you didn't tell me that you had muppets in your classroom that laugh like they've been inhaling helium," Chardy said firmly. "What's so funny? I love jokes."

Judy was the first to stop laughing and looked confrontationally at Chardy. "We were simply telling your brother about how fortunate it is that he can see a movie this Christmas during the charity showing."

Chardy's face continued to hold a sarcastic smile. Gruhit was absolutely quiet, as were Judy's three friends. No one was quite sure of how Chardy was going to respond.

"Hmmm. Yup. I see how it is. Well, Gruhit, us good boys better get back to our fosters. They'll be looking for us soon," Chardy said. "We must say, 'Goodbye.' Farewell, to the fairy, the clown, the singer, and… oh yes, the dog… the girl dog… Do you know what a girl dog is called?"

"Yes, Chardy. I think they'll know what that would be," Mr. Wunder stepped into the conversation. "We are not going to sink to name calling here, are we?"

"Name calling is a horrible habit, sir," Judy said through a smile in her most innocent girl voice. "My dad told me that."

Mr. Wunder looked over at Judy. He now stood between Gruhit and Chardy, one arm resting on each of their shoulders. "I'm glad to hear you say that. What's your name again?"

"Judy. Judy Cr…"

"Credulent. Yes, I know your father. He's a popular man in this town," Mr. Wunder stated.

"Daddy is very important," Judy said through a bigger smile.

"Judy, that's fantastic. I do enjoy hearing when a child has learned to appreciate their parents and to respect other people," Samme said with a coy grin as Judy's smile got bigger.

"Boys, I want you to remember this moment," Samme went on. "Our dear little friend Judy here has taught us we should appreciate the good advice given to us by parental figures. We have also learned from Ms. Credulent, and her father's teaching, that name calling is detestable. It demeans another human being. Even if we don't like someone, we should never sink to name calling, or making fun of their situation or skin color."

Judy's face was starting to become pink, nearly matching her outfit. She and her friends couldn't look Mr. Wunder in the face, but instead found their feet more interesting to look at.

"Well, it was nice to meet you, Gruhit's dad," Judy said as she started to turn away.

"Actually, I'm not finished, Ms. Judy," Samme said in a serious tone. She turned to face Mr. Wunder again. "Every person will have to ask someone else for help in their life at some point. I have a friend who tells me that some kids at this school are telling him that he doesn't belong here and are calling him names. Now, I know *you* would never do such a thing. *You* would never be upset at someone asking for help. I thought maybe you could do me a favor: make sure my friend is taken care of at this school. If he isn't, I'm afraid I might need to talk to your father. As you say, he is an important man. I'm sure he will be able to stop this bullying."

"Yes, sir. I'll see what I can do to help," Judy said in a sullen voice. She kept her eyes on her feet.

"Thank you, Judy. And one more thing. You really should look adults in the eye when they're talking to you. Otherwise, someone might get the impression that you're guilty of something," Samme said pointedly. "Run along now."

The four girls couldn't get away from this uncomfortable situation fast enough.

Mr. Wunder turned around to face both Gruhit and Chardy. "Are both of you alright?"

Gruhit nodded.

"Man, I had everything under control," Chardy started to say, "but that was pretty cool."

"Well, you can thank Mal later for protecting your brother from the adults." Samme looked over at Mal still conversing with Mrs. Snow. "I overheard a part of your conversation. How in the world does that child know that you're in foster care?"

"I don't know who all knows, but I know Judy found out from Amarie," Gruhit said. He looked at Samme, frustrated.

Amarie came running over to the little group with a huge smile on her face.

"Hey! Why is everyone standing around talking? I thought I was missing something fun," Amarie said.

"I want all three of you to look at me," Samme said in a commanding and serious tone. "When you met Dragon today, you learned that you couldn't instantly get close to him. Charmyrlls demand that they learn more about you to determine if they can trust you, to see if you're a safe person. The same is true for us. We can choose what we let people know about us. The more a person has earned your trust and has proven they are safe, the more information you can share with them. The problem with telling an unsafe person too much about your life is that they now have power they can use against you. Does that make sense?"

All three kids nodded their heads. Amarie held her head a little lower, knowing what she had done to her brother.

"Good. Wunders protect each other. Sometimes that means we protect our family by carefully guarding who we tell important information." Samme looked at all three kids and added one more thought. "Understand that you are each a part of the Wunder family, and Mal and I will go to great lengths to protect you."

As Samme finished, Mal could be seen shaking Mrs. Snow's hand and heading back to the group.

"Is everyone ready to go? I could use some of the Dwarves' cider," Mal said in an exhausted voice.

"Yup. I think the Wunder clan has had enough Halloween Party for one night," Samme responded.

It hadn't been the party Gruhit envisioned. He was elated to witness Samme and Mal standing up for him. He felt safer with the Wunders right now. As they walked toward the exit, Gruhit noted one more important thing. Samme's hand was still tenderly on top of Chardy's shoulder, and Chardy was allowing it to remain there. This is how things usually happen, Gruhit thought. Unpleasant situations tend to show you who the safe people are and make you want to be closer to them.

Chapter 19
The Dwarves' Party

The back door to Big Blue flew open.

"Move! Move! Everyone move!" Malda said in a sing-song voice. "Get changed into warm and comfy play clothes that can get dirty! Quick! Woo hoo! Let's go see the dwarves!"

"Quickly everyone! Last one to the back door is a double-headed moat!" Mr. Wunder yelled with the same excited fervor as he and Mal hurried to their bedroom to change clothes.

Gruhit wasn't sure if being a double-headed moat was bad, but he knew the fosters' energy was infectious. Each kid couldn't seem to move fast enough. Chardy jumped all the way down the stairs to the basement from the landing, and Amarie was moving so fast that her feet couldn't keep up. She slightly tripped up the stairs before catching herself.

It seemed like mere seconds before everyone was meeting in the kitchen. All had changed into jeans and various colored hoodies. Mr. Wunder was the exception with his usual overcoat with many pockets. Mal had on a light green hoodie with colorful leaf patterns that danced all around the garment in an artistic style. She had also changed her hairstyle to a simple braid with artificial leaves strewn throughout.

Samme began shooting out questions before they left.

"Gruhit, do you have your sketchbook and pencil?"

"Got 'em."

"Amarie, have you been to the bathroom?"

"Went already."

"Chardy, did you check on Kieffer?"

"He's out, asleep."

"I've got the house key to lock up. Let's go!"

Mal excitedly grabbed Amarie's hand and took off out of the door with a flash. Gruhit and Chardy walked briskly to keep up. Samme brought up the rear of the small caravan.

As they approached the Lighthouse, they could see a note on the door. Mal looked closely and could see the words, "Couldn't wait. Went to the party already. Come around back. Gripple is waiting for you."

Mal turned around to face everyone. Her grin seemed almost childish, uncharacteristic from her usual controlled and elegant self. "Who's ready for an adventure?" she asked.

Before anyone could answer, Malda led the way, passing several little metal squirrels and birds on the ground. These were holding small lights in their paws or mouths to light the way.

The backyard of the Lighthouse wasn't much to look at. Toward the back, there were about eight to ten stacked rectangular metal boxes. Gruhit supposed that those must be the temporary charmyrll homes. The rest of the yard was pretty scarce. In daylight they might have been able to see grass patches here or there. The Lusplendidas clearly didn't do as much gardening as Mrs. Bang. In fact, their yard was almost the opposite of Mrs. Bang's flourishing green yard.

Mal stopped in front of a single large acorn tree in the middle of the backyard. The tree was quite impressive as it stretched high into the sky and the trunk was one of the widest and thickest tree trunks Gruhit had ever seen. It must have been growing in that spot for hundreds of years. As everyone caught up with Mal in front of the tree, she turned toward the children with a smile.

"I thought we were supposed to meet someone here," Gruhit said to Samme.

"Well, I see that Gripple at least left us some of the dwarves' special apple cider," Samme said. The tree had a ledge on which there sat five wooden mugs.

Samme handed each person one. "Here's to having faith that just because something seems impossible, it doesn't mean that it is," he said.

Amarie soon followed the fosters in taking a drink. Gruhit sniffed the contents of his mug first and could smell a pleasant scent, like apple pie mixed with warm acorns. He wasn't sure if he had ever smelled anything that made him feel so warm and cozy inside. He looked over to see that Chardy had put a finger in his mug and licked it. A huge grin suddenly came over his brother's face.

Gruhit slowly brought the mug to his lips and closed his eyes as the warm liquid made its way in. The apple cider reminded him of playing outside with other children in House Number 3. They had so much fun eating their apple snack and playing in piles of leaves. He could almost smell the crisp fall air and remember all the fun. It was like he didn't have a care in the world.

When he opened his eyes again, he could see that Amarie and Chardy both had satisfied grins.

"Who is that?" Gruhit said, alarmed.

"Oh, Gripple!" Mal said happily. "Have you been here the whole time?"

Gripple had a stern expression. He merely grunted and nodded.

Gripple was nearly four feet tall. He wore clothes that reminded Gruhit of a miner. Gripple appeared to be built and dressed for physical labor, as opposed to the little folks. He had a bushy black beard, large nose, and a very strong build.

"Kids, this is Gripple. He is one of the most talented Sunburst Dwarves in the area," Samme announced. "Well, Mr. Gripple, we have finished our cider, and it's surely been long enough. Let's get to the festival. It only happens once a year, sir. We're wasting time."

Gripple rolled his eyes at Mr. Wunder. The dwarf held out his hands. Malda grabbed one hand and Samme the other hand.

"Children, hold our hands and make a circle," Samme instructed.

As they did so, Gruhit whispered, "Why do we have to do this?"

"Well, you heard that we drank dwarf-made cider, right?" whispered Samme.

"Yes."

"It has been a few minutes now, so the drink has been absorbed inside our bodies."

"Okay? What does that mean?"

"Oh, didn't the Lusplindidas explain this to you?"

"Explain what?"

"Malda, you didn't tell them that Sunburst Dwarves can shrink dwarf-made objects?" Samme said, surprised at his wife.

"Wait, what?" Gruhit exclaimed.

Before anyone could react, there was a *SNICK* sound and Gripple had successfully shrunk the entire party to no more than about one foot tall.

"Amarie, dear, are you okay?" Mal said, looking concerned.

"I'm great. Can we do that again?" Amarie said. She was giggling and looking around the world from this new height.

"Oh? I thought I heard a high-pitched scream," Mal said, relieved that Amarie was okay.

"It wasn't me. Gruhit?" Amarie said, looking at her younger brother.

"Hey, just because I'm the youngest, doesn't mean it was me. Right, Chardy? Chardy?"

The group looked toward Chardy in unison. He was shaking, and his face was pale. Everyone suppressed grins, except Mrs. Wunder.

"Chardy? I'm sorry, kiddo," Mal said. "We should've better warned you that the dwarves can apply their shrinking ability to humans as well after ingesting dwarf-made cider. We're perfectly fine though. After the festival, Gripple will take us back to our original heights. You're okay."

"N… no. I'm f-fine. I've always wished I was the size of someone's nose hairs," Chardy said, trying to sound convincing.

"Oh, come on now! You're still way taller than a nose hair," Samme joked.

"¡Hola, compadres!" A deep but excited voice could be heard from the base of the tree.

Everyone looked to see Mr. and Mrs. Lusplendida, who were shrunk as well, standing by a concealed doorway in the tree trunk. As the doorway opened, light emitted into the dark backyard. Gruhit thought it was so strange to be under a foot tall right now. He looked up at the sky. The moon and stars looked bigger to him. The acorn tree was absolutely huge. Before Gripple shrank them, they stood right next to the tree, but now at their shrunken size, the tree seemed to be a ways in the distance.

The group jogged over to the door as Mrs. Lusplendida called out, "Oh, good! I'm so glad you saw the note on the door. Come on, the festival has already started. Vamonos!"

Mr. Lusplendida had to duck his head a bit to get through. The closer Gruhit got to the door, the more he could hear instruments playing fast-paced and melodic music with a folk sound to them. As he walked through, he was greeted with a thousand scents. Gruhit was immediately amazed to see that the inside of the tree had been carved out to reveal a network of support beams, concealed windows letting in the moonlight, and splendidly decorated devices. The stairs went up three flights to ledges that wrapped around the edge of the tree, leaving the center vacant. Gruhit could only see a few dwarves on each floor talking and laughing together. All of them seemed to hold a wooden mug. Along the side of the tree, he could see candles held by expertly carved holders in the shape of various animals, so it appeared that an animal was holding the lit candles by the wall. It was all wonderful and peculiar.

Gruhit had so many questions. Why were there only a few dwarves at the festival? Were there only a few dwarves in existence? He didn't see a band, so what was making the music? Where was all the food he was smelling? How was the tree so bright on the inside with only candles?

Gruhit looked straight up. He could see strange mechanical glass lenses decorating the ceiling of the tree. The glass seemed to shift slightly and sparkle with the ambience of the moonlight streaming in through the highest windows.

"Look! Look! It's beautiful, no? The lenses magnify the moonlight so that the caverns below are properly lit," Mrs. Lusplendida explained.

Gruhit had been so busy marveling that he hadn't looked downward once. As he followed the silvery moonlight, he saw that the stairs continued for ten flights below. He could barely see the bottom. However, he was just barely able to make out a floor with a medallion carved into the wood. The medallion was in the shape of a circular compass with a handful of small stars and one large, bright star in the center.

"Enough staring! Let's go have some fun!" Malda said gleefully.

Cindy grabbed Mal's arm, who in turn took Amarie's hand. The three ladies walked briskly down the stairs smiling. They could hear Amarie exclaim her popular, "Wee!"

"*Vamonos*! If I know Mal and Cindy, they won't save any cider for us!" Mr. Lusplendida declared. He grabbed Chardy's arm to chase after the girls.

Chardy was still a bit shocked but slowly coming to his senses. Everything was happening so fast. He barely had time to take everything in before the adults moved to the next thing. Gruhit wasn't worried about him, though. Even though he was less than a foot tall now, this seemed like a safe place to be. He didn't know why. He wondered what Constance would say. Not that he would tell her, but it was interesting to think about. He was starting to descend the stairs with Samme when he felt a small twinge of sadness. Was his mom having a good evening? Was she celebrating Halloween? Was she having fun? Would she like this place?

"... sketchbook," Sammed had said something but Gruhit had missed it.

"What?" Gruhit asked.

"Did you remember your sketchbook? This festival only happens once a year, so you need to capture this," Samme said. He motioned to Gruhit to keep up with everyone else.

"Why is it only once a year? Is it like a religious holiday or something?" Gruhit questioned.

"No, not at all. The end of October is the only time that all fleet birds naturally rest for the night. The birds rarely rest, but for some strange reason, they all do it in unison on this night. Some have guessed it's to give the dwarves the night off."

The music continued to get louder as they moved down the stairs. Gruhit could hear a distinct voice mixed with laughter and cheers. Finally, when he set foot on the medallion that he had seen from up above, he looked over to see a large cavern that extended up three floors. The room was beautifully lit with a series of mirrors and lenses which captured the moonlight.

Gruhit looked out over the seemingly endless sea of dwarf men and women. Some were sitting at long ornately carved benches and tables. They were drinking what looked like the same cider he had just a few moments ago. There were pies and puddings, different kinds of meats and vegetables, and some unfamiliar fruits.

Along a wall at one end, was a large stage that stood above the crowd. A band of six or seven dwarves were playing handmade wooden instruments. A crowd in front danced fiercely with great fun. Other dwarves had formed a ring around the dancers and were clapping their hands to the music.

Nearby, all sorts of games were being played. There was one that looked like participants had to balance a single acorn on their nose. There was what looked like a pie eating contest with about five dwarves savagely devouring pies. Another game looked like a race to make holes and mount a series of rockets into the ground. Gruhit wasn't sure how it worked, but it looked like the first participant to mount ten rockets in the ground would win. The last game featured three dwarves racing to climb a tall wooden pole.

The whole cavern was filled with laughter, music, and cheering. It was really too much for Gruhit's ears and eyes to take in. He forced his body to be comfortable so that he could experience it. Gruhit found that focusing on walking and drawing kept his mind from overloading.

"Alright, let's do this! All kids stay with a buddy because there is no way we will be able to find you if you get lost in the crowd," Malda said.

"Chicas stick together! Let's go dancing!" Cindy said, pulling the two ladies with her and saying to Amarie, "Mr. Lusplendida will never go dancing, so I need to get my fix now."

The trio disappeared into the crowd when Mr. Lusplendida looked down at Chardy. "You're with me, Chico," he said. "Let's go eat our weight in acorn and chocolate pudding." They walked happily off toward the food lines.

Samme asked Gruhit, "What do you say? Let's head over to the climbing contest, and we can do some sketches."

As they approached the crowd, Gruhit could see two women and one man getting ready. Gruhit quickly took out his sketchbook and drew anything that he could see. He noticed that all the men and women wore clothes that were a cross between a lumberjack and miner.

"Most of the games are fashioned from activities that the dwarves have to do when saving fleet birds falling from the sky," Samme explained, watching Gruhit draw. "They have to climb trees often, but dwarves typically hate heights. That's why we're underground."

"Do you see the rockets over at the other arena?" Samme mentioned. "Those are the ones that save fleet birds. They have a glass globe in the center which contains pure sunlight. The loud bang of the rocket wakes up the bird, and the explosion breaks the glass globe to provide sunlight."

Gruhit couldn't move his hand fast enough to sketch everything. He was already on his fifth drawing. He was amazed at the physical strength and build of the dwarves in front of him. He watched a female dwarf scramble easily to the top and raise her hands in triumph. The crowd cheered.

Just as Gruhit was putting the finishing touches on his eighth drawing, the candles along the walls started to flicker. The ambient light in the room did the same. The band suddenly stopped playing. All activities slowly ceased. There was a definite cool breeze blowing through the cavern.

Samme stood up in alarm and looked around quickly for the ladies. He spotted them by the dwarves who had been dancing just a moment ago.

"Gruhit, come with me now!" Samme helped Gruhit get to his feet and led him through the crowd.

Yet, despite Samme's alarm, the dwarves were not panicking. Many of them were simply looking toward the stage, while others were looking around.

As the two approached the stage, Gruhit could see that all of the adults were tense. Shortly, Mr. Lusplendida and Chardy came to join them.

"Jon, you know the dwarves the best. What do you make of this?" Samme said. At that moment, a small whirlwind formed in the middle of the stage.

"This is not the dwarves' doing," Jon replied. "Look! No one seems to be scared. It doesn't mean that we shouldn't keep our guard up, though. I can't explain it, but I feel that we are fine."

"I agree with Jon. This seems odd, but something is telling me it's alright," Malda said.

"*Si*. I'm feeling that too. I know it looks scary, but it seems okay," Cindy agreed.

"I get it; I think I'm getting a feeling too," Chardy said.

Samme wasn't sure what to think. The wind was definitely picking up. The whirlwind on the stage was intensifying. Samme wanted to believe the others, but felt uneasy.

"If we need to, we head for the secret tunnels and make our way to Priscilla's house," Samme told the group. The adults all nodded.
Gruhit and his siblings were absolutely bewildered. The adults clearly knew something that they weren't saying.

Before Gruhit could ask, the candles all went out. Instead of hearing cries of panic, the dwarves calmly walked toward the stage to stare at the whirlwind.

WHOOSH!

The whole cavern was plunged into darkness. Gruhit couldn't see his own hands in front of his face. Only one sound could be heard - the quiet fizzle of what sounded like a sparkler. Gruhit swallowed nervously. The fizzling sound became louder and faster.

Chardy's hand found Gruhit's shoulder as Chardy said, "It's alright Gruhit. Can't you feel it? In your gut? Everything is fine."

Gruhit had no idea what Chardy was talking about. The fizzling was almost deafening. It had almost reached them. With a sudden *WHOOSH* and crackle, a red ball of energy flew into the cavern and raced around the perimeter. There was a small laugh. Cheers came here and there as dwarves tried to jump up and grab at the ball.

The ball suddenly took a sharp turn and headed straight for the whirlwind. The two forces joined together in a strange marriage as the ball of energy grew brighter and spun violently. There was a large flash. The room was lit up by smaller balls of energy in various red hues. They could now see a tall female figure with large butterfly-like wings protruding from her back.

"Is that...?" Samme nearly stuttered and peared at the figure in total wonder.

"Hot diggity dog! Sorry I'm late, but who doesn't love to make an entrance?" the woman declared. "It's an honor to be with you, my dear Instinctuals, during the 300th Sunburst Dwarves Fall Festival! Enough niceties! Get this gal a good cider. It's time to crack up and cut a rug! The night is young, and adventure can still be found."

The dwarves all cheered and clapped for the woman as several big mugs of cider were passed through the crowd toward her. She took one in each hand, before downing a generous swig and hoisting a mug into the air in a triumphant manner. The dwarves clapped even louder.

The woman reminded Gruhit of an old time adventurer he had seen in his history book. She appeared to be wearing something like a bomber jacket, along with form-fitting pants. She also wore an old-fashioned aviator scarf, and goggles were resting on her forehead. Her wings looked similar to those of a tangerella, only much larger. Was this a fairy?

The woman gulped down the remainder of her cider and handed the empty mugs to a dwarf. It was then that her gaze happened upon Amarie.

"Well, I'll be a flobberworm. Do my peepers see a Sentrite at this shindig?"

Everyone grew quiet and looked at Amarie, Gruhit, and Samme. No one looked upset, but this many eyes on him made Gruhit very uncomfortable.

"Well, don't just stand there collecting dust aces. Swagger up here and let's get a look at ya."

The whole company walked toward the woman. The dwarves parted in front of them to let them walk through. As they drew closer, Gruhit noticed how unbelievably tall and powerful the woman looked. In fact, she was so magnificent and beautiful to look upon that Gruhit had to forcibly keep himself standing and fight the urge to simply kneel.

"Welcome, children of Victus from the Orders of Timorines and Sentrites. It is always good to have visitors from my brothers' orders with us. I am Ira, one of the three leading Messengers of Victus and overseer of the Order of Instinctuals."

Chardy fell to his knees and looked at the ground. Gruhit would have thought this was strange except he felt that he must do the same thing. Amarie suddenly followed Chardy's lead and was now also kneeling before Ira.

"Aren't you two aces absolutely precious," Ira said. "A couple of killer dillers. Holy Mackerel, please get up. Kneeling in my presence is a really cockeyed notion. I'm just a messenger and overseer. Folks really get everything jimmy-jacked when they think that they need to kneel before me.. Now enough with the stiff lips and let's start jabbing. What's buzzin', cousin? What brings humans to the Festival of the Dwarves?"

Malda nodded her head in respect toward Ira and started. "These are the children we are watching over at the moment. We are teaching them about the Kingdom of Victus and what we know about magical creatures."

"Malda Wunder, and the Lusplendidas," Ira said with a wide smile. "You're all distinguished in the magical community. I know the names of all humans and creatures in the Order of Instinctuals who are about the business of Victus. You all have a lot of moxie."

Ira looked from the adults to Chardy, who was on the verge of crying.

"My eyes are bamboozled by you, young man. It is a talent of messengers to recognize the orders of others and my right as an overseer to know those that move to the beat of the drum heard by Instinctuals, but I do not know your name," Ira said.

Chardy bowed his head lower in embarrassment.

"Don't worry, young crackerjack," Ira went on. "I have a feeling that one day I will know your name."

"Please, ma'am," Amarie got the courage to quietly ask Ira a question. "Why can't I belong to your order? Why can't you know my name? Did I do something wrong?"

"Ah, listen to me, cookie. Don't ever doubt how unique you are because all humans were made to have a special place," Ira explained. "When the universe was just a young rookie, Victus created his messengers. There was Fridgita Mortes. Underneath her, he created myself and my two brothers." Ira held out each of her hands face up. Balls of red energy formed on her palms and morphed into two different figures of fairies.

"Victus, being the original hipster, was inspired by our unique personalities. He fashioned humans and magical creatures in variations of our diverse dispositions. There is the Order of Sentrites, which is overseen by my brother Sentire. The creatures and humans of this order tend to live life through their feelings. These are the folks that impact your world with the heart, and tend to be concerned with appearances the most."

Ira leaned forward once more and looked over Amarie again before going on.

"I may not oversee my brother's order, but I can see that you, little chipmunk, are a darling part of it. The tangerellas and little folks of this world are also part of your order. Learn to have empathy for other critters and think about others first. Feelings can be a great motivator in this order and will make you a great force for good or an awful villain. Remember that, cookie."

Ira brought forth her other hand as she stood up once again.

"Timor is my other brother. He's a planner and a wise man; a real egghead. His order is made of those creatures and humans who impact this world through thinking and planning. Malda, your husband is no doubt a Timorine. I can also see that this young boy is a Timorine. Be careful, both of you. While humans and creatures in this order bring great joy through their thoughts, fear and pain can be their undoing. Never avoid fear. Don't live with it either. Charmyrlls, dipsy toads, and the drlecks call this order home as fear motivates them to do amazing things.

"The final order was created after my own personality. The Order of Instinctuals tend to live life by their gut, to be real eager beavers. We love to be honest and blunt. Life is simply too short for mortals to be flapping their gums with useless lies and tip-toeing around the point of the conversation. Those creatures who call my order their home are motivated most by their response to anger. There can be just anger that wants to see wrongs put to right. However, all must be sure not to be consumed by anger. There are plenty of folks who I have seen get jimmy-jacked by anger and turn into real knuckleheads. Naturally, the Sunburst Dwarves are overseen in my order, as are the fleet birds, guardlings, and even golems because they all have great instincts and the ability to use anger to lead on to greatness.

"These are the three orders in the Kingdom of Victus. None are better than the others and all are special in their own right, for we are children of Victus. We are all at our best when we rely on the strength of the other orders. We are most comforted when we share our concerns with people from our own order."

Ira extinguished the figures of her brothers in her hands and looked intently at Samme as though examining his thoughts. Samme was quite nervous. Finally, she smiled and spoke again.

"Sharing our burdens with all people in different orders isn't just gobbledygook, or a way to pass the buck; helping each other and creating strong relationships makes us the strongest. Remember: you are a child in the Kingdom of Victus. You were created to relate with him and other creatures in his Kingdom."

Ira looked away from Samme to his relief. She looked toward her empty hand and declared, "Where's the cider? I've got bupkis aces. It's a crummy way to find yourself at the Festival of the Dwarves. I don't want to bust anyone's chops, but can I get some refreshment here?"

With that, she descended the stairs. After reaching the floor, she turned and added, "Hey aces! Don't forget that there is always hope. Just because you can't see something, doesn't mean it's not possible."

Then Ira disappeared into the sea of dwarves. The festivities returned to the way they were before. The candles relit themselves. Ira's red balls of energy could still be seen around the cavern. Gruhit could still see her most of the time due to her size and height.

It was almost 11 PM. Even Gruhit had to admit he was feeling very tired. He was amazed he could still hear Ira's uproarious laughter occasionally. She never seemed to run out of energy. The Brown Place crew were sitting at a long bench eating various savory meats and delicious puddings. Amarie barely had her eyes open as she tried to sleepily get the last bit of pudding to her mouth.

"Samme?" Gruhit inquired. "Why does Ms. Ira know what orders we are in?"

"I'm assuming it's because of her duties as a messenger. I've never met one before tonight. They're talked about all the time, but we usually don't see them. It sounded like she was here because of the special age of this festival."

"So did you know about the orders before tonight then?" Gruhit asked.

"Sure. All of the creatures know about them and have educated us on such. There is at least one creature from each order that has the ability to tell which order someone belongs to. The creatures around our area are the little folks, guardlings, and charmyrlls. They can tell in different ways. For example, Mrs. Snickelfritz can make a mixture that, when drunk, will cause colored steam to come out of your ears. Red steam for Instinctuals, blue steam for Timorines, and yellow steam for Sentrites. Charmyrlls are able to tell when they know you well enough. They, of course, present their answers in different images. A flame for Instinctuals, a book for Timorines, and a heart for Sentrites. You kids really are fortunate to have been told by an actual messenger."

"Oh no, little one!" Cindy declared as she began dabbing Amarie's face with a napkin. "She fell asleep in her pudding."

"Samme, I think it's time we started walking outside. It's very late," Malda expressed.

Samme nodded his head in agreement. "I'll get Gripple. He told me he would be working by the apple cider stand tonight. I'll meet everyone upstairs."

Even Chardy yawned a bit as he got to his feet. Gruhit gave his mug of cider one last sip. He gently placed his sketchbook in the cargo pocket of his jeans, now full of new drawings.

They were greeted by a young dwarf woman upon reaching the stairs. She was dressed in dark green work pants and a dark orange long-sleeved work shirt with several pockets. Her dark auburn hair was done in a simple braid and hung down her back.

"Will you be taking the stairs or the railing tonight?" asked the woman.

Mal looked at the children and then back to the dwarf. "I think some of us are so tired that we would never make it up ten flights on our own. We'll take the railing please."

"Let me get a gyro-ball, please. Since we have non-dwarf riders, has everyone had some apple cider recently?" asked the young woman.

"*Si!* We just came from the food benches. It was all very delicious," Cindy said thankfully.

"Good," said the dwarf. She grabbed a small, clear ball from a cupboard next to the stairs. "Everyone join hands please."

Everyone joined hands as the dwarf set the ball on the floor. Gruhit could see it had several gears and wheels around it with a small door on its side. As he observed the curious little ball there was a quick sound.

SNICK!

Gruhit looked around. They had become even smaller, the stairs were now gigantic before them. Chardy looked like he might be sick.

"Can I just know? Are we getting any smaller tonight?" Chardy said as he fought being ill.

"Everyone on board, please." The young dwarf held the door open for the six humans as they got into the clear ball and sat down.

As soon as they were all settled, there was again the sound… *SNICK!* They had shrunk again, and now were looking at the dwarf woman's boot. A giant hand came down and grasped the ball. It was Gruhit's turn to feel ill as the ground below became more distant. The ball was placed inside a hole in the stair railing.

As Gruhit looked up the dark cavernous railing into the unknown, he heard a third *SNICK!* The young dwarf blew into the railing like it was a large straw, sending the ball flying up the railing. Gruhit couldn't see a thing for about a minute, but could hear the wheels rolling ferociously. Then a light appeared at the end of the tunnel. The ball flew out of the opening and landed in the hands of a male dwarf, who gently set it on the ground.

With a fourth *SNICK* the ball grew larger. After exiting and joining hands with the male dwarf, a fifth *SNICK* brought the group back to their festival size.

The dwarf looked up at them. "Thank you for coming to the festival tonight!" he said.

"I think next time I'll be taking the stairs," Chardy said in a shaky voice.

Everyone huddled together inside the tree's doorway, when suddenly Gruhit could see another ball arrive from the railing. It enlarged with a *SNICK* and then opened, revealing Mr. Wunder and Gripple who returned them to the height of their companions.

Gripple still wore a stern look on his face and walked past the group without saying a word. He opened the door and urged everyone to follow him outside. They held hands and formed a circle. As they did so, Gruhit noticed several dwarves mounting rockets on the outside of the tree and pointing them up toward the moon.

Samme checked his watch. "We have less than a minute until eleven o'clock, Gripple."

And with a *SNICK* the party of seven people and one dwarf found themselves at their normal heights once more. Gruhit thought the world looked a little less magical now and more ordinary.

"Everyone look at the tree!" Mal exclaimed.
Suddenly the rockets came to life and went whizzing into the stratosphere. Gruhit watched as they quickly went out of sight and into the dark night sky before…

BOOM! BOOM! BA-BOOM!

The explosions filled the night air with flashes of lightning. If Gruhit hadn't seen the rockets before, he would have thought it was a normal October storm. As the lightning subsided, rain began to pour down.

"Gracias to everyone for coming with us to the festival!" declared Mr. Lusplendida, shaking everyone's hands. "Samme and Mal, it was another great year!"

"*Si!* Next year we must talk Priscilla into coming with us. I know she doesn't like being underground or out so late, but she is going to hate that she could have met a messenger tonight," said Mrs. Lusplendida.

"Goodnight, dear friends," Mal replied. "We will see you later. Come everyone, off to bed," she said as they led the children toward Big Blue.

Once inside, Mal instructed everyone to get their pajamas on and go straight to bed. No one objected. When Gruhit was finally under his covers, he thought about what Ira had told them. He felt more connected to people and creatures than he had before. Gruhit reflected on how people who were different from him could help make him stronger when he was weak. This meant someone like Judy Credulent had a purpose and role in his life. He wasn't thankful for being bullied at all. However, Ira had said that fear, anger, or feelings had the power to motivate, or make someone into a villain. Which would Judy choose?

It was odd that even though he felt more connected to others, he also felt more disconnected from his mom. Before falling asleep, he spoke into the darkness: "Victus, if you listen to any of us, and if you're real, please take care of my mom."

Chapter 20
The Tacet Stone

Amarie was excited the next day because Mrs. Snickelfritz and Mrs. Dickelbutton had written to her the night before. She enjoyed her pen pal relationship and was delighted to hear that Mrs. Snickelfritz was feeling much better than she had been the previous morning. For the last few weeks, she had written to them almost nightly. With permission, and a little help from Malda, she made little treats for them periodically. One night she helped Malda make a cake for the whole Wunder family, but used the last of the cake batter to make tiny cakes with dabs of frosting on top for the little folk families. Amarie even took an index card, scissors, and tape that same day and created two small cake boxes.

If this wasn't enough to make her sing and dance all day long, she was also becoming better friends with Sparkles. Mrs. Bangs had suggested that she pick one flower from her garden every other day and sleep with it in her hair to see if Sparkles would feel more comfortable. The gesture seemed to work. Sparkles infrequently came to Amarie's bedroom while she was about to fall asleep. It was so difficult for Amarie not to talk incessantly to the tangerella, but she didn't want to scare her off either. She reported to the Wunders that she would greet Sparkles and say goodnight. She planned to help Mrs. Bangs tend to her flower garden the following weekend so that they could look for more tangerellas.

After finishing his chores for the day, Gruhit spent most of the morning looking over his sketchbook. He added notes about the drawings, or things he had learned the night before that he didn't want to forget. He was content to work quietly and by himself because his brain felt a bit foggy. He wasn't sure if this was because he stayed up so late, or because a walluping wallop visited him last night. Even after being awake for several hours, he was still rubbing his eyes and finding a sandy-like substance around them. It was strange that most foster homes gave him many reasons to have nightmares, but this home gave him good dreams.

Gruhit had to laugh a bit at his fosters. They sat for the longest time at the dining room table with large mugs of coffee saying things like, "I'm getting too old to be out that late," and "Why am I so tired this morning?"

Samme continuously rubbed his temples while nursing his coffee. Gruhit was impressed with Malda. Most people would simply wake up with bedhead hair. She had styled her hair so that it was twirled, spiky, and frizzy all at once. Gruhit noted it looked like a mess but beautiful at the same time. All three of them were sitting around in their pajamas.

"Samme, did you remember that Constance is picking up the kids this afternoon? They're getting an extra visit this week," Mal said.

"An extra visit? Are things going well?" Samme asked. Gruhit perked up his ears while pretending to be very intent on his sketchbook. Amarie too seemed to appear from out of nowhere to sit quietly at the table and listen.

"Who knows. With as much information as we are told, I think we know less about the situation than the children sometimes. Constance just said this was an extra visit. She said in the winter with storms and icy roads they might only have phone calls. This gives them a chance to see their mom now. Constance made it seem like their mom is having some problems getting everything completed for the children to move back home. She's trying her hardest, so that's good news. But there were some setbacks. Maybe the extra visit will lighten her spirits."

"It's almost time for lunch, and we're all still in our sleep clothes," Samme said. "Is Chardy even awake yet?"

"I haven't seen him yet today," Malda said.

"I'll go tell him to get the day started," Samme said as he struggled to his feet and walked toward the basement.

"You two need to get ready to see your mom. I want you washed up with nice clothes on. I don't want her worrying that you're not being taken care of," Malda stated before taking a good long sip of coffee.

Gruhit and Amarie both got up out of their seats and headed toward their bathrooms. While Gruhit brushed his teeth, three of the drleck appeared and began hitting the toothpaste cap around like an odd-shaped volleyball.

After showering, Gruhit said goodbye to the drleck. They were the first creatures he had truly observed and captured in his sketchbook, so they held a special place in his heart. He felt even more connected to them now that he knew they were in the Order of Timorines too. He always wanted to know what was going on around him so that he wouldn't be scared. He liked to know what was going to happen and make plans. For him, the best adventure was the carefully thought-out one. He knew the drlecks also hated to feel anxious and fearful. Afterall, this is why they dispelled their magical calming lavender scent.

After getting dressed in a new long sleeved t-shirt Mal had picked out for him and some newer looking jeans, Gruhit made his way back to the dining room table to look at his sketchbook. He found Amarie and Chardy in the middle of an argument.

"I wouldn't go into your smelly old room even if you promised me I could have wings like a tangerella," Amarie said with a stern face and attitude.

Chardy turned to Gruhit. "Did you come into my room last night and leave all sorts of trash? I *know* one of you did something."

"Why would I go all the way downstairs to put trash in your room?" Gruhit said defensively.

"You know what, no one wants to admit what they did? That's fine. Both of you go to your rooms then," Chardy barked at his siblings.

Gruhit started to turn to walk away. For years, he saw Chardy as a father-figure and did what his brother said. Then he stopped. "No. I don't have to do what you say. You're not the boss of me, and *I didn't* do anything."

"Are you talking back to me?" Chardy asked with a scowl on his face.

"Yes, he did," Amarie put in. "And I'm with Gruhit. You're not the boss of either of us. Just because you can't clean your room doesn't give you the right to yell at us."

"I don't know what has gotten into both of you, but I will not be ignored. I took care of you for years, and you will listen to me. You will…"

"You will all sit down at the table now," Mr. Wunder strode urgently into the dining room. "Malda! We need a family meeting."

All the kids quietly took seats at the table. They had never seen Samme this upset. Like any other foster, he had raised his voice at them when he was frustrated, but this was a whole new level. Samme placed a couple of buttons, some string, yarn, paperclips, thimble, part of a broken comb, and lots of dust and dirt all over the table.

"Now you two are going to get it," Chardy whispered to his siblings. "That's the trash from all over my floor."

Gruhit was worried as Mal entered the room and took a seat. She obviously didn't know what was going on. Gruhit feared he was about to be blamed for something he didn't do. When other fosters got this frustrated, this was the moment they told them they were leaving the house. Gruhit could see in her face that Amarie was nervous about this too.

"Samme, what is all this?" Mal said. "I can't believe you would put this all over the dining room table. We eat our food off this table."

"We need to talk about something very, *very* serious. Right here. Right now. And someone is going to have to give some answers," Samme said sternly, "Mal, Chardy, where have you seen these items before?"

"It's just the junk that someone put on the floor of my room. Probably wanting me to get in trouble for having made a big mess and not cleaning my room," Chardy said defensively.

Mal examined the trash on the table a bit longer, trying to see what her husband was getting at. Suddenly her eyes got large, and she put a hand over her mouth. "Is… is that the… I know I didn't like it, but…" Mal couldn't finish her sentences.

"Yup. It's the golem alright. I recognized the buttons it used for eyes immediately. It has been fizzled out," Samme said sadly, but still stern.

"But… I didn't think anyone could hurt a golem. They're supposed to magically regenerate their body if they get hurt," Gruhit reported.

"If something saps all the sundust from them, though, I'm afraid it simply ceases to exist," Samme explained. "This is just a pile of trash now."

"I never liked it, but I never wanted this," Mal said again, shocked.

"There's more," Samme said. "I went into Chardy's room to check on Kieffer. He's worse. His breathing is more labored, but he isn't sick. He's fizzling out slowly. His tail has already disappeared and the rest of his body is becoming transparent. I don't think we noticed last night because his bed is in the shadows on the floor. As I bent down to pet him, I noticed something shiny coming from underneath the bed. The golem must have found it and dragged it there before fizzling out." Samme removed a handkerchief from one of his pockets and quickly unfolded the material to reveal a jagged, dark green gem. It was a bit smaller than his palm and radiated an eerie glow in its center, which twinkled in the gold wire-wrapped setting of its necklace.

"Is that a tacet stone?" Mal said. Gruhit could see the fosters' fearful expressions, but had no idea what this item was.

"What's a tacet stone?" Amarie asked.

"Well, it's made from a beautiful gem, but it is empowered with dark magic. There are only a few in existence. Whoever holds the stone is invisible to magical creatures," Malda said.

"Well, that's not so bad. Why are you both so scared of this thing?" Gruhit said, still confused.

"Because, Gruhit, the stone cannot produce this magic on its own. The only way the stone can power itself is by stealing the sundust energy from the magical creatures around it," Samme said sternly.

Samme slammed his hand down on the table, causing everyone to jump back in their chairs. "This is why the poor golem is no longer and why Kieffer is fizzling out downstairs. From the way the discarded items were spread across the floor, it looks like the golem was trying to move the stone away from Kieffer before fizzling. This creature fizzled out because someone has brought this necklace into our home, and I want to know who it is, and now!"

Mr. Wunder glared around the table from child to child. Malda continued to look at what was left of the golem, still in shock. Amarie began to cry. The tension was too much for her. Malda slipped her arm around her in comfort.

Mr. Wunder was still expecting an answer. The children could see that he had almost worked it out. "It *was* you, wasn't it, Chardy?" he asked. "Just because it was in your room, I didn't want to jump there but… it all works out. It has been colder in your room than the rest of the house. I just thought it was the heater not working or this old house being drafty. No. Evil magic is from Fridgita Mortes and always gives off coldness. Your bedroom has been cold this whole time because of the tacet stone, hasn't it? You've been using it to hide yourself from Kieffer so he can't watch you at night. I'm right, aren't I? Where did you get this? Why are you using it?"

Mr. Wunder stared at Chardy. Gruhit kept waiting for Chardy to say that this was all made up, but he never did. Chardy just stared coldly at Mr. Wunder and refused to talk.

"Chardy, tell them you don't know what's going on," Amarie said through tears.

Gruhit watched as Chardy stared at the table. Minutes ticked by in awkward silence. It seemed like hours.

"Tell me where you got this now!" Samme demanded.

"Samme, I think that it's time to back down a little," Malda said.

"Back down? Mal, do you know what this means? Fridgita Mortes could have access to our home. At the very least, the other creatures here are in danger. And that's just the beginning. If Fridgita can collect enough sundust, even the people in our neighborhood are in danger. Our family has been protecting magical creatures for generations. Fridgita will be sure to make us a target simply because we are the biggest threat to her in the area."

"Will Kieffer be okay?" Chardy said timidly.

Gruhit could tell that his brother really did like the guardling. Samme was still so angry that he couldn't look Chardy in the face. Gruhit had only seen a foster this angry once before. That was during the kissing incident with Chardy and the foster's daughter.

This would be it. Samme and Malda would ask them to leave the house for sure.

"There is always hope, Chardy. Always!" Malda said. "We don't know exactly how the tacet stone got into the house, but we are a family. That doesn't mean we don't make mistakes. It means that we stick together and protect each other the best we can."

"You're the Timorine, right?" Malda asked, standing up and looking directly at her husband. "Aren't you supposed to be good at thinking things through and planning? Well, how do we destroy the stone and keep Kieffer from getting worse?"

Samme stood. Everyone could see him thinking things over before he spoke. "Stabilizing Kieffer is the easy part. We need Mrs. Snickelfritz to make a bit of the sleeping draught. It seems to be working for her husband at the moment. As far as getting rid of the tacet stone, I don't know. There are only a few of them in existence. I'll look through my books and question our friends."

"What do we need to do?" Gruhit said, concerned.

"Be ready to visit your mom and make sure she knows how much you love her," Malda said. "When you get back home, we'll find some other things you can do to help. For now, having the best visit you can with your mom is what you are meant to do."

"There is always hope, Wunders," Malda went on. "As long as we have hope, Fridgita will never win. Now, we can choose to mope around and be scared or let our anger consume us. However, if I were an evil being looking to destroy the world, I would want to get them to do just that. There is *always* hope."

"Can I go give Mr. Kieffer a hug and a kiss?" Amarie asked.

Samme looked touched by her request. "Of course. I would actually love it if you would watch him while I call for Mrs. Snickelfritz."

"I'm on it. Nurse Amarie to the rescue," Amarie sang as she started running toward the basement steps. "I'm going to make a quick card for momma before we go, too. There's *always* hope!"

"Mr. Wunder?" Gruhit said. "I'm going to help Mrs. Wunder get lunch ready.

When we get back from our visit, I want to help look through books for a way to destroy the tacet stone."

"Gruhit, get some frozen vegetables out of the freezer. I'm going to write a quick note to your mom before Constance arrives." Mal declared. "After the children leave for their visit, I'll notify the Council about the situation."

Soon everyone was off doing their various tasks. Samme and Chardy were the only two to remain. They both stared at each other, not knowing what to say.

"Do I need to pack my things?" Chardy asked nervously.

"No," Samme said. "When you know that you're moving back home with your mom, then you will pack your things. Not before."

Samme continued to stare at Chardy. The tension and awkwardness in the room was very strange and thick.

"I'm sorry, Chardy. I should not have yelled and carried on the way I did. However, I'm not sorry for being concerned about our family. You need to know how serious this all is."

"Will Kieffer really be okay?" Chardy asked again.

"You heard Mal. There's always hope. If only we knew where the tacet stone came from. It might help us destroy it and give us a hint on how to restore Kieffer and Mr. Snickelfritz. I don't think that there is any way to help the golem though. He's completely fizzled out. It's like he doesn't exist anymore."

Samme paused for a moment, hoping Chardy might have something to tell him. It soon became clear Chardy wasn't going to say anymore right now.

"Well, I need to get word to Mrs. Snickelfritz," Samme said at last. "If you think of anything, Chardy, please tell us soon. Everyone makes bad decisions and mistakes. Bad decisions are choices we make and actions we do; the actions are not who we are but reflect what we believe. A family still loves and accepts someone for who they really are. Chardy, I'm very glad to have your Instinctual spirit here in our home; I'm glad you're part of the family."

Chapter 21
Nathan's Grandma

Gruhit took his seat in Mrs. Snow's classroom. He still had about ten minutes before the school day began. Most of the students hadn't arrived yet. There was a small group in the back watching one student play a math game on the computer. One boy was nervously sitting at his desk and trying to complete a homework assignment. Some girls, including Judy, were sitting on bean bag chairs in the reading corner.

Judy hadn't been bullying him as much since the Halloween Party. However, she didn't miss a chance to whisper, "Cheesehead," when she passed. She kept her distance for the most part. That was fine with Gruhit. But out of fear, he still kept an eye on where she was. He was the prey and needed to know where the predator was at all times so he could protect himself.

Gruhit pulled a worn book out of his backpack and began reading while he waited. It was titled *Curious Plants* and was more of an old sketchbook and journal written by one of Mr. Wunder's ancestors. He wanted to find something to help Kieffer. It was difficult to read because the writing was in cursive. The drawings were interesting to look at though. There was very little that was useful for Kieffer, and some of the more promising plants were reported as being nonexistent. They were only recorded in the book because older magical creatures were able to describe them and explain their properties to the author.

Gruhit glanced up at the clock. A few more kids came into the classroom and were laughing and talking loudly. Gruhit's mind wandered to the last visit with his mom last weekend. Even though news of the tacet stone in the house had been horrible, it didn't impact the time with his mom too much. Mrs. Wunder put the stone in a thick-walled safe in the corner of Samme's office. This was to deter magical creatures from accidentally happening upon it, and the thick walls seemed to dampen its power. Though this was good progress, all three kids were rather gloomy and on edge when Constance picked them up. During the drive, Constance kept asking why they all seemed so glum. Even Amarie was quiet. She was sad, but mostly frustrated with Chardy. Not only had he been trying to parent her and Gruhit, but she was pretty sure he had brought the tacet stone into the house.

Amarie told Constance she was so quiet because she was thinking about the perfect way to give her mom a card she had made. This was partly true and seemed to stop Constance from asking more questions.

Their mom was waiting for them at the front of the restaurant. Gruhit thought his mom was wearing a bigger smile than usual and giving each child more compliments. She always hugged and kissed them and told them how proud she was of them, but this time she talked about everything from how tall or pretty they had become to how clever or brave they were. Gruhit also noticed she seemed to be thinking about something important.

Everyone sat in their usual places at a long table in the restaurant. This time Amarie didn't play at all on the playground. Their mom was happy to get the card from Amarie and repeatedly said how creative and thoughtful Amarie had been to make it. This led into a long conversation about good times when they all lived together. All of them were laughing at the old stories; even Constance was having fun. Every time someone told a fun story, Gruhit's mom would say, "Don't you kids ever forget that story," or "Please, remember that story when you think about me."

Toward the end, Gruhit handed the latest letter from Malda to his mom. She took it a bit reluctantly, promising to read it when she got home. She looked at the letter in her hand for an unusually long time. This was followed by a round of compliments to Gruhit about how responsible he was becoming to deliver a letter for someone else. It was soon time to leave. All the kids got hugs and kisses. Gruhit couldn't remember when he had felt a bigger or deeper hug from his mom. As they drove away from the restaurant, she waved goodbye with the biggest, most loving smile he had seen.

Constance was quiet on the way home. She seemed to be deciding something. It was odd that she was bothered when they had such a great visit. Why would she be so fidgety right now?

"I want to say that I'm so proud of each of you for making this time so special for your mom. She really needed that," Constance finally stated. "Your mom is having a really rough week. You know she lost one of her jobs, right? Well, she thought she had found another, but they called her yesterday to tell her she didn't get the position. Another worker at my office is now trying to help her find a better paying job so she can spend more time with you kids. She also thought she had found the perfect place for all of you to live together, but when the landlord heard she had lost multiple jobs in a short period of time, he wanted the first two months rent up front. Your mom simply doesn't have that kind of money right now. She's trying so hard, too. Anyways, I probably shouldn't have worried you kids about all that, but I just wanted you to know that it touched my heart deeply to see you all getting along and being loving to your mom today."

Even as he sat in class, Gruhit got a good feeling when he thought about helping his mom. The school bell suddenly rang, snapping him from his thoughts. Mrs. Snow told all the kids to take their seats with their reading books.

At recess, Gruhit planned to sit by himself along the side of the school building again. This time he wasn't going to watch the other kids playing. He planned to look through the old sketchbook on plants and see if he could find a cure for Kieffer.

As he began to head toward his favorite spot near the monkey bars, he saw another boy sitting there. The boy was sitting with his legs folded up to his chest, his face buried in his knees, and his arms wrapped around his legs. Gruhit could tell from the curly, dark brown hair though that it was Nathan.

"Nathan, you okay?" Gruhit asked softly.

Nathan slowly lifted his head. You could see that he wasn't crying but looked really upset. Gruhit sat down next to the only person that he considered to be a friend at the school.
"What's wrong?" Gruhit asked again.

Nathan sat in silence as he looked at other boys playing soccer on the soccer field.

"You remember when I came over here and told Judy to take a hike that day?"

"Sure. I remember."

"Well, do you remember that she said something about missing seeing my grandma around?"

Gruhit had to think for a moment. He had been so concerned about his misery at the time that he didn't remember that detail.

"Well, anyways, she said that to make me mad, too. A few years back my mom and dad both had good jobs working at the factory in town," Nathan said slowly and in a weak voice.

"You mean the Wunder Shoe Factory?" Gruhit said in amazement.

"No. I don't even really know about that place. It was closed a long, long time ago. I've just heard people talking about it every once in a while. I'm not sure what my mom and dad did at the factory actually. Well, the factory closed down, and so they were both out of work. It was bad. Neither one of them could find work anywhere. After a few months, money started getting tight. Our electricity and water got shut off. They had trouble getting food for us and started getting letters from the bank about losing the house. I'm not sure how it all happened, but a lady and a police officer showed up one day. My parents said they wouldn't be able to take care of me until they could afford food and to pay for our house."

Gruhit's eyes got wide. "Did you have to go into foster care?"

"Nope. My grandma took me to live with her in the next town over, but she made sure that she drove me to school every day so that I could still keep coming here with my friends," Nathan explained.

"You live with your folks again though, right?" Gruhit asked.

"Yeah. They had to work hard, but they both got jobs and paid off their debts. But Judy saw my grandma bring me to school a lot. That was the first thing she thought of to hurt me when I talked back to her that day. Only it doesn't make me mad."

"It doesn't? I mean she is so mean sometimes."

"My mom and dad told me that everyone needs help sometimes, so you should never look down on people that ask for help or need it. Some day we are all going to ask for help. I'm proud of my mom and dad. I'm proud of my grandma for looking after me. That's actually why I'm a bit sad."

"I'm not getting it. Why are you upset if you're not mad at Judy?"

"My mom told me before we left for school this morning that Grandma is in the hospital with pneumonia. Everything will probably be fine, and mom said she got into the hospital very early before it got too bad. It's just... well... my grandma is kind of like a second mom to me. I can't stop thinking about what life would be like if she weren't here. It's silly, I know."

"Nah. That's not silly at all. I think about that all the time. I mean, not about your grandma, but about my mom. I mean she is trying really hard to get us back, but she keeps having setbacks. She just lost one of her jobs, too, and we can't move back home until she is able to make enough money and find a good, safe place for us all to live together. If we're talking about 'silly,' then I'm the silly one. Sometimes I think I should give up hope."

Gruhit looked at the ground, feeling the weight of his own situation. He started to feel numb. He never really realized how much work it was to think that he was going back home with his mom. Once he let the hopelessness take over his thinking, he knew how easy it would be to just give up and sit on the ground. He almost thought he heard a woman's voice in his head telling him that it was alright to give up. He slouched a bit more. He wanted to let his emotions go numb, to stop caring about his mom and siblings. It didn't feel good, but the numbness didn't make him hurt either. He didn't feel at all. No. That's not true. He could feel the air get cooler. The colors around him seemed to be more dull and faded. He was less aware of others nearby. For once in a long time, he didn't feel any negative feelings. He simply didn't feel. There was only hopelessness and the growing icy feeling all around him.

"Hey! Don't go there!" Nathan slightly yelled as he shook Gruhit back to the moment. "You were thinking about giving up. I could see it. I've been there. Don't do that! Grandma always told me that the best things in life are worth working and fighting for. She also said that no one was ever promised to have an easy life. Everyone has something going on in their lives. Even someone that seems so goody-goody like Judy Credulent. If there's one thing I've learned, it's that my mom and dad need me to do my best to hope for the future. Everything doesn't always turn out the way we want it to. You can never stop hoping. There's always hope, Gruhit. Your mom needs you to help her hope, especially if she is feeling down."

Gruhit stared at Nathan for the longest time without saying anything. He began to feel strength and feeling come back into his arms and legs. The world felt fresh and warm again. He wouldn't say that he felt happy but… he felt again. It was good to feel again.

"Thanks, Nathan, I needed that. Thanks for being my friend," Gruhit said.

"You bet. Look, not many people get you and me. We have to stick together, right?" Nathan said with a smile.

Gruhit nodded and smiled. He would remember today as the one where he made a good friend and never had to spend lunchtime in 2nd grade alone again.

Chapter 22
The Snowflake

It was a lazy Saturday. The cool October air had given away to chillier November weather over the past couple weeks. It was still a ways away from being cold enough for snow, but it was cold enough that Gruhit had to wear sweatshirts instead of tshirts from now on.

Amarie had officially made friends with Sparkles. Well, maybe not quite friends, but the tangerella was comfortable to stay with Amarie while she was awake and active. Amarie would join Mrs. Bangs in her garden on Saturdays. The two of them worked to prepare the flowers and the small pond for the coming winter months. Amarie was happy to report that Mrs. Bangs was going to show her how to assemble a small portable greenhouse to cover the pond and a portion of the flowers. This would make it easier on the dipsy toads as they hibernated, and provide some extra warmth for the tangerellas' flowery homes. Today they were pulling weeds, pruning plants, and cleaning around the pond. If they had enough time, Mrs. Bangs wanted Amarie to help her harvest some of the dipsy toad saliva so Malda could make more nighttime salve.

Gruhit had decided to spend the day studying books in Samme's office. They had poured over a handful of titles on various creatures, plants, and even different kinds of stones. Gruhit was amazed that Samme always had more books that came from who knows where. There were a few in his office, but they all had to do with design work. Yet, there seemed to be an endless supply of books written by his late relatives.

"What will happen to my sketchbook?" Gruhit asked Samme as he sat at the smaller desk adjacent to Samme's drafting table.

Samme sat up straighter in his chair as he swiveled to face Gruhit. "I'm not sure I understand what you mean."

"Will my sketchbook have to stay here? What happens when I go home?"

"I gave you the sketchbook, Gruhit. You decide what happens to it. If you want it to stay in the house with the others, it will. If you want to take it with you, you can."

"Aren't you worried about other people finding out about magical creatures though? And my sketchbooks aren't as good as these, right?"

"The goal has never been to keep magical creatures a secret. It's part of reality. It has always been about trust. Who can we tell that will protect and take care of these creatures? I mean, unfortunately there are those who would want to do experiments on them, dissect them, or do other nasty things instead of living in harmony with them. However, to keep them a secret would be like not telling other people about what is really happening in the world. Think about it, Gruhit. All those other homes you lived in, they would have thought we were nuts for believing in tangerellas or dwarves. They're the ones living in a fantasy world. It sounds funny, right? Again, it's all about finding safe people who are open to learning something new about the world. So many people act strangely around something they don't understand. They will either want to destroy it, belittle and control it, or simply ignore it. Does that make sense?"

Gruhit nodded.

"To your second question about your sketchbook. Every book that we have here is great for one reason or another. The one you're reading was done by a man who was very good at sketching pictures. But his descriptions are not very helpful. The book I'm reading has very simplistic pictures. The woman who penned it, though, was very good at describing every detail she has seen. My point is that your sketchbook, like all of the books, will bring about its own unique view and interests to teach people about the magical creatures you have seen. We need all the viewpoints to better understand our world."

This all made Gruhit feel good. He felt like he was a piece of something bigger.

"We've been looking through books for weeks now, though. Do you think we'll find something to help Kieffer?" he asked.

"I think you know what I'm going to say," Samme said with a grin as he looked at Gruhit.

"There's always hope," Gruhit mocked.

Gruhit and Samme went back to reading. Gruhit grabbed a new book to give himself a break from reading about plants. This one described various creatures. He opened the book to some pages talking about a doat, an animal about the size of a golden retriever with a goat-like and lion-like appearance. Doats are known for their food tracking abilities. Each doat only eats one type of food. When hungry, a doat will send itself into a trance to locate the source of the food it craves. From Gruhit's reading, early American settlers used doats to find food sources for them so they wouldn't go hungry. Gruhit was sure this wouldn't help Kieffer at all, though it was very interesting.

"Samme, do you think if we destroy the tacet stone, it will help Kieffer or Mr. Snickelfritz?" Gruhit asked as he finished reading about doats.

"I'm not sure. I did find a special brew, a potion that little folks are known to make. Mrs. Snickelfritz is quite good at making all sorts of potions, brews, and home remedies. Look, here it is," Samme had grabbed a book entitled *Little Folk Potions*.

"I was excited to find this potion the other day. It's specifically for destroying tacet stones. What is the one problem that you can see here?" Samme asked as he laid the book in front of Gruhit.

Gruhit scanned the pages. He saw instructions for how hot the brew needed to be and how to stir the potion. So far, not overly complicated. In fact, it appeared like something he could do if he followed the directions well. The ingredients weren't out of the ordinary either. They would be able to easily get water, honey, tea leaves, and few other things like dipsy toad saliva. The tacet stone had to be touched by a walluping wallop's tentacle, which would instinctively turn a small part of the stone to dust. It was important that the dust be used in the brew. It would be difficult to find a wallop, although they at least knew some inhabited the Wunder house.

Then he saw it. The most important ingredient for the potion that makes it work is a hair from the creature which made the stone.

"It's the hair, isn't it?" Gruhit said downheartedly.

"Exactly. I knew I had heard about this potion before, and it's the reason I wanted to know where the stone came from so that we could possibly get the hair," Samme explained.

"Mr. Wunder, you know that Chardy did it, right? I know my brother. It seems like something he would have done," Gruhit said, not wanting to sound like a tattle-tale but wanting to help.

"No one can make Chardy tell us if he has been up to something. We have no proof. I know that he seems to be awfully concerned about Kieffer, and he has been very helpful to Malda lately. He might be trying to make up for something, or he might be really sad. Kieffer and he were close friends. I don't want to be the person accusing him of something again if he was innocent all along. We're family, Gruhit. We believe in each other and support each other. But, I have to admit there was something strange about Chardy's behavior."

Gruhit grabbed his sketchbook and started to flip through its pages as he continued to think of a way to move forward in assisting the guardling.

"Stop!" Samme said in alarm, scaring Gruhit. "What is that?"

"It's a picture of Dragon as he was making his cloud images," Gruhit said, confused.

"I see that it's Dragon, but what are all those? Is that a snowflake?" Samme asked quickly.

"Yeah. I drew a picture of everything that Dragon showed us in clouds that day," Gruhit replied.

"It was only a month ago, right?"
Gruhit couldn't tell what Samme was getting at. "I think so. It was the day we

went to the Halloween Party," he replied.

"It was also the first day that we noticed Kieffer was fizzling out. What is this symbol?"

"That's the factory across the street. My picture isn't that good, but Dragon made a very detailed image of it. We were all pretty amazed. Well, everyone except for Chardy. He actually got really upset after Dragon made that symbol and tried to make Amarie and me go into the house away from Dragon."

"Did Dragon make the snowflake after or before the picture of the factory?" Samme asked.

"After."

"Were you talking about snow or winter or anything like that?"

Gruhit thought for a bit back to that day. "I don't think so. He just kind of made the snowflake after Mal told Chardy to go to his room. Actually, I think Mal and I might have been the only ones to see the snowflake."

"Of course, of course... Why hadn't I seen it before?" Mr. Wunder started rifling through his overcoat pockets as he walked quickly out the door. He didn't stop until he was at the window in the basement living room.

Samme pulled out a small collapsible scope and peered over at the shoe factory across the street. Gruhit quickly chased after his foster, hoping to hear more about what he was thinking.

"Samme, what is going on?" Gruhit asked eagerly.

"Dragon naturally talks in symbols. The factory image is self-explanatory. He was trying to tell you all something about it. My guess is that's what made Chardy upset. He realized that Dragon was trying to tell everyone he had been over at the factory."

"I thought he was just showing us how he could make images."

"I think Dragon could tell he wasn't getting through to you all, and when Chardy went away, he was trying to tell you that your brother must be involved with Fridgita

Mortes, or maybe a dark messenger. Fridgita Mortes' name means 'cold death' to all the creatures. I think the snowflake was Dragon's way of trying to warn you."

"Do you think there is something evil over in the factory?"

"I can't see anything over there. I don't know..." Samme slowly took his spyglass down and placed it back in his pocket. "It all makes sense, though. If Chardy were sneaking over to the factory, which I still don't know for sure, he could have used the tacet stone to hide from Kieffer, and Kieffer couldn't protect him."

Gruhit let this information sink in before saying, "Except, where did Chardy get a tacet stone in the first place? I'm guessing there wasn't one hiding around here, and he didn't have another opportunity to go over to the factory alone. Kieffer has been with him every single night since we got here."

Samme and Gruhit both looked at the ground in thought. Gruhit wanted so badly for Samme to be right so that they could help Kieffer. At the same time, he was glad there was a chance his brother didn't cause this situation.

"No, Kieffer hasn't always been down here," Samme finally said. "Remember Kieffer was to guard your brother against the golem. There was one night Mal and I determined that the golem had somehow gotten to the second floor to terrorize you sister. She had an absolute meltdown, so we had Kieffer sleep in her room."

Gruhit's eyes became wide. "So you think that Chardy snuck over to the factory that night? Do you think that he made the golem go upstairs?"

"Whoa, whoa, I'm not suggesting anything. I'm just saying the possibility of this happening was present. The tacet stone might have come from an evil entity at the factory. I want to observe the factory to see what I can find out. This would all be easier if Chardy would just talk to us."

"You don't think Fridgita Mortes is over there, do you?"

"Gruhit, I said I would always be honest with you. The truth is that I don't know. Could be. That's the worst case scenario. Don't forget that at the best, she is only a dark messenger."

"But I've never even seen Victus. Does he even care about what is happening to us? Why doesn't he just save Kieffer and Mr. Snickelfritz? Why doesn't he just imprison Fridgita Mortes?"

"Look, there are a great many things that are complicated in this world that even adults have to find the answers to. Do I know that Victus exists? Sure. We just met one of his messengers a couple weeks ago. Do I think that he is watching us and concerned about us? Yes. Until you came to our house, you didn't even know about the existence of a dipsy toad or little folk. It doesn't mean they didn't exist or were not going about their work. Just because I have never personally met Victus or seen what he is doing, doesn't mean he isn't working things out for us. It's his world, Gruhit, and I'm guessing he is giving us the chance to pick a side ourselves. There is always hope."

Samme looked down at Gruhit's sketchbook in the boy's hand.

"Can you see how much you were able to help from sketches that you thought were worthless?" Samme asked. "I don't want you ever doubting your abilities again. You might have literally saved the day here."

"What are the next steps? Are we headed over to the factory?"

"Now, don't get any ideas. My responsibility as your foster dad is still to protect you the best I can. You're an adult-in-training—otherwise known as a child. The job description that goes along with that is to learn and listen to the safe and caring adults in your life. You still have a lot to learn before coming along on such a dangerous pursuit. When you're at school, I'll work on a plan with Mal, Mrs. Bangs, and the Lusplendidas. Don't worry, I'll be sure to let you kids know what is happening."

Samme pulled a pocket watch from his coat.

"Have we really spent most of the day looking through this book? Thank goodness we still have a little extra time before dinner." Samme started to walk back to his office before pausing. "Extra time…. extra time. You have another extra visit with your mom tomorrow; it's the last extra visit before Thanksgiving. Perhaps we'll meet with everyone while you kids are there."

"Good! I can't imagine having to wait a whole week before we help Kieffer," Gruhit said happily.

"Me neither. This is great timing. Okay, I'm going to think about a plan while I clean my office," Samme stated. "Why don't you take off and do something fun before dinner?"

Gruhit briskly walked out into the small hallway. Across the way he could see Chardy's door was cracked open and a light was on in his room. It seemed like ages since he had really talked with his older brother.

As Gruhit approached the door, he could hear a soft voice. Gruhit peered through the crack and could just make out his brother sitting on the floor next to Kieffer, stroking his fur. He was mumbling something in a melodic voice to the point that Gruhit thought that there might be someone else in the room. He began to hear Chardy singing.

"I am here while you sleep,
While being away makes me weep.
I'm glad to see you now at peace,
More peaceful than the trees.
I hurt every second to leave you alone,
But I must work my fingers to the bone.

One day you'll know how much I care,
But for now the distance may just scare.
I hold onto a future for you and I,
One where our hopes and love can fly.
Until then we'll just have to make things work,
And keep hopelessness away as it lurks."

Gruhit was shocked. It was the same song his mother had sung to them many times. Gruhit could remember the familiar scent of his mom mixed with scented lotion. She would often come home hours after all three kids were in bed asleep and sit on the edge of the bed. His mom would kiss each of their foreheads and then sometimes, if they were lucky, she would sing this song she had created. If Gruhit woke up, she sometimes would play with his hair to send him back to sleep.

Gruhit watched Chardy affectionately pet the guardling. As he listened, the dam holding back many of his emotions broke, and Gruhit could feel floods of sadness and anger, but mostly fear, roll over him all at once.

He was scared about losing his mom. He was terrified that there might be a creature across the street that could end them all. He was scared of losing Kieffer. He was hurt that his brother wasn't talking to them and that he could have caused all this mess. He felt angry at the people who made him leave the apartment where they had all been together. He was hurt that his mom hadn't fixed things yet.

Gruhit froze to the spot where he was standing. He wanted to run from the feelings and the painful memories, but he couldn't move. He didn't know how to even explain how he was feeling. The painful memories reminded him of everything he had ever lost: his mom, his home, his old friends, and now new friends.

Gruhit kicked Chardy's door open so hard that it hit the bedroom wall and bounced off of it with a great *THUD*. Chardy was shocked. He stopped petting the guardling and slowly stood up.

"Gruhit? What's... what's going on?" Chardy said, confused.

"I hate you!" Gruhit screamed. "You know what's going on here! You won't tell us! You know why Kieffer is fizzling out, and you won't tell us! You know why we were taken from mom, and you didn't stop it! I hate you, Chardy Brown! I HATE YOU!" The venomous words spewed out of his mouth.

Gruhit wanted to lunge at his brother and hit him. Before he could, Samme's voice came from behind him. "Gruhit? Hey, what's wrong kiddo?"

Gruhit whipped around quickly and kicked Mr. Wunder in the shin as hard as he could. Samme called out in pain and fell to the floor while holding his leg. Gruhit ran past him up the stairs. At the top, Gruhit could see Malda running toward him.

"Gruhit, what's going on? Is everyone…" Gruhit shoved his foster mom out of the way and continued his race to his bedroom. He quickly slammed and locked his doors, then jumped onto his bed and burrowed under the covers.

All of his emotions, which had welled up quickly moments before, now slowly slipped away. He hadn't wanted to get away from anyone. He loved his foster family. He loved his older brother a lot. He was getting away from the hurt and the fear, and his body decided the best place to hide was under nice, heavy, soft blankets.

Chapter 23
The Protection Of A Timorine

As his emotions calmed down, he could hear footsteps coming slowly and gently toward his door. These were closely followed by smaller footsteps. He could hear Amarie talking frantically through sobs.

"Don't make us leave, Mal! I don't know why he kicked him or pushed you! Please don't make us move again!"

Gruhit heard Mal say something soothing to Amarie, and then his sister's sobs got further away. He really wished he could hear what Malda had said to his sister. He could make out a shadow through the crack at the bottom of his door.

"Gruhit? Gruhit, I'm unlocking the door, okay? I'm just checking to see if you're okay," Samme announced before Gruhit heard a key jiggling in the doorknob.

The door to the bedroom slowly opened, and before long, Gruhit could hear footsteps walk across the room with an odd rhythm. Mr. Wunder must have been limping. A chill went down the back of Gruhit's neck. He figured they would tell him to pack up and leave. He could feel the emotion of fear once again entering his body. This time it was manageable and not overwhelming like it had been just a second ago. It still made him burrow under the covers all the more. He thought it was ironic that he had been afraid Chardy's actions would get them removed from the house.

The bed mattress sank down on one side near the edge. He knew Mr. Wunder was there now. Gruhit refused to leave the safety of the blankets.

"Gruhit, I need to see your face and eyes, please," Samme said gently without a sense of harshness. Gruhit didn't move or make a sound.

"Gruhit, I can't have this conversation with a pile of blankets. I need to see your face," Samme said, still in a soothing voice. Gruhit was still scared. He felt safe under the blankets. He simply didn't want to move.

"Gruhit, I just want to see if you're okay," Samme said. "Look, I told Chardy earlier, and Mal just told Amarie. You three will not be moving from this house unless you're moving back home with your mother. You could be in this house for quite some time, so I can't imagine wanting to spend that time under blankets."

Gruhit considered leaving the safety he had built under the covers. He began to realize that maybe it was alright to face the world again. Mr. Wunder didn't sound angry. It sounded like there were no plans to move the three of them.

"How did you know that I was scared about moving?" Gruhit asked in a small voice as the blankets came down from over his head.

"Well, let's see. You have been in several homes in a short period of time and have had to move for various reasons. Chardy asked me the other day about having to pack up and move. Amarie just saw this chaos and was worried about the same thing. It seems this is a concern on each of your minds. Now, a little while ago I saw a little boy yelling at his brother and attacking people. These are things that the wonderful, creative Gruhit does not do. What happened?"

Gruhit couldn't look Mr. Wunder in the eyes. He felt guilty and embarrassed. He looked at his hands in his lap and sheepishly spoke. "I don't know. I was really angry at Chardy for singing a song my mom sang to us at bedtime. He was singing it to Kieffer."

Samme peered at Gruhit in the bed and studied his face before saying, "Hmmm. Anger? That doesn't sound like the Gruhit I know. Tell me, young Timorine, are you sure you weren't scared about something? Or feeling hurt?"

Gruhit thought for a bit. All the fearful and painful thoughts from a bit earlier raced through his mind briefly. Before he knew it, he was on the edge of crying again.

"Timorines usually get that angry like you just did for one reason. They're protecting themselves. Anger is the emotion a Timorine uses to keep everything away. We rarely use it for something good. I get it." Samme paused shortly and looked intently at Gruhit. "The best way to make sure that it doesn't happen again is to talk about what made you scared, if you can remember."

Gruhit slowly steadied his emotions so that he could try to talk, "I don't know. I heard Chardy singing the song and… what if I never hear my mom sing that again? What if we lose Kieffer?"

"Are you scared about those things?"

"Of course! Aren't you?"

"Absolutely. What will happen if either one of those things happens?"

"It would be horrible. I don't wanna think about it."

"Now, hold on. I'm right here, Gruhit. There's nothing to be scared of because we're just talking about it. Just talking about it doesn't make it real or mean it *is* going to happen. I agree with you. In either one of those situations, you would be very sad. I would be very sad. While you're sad, you'll have Mal and I to help you. I know you will help me if we lose Kieffer. I want you to know that if you can't go home, Mal and I will do everything we can to make sure you stay in touch with your mom."

Gruhit looked at Samme and realized something he didn't think about before… Maybe Samme was scared too. He just figured that adults knew what to do and never got scared.

"How do you know all this? It's like you know what I'm thinking. Are you sure you're not magic, too?" Gruhit said, but still not looking at Mr. Wunder.

"Do you remember what Ira said at the party, though? All of us are strongest when we work together with all the other orders and find comfort in those from our own order. They understand us the most. I'm Timorine, too. Fear can cause me to lose my mind, but talking about my fears can help us get motivated to improve ourselves… and the world."

"I don't want to be scared anymore, Samme," Gruhit said, finally looking up at his foster.

Samme nodded. "I know. Me too. Do you need a hug?"

It wasn't exactly what Gruhit was hoping for, but it was nice to feel that he wasn't trying to go through the scariness alone. He leaned over and wrapped his arms around the middle of Samme while his foster placed one arm around him.

Samme added, "Tomorrow is a new day with its own thoughts, adventures, emotions… and above all, new hopes."

Chapter 24
Amarie, Expert Mail Courier

"Amarie?" Mal called throughout the house. "Amarie, come here please."

The sounds of thuds could be heard coming down the stairs as Amarie sang one of her little tunes. She found Mal at her writing desk in the kitchen by the basement stairs. Mal swiveled in her compact chair and turned to face Amarie.

"Is that another letter for momma?" Amarie asked, fidgeting in place.

"Can you please make sure that your mom gets this?" Malda asked.

"Yes, I can! Amarie, expert mail courier at your service," Amarie said while playfully saluting Malda.

"Thank you, ma'am. Do you know if your mom has been reading my letters? I thought maybe I would be getting a phone call or response back," Malda asked.

"I dunno. I see her take them but then I'm usually playing," Amarie said before her eyes lit up. "Maybe she reads them while I'm playing. It probably gets boring just sitting there with the boys and Constance without me."

"Well, if you remember, please remind her that my phone number is written on the bottom of each letter, okay?"

"Of course. There is no bit of information which Amarie, expert mail courier, cannot relay," Amarie said in a playful and heroic voice before continuing. "Do you like writing letters because of the little folks?"

"What do you mean?"

"Mrs. Dickelbutton and Mrs. Snickelfritz write letters to me all the time now. Especially when they know I've been sad. I just thought maybe they taught you to write letters," Amarie said.

Malda chuckles a bit before stating, "I learned to write letters in school just like you did, pretty girl."

"Oh, right. I like getting them, but I wish they would just talk with me," Amarie stated.

"I suspect that they still have a lot going on. I'm sure Mrs. Snickelfritz doesn't want to leave her husband's side for too long and Mrs. Dickelbutton has two children to care for now. I'm in high hopes that one day we will see the little folks around the house again. They normally come around in late evenings when predators would be asleep."

"I hope Momma is doing well this time. Do you think she might have a new job?" Amarie asked hopefully.

"I think Constance would have told us about your mom getting a new job. Although, I could be wrong. It would be wonderful if the agency helped her find a new job that could replace all of her jobs. I think she will be doing well today because she gets to see you three. Make it the best time she has ever had, okay?"

It was not long before Amarie, Chardy, and Gruhit sat on the steps of Big Blue waiting for Constance to arrive. The weather was just slightly too chilly to stay outside for long. Luckily everyone had on extra warm sweaters, thick socks, and hats. Well, everyone but Malda wore a cap. She wore earmuffs over her elaborately done hair. Samme was telling them a hilarious story about a tiny charmyrll named Fireball, who was accidentally catapulted across a farm when it lit itself on fire next to a flatulent cow. While everyone was laughing, Gruhit kept looking across the street at the abandoned shoe factory. He knew it might not be abandoned anymore. There could be a being there planning something heartless. At one point Gruhit, swore he caught Chardy looking at the factory's second floor. Gruhit could make out an emergency metal staircase leading up toward a green door. He gazed at the faded green door and the rusty stairs.

"Constance!" Amarie squealed as she stood up and ran toward the sidewalk as the caseworker's car slowed to a stop.

Chardy and Amarie immediately got into the car and readied themselves for leaving. Amarie was waving wildly back at Mal. As Gruhit stood up, Samme whispered in his ear, "I will assemble the team as soon as you leave. We'll be meeting here in the dining room. Enjoy your visit with your mom, and we'll fill you in when you get back."

Gruhit nodded, hugged Mr. Wunder and ran to Constance's car. Constance quickly stepped out of the car and yelled, "We should be back in about three or four hours. Thank you for letting us do this visit. I've had years where the snow storms during the winter were so bad that some children lost out on visits with their parents for two months."

"Absolutely understandable," Malda responded. "I gave Amarie another letter. Can you please make sure that their mom gets it?"

Constance nodded with a smile as she ducked back into the car. Soon after, the children were on their way.

"Darling, would you be kind enough to make some coffee for everyone? We only have three hours to figure out how to smoke out the fox in the hen house," Samme said as he looked over at the factory.

"Yes," his wife replied. "Get the neighbors. I'll have the Dickelbuttons alert the representatives. If there is a dark messenger plotting against us, they're about to learn that the creatures of Victus here are not to be underestimated. Let's hurry to get started. I'm feeling incredibly hopeful today."

Chapter 25
The Council of Brown Place

The smell of coffee wafted through the air of the Wunder dining room. Everyone who was assembled seemed to have an odd mixture of confidence and
anxiety, almost like actors about to perform a play.

Surrounding the table sat the Lusplendidas, Mrs. Bangs, Mal, and Samme. Gripple was next to Malda in a chair outfitted with a small wooden box to boost him
a bit in his seat. Gripple refused coffee but took out a flask of dwarf cider from
within a hidden pocket of his shirt and poured it into one of the mugs.

In between the Lusplendidas sat Dragon. Dragon's chair had not only a box, but
also a cookie sheet with a flame retardant blanket over it. This was a highly unusual circumstance in which Dragon was allowed access into the Wunder home. The
Lusplendidas insisted that Dragon sit in between them so that they could handle
the unlikely situation that he would burst into flames. Mr. Lusplendida had a fire
extinguisher below his chair, and Mrs. Lusplendida had her gloves ready on the
table. Everyone at the table had known each other for years, so Dragon undoubtedly should be comfortable enough to control his magical abilities.

On top of the table sat a miniature table that someone might see at a craft store for a Victorian dollhouse. At the moment it gave seating to Mr. Dickelbutton, Mrs. Snickelfritz, and Sparkles. It was good to have a tangerella representative at a Council meeting for the first time in ages. The occupants of the smaller table each had a little folk-made mug in front of them with hot coffee. It was odd to not see Mrs. Dickelbutton there, but she had chosen to stay with her children and keep them away from the conversation.

The Lusplendidas, Mal, and Gripple, being in the Order of Instinctuals, were all anxious to right the wrongs of their small neighborhood. Mr. Lusplendida especially seemed a bit antsy, as though he were ready to march over to the factory and demand answers for the injustices his friends had suffered.

Mrs. Bangs, the little folks, and Sparkles were all caught in a conundrum of wanting to enjoy the conversation while also knowing there were chores to be done. Samme chuckled inwardly to himself. It was the classic sign of a creature or person in the Order of Sentrites. While they all enjoyed experiencing feelings and emotions, they all also seemed to value the productivity of a good day's work. To ask them to take the day off would be like asking them to jump off a building. They simply would never dream of doing either.

Samme peered over at Dragon, whose eyes were darting from person to person. To anyone unfamiliar with charmyrlls, they would simply think that they were looking at a very adorable and large rabbit. However, as a Timorine, Samme knew that Dragon was going through the same thoughts and calculations as himself. Their order did their best to avoid pain and fear through careful planning and thought. Samme knew that Dragon would be assessing the strengths and weaknesses of the group. Samme himself was considering how well everyone would work together and whether there would be arguments about the next course of action.

Samme took out his pocket watch and glanced at the time. He then withdrew a small gavel from his overcoat and gently banged it against the table.

"Good afternoon to you, friends," he declared. "Before we begin, I think we can all agree it has been too long since we have all joined together like this. Let's not let time lapse like that again. I would also like to welcome Ms. Sparkles to our Council. It is more than good to have a representative of the tangerellas among us."

He reached over to his large, ceramic mug filled with hot coffee and raised it high. "Let's get our mindset right. I want to toast to Victus. We remember we are his creations and that we serve each other in his world to give everyone hope. We are all his beloved, sacred creatures. No more but no less. He has always protected this world against the plots of evil. Without him we are nothing, but with him we are everything. Friends, I ask that we hold our mugs high and toast to Victus."

Every person and creature raised their mug high and in unison declared, "THERE'S ALWAYS HOPE," except for Gripple who merely grunted.

Samme looked proudly at everyone. "You all know that a tacet stone was found in the Wunder home recently," he went on. "It is true that it has begun the fizzling out process of Kieffer. This brings us to two of our own which are succumbing to fizzling out, in addition to those we have already lost."

"The dwarves give us news that more creatures are disappearing a mere ten miles from here," interjected Mr. Lusplendida. Gripple grunted in agreement with this news.

Mrs. Bangs was next to speak up quickly. "The tangerellas also have warned me of similar disappearances within the same distance."

"Oh no, no, no. It all gets so close to us, I think," Mrs. Snickelfritz said.

"It was inevitable that we would have to deal with this situation sooner or later," Samme stated. "We have one of the biggest and strongest communities of humans and creatures working together for hundreds of miles. When we all began to hear about creatures fizzling out, we all knew something would try to destroy our community."

"Have we communicated with any of the other Councils that we are familiar with?" Mrs. Lusplendida asked.

"I've thought about it at least a few dozen times," Malda said, "but being a new mom this year, I keep forgetting to send out a message."

"Stop, now, we are not going to blame ourselves for anything. We are all on the same team," said Mrs. Bangs.

"We have reason to believe there might be a dark messenger stationed inside the factory across the street to spy on and possibly harm our community," Samme said. "Dragon, is it true that you think that Chardy got the tacet stone over at the factory when he snuck out one night?"

He paused as the cute creature sculpted steam from its ears. A small check mark appeared, signalling his agreement.

"If Dragon saw the boy, then let's stop talking and get over there, seize the factory, and stop this bully," Mr. Lusplendida announced impatiently.

"Hold on there, friend. It is my suspicion that Dragon saw Chardy at the factory and with the tacet stone. What we don't know is if he obtained the stone at the factory, and if he did, if it was from a dark messenger or Fridgita Mortes herself," Samme said.

More white steam went up into the air in the shape of a check mark to confirm Samme's statement.

"Now, all of you know the best way to destroy a tacet stone is to brew the little folk potion," Samme went on. "It requires a hair from the being which created the stone. Our best hope is that there is a dark messenger over at the factory, which we can sneak a hair from and make the potion. With a bit more hope, and maybe a little luck, the destruction of the tacet stone will bring Kieffer back and maybe even Mr. Snickelfritz."

Samme looked over at Mrs. Snickelfritz and could see a glimmer of hope in her eyes.

"Sneak a hair from a dark messenger? Does anyone know anything about them? I mean, their name alone doesn't sound like they will be very warm and fuzzy. I don't imagine that we can just knock on the factory door with a present in our hands and say, 'Oh, hello. We're your neighbors across the way. Do you mind if we borrow a couple of eggs, a cup of flour, and oh, one of your hairs if you don't mind?'" Mrs. Bangs said in a worried and sarcastic tone.

"Dark messengers are foul," explained Mr. Lusplendida. "The dwarves have many stories of them. Just like Fridgita, they talk in half-truths. Remember, they were all once messengers and perfect creations of Victus. Just because they're evil now doesn't mean they look disgusting or menacing. So if you have this notion that you will see a deformed creature covered in grotesque boils, you can stop now. They are likely to be something that we think we can trust and who talk sweet-ly. They have all sworn to rebel and end the ways of Victus, and Fridgita hates humans most of all. Don't for one second think that a dark messenger won't do whatever it takes to please her and destroy anything that is on the side of Victus."

"I agree with everything that Mr. Lusplendida just said," Malda added. "But also, they are *just* dark messengers. They would like to think that they are gods but all they are, and can ever be, is what they were created to be. A fish cannot be a cat. We all know Victus is the only true being who has the power to create and sustain. Don't you see this is their downfall and might give us an edge? The dark messengers are blinded by their arrogance."

"*Si! Bravo!*" Mrs. Lusplendida exclaimed. "However, time is of the essence. Every second that the stone exists is dangerous. Our two little friends still must be saved from fizzling out. We need to get over to that factory and find out if we're dealing with a dark messenger or Fridgita Mortes herself."

"The floor is open to ideas on safely searching the factory. I think we all understand that this must be done in secrecy, and it must be done without being found out," Samme declared.

As if he had been waiting for an invitation, Dragon began to pump white steam images into the air above his head.

"He's making figures. But… they're moving. I didn't know charmyrlls could animate their images," Malda said in amazement.

They all watched as the factory appeared with a noontime sun over it. An image came of Gripple and Mr. Lusplendida running to one of the side doors which had a small hole on the left bottom side. The image showed Gripple quickly shrinking the two figures before they disappeared through the hole in the door. Toward the top of the factory, an image of Sparkles passed through the building.

"*Si!* Send me over now. Are we going over unarmed?" Mr. Lusplendida asked.

The Council once again looked above Dragon's head as they watched the small shape of Mrs. Snickelfritz creating potions and placing them in small glass balls.

"Yes, yes, yes," Mrs. Snickelfritz said. "I can make a collection of different potions for you to take with you. I think it would be good to have my sleeping draught, as well as my special 'memory fogging' potion. It's made to help you forget troubles for an hour so you can destress a bit. I think if I make it potent enough though, it could make it difficult to think. Yes. Yes. Yes. That will be very useful if a dark messenger sees you so you can get away. Might only work for a few seconds though."

Lastly, the Council could see the images of Gripple, Mr. Lusplendida, and Sparkles fleeing from the factory as a monster burst out of the wall. A spry image of Dragon hopped toward the monster and a giant ball of fire engulfed him.

"Good," Samme said. "Dragon is indicating that he will be on standby outside in case you are found out. He will set off his natural defenses. We hope that this will scare the dark messenger enough for you to escape or actually harm it. Is everyone in agreement with this plan?"

Everyone nodded.

"Mrs. Snickelfritz, how much time do you need for the draughts and potions?" Samme questioned the little folk.

"Hmm. Oh my. Yes. I think two days is fine. Yes. Yes. Yes," she said with thoughtfulness.

"Right," Samme said. "Let's all meet back together then on Wednesday at 11 AM to help our comrades prepare for this task. Remember the mission at this point is to simply see what is there, and hopefully what made the tacet stone. After we know more, we can make plans for getting the hair and destroying the stone. If anyone disagrees or thinks we need to back out, now is your time to say something."

The silence was audible. Everyone looked at their neighbors. Samme knew this was a dangerous endeavor and gave everyone almost two minutes to consider.

"Very well," he said. " If no one has any arguments, then we are all assumed ready to move forward with this plan. My dear friends, tomorrow is another day full of adventures, dreams, thoughts, and most of all..."

"HOPE!" everyone with a voice cried in unison.

Chapter 26
The Half-Fizzle

Most of the Council had left for their respective homes. Mr. Lusplendida had put on his fire retardant gloves and carried Dragon to his home in the coal room before walking to the Lighthouse to check on the other charmyrlls. Gripple decided to join him, since dwarves were always needing to get some sort of work completed. Mr. Dickelbutton wanted to get home to be assured that his wife and children were doing alright.

As for Mrs. Snickelfritz, this was the longest amount of time that she had been away from her husband's side since his incident. She was very anxious to get back to him as his condition had slightly worsened. Mrs. Luspendida, Mrs. Bangs, and Malda chatted for a bit while Sparkles listened. Mrs. Lusplendida eventually decided that she must get home to finish up some of her household chores. As she went out through the front door, Sparkles waved goodbye to everyone and phased through the walls as she returned home to Mrs. Bangs' garden.

This left Samme, Mrs. Bangs, and Malda at the table, sipping coffee and sharing interesting stories from the past few years. In the middle of one, Malda's phone gave a gentle buzzing sound. She glanced over at the screen.

"It looks like Constance and the children are almost here," Mal expressed.

Samme looked up at the clock with a puzzled expression. "They're getting back almost a full hour early."

"Did they have car trouble or something?" Priscilla asked.

"Constance didn't say. She's just giving us a heads-up that Amarie is pretty upset," Malda said.

The three adults were still wondering about the message when the front door burst open. A frantic Amarie entered and ran straight for Malda.

"Mal, oh, Mal! It's bad! I never want to go on another visit again. Never! I hate it!" Amarie said through sobs as she lunged herself into Malda's arms.

Everyone looked confused. There was no asking her clarifying questions because she was crying so hard. The tears were coming so fast that occasionally she paused to deeply inhale.

Gruhit and Chardy appeared at the door. They were both in a mood that was beyond glum. Constance was right behind them with her hand on either of their shoulders for moral support. All of the adults looked at Constance and waited for her to say something.

Constance looked out over the group. She had a lot that she wanted to say but was holding back. Even her mood was discouraging. Her face looked like that of a mother who was worrying about a lost or runaway child.

Finally, Constance spoke. "Mom didn't come to the visit," she said.

The words were so heavy they almost physically hung in the air. Mrs. Bangs had tears forming in her eyes.

"But… she's never missed before. Maybe… was she just running late?" Samme said, hoping that this would explain everything.

"No," Constance said. She's always the first one to arrive at a visit. When we had waited twenty minutes, I texted her. She responded back that she wouldn't be coming." She paused before she continued. "I'm going to go to her apartment tomorrow and see what is happening. This is unlike her."

It was bad enough that Gruhit had to live through this experience, but now he had to listen to it being told to his fosters. He looked down at his feet and fought the urge to scream, to run, and to hit things. Constance's steady hand on his shoulder was the only thing keeping him calm. Still, he could feel fear rising up in him, as it had the whole car ride back. Had his mom abandoned them? Would he never see her again? What would happen to him and his siblings now? There were so many questions.

"I was thinking tonight would be a good movie night," Malda softly said. "It would be good for everyone to get into comfy sweats and PJs. For dinner, let's have nachos. I have all sorts of delicious cheeses we can melt together, and I'll throw some yummy veggies into the mix."

"Sounds like some great comfort food. It seems like you have everything under control, I'm going to get out of your hair," Constance said to the Wunders before addressing the children. "I will let Mr. and Mrs. Wunder know of any news. You can talk about anything with them, but you can also call me. You all have been through enough today though. Goodnight, everyone." Constance walked out the front door and got into her car before driving off.

Without the support of Constance's arm, Gruhit went over to the couch and sank himself into it. Chardy stayed frozen to the spot, unable to move or talk. He simply looked at the floor.

"I should probably get out of here too," Mrs. Bangs said softly to Mal while massaging Amarie's back.

"You won't stay with us? Can she stay, Mal?" Amarie asked through sobs.

"Of course Priscilla can stay. Let's ask her, though, because she might have other things she needs to get done today," Mal explained.

"I actually need to check on the dipsy toads and the pond. With the weather getting colder, I want to make sure they have enough food and that the fountain is keeping the water from freezing over," Mrs. Bangs explained. "Tell you what, I'll check on the toads and throw some laundry in the dryer. Then I'll get some sweats on and be over here in time for nachos, okay?"

Amarie nodded her head as her sobbing began to subside. Mal ran her fingers over Amarie's scalp in a massaging motion in hopes that she would continue to calm down. Samme walked over to Chardy who was still standing tensely.

He carefully put his hand on Chardy's shoulder and looked him in the eye. "What do you say, Chardy? We could catch up on a couple episodes of that second superhero miniseries that came out on streaming."

Chardy shrugged his shoulder forcefully in an attempt to remove Samme's hand as he declared in a low voice, "Don't touch me."

Samme removed his hand. He could see that Chardy's face was a mixture of sadness, anger, and hate. Chardy was almost trembling. Samme became concerned that Chardy's anger would explode.

"Here. I never got to give the letter to momma," Amarie suddenly said.

"That's fine darling," Malda replied. "Amarie, expert mail courier, still did a great job. We'll see if we can give it to her another time."

Samme and Gruhit then saw Chardy's head rise up and turn to look at Mal and Mrs. Bangs. "You witch!" Chardy screamed in a hateful voice and started to run at Mrs. Wunder, who calmly maintained her position at the table.

Samme quickly caught Chardy in one arm. Chardy spun around to face his foster. He took a step forward to be sure to get in Mr. Wunder's face. He was so angry that he almost didn't look like himself any longer. Chardy said quietly but in a threatening voice, "I said, DON'T TOUCH ME."

Samme returned Chardy's stare. "And I say, there will be no intimidating people in this house," he said firmly.

"Oh yeah," Chardy said, still mere inches from Mr. Wunder. "Tell that to the witch sitting at your table."

Mrs. Bangs stifled a gasp. Gruhit's eyes got bigger, and his mouth dropped open. Amarie could feel her stomach tensing up. She was queasy about what was going to happen next.

"Chardy, I will not have you calling Malda…" Samme began but was quickly cut off.

"A witch? Why?" Chardy's anger was rising. "We see what you all do here. We see that you're friends with magical creatures. That witch writes letters to our mom before every visit. Momma reads them; I see her read them, and she gets sad. She doesn't want us to see that she is bothered by them, but she is. She hides it. Momma has always come to a visit with us. ALWAYS!" Chardy's eyes darted around the room as though he were an injured animal looking for a predator.

Chardy's rage took Gruhit's fear to the next level. He felt a chill go straight up his back and shivered. Gruhit didn't like any of this. Even though his mom seemed to be the source of this all, she was also the one person he wanted most right then.

"Our momma loves us! She wants us!" Chardy yelled so loudly that Amarie covered her ears and resumed crying.

"Stop Chardy! You're scaring me!" Amarie pleaded between breaths.

Mrs. Bangs picked up Amarie and set her on her lap. Amarie curled herself into the fetal position and cried. Her emotions were getting to be too much for her. Even Mrs. Bangs was finding it too much to handle; Priscilla really felt like crying with Amarie. Instead, though, she began rubbing Amarie's arms to help soothe her.

"What did you write in those letters? What have you been telling her? Momma never, NEVER missed having time with us until you came along. Did you put a spell on her?" Chardy continued to yell as his hands were curling into fists.

"What? No. You know perfectly well that I can't, and wouldn't, put a spell on anyone. I'm only human," Malda said in a slightly surprised but steady voice.

"Answer my questions! What did you do to her?" Chardy's scowl was now contorting his face so that he looked like a completely different person.

"You know very well what I've said in those letters," Malda quickly responded. "You delivered a couple for me. If you weren't causing such a scene, your sister would be able to tell you she even watched me write the letter. My letters are words of encouragement for your mom. I feel nothing but the deepest sadness for her having to live without the three of you. I have been trying to befriend her."

"Befriend? Hmmph," Chardy chuckled with a malevolent overtone that his siblings had never heard before. "I know what you are, witch. I know what all of you are. If this is how you 'befriend' us, then by all means let me return the favor."

Chardy paused and looked at both of his fosters with a menacing grin. Gruhit noticed that his brother seemed to have completely forgotten about him and Amarie. He only saw the adults in the room and directed hate at each of them. Gruhit's stomach was turning in knots. He folded his arms around himself to feel comforted and warm. That's when he noticed the room had become chilly. Gruhit instinctively looked at the door; it was securely closed.

"Samme?" Gruhit said, just loud enough to get the attention of his foster dad.

Samme immediately noticed the chill in the room, prompting him to discreetly gesture as though he were drinking an invisible cup of tea toward Gruhit. Gruhit looked puzzled at his foster dad for the first few repetitions of hand motions until it dawned on him what Samme was trying to convey. Gruhit jumped up from his spot and ran for the basement. Everyone including Chardy assumed that Gruhit was too upset by what was happening to remain in the room.

"See! This is YOUR fault," Chardy yelled. "My sister is sitting there in a mess, and Gruhit is scared of everything. You have damaged my family! Let me tell you how I've been damaging yours so that you can hurt like we do."

"Chardy, stop this. You must see that we are *not* doing anything but trying to help you," Samme said, attempting to reason with him.

As Samme spoke, he swore he could see the lights dim slightly. He could be imagining things, but he thought he heard a soft and silky voice say, "Liars, all liars." Just then he spotted Mrs. Bangs looking around too: he wasn't hearing things.

Chardy continued to spew his hateful talk as he explained how he had been hurting the Wunders.

"You're so clever, Mr. Wunder. You figured out I've been sneaking out to the old factory. I was the one who sent the golem to the second floor so Amarie would have a meltdown that night. I knew she would get worked up from the pranks it would pull on her. I also knew you two would send Kieffer upstairs to keep her calm. That got the guardling out of the way so I could explore the factory. I was hoping to have some fun away from all of you, but then I met her, and my eyes were opened about your family."

"You met someone? Chardy, what are you talking about?" Malda asked urgently.

Malda was the last person to notice that the temperature was dropping, and the lights were dimming in the room. Her eyes widened as her natural bravery faltered.

"I don't think we're alone at the moment," Samme said in a slightly timid voice.

"No. She's here," Chardy stated. "She has always been watching you, Mr. Wunder. She told me how you and the other creatures nearby work to stop her. She only wants humans to get what they deserve. She showed me power, Mr. Wunder. She showed me the power we could have if they were in charge. But all of you want Victus in charge. With him we are nothing but ordinary. With her we could be the most powerful beings in the world. She gave me the tacet stone. All I did was tell her how hard it was to sneak out, and she gave me the power to overcome it. She says it's just a small taste of what I will get if she wins. It looks like none of us win now though, right?" His tone began to turn to sadness. "I'll never see my mother again. My brother, sister, and I will always be in foster care and possibly separated some day. It's all stupid. I hate it all. If there's no hope for us, I'm glad I can finally call you all out for what you are—witches trying to destroy the nobility of the Empress of the Universe."

"Enough! Chardy, remember how I said you would never leave this home unless it was back with your mother? If you can't ever live with your mother again, Mal and I will become your family if you wish. You kids are already a part of ours," Samme quickly explained to Chardy. The room became darker and colder as white wisps of air began circling Chardy's feet, rising up to his waist.

"It's too late," Chardy said in despair. "I've done too many things. I might have destroyed Kieffer. It's all my fault, and it's all hopeless."

"Chardy, listen to me," Malda said earnestly and with great concern as she cautiously rose from her chair. "It's never too late to do the right thing. Tell us the name of this dark messenger, or was it Fridgita Mortes that you met in the factory?"

The white wisps slowly spiraled upward around Chardy's head. Mrs. Bangs clung to Amarie. Malda was now able to see her breath. Chardy glanced from the adults back down to the floor with a look of total defeat and hopelessness. He started to open his mouth to answer Mal. Just then, his body completely froze in place; he was unable to move, and there was a great fear in his eyes.

The white wisps now formed a shadowy outline of a woman-like creature with giant wings. She skillfully swooped around Chardy's inanimate body. Everyone could hear a silky voice saying softly, "Dear Chardy, There's no need to tell them my name. There's no fun in telling them that. Hello, Samme, Malda, and Priscilla. You've all been doing so well with these children, but this one is mine. I like him a lot. He's so full of anger and hate. I was able to persuade him to do anything for me. I told the poor darling that I would give him the power to be invisible to the guardling. Too bad he didn't know a tacet stone also steals life from magical creatures who defy the Empress."

Mrs. Bangs clung to Amarie even tighter. Malda immediately took a step forward, outraged that a dark messenger would dare to come into her home and terrorize her family. Samme kept looking at the kitchen door as though he were waiting for something.

"Hehe. I'm so glad all of you are here to play with right now," the voice spoke. "My Empress will no doubt be so happy with me for collecting more trophies. Let's see. I think stealing the hope from a couple of Sentrites would be just what I need to regain most of my former power and beauty. Oh, don't get me wrong. A few little folks, tangerellas, and dwarves here and there have been great for regaining my physical strength, though, I would like to have my more playful powers back. Until my dear little Chardy just began to give up his essence to me, I forgot how deliciously destructive stealing human hope can be. I'm quite hungry for more, and emotional Sentrites would hit the spot right now."

"No, please, get back and leave the child alone," Mrs. Bangs pleaded with the wispy shadow figure which was moving slowly toward them with evil, hungry eyes.

"Not today you horrible, horrible creature!" a voice cried out from the direction of the living room window.

Mrs. Snickelfritz had emerged from a knothole door in the window frame. She ran quickly across the arm of the couch and leaped in a most powerful way. She landed on the statue-like head of Chardy and dumped a flask of her sleeping draught down the throat of the young boy. Chardy remained magically frozen, though his eyes slowly drifted shut, and he began to breathe deeply. He was asleep.

The creature turned and moved slowly toward Mrs. Snickelfritz, who stood with a rebellious look on her face. The dark messenger smiled a wicked grin and laughed eerily as her body became a bit more transparent. "Oh, no, hehe. You ruined my fun. You may have found a way to keep me from draining the final hope from this one to complete the process for now, but you know where I'll be waiting for you all. This isn't over. None of you are safe. Now that humans know about our hideout, the Empress will want to begin the war. We are more than ready to have fun with all of you. You'll never be safe. Your children will always feel scared. Just wait until…"

Suddenly, a flask flew through the air and hit the center of the shadowy face. The wispy air instantly disappeared, and the light and warmth slowly returned to the room again.

"Yes, yes. yes. I think these things talk too much. Look, now I've gone and thrown and damaged my best flask," Mrs. Snickelfritz declared to the group. "Now, if it's all being good, Master Wunder, I must return home at once," she announced as she climbed down from Chardy's head and darted for the couch.

Gruhit ran back into the room to the sight of his family trying to recover from the fear and anxiety they had just experienced. He barely caught a glimpse of Mrs. Snickelfritz as she scampered back through the knothole door in the window frame. Gruhit looked around as everyone in the room was collecting themselves and consoling each other, except for his brother.

"Samme! What's wrong with Chardy?" Gruhit exclaimed.

Samme touched the boy's face. It was like touching ice.

"It's as if he's half-fizzled out," Samme said astounded. "This is so rare. Most people in olden days followed Victus and never had to fear a dark messenger having enough power. It was only speculated in books but…"

"What do you mean half-fizzled?" Mal said in shock.

"Humans are not dependent on sundust to keep us alive," Samme explained. "We can't have the dust stolen from us and stop existing. What makes humans so special is our ability to maintain and create hope. Take all the hope out of a person and a dark messenger can fizzle them. Chardy is essentially half-fizzled inside… frozen. He can't move. Almost like a living statue that will never hope again. Well, that is if Mrs. Snickelfritz had not used her sleeping draught at the last minute to stop the process."

"Half-fizzled? Is he stuck like this forever?" Gruhit said fearfully.

"I… I don't know. I mean… I've never seen this happen before," Samme said, not entirely sure what to do next. "The best thing to do is still to destroy the tacet stone. You heard that thing. It's causing all the disappearances by feeding off sun-dust and hopelessness. I'm guessing it's trying to regain strength because a tacet stone is powerful and old magic. They would need to consume a lot of power to create something that strong. What I'm trying to say is, if we can't destroy the tacet stone, maybe we can weaken the creature enough to reverse the fizzling process of our three friends somehow."

"What if you're wrong?" Gruhit demanded.

"Then we have to cling to hope that Victus will lead us to an answer," Samme said.

"Well, what are we waiting for? Let's get moving now!" Malda said sternly.

"What now? What about the plan we just all agreed on earlier?" Mrs. Bangs questioned.

"That plan assumed we didn't know who made the tacet stone, or what was at the factory," Malda said. "We know now. Poor Chardy, he had no idea he was being tricked. We all heard that Fridgita plans to start a war. I want to end the threat here quickly before they have time to act."

"Mal's right. We need to get a move on," Samme said quickly. "Malda, alert Dragon and the Lusplendidas; have Gripple meet me at the castle. Priscilla, please alert the tangerellas. I'm not sure if any of them will join us. Please take Amarie with you. Sparkles seems to be particularly attached to her, and I think she will join the battle if Amarie asks her to help."

"Sure… but you want me to take Amarie," Mrs. Bangs said. "Are you thinking that the children will go too? They're children, and you saw how powerful and dreadful that thing was, right?"

Amarie, still sitting in Priscilla's lap, was becoming less frightened. Gruhit could see she was mad enough to try to take on a hundred dark messengers by herself. He didn't think that was wise, but he wouldn't dare tell his sister what she should do when she was in such a mood.

"The children come with us," Samme replied. "Don't you see? Fridgita Mortes is after the destruction of humans, magical creatures, and ultimately all created things. This dark messenger is specifically targeting us because we are working against it. But mark my words: everyone in this town is in danger, and they don't even know it. They would never believe us if we told them the truth."

"I agree. The children must come with us so we can protect them," Mal said. "I'm off to rally the rest of the Council. I'll let everyone know to meet back here as soon as possible."

Malda dashed through the kitchen and out the back door. Mrs. Bangs stood up and carefully set Amarie on her feet.

"Well, dear, should we go see if Ms. Sparkles would join us?" Mrs. Bangs said tautly while looking at Amarie.

"Let's go. This thing picked the wrong family to mess with," Amarie said angrily. She headed toward the front door with Mrs. Bangs chasing quickly behind.

"Gruhit, I need you to stay close behind me. We have a lot to do before Gripple gets here," Samme stated as he picked up Chardy's inanimate, sleeping body and headed for the basement.

"Where are we going?" Gruhit called after his foster dad.

"I want to get Chardy into bed," Samme called back. "Then we need to get to the secret tunnels in my office."

Chapter 27
The Hidden Room

Samme gently laid Chardy on his bed and pulled the covers over him. Gruhit looked at his brother's saddened, sleeping face. He reached out to touch his hand, but quickly withdrew it. His skin was ice cold. Gruhit couldn't believe everything that was happening. He had these odd conflicting feelings where he was glad to be with people who were fighting for good, and yet he also felt great despair. In a way, he envied Chardy at the moment. He wanted nothing more than to lay down and do nothing. Everything seemed so humongous right now. The problems were big. His emotions were big. His stress was big. It would be easier to just hide in bed.

"But then Fridgita wins," Gruhit mumbled to himself.

"In here... hurry!" Samme called from across the hall in his office.

Gruhit had been so lost in thought that he hadn't noticed Samme leave Chardy's room. Gruhit looked at Chardy and then Kieffer with the deepest of sympathies.

"Don't worry guys. I'm not giving up. We have a plan to help. Don't lose hope," Gruhit said quietly to the room, not sure anyone could hear him.

Gruhit ran over to Samme's office. The lights were on, but he didn't see anyone inside. He briefly wondered if his foster dad had gone back upstairs without his noticing. Then suddenly a head poked out of the closet. Samme had a pair of work goggles on his head and tossed another pair to Gruhit.

"What are you waiting for? Put those on and let's get going!" Samme said urgently.

Once inside the closet, Gruhit could see a small shelf which appeared to hold boxes of knick-knacks and memorabilia. There were three empty hangers hanging from the bar.

"Are you in?" Samme asked. "Close the door. Quickly! The security system doesn't allow the other door to open until this one is closed."

Gruhit hastily closed the closet door with confusion. It looked like a basic closet. However, if he had learned anything while living in Big Blue, it was that he should never doubt the ordinary.

Samme pushed on the side wall. It smoothly gave way and pivoted to reveal a hidden room. He motioned for Gruhit to promptly get through the opening before he followed in after him.

Once they were through the threshold, Samme turned to close the revolving door. Gruhit gasped in wonder at the sizable room in which he found himself. There were stone walls all around him except for the one on his right which was constructed of cement blocks. The space was lined with old sconces from the early 1900s that gave a barely brighter than dim glow throughout the room.

Standing majestically in front the concrete wall was an ornate, Victorian roll top desk. It was meticulously built from dark stained oak that had withstood the test of time aside from sporadic nicks and scratches. It was adorned with fanciful carvings of creatures like those that Gruhit had seen in the woodwork throughout the house. There were books and papers stacked all over the workspace and certain drawers inside the desk were left open haphazardly with their contents sticking out here and there. The chair and lamp behind the desk were in surprisingly good shape for their age as well.

In a corner on the far side of the room, a stainless steel examination table was positioned adjacent to a small scrub sink. There was a medicine cabinet above the table containing various bottles of salves, medicines, and dried herbs. Located on the other side of the sink was a storage cupboard for medical supplies and equipment.

On the longest wall was the most amazing sight in the room. An immense oak bookcase that complimented the desk in age and design. It was almost completely filled with books, most of which were homemade journals and sketchbooks.

"This is where all the books have come from," Gruhit said in awe.

"Yes. My great-great-grandfather had this room built in secret when he first built the house. He wanted a place where he could study magical creatures without a neighbor or visitor finding his research and thinking he was crazy. He used it to meet with befriended magical creatures. My grandmother would perform first aid on dwarves, little folks, and so on."

Samme ran over to the desk and ruffled around before he pulled out a medium-sized mug. He then searched through his pockets until he produced a small flask of liquid.

"Drink up. Quickly, now. We need to be ready to go when he gets here."

Gruhit took the liquid and drank the familiar apple cider. It once again made him feel warm and reminded him of fall.

"Who's coming, Mr. Wunder?" Gruhit asked his foster dad.

Before Samme could answer there was a low grunt from the wall behind the desk. Gruhit turned his gaze toward the sound and noticed that there was a relief sculpture of a castle carved in the blocks, slightly raised from the flat surface of the wall. It depicted a gatehouse, several towers and turrets with flags, and a courtyard nestled behind the curtain wall. The castle's base formed into a pile of large rocks jutting out from the floor below. The carving was very intricate; it seemed as though each stone of the castle was hand chiseled with purpose and care by the sculptor. The most fascinating aspect of the carving was the operable, arched oak doors of the gatehouse that were about waist high to Mr. Wunder. At the bottom of each opening descended a winding and very steep staircase that snaked around until it came to the floor. The left door opened to reveal Gripple. He was only about ten inches tall. When he reached the floor a loud *SNICK* brought him to his full height.

Gripple grumbled something under his breath.

"Yes. We're ready to go," Samme stated.

Gripple grumbled again toward Samme.

"Yes. I'm aware that they sell human-made apple cider at human stores. Like I said we're ready to go," Samme started with a little frustration.

Gripple let out a series of high-pitched, sad grumbles.

"Yes, I know it's a cheap imitation of the dwarf cider," Samme stated. "I promise never to drink it again. Look! Gripple, we are sort of working through an emergency here."

Gripple roughly grabbed the hands of both humans. With a *SNICK* they were all shrunk down to less than a foot tall. The dwarf was the first to run up the opposite set of stairs than those he had originally descended. Samme and Gruhit followed Gripple through the doorway once they reached the top. Gruhit couldn't see much of anything except for what the light from outside allowed him to see. He could make out a concrete floor and a block wall. Samme fumbled through his overcoat and pulled out a headlamp before handing Gruhit a small flashlight. Gripple detached the lantern that was fastened to his belt and placed a small radiating feather from his pocket inside of the globe. Gruhit knew it must be a fleet bird feather. It gave off a warm glow, making Gruhit feel content.

"There it is. Get in, everyone," Samme instructed as he moved toward an old metal lunch pail in the middle of the space in the wall.

Gruhit had seen these in old movies and even a picture in a history book at school. Samme climbed into the pail, then turned to help Gruhit and Gripple inside. The handle of the pail was positioned above them and attached to a complex system of ropes and pulleys made from various items that one might find lying about.

Pierced through the bottom of the pail were two holes, just big enough for the rope to pass through. The rope extended upward into a hole drilled through a cement block above them. Samme and Gripple took hold of the ropes and began pulling. Immediately the pail began to rise through several cement blocks. Gruhit was glad that he couldn't see below because he was sure he would be frightened by the height.

Finally Gruhit noticed that the hole they passed through was bored out of a wooden material. The pail suddenly came to a halt. There was the faint smell of pine all around. He could hear Samme climb out of the pail and began wrestling to move something. There was a *CLICK* and light flooded the area.

Samme appeared above him, having just switched on an ordinary-sized lightswitch before helping Gruhit and Gripple back out of the pail. They were in a narrow passageway with wood on one side and drywall on the other. The light was coming from strings of Christmas lights which were strung along the length of the wall.

"We're inside the walls, aren't we?" Gruhit said as he looked around the passageway.

"Yes. You are now in the realm of the little folks. There is a network of paths that cover the entire home and hundreds of doorways to get into the main part of the house. You'll find that while the dwarves are hard workers, the little folks are fantastic at creating contraptions. Look over here, we have a ride." Samme walked over toward an old metal roller skate. "Gripple, can you wind up the vehicle please?"

Mr. Wunder helped lift Gruhit onto the skate. Gruhit could see that there were paper cups cut up and crafted into seats, complete with cushions. In each one of the seats was a helmet fashioned from a nutshell. Gripple jumped on the back part of the skate. It was fabricated with a wind-up key. The dwarf started to wind the vehicle. Gruhit could feel something moving under the skate. Samme took his place in the driver's seat and tested out the steering wheel which was made from a bottle cap.

"What's Gripple doing? Is this thing a wind-up toy?" Gruhit asked.

"It's a lot more complicated than just a wind-up toy," Samme reported. "It has a series of gadgets and pieces underneath the skate which utilize rubber bands to handle the propulsion of the machine and the steering of the wheels."

Gruhit stared at his foster dad for a few seconds before saying, "Right. So it's a wind-up toy, right?"
"With a fancy handle right here for the brake. And they painted racing stripes on the side," Samme said with a big smile and excitement. "Get your helmet on. Gripple will be done soon."

Gripple gave a loud grunt to indicate the vehicle had been adequately wound as he secured himself into his own seat.

"Alright, Gripple. Ready, Gruhit?" Samme asked.

Gruhit quickly put on his helmet and made sure he was deep in his seat.

"Release the brake! Hold on!" Samme yelled.

The skate leaped into action with great speed. The lights passed in a blur. Gruhit could feel the wind whip against his face. He tried to sink deeper into his seat as he gripped the sides tightly to ensure he didn't get knocked out. To say that Gruhit was nervous would be an understatement. Mr. Wunder looked over at Gruhit.

"WOOHOO!!" Samme exclaimed as they zipped along the passageway.

It had only been about thirty seconds in the little folk vehicle, but it felt like a thirty-minute trip to Gruhit. He definitely wanted to talk to Samme about walking next time instead.

"Engaging break! Hold on!" Samme screamed.

Gruhit had just enough time to brace himself before the skate came to a grinding halt next to another metal lunch pail dumbwaiter lift. Just beyond that was a home. It took up nearly the entire passageway, with just enough room to walk by the house and continue down the corridor. The home was only one story tall. Gruhit guessed that the house was mostly made from discarded wooden objects, such as popsicle sticks. The windows and doors were circular. The top of the house was created from various pieces of broken pottery. A thin wire was running into the roof from high above.

"Everyone out," Samme said. "Please leave the helmets in the seats. As you can see, Mr. Snickelfritz has outfitted the little folk homes with electricity. I'm told that this is unusual. Most just have candlelight. There are so many fires because of unattended candles. Mr. Snickelfritz has always been good with gadgets and tools, though."

"So this is the Snickelfritz's home? What are we doing here?" Gruhit asked.
"Well, we had originally given Mrs. Snickelfritz two days to prepare her potions," Samme said as they walked up to the door. "I now need to see what can be done

immediately. We also need to alert the Dickelbuttons to the current situation."

Gripple rang a doorbell. They could hear a chair moving inside and light footsteps coming toward the door.

"Yes, yes, yes, who's there? Mrs. Dickelbutton, I wonder?" Mrs. Snickelfritz said as she opened the door.

"It's Samme, Gripple, and Gruhit, Mrs. Snickelfritz," Samme announced.

"Master Wunder, and Master Gruhit with Mr. Gripple? I wasn't expecting you."

"Plans have changed, Mrs. Snickelfritz," Samme said. "May we come in? I'd like to share with you a few details you didn't catch before leaving."

"Yes, yes, yes. Of course, you may, Master Wunder. Should I put my tea pot on?" The woman stepped aside from the front door and motioned for them all to enter.

"No. There's no time for tea, unfortunately," Samme said. "I'm afraid we only have a moment to fill you in, and then it will be time for action."

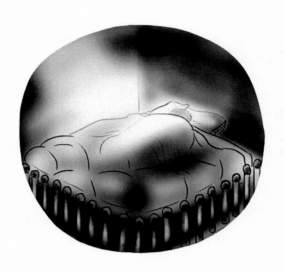

Chapter 28
The Snickelfritz Home

As soon as they stepped into the Snickelfritz's home, Samme launched into an explanation of the conversation that took place after Mrs. Snickelfritz had returned to her husband. Gruhit only half-listened to the conversation out of fascination for the house. It was full of paradoxes—things that don't seem to be able to exist at the same time but they do. For example, the home was a very warm and comfortable place. There was a cheerful fire dancing in the woodstove and pleasant fragrances all around from the homegrown potpourri, herbs, and spices hanging in the air. At the same time, the room felt very lonely. Cobwebs were forming on one of the two kitchen chairs, and a jacket hanging on the wall was collecting dust.

The home reminded him of a time long ago. The stove was not gas or electric but rather a wood-burning stove that was for both heating the home and cooking. Everything he saw looked to be built from discarded items. Yet, everything was very detailed and sophisticated. The stove was a far cry from just being a bunch of items glued together. There was a special door which had hinges on the front for putting wood in. He could also see that the bottom of the stove had a special apparatus for getting rid of the excess soot. There was a homemade broom sitting in the corner of the kitchen, which was constructed partially from an unused toothpick, and mugs on the counter made from sealed up thimbles.

Given the style of the furniture, Gruhit would have guessed that they were in an early American pioneer's home. Yet, there were working lights hanging from the ceiling. They appeared to be smaller Christmas lights. There were even half-ping pong balls around each bulb, so they looked like ones in any human home.

"Oh dear. Me thinks… oh dear," Mrs. Snickelfritz expressed.

"Everyone is coming over to the house now. I need to know what you can give us to defend ourselves. Do you have anything that we could use?" Samme implored the woman.

Mrs. Snickelfritz paused for a moment before replying.

"Yes, yes," she said at last. "I think I have enough sleeping draught for you to take with you. I've been making much of it in case we have to put more friends to sleep. Though it doesn't work unless it is ingested, and I don't think your enemies will much want to drink it,"

"We'll take it. I don't suppose the memory fogging potion will be ready quick enough, will it?" Samme inquired.

"No, no, you are right, but I have already made a batch. It must sit and age for two days to be powerful enough to cause someone to forget, but it might be strong enough to make someone confused for a few seconds. You are welcome to take it. You simply have to throw the liquid on them, so it is better, I think, for defending yourself," Mrs. Snickelfritz explained in a calculated manner.

"I was also tinkering with making this anxiety salve," Mrs. Snickelfritz explained. "It is the recipe for my dipsy toad salve. I only replaced the dipsy saliva with my homemade chili powder and teardrops created from a fearful moment. You don't want to get this on your skin. No, no, if it gets on you, it will make you scared and worried for maybe five minutes."

"If you've never made it before, though, how do you know it will work like that?" Gruhit interrupted.

Everyone stopped talking and looked at Gruhit. For a brief moment, Gruhit thought he said something wrong.

"Gruhit," Samme said with a small chuckle, "It's magic, afterall. Magical talents don't always follow logic and don't need explanation."

Gruhit rolled his eyes. He should have known this would be the response. He wasn't sure when it was going to sink in for him that there were times when odd things would happen and this would be considered normal. Also, there were times when he just had to trust that the adults knew what was happening.

"Gripple, can you load these potion jars and salve onto the skate?" Samme asked the dwarf.

"No, no, no, the skate is too slow," Mrs. Snickelfritz responded.

"Too slow?" Gruhit exclaimed, louder than he had meant to.

"Take the lift up one level and use the second door on the right," the woman explained.

"In that case, Gripple, please get the lift loaded with all of these items," Samme said. "We also need to call the Dickelbuttons. I'm assuming you want to stay with Mr. Snickelfritz. Can I see him before we go?" Samme asked.

Mrs. Snickelfritz's demeanor saddened a bit. "Yes, yes, you never have to ask this. Please go in the bedroom. Be needing to call the Dickelbuttons. I think you will want them for this mission, yes?"

"Yes. Thank you, Mrs. Snickelfritz. We will meet whomever is coming with us at the lift," Samme said gratefully.

Gruhit followed Samme into a dimly lit bedroom. There was a bed made from a large pincushion and supported by a matchstick frame. Gruhit could make out a lump of a man's shape under the comfortable quilted blanket. The shape was the only way Gruhit could tell there was a little folk there. Mr. Snickelfritz had become very transparent so that in the dim light of the bedroom, Gruhit could barely see anything. Well, he could also tell someone was there from the rough snoring.

Samme tenderly touched the top of the man's head and peered down at him.

"He looks so peaceful, doesn't he?" Samme said. "I'm glad that he doesn't appear to be in any pain or fear. His skin though, from what I can still feel, is ice cold."

Gruhit looked at the little folk and was reminded of Kieffer and Chardy. They were both unknowingly in a magical sleep and unknowingly fighting for their lives.

"We will be able to save them, right?" Gruhit said to Samme.

"I have no idea Gruhit. I have hope but…" Samme stopped, as though he didn't want to share what he was thinking.

"What is it?" Gruhit asked his foster dad.

"Well, if we do destroy the tacet stone, it should help Kieffer and Chardy. They were both harmed by the stone. However, Mr. Snickelfritz…. he was not harmed by the stone. It was his own hopelessness and maybe even Fridgita herself that did this."

"You don't think Mr. Snickelfritz will make it, do you?" Gruhit asked with a bit of shock.

"I don't know what I think. I just hope that something amazing happens as the events roll out," Samme said.

Samme took Mr. Snickelfritz's hand in his own and gave it a few pats. "Hang in there, old friend. Try your best to hang in there a bit longer. Give us a few more days."

With that, Samme and Gruhit left the home of the Snickelfritz's.

Chapter 29
The Quest Begins

T he small community of humans and magical creatures were gathered together in the dining room of Big Blue. All of them were in various states of nervousness or fear, and some were simply longing for justice.

Mr. Lusplendida paced back and forth, unsure if he was waiting for a meeting to start or for someone to finally decide to jump into action. His wife sat at the dining room table, peering out a window at the old factory across the street as though she could will her eyes to shoot lasers and do some damage.

Priscilla sat next to Mrs. Lusplendida and almost felt ill to her stomach. Not only was she very worked up, but she could feel the anger and aggression coming from the Lusplendidas. Mrs. Bangs knew that there would be a big confrontation coming. She absolutely hated the feelings of confrontations most of all. She bit her lip hard to keep herself from crying as she thought about all the big emotions flooding her mind and body.

The news and emotions seemed to be bothering Sparkles too. She flew above the group in a figure-eight path. She didn't stop zooming around as she kept wringing her hands in a nervous fashion.

Malda sat at the table looking around at her friends and tapping her foot anxiously. It wasn't that she didn't have any fear of what might happen tonight. She was furious that someone would dare to try and hurt her closest friends. Mr. Lusplendida's pacing was making her more anxious. She knew that he was very close to leaving the group and heading over to the factory by himself. Mal glanced at the clock, wondering what was keeping Samme.

As though Samme could read his wife's thoughts, a small wooden door opened on the bottom sill of the decorative window in the dining room. Out stepped Gripple, Gruhit, Samme, and Mr. Dickelbutton. Samme carried a basket full of various bottles and containers. Gruhit himself had a basket as well and could barely hold onto it as it was nearly three quarters of his size. Gripple grabbed Gruhit and Samme's hands. Together they leaped off the window sill toward the floor. Gruhit was absolutely terrified. At his current height, it appeared as though they had just jumped off a five-story-tall building. Before Gruhit could open his mouth to scream, there was the familiar *SNICK*, and the three beings were back to their original heights, standing by the table in the dining room.

Gruhit immediately noted that none of the salves and potions had grown with them. Samme took the now tiny basket from Gruhit and put both on the table in front of everyone.

"Samme! Let's hear a plan, or else I'm ready to march across the street myself now! This thing doesn't scare me," Jon yelled in an enraged tone.

"Jon, you're my dear friend, but you're a fool to not be scared of this thing," Mrs. Bangs announced. "You weren't here; I was. I could sense its emotions. It didn't care about any of us at all. But it didn't want to just destroy us either, no. It wanted to make us hurt for its own entertainment first before it caused any real damage." Mrs. Bangs was getting more worked up and stopped talking when Malda put her arm around her shoulder.

"Keep the hope everyone!" Samme directed. "I know that we have a lot to deal with tonight. Let's not forget our hope. Also, need I remind you that at fearful times, it falls upon Timorines to plan how to avoid dangerous situations? Dragon gave us a good plan for entering into the factory. I suggest we alter it a bit to allow all of us to go over."

"Ahem," said Mr. Dickelbutton in the loudest tone he could muster so that the entire room looked at him. "Master Wunder, may I suggest that I take all the extra humans over on the birds? The sparrows haven't quite gone asleep for the night."

"Excellent idea," Samme said quickly. "Mr. Lusplendida, I want you to enter the first floor with Gripple as originally planned. I don't see Dragon here. Will he be joining us? What about the rest of the dwarves?"

"Si. Dragon is already waiting for us outside," Jon gruffly commented. "The dwarves will not come. Except for Gripple, they claim they are all needed to watch the skies for falling fleet birds. They were actually very upset with Gripple for abandoning his post tonight."

"That's a bit disappointing given the severity of the situation," Samme said. "I'm grateful for all the help we have at this point. Priscilla, I want Amarie to stay with you and Mal, Gruhit should be with you as well. If that thing is going to go after any of us, it will be me, the one with generations of family knowledge about the magical world."

"Don't forget to have hope, everyone, please," Samme went on. "I won't sugar coat this. Our mission is fragile. While we have a plan for getting to the factory, none of us knows what to expect inside or what kind of attacks will come. The goal is to get the hair of the dark messenger. We're not even sure if destroying the tacet stone will fix anything. I'm asking for all of you to blindly chase after a chance, a hope. But I want you all to think of this: while this mission might require everything from you, failure will lead to the destruction of everything you know."

Samme began motioning for every adult human to take an assortment of potions, salves, and magical products. He explained how each was to be used. While he was doing this, Gripple escaped to the kitchen and returned with a large glass jug full of dwarf cider.

"Oh, good. I didn't know if you would be able to see it on the shelf," Mal said.

Soon mugs were passed around, and all were expected to drink. Gruhit wondered if he would ever grow tired of the warm feeling the cider gave him.

After everyone finished, Samme instructed, "Quickly, everyone to the baseboard in the kitchen."

They followed Samme and watched as he stared at a piece of baseboard trim. Before Gruhit could ask why they were staring at the floor, a knothole door opened. Mr. Dickelbutton stepped out and peered at the group of humans. Suddenly, Gripple shoved his way forward and grabbed the hands of Mr. and Mrs. Wunder. Everyone followed suit joining hands and then *SNICK* they were the size of little folk.

They each looked around to be sure that everyone had shrunk to the right size. Sparkles was the only one who didn't need to shrink. Gruhit could now see the intricate and fine designs on her translucent wings as they sparkled in the light.

"Quickly! Come this way," Mr. Dickelbutton said, motioning for everyone to climb into the walls.

Sparkles immediately flew in the direction of the door, but at the last second, phased through the wall.

"Hmph," Gripple grunted.

"*Si*, Gripple and I are sticking to the original plan. We will be going across the street at full height and shrink once we get to the factory on the ground floor. We will find you all over there for Gripple to restore your height," Mr. Lusplendida explained.

"Sounds great. We will probably be better undetected in smaller numbers too," Samme said as he gave Jon a friendly, parting handshake.

As soon as they released their hand grips, Samme turned to walk through the knothole doorway and followed half of the group which had already gone into the walls. Gruhit turned to look at Gripple and Mr. Lusplendida. He heard the familiar *SNICK* and saw four large shoes standing before him. The giant-looking men walked toward the back door to meet up with Dragon, who was waiting for them outside.

"Gruhit! Come on!" Amarie yelled. She grabbed Gruhit's arm and pulled him through the door. He could just barely make out several figures climbing into a lift pail. The passage above went further than Gruhit could see.

Chapter 30
Into The Factory

When the lift pail stopped rising, Gruhit still couldn't see a thing. All he knew was that they had risen for what felt like ages, and using the flashlight that Mr. Wunder had provided him earlier was out of the question for fear the light may startle the birds.

"Yes, yes, attic floor. Everyone is getting out now, quickly," announced Mr. Dickelbutton. "Follow me please. We have to uh… be quick… yes. Yes, yes, quickly now."

Everyone clumsily piled out of the lift pail in darkness. Gruhit's eyes eventually began to adjust enough so he could follow Mr. Dickelbutton. It was strange to be scurrying across the floors of the attic at this size. He felt like they were a pack of mice running for their lives from an invisible terror. Gruhit could see a vented window-like shape ahead of them with moonlight streaming inside. Mr. Dickelbutton grabbed the side of the vent and pulled with some effort inward. The vent swung toward the group like a door and revealed the starry sky outside.

Mr. Dickelbutton poked his head out and quickly glanced around for something. Gruhit was close enough to the opening to be able to see the edge of the street. Down below he spotted Mr. Lusplendida, Gripple, and Dragon speaking to each other. The charmyrll had just completed making the cloud-like shape of a stoplight with the green light area indicated as being lit up. Suddenly, the human and dwarf shrunk down to a smaller size and hurried onto the back of the charmyrll. Dragon hopped swiftly across the street toward overgrown weeds near the edge of the factory.

"Hmmph. He thinks he's hot stuff riding a charmyrll," Mrs. Lusplendida said under her breath, "More talented people than him have had their bottoms burned from trying that stunt."

Gruhit stifled a chuckle. He looked back over at Mr. Dickelbutton, who was now searching through his pockets. He pulled out an object, fashioned from what looked like the plastic barrel of a pen. It was narrow at one end and grew slightly wider at the other. Mr. Dickelbutton blew into it with great force. Immediately, a fluttering whistle noise was released into the night air.

"Stand back, stand back," Mr. Dickelbutton instructed.

Everyone hopped back a bit and stared at the window. Gruhit waited in anticipation for something to happen. All he saw were stars looking back at them. A breeze blew into the attic. It was a cool breeze which reminded the group winter would soon be in full force. However, Gruhit couldn't help but wonder if it was a drop in the temperature they were feeling. Did Mr. Dickelbutton suspect an attack from the dark messenger already?

No sooner than Gruhit could put those thoughts together, he heard the pounding of the air and strange noises. Afraid, he took another step backwards just as three sparrows and two finches swooped through the open vent and landed in front of the group. Mr. Dickelbutton approached the first sparrow and began petting it. The birds all seemed to be interested in Mr. Dickelbutton. He spoke to them in a low voice and the birds began cocking their heads as if in disbelief at what he had to say.

"Yes, yes, they have agreed to take us all over to the factory," Mr. Dickelbutton said. "They will not stay. They are worried about this dark messenger. They will be getting us there, but we need to find our own way home."

"This whole plan is based on hope. It sounds like the best option we have, so I say let's get going," Samme replied.

Everyone started mounting the birds and assured they had a good grip on their feathers. Amarie was sitting in front of Mrs. Bangs on a sparrow. It was difficult to tell who was more frightened, Amarie or Mrs. Bangs. To Gruhit, they both seemed to be feeling all sorts of emotions and were very pale. Mal and Mrs. Lusplendida were ready for action and climbed on the back of a finch. Mr. Dickelbutton was already mounted on a sparrow. He seemed very familiar with it and continued to speak to it in a low tone too quiet for the rest of the party to hear.

Samme guided Gruhit over to a finch and helped him aboard. The feathers were warm and soft. Under different circumstances, Gruhit might have been able to fool himself into thinking he was on a comfy mattress.

"Hold tight, but none shall pull out a feather!" Mr. Dickelbutton yelled to the group. "Swiftwind will go now."

Mr. Dickelbutton's bird quickly hopped over to the open window and launched out into the night. The other birds immediately followed. Gruhit gripped the feathers, more scared of falling than he had anticipated. He now understood why Gripple did not want to take the birds.

Mr. Wunder extended his arms and gripped the feathers on either side of Gruhit to help him feel protected. Gruhit had to squint in the wind. Up ahead, he could barely see Swiftwind gliding toward a massive shape. A few seconds later, Gruhit could make out the brickwall of the factory. The birds were moving toward a window sill.

They landed so lightly that the passengers could barely feel it. Gruhit was one of the first to dismount. The ride was thrilling, but he wasn't sure if he wanted to travel this way all the time.

Mr. Dickelbutton was the last to dismount after he was sure everyone else was safely on the window sill. He patted Swiftwind while speaking to the flock of birds before they took off, creating a small breeze.

Mrs. Lusplendida was already crawling through the window into the dark factory interior. Suddenly, this was all becoming more real for Gruhit. They had no idea what was going to happen to them when they entered this factory. They weren't sure if they were going to face an army or Fridgita Mortes herself. If they failed, Gruhit might never speak to his brother again. He could feel fear rising up inside of him, causing his stomach to feel fuzzy and weird.

"We're all scared, Gruhit," Samme said from behind him as if guessing his thoughts.

"You can tell that Mrs. Bangs is feeling the same way. I'm very nervous too. We just have to be brave enough to take one more step. Don't forget, our friends are counting on us."

With this small pep talk, Gruhit walked toward the crack in the window behind Amarie. When he crawled into the factory, he instantly noted the smell of rusting metal and rotten wood. It was as if soil was in the air and entering his nose with every breath. There were no signs of life as far as Gruhit could tell, not even mice or spiders. It was very quiet, and he felt like everyone within a mile of the factory could hear his breathing. He wanted so much to retreat back outside to the night air where the birds were flying and the beautiful stars were sparkling.

"I don't see a thing," Mrs. Lusplendida said in a hushed tone. "Everyone should be ready to use their potions if needed. That thing could be anywhere in here. Let's climb down to the desk. My husband and Gripple will be on the first floor. We should get to them while we search."

Everyone treaded lightly over the sill to the string of an old window blind hanging haphazardly from up above. They took turns sliding down and safely jumping off onto an old metal desk. There were various dust-covered papers laying around the surface.

"Over there!" Samme said as he proceeded toward a group of metal chutes by the desk.

"This is where they sent messages throughout the factory," Mal explained. "You would put a message in a tube and then place it into the chute. Air flow would then carry the tube to the other end of the chute for the person waiting there."

"Right. This one is labeled, 'Front Desk.' That seems like the place we might need to go to find the others. We should just be able to slide down the chute," Samme said as he opened the door.

Samme peered down the dark chute, trying to assess how safe it was. Then, as though he didn't want to think too much about things, he jumped into the chute. Sparkles took flight then phased through the desk and floor to follow Mr. Wunder. Malda quickly went over to the side of the chute and peered in it herself.

"Samme?" Mal whispered as loud as she could.

There was a pause before they heard Samme's voice whisper back. "It's a bumpy ride, but it's safe. Get down here quick and mind the dust. Gripple and Jon are already here, and Sparkles just phased through the ceiling."

Chapter 31
The Empress Summoned

Gruhit was jolted around as he flew down the dark chute that nearly went straight down. He was so scared he might get hurt; although he knew that several others had already done this, including Mrs. Wunder and Amarie. It was just himself and Mrs. Lusplendida left. Just when he thought he might start screaming from the fall, the chute curved into a long slide and soon became horizontal with an opening above him. He slowed to a stop and looked up to see familiar faces staring down at him.

Once everyone had made it onto the desk, they slid down the handle of an old dusty broom leaning against it. Gruhit was handed a small flask of dwarf cider when he joined the group on the ground. Before too long, Gripple had returned everyone to their proper height. Sparkles was resting on top of Amarie's head, while Mr. Dickelbutton had been placed inside the front pocket of Mrs. Lusplendida's coveralls. It seemed as though everyone was waiting for a command, and fearing it was unwise to grow to their full size again.

"There's nothing in this front area. It's just dust and old office supplies," Jon relayed to the group.

"That makes sense," Samme said in a whisper. "If I were this thing, I would be in the production area. It's completely open with few hiding spots. Factory foremen needed the area set like that so they could observe what was happening at all times."

"Well, unless that sign that says 'Production Area' above that door is incorrect, I'm guessing we have to go this way," Malda said quietly.

"Right," Samme replied. "Remember, Amarie stays with Priscilla. Gruhit stays with Mal. Everyone stick close to the walls. There are large windows near the ceilings that will let in the moonlight. Our best chance of not being seen is to stay in the shadows around the perimeter of the room. Remember your potions. Also, Dragon is outside and ready to light this whole place on fire if it comes down to that."

Jon took this as his moment to act. Everyone could see that he was dreadfully tired of sneaking around. He wanted to take action. He moved on his hands and knees in the direction of the door leading to the production area and opened it just enough to stick his head through. After a few seconds of quiet, he quickly crawled through the door and was gone.

"Well, it looks like we all need to get moving if we want to keep up with Jon. Gruhit, get behind me. Here we go," Mal said as she got on her hands and knees and quickly crawled through the door.

Gruhit was moving before he could think too much. He was worried he might get left behind. It was his luck he was paired with an Instinctual. Gruhit knew he should be brave and react quickly.

Gruhit was now in a wide open room with a ceiling two or three stories tall. It was just like Samme said. There were windows everywhere, and the moonlight flooded the entire space. They all crawled around the dark edges. In the middle of the space were several large machines for making shoes. Gruhit didn't have a clue what most of them did. He could see one was a cutting machine and had a spare piece of leather still hanging from it. Throughout the rest of the production area were assembly conveyor belts. These were designed to move partially made shoes so that people and machines could complete the process. Everything was covered in inches of dust and cobwebs. The smell of rust and decay was strong here.

"Look, there's the foreman's office," Samme whispered, pointing to a small box-like office up above the production area. "The stairs are over there. If we can get to the office, we will be able to see almost everything from up there."

"Good. Let's go!" Mr. Lusplendida whispered back as he hurriedly crawled along the outer walls to the stairs.

Gruhit thought how unlucky it was that the stairs were at the other end of the factory. At their present speed, it would take them thirty minutes to get there, and they had no idea if they were being watched at this point or not. This area seemed to be slightly cooler than the front office had been. Gruhit reminded himself the broken windows above would be letting in the cold night air. Periodically, he could hear stifled whimpers from Mrs. Bangs, who was trying to be brave enough to continue moving forward. Sparkles stayed hidden in Amarie's hair and was too scared to fly.

The shadows in this room were the worst. The moonlight created scary silhouettes on the floor. They were just passing an outline that looked like a dog with its mouth open. Then, to make his mind play even worse tricks on him, the breeze would slightly move various pieces of old machinery, causing the shadows to move.

Gruhit closed his eyes and began to tell himself that everything was fine. He was with people who would protect him. He tried to put aside his fears and opened his eyes. He immediately saw a bat-like silhouette on the ground which seemed to be moving.

"I'm not afraid of you," Gruhit whispered.

The shadow continued to move, then grew a bit larger. Gruhit felt as though he were in a battle of wits with the shadow on the ground.

"I'm not afraid of you!" Gruhit said a bit more intensely, but still in a hushed tone.

Gruhit's talking didn't go unnoticed this time.

"I'm not afraid of you!!" Gruhit said so forcefully that he almost spoke in a slightly higher than normal voice.

This time everyone stopped moving and looked at Gruhit. Mal turned her body to console him. As she reached for her foster son, there was a deafening flapping of wings soaring through the air. The temperature dropped severely. Mrs. Bangs and Amarie both hugged each other for support.

From the ceiling, the silhouette of a large winged creature suddenly came into view. Everyone froze. It was the dark messenger. They could hear the icey cackles now as she began to fly around in a circle slowly. The shape high above began to encircle the room in faster and tighter circles. Had she seen them? Did she know they were there?

The great flapping of the wings began to move the air and dust in the room. A small whirlwind appeared about ten feet in front of where the group lay in wait. There was cackling that could faintly be heard from up above. Mr. Dickelbutton buried himself deep into the pocket of the coveralls. Sparkles flew out of Amarie's hair and hid behind a conveyor belt in front of the group. Gripple shrunk down to the same size as the tangerella and ran to Sparkles to comfort her.

It was becoming more difficult to see as the wind intensified and dust began pelting their faces. Gruhit could make out the shape of the dark messenger as she descended to the ground nearly in front of them. She touched down lightly as she watched her whirlwind of dust quicken. Her back was to the group, which gave hope that she wasn't aware of their presence. Gruhit was sure that his loud exclamation had caught the attention of the dark messenger. Samme quietly motioned for everyone to remain silent and press as closely to the walls as they could. There was nowhere to go now. Any movement would alert the dark messenger of their location. They had to hope that the shadows and dust would keep them concealed.

The dark messenger was a bit shorter than Mrs. Lusplendida when she stood straight and tall with her wings stretched out to their full span as she raised her arms upward. Even without being able to see her clearly, Gruhit could sense the immense power of her presence. Her wings looked as though they could kill him with just one flap.

The dark messenger let out one final cackle, sending a chill through everyone.

"Come grace me with your presence, my Empress! The rightful ruler of the universe… FRIDGITA MORTES!" yelled the dark messenger as she bent down on one knee in a bow of respect and fear.

The whirlwind immediately stopped swirling. A blast of wind shot upward from the floor, hitting the high ceiling with a mighty blast. There was dust and dirt everywhere. When things finally cleared enough that Gruhit could see, some of the dust still hung in the air, animated to form the shape of another female messenger. While the first dark messenger appeared to be feminine and graceful, this one was extremely tall and muscular. She looked to be at least eight feet tall and strong enough to lift a horse.

"Esna, my little imp of mischief and deception. You better have a reason for distracting me," Fridgita said to her minion with a surprisingly pleasant, albeit commanding, voice.

Esna refrained from looking up at the image of Fridgita. Esna was smaller in stature. She was garbed in a long flowing tunic that complimented her graceful movements. Her wings, while bat-like, flapped as precious silk linens blowing in the wind. Her face contained the feminine beauty of a human woman with short and shiny hair.

Fridgita's presence, on the other hand, commanded attention and resembled power. She was clad in a tunic and leggings interwoven with chainmail armor pieces. She appeared to be more like a warrior than a messenger with her dragon-like wings and was equipped with a long spear. Her headdress was spiked and doubled as both a crown and a helmet that contained her straight, shoulder-length hair. Her face was angular and stern, which matched the rest of her body.

If this was merely the image of Fridgita that Esna called here, Gruhit worried what the real thing would be like to encounter. Gruhit could feel the temperature drop every second that Fridgita's image remained in the room. It was so cold his teeth began to chatter. He looked across the way to where Sparkles was hiding. The tangerella was so scared that she was openly crying.

"Empress, I have used the Chardy boy to gain access to the Wunder home like you commanded. The tacet stone will soon complete the fizzling process on the guardling and the Chardy boy who began to lose all hope for me to steal," Esna reported, trying to keep her voice from shaking. Perhaps she too was frightened of Fridgita.

"You talk to me like you have done something well, Esna. Tell me... what is so good about this situation?" Fridgita asked. She leaned over to put the image of her face closer to the kneeling dark messenger.

"I... the Chardy boy's fizzling should give you more power..."

"Power? Power? You made a tacet stone, yes?"

"Yes, Empress."

"Those take a great deal of magic and power to create, yes?"

"Yes, Empress."

"I suppose you feel weakened from this, yes? Can't do all of your tricks like you're used to, yes?"

"Yes… yes, Empress. But it is worth it for the cause of my Empress."

"Idiot!" Fridgita yelled so ferociously that she was spitting while she talked. "I know you would use the essence to regain your own power. You would take what is mine!"

"No… no, Empress."

"Tell me, Esna. Your victims haven't completely fizzled out, have they?" Fridgita said cunningly while she stood tall.

"No, Empress. The community used their sleeping draught on them both to slow the process. I thought maybe if I called upon you, my Empress would help me…"

"Ha! Well you 'thought' did you? Esna, let's be clear. I only allow you to breathe because I simply cannot be everywhere at once. You had one job: to watch over the Wunder community and cause mischief, maybe even convince some of them to lose hope. You were to do all of this undetected." Fridgita extended the tip of her spear so that it rested under the chin of Esna. The smaller, frightened dark messenger shook more. Esna intensely attempted to hold back any signs of fear. Even though Fridgita herself was not there, the spear tip felt just as sharp as a real one. The blade lifted Esna's chin so that she was forced to look at the eyes of the powerful being in front of her.

Simultaneously, large balls of dust rose out of the floor all around Esna, quickly becoming nearly as tall as Gruhit. The balls of dust shivered on the ground as arms and legs made of dirt particles poked out. Then a mouth and pair of eyes formed on each. The creatures opened their jaws to reveal sharp teeth. Gruhit could hear stifled cackles coming from the creatures as they looked about mischievously.

"I fear that I thought too much of you, Esna," Fridgita said. "At the first sign of an intruder, you showed yourself. You even weakened yourself by creating a tacet stone. Now you have nothing to show for it. You can't even utilize some of your more deadly, deceptive powers. The Wunder community knows we're watching them, and your victims are being sustained by a magical sleep."

The odd looking dust creatures continued to cackle slowly as they watched Fridgita. A few of them snapped their jaws at Esna.

"And now, dear Esna, you have allowed them to see what I, Fridgita, Empress of the Universe, look like," Fridgita said slowly.

Gruhit could feel his heart racing. He longed so much to be anywhere but here. He was so scared and cold he couldn't even remember the warm feeling he would get from drinking dwarf-made apple cider. He looked over at Mal next to him. Mal and Mr. Lusplendida were both crouched down low, looking like cats ready to pounce. Their hands held tight to potion bottles. Gruhit could see Mrs. Lusplendida spreading salve on her gloved left hand. Mr. Dickelbutton was still buried deep in her front overall pocket and couldn't be seen.

Esna looked shocked and spoke defensively, "I… no… I would never reveal you to them, Empress."

"Really. Poor, dim Esna. If you're as loyal as you claim to be, then why is most of the Wunder community staring at me from the shadows of the room," Fridgita asked calmly. She pointed her spear in the direction of the group. "Dust-Wumps, get them. Now!"

Mrs. Bangs quickly yanked Gruhit and Amarie's arms, pulling them down the wall to the opposite corner. Mal and Jon leapt upward and ran directly toward Esna. Both wore a look of determination and clutched bottles as the dust creatures moved toward them. Mrs. Lusplendida was right behind them, spreading salve on her other gloved hand as she ran. Her eyes were fixed on the image of Fridgita.

Jon plowed into the first dust-wump. The creature didn't have time to react and was forcefully shoved into several other creatures. Mal locked eyes on a dust-wump that was chomping its jaws and walking toward her. Since the creature was half her height, she was able to use her speed and agility to jump over it without getting entangled in its arms. Gripple, longing to help his friends, grew to full height and charged behind his comrades who were now mere feet from Esna.

Mr. Lusplendida was the first to launch a bottle of the memory fogging potion toward Esna. At the last second, the dark messenger skillfully batted her wings, knocking the potion bottle away and breaking it to pieces. Mal vollied another bottle at her, only for the same fate to befall that potion as well.

Esna wrapped herself in her wings as Jon and Mal continued their swift advance. The dust-wumps had recovered and were chasing after them. Esna let out a loud roar as she threw her wings outward, creating a violent burst of wind.

Jon, Mal, and Gripple were hurled backwards. As Jon fell, the second bottle of potion was dislodged from his grip and hit him squarely on the top of the head. The memory fogging potion created a great cloud around him that he breathed it in.

As the gas cleared, Mal turned on her side. Gripple lay unconscious next to her. A few feet away lay Mr. Lusplendida.

"Jon! Are you alright?" Malda yelled.

Mr. Lusplendida sat up quickly and surveyed the area. He stared at Malda, then looked shocked at Esna and Fridgita before immediately getting to his feet.

"What is this? What's going on? Get away from me, all of you!" Jon yelled, backing up to the exterior wall.

Esna let out a maniacal laugh at the sight of Jon. "Ah, your memory fogging potion backfired on you, didn't it?"

Mrs. Lusplendida continued to run around the pack of dust-wumps and stealthily slipped in behind Fridgita. Fueled by anger, she leapt at Fridgita's left arm. With her salve-soaked gloves, she clutched onto the evil messenger with a vice-like grip.

Fridgita looked shocked that a puny human could have gotten so close to her. The evil messenger raised her arm for inspection. Mrs. Lusplendida refused to let go; she knew time was needed for the salve to have a better chance of working. Fridgita's worried expression turned to a sly smile.

"Pathetic," she said. "Did you think your magic tricks would work on me? Idiot! Too bad I'm not actually there."

Mrs. Lusplendida's eyes widened as she realized the awful predicament she was in. Fridgita ruthlessly spun around as Mrs. Lusplendida held on for dear life. Fridgita abruptly stopped, catapulting Mrs. Lusplendida through the air before she hit the wall with a loud thud.

Gruhit, still huddled in the corner with Amarie and Mrs. Bangs, watched as Mrs.

Lusplendida's limp and unconscious body slid to the floor a few feet away from where Mr. Lusplendida was still feeling the effects of the memory fogging potion. Four dust-wumps encircled Malda and forced her to her feet, holding her tightly. Two others collected her potions and salves. The smallest creature made an evil cackle as it shook loose the contents of a bottle into Mal's face.

Mal struggled to get loose. But just as quickly as she was enraged, her face changed to fear and panic.

"No! NO! Get away from me! I'll do what you say! Please! No! Help! Help me!" Malda screamed as the anxiety salve began to take effect on her.

Sparkles couldn't accept Malda's terror. Without thinking, she flew from her hiding spot and went to aid her struggling friend.

The tangerella curled her small hands into fists and held them out in front of her face. It looked like she was going to ram one of the dust-wumps in the eye. Suddenly a dust-wump grabbed one of her tiny wings and laughed.

Sparkles struggled against her captor. It tilted its head back and opened its teeth-filled mouth. Mrs. Bangs' eyes filled with horror. She looked around for some way to help. Then the dust-wump let out a shockingly loud belch, echoing throughout the production area. All poor Sparkles could do was cover her mouth and nose to keep from vomiting.

Two more dust-wumps came over to join in the tormenting. They all laughed at the sickened Sparkles. When the dust-wumps saw her duress, they began poking and prodding her. One of the evil beings decided to take it a step further. It sharply ripped one of the many flower petals that made up Sparkles' dress.

Sparkles' face turned to shock and then complete rage. She scowled and gave the dust-wump a seething stare. Her skin turned to a dark pink color. A small stream of steam rose from the tangerella's body.

"Oh, they've done it now," Mrs. Bangs stated. She urged the children to stay as tight to the shadows as possible. "Tangerellas are sworn protectors of their beauty. Ripping their garments will be seen as more than just an attack on her. She is from the Order of Sentrites. Believe me, you don't want to get us blind with anger."

At that moment, Sparkles pulled her wings free from the dust-wump. Her skin and body was now so red it resembled hot iron just pulled from a fire. The tangerella took off flying with such great speed that all one could really see was a streak of crimson. She flew back at the first dust-wump and through the center of the creature. She tore a hole completely through the dust-made being. It retched in pain before poofing out of existence.

Gruhit barely had time to figure out what happened before Sparkles tore through another dust-wump, then a third, a fourth, and so on. There were now only ten of the evil creations left, all running toward Esna and Fridgita for protection. The tangerella could not be deterred, flying toward the remaining creatures. Gruhit wasn't sure Sparkles knew what she was doing. He knew that when anyone gets this angry, they don't think about the fine details. They only have one thought on their mind.

Fridgita surveyed the battle. She kept looking back and forth for something, now frustrated. She glanced down and saw her dust creations running in a panic toward her while two of them fought to keep Malda under control.

"ENOUGH!" Fridgita bellowed in a prolonged tone as she stomped her mighty right foot on the floor.

Everyone was thrown back violently by the force of Fridgita's yell. The whole factory shook as though there had just been a small earthquake. Both Amarie and Mrs. Bangs were dazed from colliding with the wall, though Gruhit landed softly on them both in a heap. It appeared that the rest of the adults had been knocked unconscious. Dust fell from everywhere. Chains hanging above her clanged. A few of the smaller machines toppled over.

Things seemed dismal. Gruhit was sure this would be the end of them all. He wished they had never come to this stupid factory. But then he thought about what Samme had told him. If they didn't fix this problem right now, the whole town would be in danger. But where was Samme?

As though Fridgita knew what he was thinking, she began to fervently scan the area. "Wunder! Esna, where is Wunder? Did you let him escape? Tangerellas and dwarves are useless to me. The little child over there is still awake. Bring him to me. I'll rip out his tongue if he doesn't tell me where Wunder is."

As a few dust-wumps began to walk in Gruhit's direction, his heart began to race. He could barely breathe; he was so scared. Then Samme stood up proudly from the opposite side of the room behind Fridgita.

"You will not harm the boy or any of my friends!" Samme said in a commanding voice.

"Hiding behind me? Letting all the others do the dirty work, eh? Is this pathetic human really from the 'famed' line of the Wunder clan?" Fridgita said in a mocking and sarcastic tone.

"You don't believe that, Fridgita," Samme said. "If you know of my family as well as you suggest, then you know that I'm not going to divulge the plans that find me behind you. However, here I am now with all the information I have learned as a boy about the magical world. Facts and observations made by my family for generations."

"I don't need you," Fridgita said firmly. "I am the Empress of the Universe. You are in my domain."

"And yet you weren't there at the beginning," Samme said. "You were created just like the first humans. You don't carry all the knowledge of the ages. You can't. You weren't there to witness the beginning. There is knowledge that you don't have in that evil head of yours. There must be, or I would be dead. But here I stand, still breathing."

Fridgita stared harshly at Mr. Wunder in silence. If Gruhit didn't know better, he would have guessed they were speaking to each other telepathically. Fridgita gripped her spear with both hands, determining if she needed to keep this human alive, or if she could kill him immediately.

She swiftly turned back to look at Esna. "Seize him!" she commanded. "Put all of the big humans into a cell! You have a prison here, yes? Or did the tacet stone steal away so much power that you couldn't concoct one?"

"Yes... yes, Empress. I've already fashioned a holding cell out of the large fireplace in the back," Esna said fearfully. "I chose it because if the prisoners have a cold attitude toward me, I can be hospitable and warm them up."

The dust-wumps began collecting the adults and taking them out of the room. Samme looked at Gruhit as he was being led away. He had time to wink encouragingly at Gruhit and silently mouthed, "There is always hope."

"I have made quick work of everything you could never do, Esna. Now, you have interrupted my journey and my business long enough. I assume you can handle the little humans and other creatures by yourself?" Fridgita lowered her powerful head toward Esna's face. "Get from him what I need and don't interrupt me again. You know the stakes."

Esna kneeled before her. "Yes, Empress. I won't fail you again."

Fridgita stood tall. "You're an idiot and pathetic, Esna. Make sure that you don't disappoint me. There is no good future for you without me. I leave you the gift of my dust-wumps to aid you. Not that you have ever done anything to deserve my help."

With these final condescending words, Fridgita raised her hands toward the ceiling. A rush of wind came from the floor, and an intense column of dust appeared. This time, when everything settled, there was nothing where the powerful, evil messenger's image once stood.

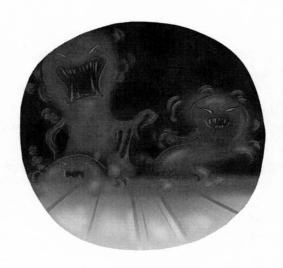

Chapter 32
Esna's Dinner Helpers

Esna got to her feet and regained her composure as she studied her captives. The fear and serious features of her face were soon replaced by a devious smile as she plotted their demise.

"Dust-Wumps! Search the captives and relieve them of any weapons and magic potions," Esna yelled. "Tsk, tsk. tsk. You humiliated me in front of the Empress. I shall have a punishment for all of you."

The dust-wumps began searching each of them and taking away potion bottles and salves. They confiscated several tools from Gripple, but allowed him to keep his flask. They searched Sparkles delicately and quickly. None of the monsters wanted to anger the tangerella after they witnessed exactly what she could do to them.

"Keep your hands away from there!" Mrs. Lusplendida demanded. She slapped a dust-wump who was trying to search her overalls.

The dust-wump looked taken aback. Luckily, the creature seemed to be content with its search and moved on. After a few moments, Mr. Dickelbutton's head emerged from Mrs. Lusplendida's front pocket. He carefully assessed the room. He did not want to be detected. When he could see each dust-wump was occupied with searches, he skillfully climbed out and navigated his way to the floor. He made a mad dash toward Amarie. She scooped him up and gently slipped him into the pocket of her hoodie.

Esna danced around, taunting her prisoners while they were being searched. When she was satisfied, she barked more orders in a deranged voice. "Now we're all ready to have some fun. Take the big humans to the holding cell! Don't light it just yet; I still need something from that one."

Esna pointed at Samme. The dust-wumps snapped into action and seized all the adults, forcing them out of sight. Mrs. Bangs was overwhelmed with being separated from the children. She twisted, turned, kicked and did whatever she could to try and hold onto Amarie and Gruhit. In her tired and weakened state, the dust-wumps were ultimately able to subdue her and take her away.

A dust-wump approached Esna and spoke to her in low hisses and growls.

"What a fun idea? Yes. Put the tangerella in this potion bottle," Esna instructed as she cast a barrier spell over the empty container. "Be sure to put the lid back on tight and place her next to my throne. I think it might be delightfully fun to watch her struggle to escape as her beauty slowly fades away."

Esna turned her attention to Gruhit and Amarie. She smoothly glided across the floor and stopped right in front of them as she smiled her lunatic smile.

"Little humans, I'm afraid that all of this commotion has made me hungry. My dinner was never prepared," she said. "I want you to make me something delicious. There is a kitchen in the back that still works well enough. And as if I'm not already being too kind, teaching you how to cook, I'll allow you to take the dwarf along for any heavy lifting you need."

Gruhit looked at Esna's short and shiny hair, now just mere inches from him. He thought about reaching out and grabbing a handful, but he wasn't sure what to do then. There was no way he could get outside safely. Even if he could, his only defense would be Dragon lighting the factory on fire. The others would still be inside.

"If you pass this lesson, little humans, I might let you work for me," Esna said sternly. "But if you don't, I have enough power to make another tacet stone. Then you can watch your dwarf and tangerella friends fizzle out of existence."

Amarie began to protest in a timid voice. "But… but you're not to make another tacet stone. We heard Fridgita…"

At the sound of her Empress' name, Esna lifted her arm in a graceful fashion and smacked Amarie across the mouth.

"QUIET! Quiet! Hehe. The first lesson you will learn is your place in this world," Esna said, seething. "You're a human. A little one at that. You have nothing to offer us and are undesirable. You will never…NEVER speak the name of the greatest being that has ever lived. I'm sure that my Empress will overlook the creation of another tacet stone when I have fizzled out more creatures."

"I thought Victus was the greatest being ever known," Gruhit said as bravely as he could.

Esna's eyes narrowed. Her face looked demonic as she replied. "Get the little ones and dwarf to the kitchen. If we cannot teach them lessons swiftly, we will need to start playing our torture games."

Dust-Wumps grabbed Amarie, Gruhit, and Gripple and then forced each one of them to walk through a darkened doorway into the back kitchen.

Chapter 33
Honest Feelings

A light switch clicked on, illuminating the kitchen. Gruhit was amazed the factory still had any kind of working electricity. He wondered if it was really Esna's magic. It seemed silly to even consider discrepancies now. He and his sister were being forced to cook for a being he never would have believed existed a year ago and who was threatening to torture many of his dearest friends.

Gruhit surveyed the kitchen as his eyes adjusted to the light. There was a long, metal preparation table with a sink in the center of the room and a commercial oven to the right. Along the rest of the wall, a table held mixing machines and other cooking devices. There were many shelves filled with old glass jars of various sizes, shapes, and hues. Some of the glass jars had fallen to the floor and were broken. The whole room had a good coating of dust and cobwebs, just like the production area.

Along the wall to his left, there were small sacks of herbs, spices, and a variety of other food goods. There was even a small pantry storing various fresh fruits and vegetables. It seemed as though Esna kept her supplies in good stock, despite the filth.

The dust-wumps released the children and Gripple from their holds and stood guard in front of the door, the only exit out of the room. One of the creatures hissed at Gruhit and pointed at the food. It then motioned to his wrist as though it were pointing at a watch. The hand gestures were clear. They had one hour to make dinner for their callous host. The door was closed and locked. They could hear a couple of the creatures right outside of the door conversing with each other in their hissing voices.

Mr. Dickelbutton jumped out of Amarie's hoodie pocket and scurried down the leg of her pants until he reached the dirty floor.

"I'm going to search the room and see if I can find any way for us to escape out of here," he said. "Gripple, I thinks you and the children should begin preparing some sorts of food in case I cannot figure out how to get us out."

Gruhit had no idea how a creature so small was going to be able to help. However, he very much admired the little man's spirit and loyalty. The dust-wumps had no idea Mr. Dickelbutton was even a part of their company. He was small enough so he could simply find a hole or a crack in a wall and escape. It would be easy enough for him to run back to Big Blue and spend the night with his wife and children.

Gruhit and Gripple immediately began assessing the food supplies to see what could be done. While he was picking up a head of cabbage to look it over, Gruhit realized Amarie was crying. He exited the pantry to see his older sister standing by the preparation table with her arms enfolded around herself. Gruhit could only remember seeing Amarie cry a handful of times in his life. She was usually so happy.

"Amarie?" Gruhit started as he approached his sister.

"I know, I know, I need to help, and I need to stop crying," Amarie said through sobs.

"I didn't say you needed to stop crying," Gruhit said.

"Of course I do!" she said through sobs. "Good things never happen to people who are sad or angry. Adults always want a happy kid. Don't you hear them all the time. 'There's my happy girl.' 'Amarie is always such a happy child and gets along with everyone.' How do you think I stay out of trouble, Gruhit? How do you think I've survived all these moves? How do you think I keep people from doing bad stuff to me? To us? I'm happy! As long as you're happy, the adults aren't wondering what is wrong with you. They leave you alone and let you be. If I'm happy, I don't have to talk about how I miss momma so badly that it hurts all the time.

I don't have to think about the sad feelings of our broken family. I don't have to hurt. I can just think about happy things and keep bad feelings and people away."

"Feelings aren't bad, Amarie," Gruhit said. "I'm scared. Like, I'm really scared. But that's okay, as long as we have hope that things will get better. You're a Sentrite. Feeling and experiencing your feelings is important...even the sad ones. We just can't give up on hope. Remember these scary monsters want us to believe that we're nobodies. But did you see how mad Esna looked when I mentioned Victus? They know there is a bigger being out there. I have to believe, if all of this is happening to us, Victus is also real, and things are going to work out."

Amarie slowly stopped crying so hard and wiped her eyes.

"Okay. Thanks, Gruhit. I'm scared and upset about this whole situation. I feel the furthest away from happiness that I have since we were taken away from Momma. I can try and hope that things will be better. I can do it because I have you to help me to remember to be hopeful."

Gruhit and Amarie looked at each other with half smiles. Amarie had been brave enough to share her true emotions. For the first time in a long time, Gruhit felt like he could connect with her, understand her, and say how they were both feeling. This didn't make their situation any better, but it did give them both strength. They were not alone in their feelings. Somehow this helped them both to be hopeful. Gruhit supposed it was always easier to hope when you didn't feel alone.

At that moment, a ball of light with a yellow tint glowed brightly on the table next to Amarie. Gruhit and Amarie stepped back and stared at it. Gripple, who had appeared from out of the pantry, stopped walking in shock. The glowing seemed to intensify as the ball grew from the size of a marble to that of a basketball. Mr. Dickelbutton appeared on top of the table about a foot from the glowing ball. His eyes were transfixed at the mysterious light. Gruhit was strangely not afraid, the light seemed to permeate a pleasant warmth that made Gruhit feel safe.

Just as soon as they were beginning to feel comfort from the light, it began to fade away. They were left with the cold and dirty kitchen again. In the place of the light remained an ornate glass jar adorned with detailed etchings of fruits. The jar was about the size of Gruhit's hand. To him, it looked beautiful enough to befit royalty. The jar had a faint glow. Amarie walked over and carefully picked it up. Gruhit could now see the jar was outfitted with a gorgeous gold lid. There was a decorative "S" etched smartly on its front.

"What is this? Where did it come from? Gruhit, you've studied magical creatures more than I have," Amarie asked. Gruhit could only shrug his shoulders. He was just as confused as she was.

Mr. Dickelbutton's eyes remained wide open in wonderment. His mouth let out a small gasp. Gripple slowly took the jar out of the hands of Amarie and gazed upon its beauty. He turned it over in his hands delicately, treating it as a priceless work of art. He set the jar back down on the table so that he could study it.

"Mr. Dickelbutton, do you know what this is? Where it came from?" Gruhit asked.

Mr. Dickelbutton broke slightly out of his trance. He gently ran one of his hands over the jar as he pointed to the sky with the other hand. Gruhit looked up at the ceiling, then back at the jar. It suddenly dawned on him.

"Oh my gosh! Mr. Dickelbutton, do you mean that this jar is from…" Gruhit said, astonished as he studied the relic holding the undivided attention of the little folk.

"What is going on, guys? What is this thing?" Amarie said, frustrated that no one was clueing her into the situation.

"The "S," on the jar, Amarie. This is an item sent by a messenger, and not just any messenger! Sentire," Gruhit explained.

Mr. Dickelbutton pointed to writing etched around the edge of the lid.

Amarie began to read outloud. "People are not jars with lids. They should never trap and hide their feelings deep inside. Bravo, young one on being brave enough to face your feelings and to share them with those who are worthy of your trust. I hope this empty jar reminds you. You can find something better to trap inside its magical hold. There's always hope, Sentire."

"What does that mean, Gruhit?" Amarie asked. "You're good at working out all these witty and clever riddles."

"It sounds like this is a gift to you for learning to share your true emotions with other people," Gruhit stated.

Mr. Dickelbutton agreed. "Yes, yes. Lord Sentire is overjoyed with creatures in his order when they learns to be honest about their emotions and use them as a tool for good."

"Yeah, but what's all this about finding something to put in the jar?" Amarie questioned, trying to work out the phrase in her head.

"Beats me," Gruhit said. "It's a jar, so it's not like we could fit much of anything in there. It might not even be for the situation we're in now. I mean for all we know, Sentire wants you to use this jar to collect coins."

Amarie, Gruhit, and Mr. Dickelbutton were a bit startled by Gripple, who had been strangely silent even for him, when he snapped out of a daze of studying the craftsmanship of the jar. His face had the appearance of one who had just gotten an idea. He gingerly set the jar down on the center table and quickly set off to collecting vegetables and various spices from the pantry. The dwarf hustled back and haphazardly threw the food down on the preparation table next to the sink.

Amarie, Gruhit, and Mr. Dickelbutton looked at Gripple, unsure what to think of the dwarf's newfound determination to make a meal. Gripple turned to them and grunted. He pointed at a large stock pot on a shelf under the prep table. Amarie placed it on the stovetop. Mr. Dickelbutton was directed by the dwarf to turn on the burner. Gruhit watched as Mr. Dickelbutton skillfully climbed, jumped, and dashed across surfaces with ease to ignite the stove.

Gruhit was amazed that the stove and water worked in this deteriorating building. Amarie grabbed a few carrots off a shelf that was just out of the dwarf's reach. Gruhit wasn't sure what Gripple was thinking, but set out to work helping the dwarf fill up the pot with water.

Before too long, Gripple was chopping vegetables and seasoning them with various spices. At one point, Amarie attempted to step in to help but quickly received a stern growl.

The two children watched the dwarf, not sure if it was actually getting them out of their current predicament or not. Even though Gripple was less than his height, and Mr. Dickelbutton even smaller, Gruhit had to remind himself that these two creatures were the current safe, caring adults in charge, so he would have to trust them.

Gruhit chuckled at the strangeness of the situation. It was almost like one of those odd riddles that people ask each other and you have to figure out the clever answer. Two Sentrites, a Timorine, and a cooking Instinctual are stuck in a kitchen with a magical jar. How do they get out of the room?

Chapter 34
Esna Returns

Amidst the old, dirty kitchen there wafted a beautiful aroma of vegetable stew. It was the one pleasant effect on Gruhit's senses among this cold and dark place. Gripple had an expression of satisfaction on his face. The food was ready.

"I think I have an idea. Yes, yes," announced Mr. Dickelbutton. "The beast doesn't know I'm here. I will be hiding in Ms. Amarie's hair. When the dark messenger comes in to eat her food, Ms. Amarie will give her the bowl. When we get close enough, I'll jump on her head and grab her hair. I have found one small hole by the floor near the stove that leads outside. I will be running quickly to Mr. Dragon who can get the hair back to the house. I will come back for you. However, I think while I'm pulling the hair, she will be distracted, and Mr. Gripple should try to tackle her so that you can all run out of here."

"What about the dust-wumps outside?" Gruhit said. He could name a dozen reasons why this plan wasn't a good idea.

"Let me have at them," Amarie said, punching a fist into the air. "If I'm being honest about my emotions right now, I'm mad and tired of being bullied around."

Gripple gave a rare smirk. He, himself, was also ready to battle.

At that moment, they could hear Esna's voice speak sternly to the dust-wumps outside. Amarie held out a hand toward Mr. Dickelbutton, who was climbing up to her hair in an instant. As the door opened, Gruhit snatched the Sentrite jar off the table and hid it behind his back.

Esna slammed the door shut with one quick flick of her hand. She peered at her three captives with her usual deranged smile.

"Hehe, it smells like obedience in here," she said. "It's good to know some of my new little pets can be compliant unlike those nasty bigger humans. If the food is to my liking, I will reward you by not letting the dust-wumps torture you. Dwarf! My meal, now!"

Gripple began laddling stew into a bowl. Amarie knew that the opportunity was coming. Fear rose up in her.

"After I have finished, we might take a trip so the other prisoners can see what obedient creatures look like," Esna said. "Did you know how loud your foster parents can scream when in pain?"

"What have you done to them?" Gruhit said in a whimper, unable to look Esna in the eyes.

"Me? Oh dear, little human. They're the ones playing a hiding game," Esna said. "Yes. My poor Empress simply needs the information that was taken from her. I'm just trying to be helpful and a good servant. If the bigger humans punish my Empress by refusing to give up the knowledge stolen from her, then isn't it up to me to help my hurting Empress? Maybe they'll see things differently after they wake up. They seem to pass out when exposed to too much of the anxiety salve you brought with you."

Amarie was handed the bowl of stew by Gripple. The warmth in her hands gave her a bit of strength so she wasn't shaking from fear as she approached Esna. Mr. Dickelbutton patted her head to remind her that she wasn't alone. Amarie held out the bowl. Amarie shivered as the cold fingers of the dark messenger brushed her own. Esna gracefully lifted the bowl to her lips and drank deeply. She appeared to be satisfied by the taste.

"Look at all of you. The picture of conformity. Maybe you will make lovely little pets for me," Esna said. "After all, I'm not sure you will want foster parents who have been driven insane because they choose to play the hiding game." Esna's tone suddenly turned to rage. "I HATE the hiding game!"

"Then let's stop hiding!" Mr. Dickelbutton screamed in his small voice as he launched from Amarie's head. Many things happened quickly.

Mr. Dickelbutton landed directly on top of Esna's head, who was definitely caught off guard for a few seconds. Mr. Dickelbutton took advantage of the time to hold firmly to the longest strand of hair and yank at it with all the strength in his little folk body. The hair came free, the momentum causing Mr. Dickelbutton to fall over. Esna raised a powerful arm to swat at him.

Gripple jumped into action. He ran at full speed toward the dark messenger's legs. This toppled Esna enough that she lost her balance, and they fell to the floor together. Mr. Dickelbutton was just able to recover, taking a mighty leap off of Esna's head. Amarie took a few steps back and caught the little man in her hands as he fell.

Gruhit looked at Gripple, who was now sprawled on the ground beside Esna. The dwarf gave the boy a sly look. Then Gruhit heard SNICK. Looking quickly, he finally spotted one creature, now only three inches tall, fighting off a smaller one to get to its feet.

Then a flood of thoughts came into Gruhit's head. Gripple didn't want help with the stew because it was a dwarf recipe. Gripple had been waiting for Esna to drink it so that he could shrink her. But it was when the dwarf had seen the jar that he had become so intent on cooking.

"... find something better to trap inside its magical hold," Gruhit thought about the inscription on the jar.

It all seemed to make sense now. He saw Esna kick Gripple away as she got her feet. She closed her eyes and began chanting something under her breath.

"She grows again!" Mr. Dickelbutton yelled urgently as Esna slowly grew an inch.

Before he could consider if his idea would work, Gruhit ran at Esna. He slammed the jar on the ground and knocked her into it with the lid. Gruhit quickly fixed it tightly and peered inside. A small, five-inch Esna was beating her arms and fists against the sides, trying to break out of her prison.

"Fear not, Master Gruhit," Mr. Dickelbutton said happily from Amarie's shoulder." She is stuck tight. If this is a Sentrite jar from Lord Sentire himself, there is no way she will magically or physically escape unless you free her. You realize what this means? I have the hair and the dark messenger is caught. We have won!"

Gruhit was definitely relieved like the others, but it didn't seem like a victory quite yet. They still needed to collect their companions and destroy the tacet stone.

Chapter 35
Goodnight Dad

Gruhit woke up from a deep sleep. He felt stiff. Every muscle in his body felt like it had been through an intense workout. He then realized that he wasn't in his bed and sat up startled. Memories of confronting Esna and seeing Fridgita flooded his mind all at once. He looked around in a panic and heaved a sigh of relief when he realized he had fallen asleep on the couch in the Wunder living room. Amarie was sleeping on the other end of the couch. She was snoring with Sparkles nuzzled in her hair.

He looked around. Mal had fallen asleep at the dining room table. Samme was half-awake in an oversized, comfy chair. He looked completely exhausted.

Gruhit replayed the events in his head. A full-sized Gripple had taken the jar from Gruhit and placed it in a pocket of his overalls while Mr. Dickelbutton scouted the hallway outside the kitchen door. They had soon learned that without Esna's dark magic, the dust-wumps had dissolved. The band of people and creatures was able to confidently move through the factory without fearing any harm.

Not too far from the kitchen was a giant furnace. It was connected to a large tub which seemed to hold and melt rubber to be shaped for shoes. The furnace was made of bricks and had two large metal swinging doors on the front. They didn't have to wonder long if this was the place the others were being held captive because they could immediately hear Mrs. Bangs' loud sobs.

The Lusplendidas and Mrs. Bangs were huddled together in a corner comforting each other. The Wunders were in another, completely passed out. Their bodies were unable to handle all the fear and anxiety forced upon them by their captor. When the doors were thrown open, and it was Gripple who stepped through, those who were still conscious cheered for joy. A small celebration broke out when they could see Esna apprehended in the jar.

Mr. Lusplendida had carried the unconscious Samme out of the factory, while Mrs. Bangs and Mrs. Lusplendida stood Mal up and flung her arms over their shoulders. They were all exhausted and weak but moved quickly. They wanted to be as far away from the factory as possible.

They were surprised when they emerged to see a collection of full-sized dwarves waiting outside with Dragon. Evidently, the charmyrll had pleaded for aid from the dwarves and reiterated that their safety and well-being was at stake. About fifty dwarves had come to raid the factory after their night watch had ended.

The dwarves had run up to the humans and took the Wunders from them. Together they were carried back to the house. The rest of the party walked slowly but triumphantly back to the Wunder home.

Once inside Big Blue, Mr. Dickelbutton had gone directly to Mrs. Snickelfritz's residence to deliver the hair. The tacet stone potion would need to be started immediately in an effort to not waste any time. When he returned, he reported the potion would be finished later that morning.

Once Samme and Mal were told all that had transpired, they encouraged the Council to go home and get rest. They all had been so tired that sleep eventually took everyone, except for Samme. Gruhit continued to stare at his foster father who seemed too weak.

"Are you okay, Gruhit?" Samme asked in a whisper.

"I'm fine. I think," Gruhit said as he got a blanket off the couch and brought it to Samme. "Why aren't you sleeping?"

"The truth?" Samme said weakly.

Gruhit nodded his head.

"I'm scared, Gruhit. Esna wanted something from me—some information. I would never cooperate with her, so she covered Mal in anxiety salve. She hoped that torturing her would make me talk. I know that Mal would have been angry if I had. Esna got so upset about that, that she covered me with the salve too. I think she hoped I would get so scared that I would start talking. She understands the orders well enough to know that as a Timorine, that would be a weakness of mine."

"But it's over now. Why can't you sleep if the whole thing with Esna is done?"

"I can't stop thinking about all the horrible images that went through my head. I saw my worst nightmares from my past and things that I'm scared might happen. It's like someone took everything that would be horrific to me and put them on a movie screen in my mind."

"What does Fridgita want to know?"

"I have no idea. My family has been helping the magical world forever, accumulating a vast amount of knowledge over the generations. I have no clue what information Fridgita is trying to get out of me. I need to hit the books in the basement again and figure it out."

Gruhit reached forward to hug his foster from the side for a brief moment. He looked at Samme to see if that was alright.

Samme looked at Gruhit tenderly. "Thank you for the hug," he said. "I don't know if I will be able to sleep tonight, but it makes me feel better to know that there are other people who care for Malda and myself. Now, get some sleep, either on the couch or in your bed. The tacet stone potion won't be ready for hours."

Gruhit began to walk back to the couch. He had no desire to go to his room where he would be alone. As he settled in to sleep, he said, "Goodnight, Samme... er... Dad."

Chapter 36
The Fate Of The Tacet Stone

Gruhit awoke on the couch. He could hear a small commotion. He opened his heavy eyelids to see the sun streaming through the window. He looked around the living room and dining room for the voices he was hearing but saw no one. He sat up and swung his legs stiffly over the side.

Once he was in the dining room, he could see shadows moving around in the kitchen. Mr. and Mrs. Lusplendida, as well as Mrs. Bangs, could be heard talking with Amarie and his foster parents.

"Hey sleepyhead," Mal said to him. "We were just about to wake you up. Mrs. Snickelfritz has the potion finished. She now needs the actual stone and then to have a walluping wallop touch it. Sparkles has phased up to the attic to get a wallop."

"We aren't quite sure if she is going to kidnap one and force it to help, or try to persuade it to assist us. None of us can speak in the tangerella language," Mrs. Bangs said with a chuckle.

"Come on, everyone. What are we waiting for?" Mr. Lusplendida asked. "Gripple went to help Mr. Dickelbutton and Mrs. Snickelfritz transport Mr. Snickelfritz to Chardy's bedroom. They'll be waiting for us to watch the stone be broken."

They followed Jon down the stairs and into Chardy's room. They wanted to begin celebrating, but were holding back until they knew their friends were safe. They all felt like they were at a surprise party about to yell, "Surprise!"

Kieffer was now lying at the foot of Chardy's bed. Both were still in their magical sleep. Chardy's skin had become paler and felt even colder than before. Kieffer's tail was already fizzled out. His right hind leg was barely visible. Over on a shelf built into one of the walls lay a barely visible little man. Mrs. Snickelfritz knelt next to her husband's vanishing body and held his hand. She refused to take her eyes off of him. She feared he might fizzle out at any moment and would never be seen again. Mr. Dickelbutton and a shrunken Gripple stood beside the couple on the shelf.

Samme was the last one in the room, standing just inside the doorway. Gruhit saw his foster dad rummage through his overcoat pockets and pull out the tacet stone.

As if she had been waiting for the tacet stone to be produced, Sparkles zoomed through the ceiling of the bedroom holding the tentacle of a small little creature that looked just like a jolly floating jellyfish. It was no bigger than Gruhit's thumb and looked very soft. The head of this creature was taken up by two large eyes that appeared to be soaking in its surroundings constantly. Underneath its jelly-fish-like body were so many thin little pink tentacles. They each moved about as if swimming through water.

Amarie playfully poked Gruhit in the ribs with her elbow. "They both look happy. I guess Sparkles didn't kidnap it," she whispered.

"Mrs. Snickelfritz, dear, I think we are ready for the tacet stone potion," Mr. Wunder announced.

"Yes, yes, I have it in my bag right here," said the little woman, her voice shaking from all the anticipation and worry.

She moved her hands to a brown sack. She reached in and pulled out a glass container and heaved it over to Gripple.

Gruhit could see a glowing purple liquid that appeared peaceful. He couldn't explain it, but this liquid made him feel safe. Mrs. Bangs gently took the potion from the dwarf and transferred it to Samme. In one hand, Samme held one item that had the power to take life, and in the other, the potential to return it.

"Do I simply pour the potion onto the stone?" Samme asked.

"No, no, I think it's better if you just dunk the stone into the vat, and we will wait for the potion to activate," Mrs. Snickelfritz replied. "Once it has been activated, our wallop friend needs to touch the stone like he would if he was eating a dream. Yum, yum."

"Sparkles, can you talk to walluping wallops? Can you let our friend here know what he needs to do? We don't have any room for error here," Samme said to the tangerella.

Sparkles nodded with a determined expression. She flew near the floating wallop and stared intently at it. The wallops' eyes seemed to widen more. Sparkles and the creature confronted each other in an intense staring match for several seconds. Both creatures' eyes darted here and there. After a bit, their stare broke, and Sparkles turned to face the group with a thumbs up.

"Alright. My dear, loved friends, we hold on to hope!" Samme exclaimed as he dropped the stone into the potion.

For a few seconds nothing happened. Then Gruhit could see the glowing purple liquid start to swirl around the stone. The glowing grew brighter as the liquid encircled the stone and forced its way through the stone's rocky exterior. Before too long, the purple liquid had permeated the entirety of the stone, turning the stone into a bright blue color. Gruhit wasn't sure if it was turning to ice or if it was the brilliance of the glow. Everyone looked at the stone as the effects slowed and then stopped. They all beheld a glowing blue stone in the glass container.

"Quickly now. Yes, yes, YES! The stone is activated," Mrs. Snickelfritz said urgently.

The walluping wallop, sensing the tension in the room, floated directly for the jar. As it neared the stone it began going into a trance, lifting one of its longest tentacles toward the edge of the container. Every living being in the room held their breath. They feared the wallop was moving too slow and wouldn't touch the stone while it was still activated, yet they were filled with hope.

The wallop's eyes grew very large. Its pupils began to whirl clockwise faster and faster. Soon the eyes appeared to be flickering lights. The tentacle of the small, fragile creature found its way to the surface of the stone and touched it. The eyes of the wallop immediately glowed pink. The creature seemed to be in mild pain. The tentacle slightly swelled up like an inflating balloon. Suddenly, it shot a sparkling substance out onto the stone.

The substance coated the stone and reacted to it like acid. Smoke streamed from the container as the stone's glow dimmed, then turned from blue to grey to black. It appeared like nothing more significant than a piece of charcoal.

Esna's tacet stone was destroyed.

Chapter 37
The Awakenings

Everyone was transfixed. As the seconds ticked by, the stone became even more brittle and broke apart into dust which settled at the bottom of the container.

"Is it supposed to do something?"

"Well, none of us have done this before, so I'm unsure if we will see anything…" Samme stopped talking immediately as he realized who he was talking to.

"Chardy!" Amarie and Gruhit said gleefully as they rushed to their brother's side.

Malda let out a gasp of happiness.

"Yes!" Mrs. Bangs cried loudly and unexpectedly. She couldn't help it. She simply was feeling more joyous feelings than she could hold inside her body.

"Would you all please keep the noise to a minimum?" a voice said at the foot of the bed. "Oh, my. Sir? I think I must be getting old. All of my muscles feel stiff and sore. How long was I asleep?"

Samme chuckled a bit as he looked upon Chardy and Kieffer with tears welling up in his eyes. "You still look like a young cub to me, dear friend. It's good to have you both among the living again."

Mr. and Mrs. Lusplendida hugged each other in celebration. Sparkles flew around in circles. The whole room quickly filled with cheers, high fives, and dancing. This was a welcome feeling after all the heaviness they had felt.

The celebration stopped abruptly as there was a loud *SNICK,* followed by the loudest grunt that anyone had ever heard a full grown Gripple exert. All looked in the dwarf's direction as he pointed toward the shelf.

Mrs. Snickelfritz was holding her husband's hand again. Mr. Dickelbutton put his arm around the woman to comfort her. The little woman's cry turned into sobs as her husband continued to lay motionless.

Chapter 38
Gruhit Chooses Hope

Mrs. Bangs and Amarie were the first to become attune with the emotions of the little folk woman on the shelf. They both began to tear up and cry themselves. As Mrs. Bangs put her arms around Amarie for support, the rest of the room began to feel somber and sad.

Samme slipped his hand into one of the bigger pockets of his overcoat and pulled out the Sentrite jar with the imprisoned Esna. He put the jar directly in front of his face and shot a glare at the creature. Esna was sitting cross-legged and looked up at Mr. Wunder. She wore a deranged smile as she realized that not everything was going well for the community.

"You're a part of this, fiend! Put an end to it! You know how to stop our friend from fizzling out! Stop it! Stop it!" Samme yelled at the dark messenger in an increasing volume and began to shake the jar a bit harshly.

Malda reached for her husband's shaking arm and steadied it. She removed the jar from his hands as she looked into his eyes.

Gruhit looked from one person to another and then at the various creatures. Everyone's face darkened and began to relinquish hope. Even Samme was deeply saddened. The whole room was hurt and grieving. No one knew what to do or what to say.

In his head, Gruhit quickly reviewed everything he had learned about the magical world. He was desperate to find a solution. Then it dawned on him. He was constantly questioning the way things worked in the magical realm and refused to trust. Here he was a human child who was among many fantastical creatures, all created by a being who watched over them. A messenger knew they were in trouble in the factory and helped them.

"I choose hope," Gruhit said in a determined voice. "I choose to believe that Victus can still help."

"That's noble Gruhit, but that's not exactly how it works," Malda said affectionately.

"No! I have hope," Gruhit said. "I don't know if I've ever hoped for something more in my life except for getting to go back home with Momma. I choose to hope. Victus will change this."

Samme knelt next to Gruhit. "Gruhit, it doesn't quite work that way," he said softly. "We are not like Victus. We don't know why this is happening. We can't just hope for what we want because what we want might not be the best outcome overall. We hope that the good of Victus will come through, even though we might not understand it all, even though it might look like evil has won. Sometimes a tacet stone is created. Sometimes foster children aren't allowed to go back home. Sometimes it is a friend's time to pass. Sometimes hope seemingly doesn't save the day."

"And yet, sometimes, it does," said a strong voice from behind Samme.

All noises ceased to exist. Every eye searched behind Samme for the origin of the voice. They could only see a blurry apparition. To Gruhit, it would be hard to explain to someone without them having seen it for themselves. It was almost like there was something there, maybe a person, but they were out of focus. The presence was partially here in this world and partially present somewhere else. The longer Gruhit starred, the more in focus it became. There was a brilliant blue light that outlined the entirety of the focusing shape.

"It's… it's a man, I think," Mr. Dickelbutton said.

"A messenger, actually," said the strong voice from the middle of the vision.

The apparition now became clear. It was as if from out of another dimension, there stood a messenger. He was of average height compared to an adult human man and had a fit physique which enhanced the appearance that this was a powerful being. While Ira reminded Gruhit of an old style aviator from his history books, this messenger reminded him of a tinkerer but dressed in an old-fashioned manner. His brown slacks were held up by navy suspenders. His belt was outfitted with all sorts of pockets and loops which held many odd shaped tools and gizmos. His off-white button-up shirt appeared to have seen many adventures as there were slight singe marks in a couple of spots and a few patches here and there.

The messenger's angular face surveyed the group in the bedroom. His blue eyes seemed to see more than what was physically in the room. Although this messenger felt safe as well, Gruhit was very nervous and couldn't look him in the face. He eyed the metal goggles on top of the messenger's head that also housed various lenses and magnification apparatuses. The goggles lay among short dark brown hair, combed perfectly to the right.

The messenger took a few steps into the room toward Gruhit. Everyone made way for the being as the messenger's presence commanded respect.

Gruhit now could see the strong wings that matched the fit appearance of the creature. This organic attribute was out of character by comparison of the mechanical gadgets and tools which were about the messenger's clothing.

"Gruhit, from the Order of Timorines, I have been sent here because you called," the messenger's voice stated. "I am Timor. It is good to make your acquaintance in person."

Everyone remained in utter disbelief. No one spoke a word.

Chapter 39
A Gigantic Decision

"I see that you have already worked out how to destroy the tacet stone. We were all wondering how that would play out," Timor announced.

"Excuse me! Did you say, 'We?' Who else is watching us?" Mrs. Lusplendida asked in a reverent voice.

"The other messengers of course. Don't be mistaken. There are many that have rebelled and would like to see the universe and humans destroyed," Timor explained. "Yet many are untouched by darkness and dearly love to watch this world."

"But, sir, if you were watching us, why didn't all of you help us when we were in trouble?" Amarie asked.

"I'm a messenger, young one," Timor said. "I have not been created to interfere with the events and actions of this world. However, it doesn't mean I am not concerned, or that I don't care about what happens. We are always able to see that the Creator has everything under control. I think it must be difficult for you to trust and hold onto hope when you are down here in this world. I can see so much fear when I watch. That raw fear can cause people to lose hope and do things, such as unintentionally hurt a loved one." Timor ended the last of this sentence by looking from Gruhit to Chardy.

Chardy fidgeted on the bed as the gaze of Timor seemed to look deep within his soul.

"I'm sorry. I didn't know that the stone would hurt Kieffer or the golem," Chardy said. "I just… I just wanted to be away from all of this, you know. I wanted to be away from other people telling me what to do. I have a mom. Everybody thinks they know what's best for me and are always forcing me to do stuff or not do stuff. Well, if they know everything, then why aren't we back home with our mom? Why have my siblings and I been moved around to so many homes? It's like no one can figure us out but my mom. And my mom stopped visiting us. I'm sorry I've caused so much trouble. I'm not trying to be a bad person, and I definitely didn't try to hurt my friend here."

Timor continued to study Chardy. This made the boy increasingly uncomfortable and nervous. Gruhit once again got the feeling that Timor could see more than what was physically before him. The messenger's mouth curved slightly into a smile.

"Thank you for that insight and apology, Chardy of the Instinctuals," Timor said in a steady voice. "It sounds like you have stumbled upon the lesson. One should discuss their emotions and hurts with safe people. Otherwise, those emotions will certainly overtake you and cause you to act in blind, unhelpful ways. I hear your pain. Alas, no one can change the events which have caused you pain. However, I think you will do well to learn from your brother, to hope and trust. The Wunder community is known among the messengers as good and trustworthy people. Learn from them and share your anger and your concerns before you are overtaken again. Next time, you might not have someone to destroy a tacet stone."

"Young Master, I accept your apology, and I don't blame you for what has happened," Kieffer said. He looked at Esna in the jar. "The dark messenger is a trickster and could make even the most dedicated person of Victus stumble. I vow today in this small group of witnesses that just as my tail is long that I… Ah! My tail!"

It was at this moment that Gruhit saw it. Kieffer's tail was gone. It had disappeared during the fizzling process and had not returned. Kieffer looked extremely hurt at his loss. He weakly got to his feet to pounce on the jar when he remembered he was in the presence of a great being.

"I… I beg your pardon, sir. I didn't mean to get rustled in front of you," Kieffer said respectfully while slightly bowing his head. "I don't suppose that a being such as you would be able to uh… remedy this situation."

"I hear your plea, dear one. There is nothing I can do, but there is something that Gruhit of the Timorines can do," Timor stated plainly.

Gruhit became nervous again. "Me? What can I do? I'm just a human boy."

"Because of your great demonstration of trust and hope, I have been sent here to grant one request to you," Timor said.

"A request? Like a wish? You mean, I can ask for Kieffer's tail to grow back?" Gruhit said, somewhat excited.

"You may," Timor stated while looking at the little folks. "You could also request to restore the little folk gentleman."

Timor turned his head and looked down at Gruhit and Amarie. His face became serious as he spoke. "You could also request to return home with your mother and live your life the way things had been before."

Amarie and Chardy both gasped. It was everything all three of them had ever wanted, to go back home. His siblings stared at Gruhit, not daring to speak, but willing their stares to convey their hope.

The weight of the decision quickly came upon Gruhit. Timor stared at him as though he were expecting an answer. Gruhit looked around the room from his guardling friend, to his siblings' longing eyes, and to Mrs. Snickelfritz, who was looking at her husband.

What should he do? This was surely too big a decision for a boy of his age. Yet here he was, having to make it. Finally, he reasoned out a thought and looked around the room. He knew one party would be overjoyed, while the others would be disappointed.

Gruhit looked up at Timor and readied himself to speak.

Chapter 40
The Tuning Fork Device

"Before you speak, Master Gruhit, I will make this process easier for you," Kieffer interjected. "I insist that your special request not be wasted on my situation. I might not have my tail, but I have my life. For this I am grateful and will consider myself to be blessed. I refuse to be counted among your choices."

Gruhit smiled at his friend. He nodded his head toward him as a way of saying, "Thank you."

"What is your choice then, little one?" Timor asked.

"I just want everyone to understand that I can still remember living with Momma," Gruhit stated, beginning to tear up. "She didn't have much time for us because she was always working. Yeah, we had to take care of ourselves a lot. No one was there to protect us except for each other. But Momma worked hard for us. I remember the loving way she came into our bedroom in the middle of the night. I remember her warm hugs that made me feel like all the evil in the world would melt away. I remember how she used to tell me she loved me and thought I was such a good boy. It made me feel like I was special and could do anything. I miss that… a lot. I want that back."

"However, there were still problems," he went on. "If we go back to the way things were, how long will it be until they take us away again? What if we get placed with bad fosters again? Chardy, Amarie, the Wunders love us… they love Momma. I think we have to have hope that things will get better. That might not mean we will go back home with Momma, but it might." Gruhit looked over at Mr. Snickelfritz's faint body. "I want you to restore Mr. Snickelfritz, please. There is no hope for him if he is not restored."

Timor smiled down at the young boy. "You are indeed a clever young man, Gruhit of the Timorines. Because of the hope you have learned to exhibit, I have been granted the power to give you this request."

Timor placed his goggles over his eyes and took out a glowing gadget. It resembled a tuning fork. He sharply tapped the gadget against the closest wall, and it came to life with a blue glow. This glow intensified quickly and encompassed the messenger. Timor took a wider stance with his strong legs as he kept both hands clasped on the violently vibrating gadget. They could feel a slight warmth from the ever increasing light. After a minute, Timor blurred out of their sight once more; he again seemed to be partially there in the room and partially somewhere else.

Malda gave a small gasp as she noticed the jar in her hands was also glowing blue now and beginning to fade away. Without warning, blurred shapes that appeared to be the great wings of the messenger furled outward. Mrs. Bangs and the Lusplendidas dodged out of the way and the Sentrite jar fully transformed into blue light before joining the glow surrounding Timor. The messenger lunged forward toward the shelf where the little folks stood and yelled, "For Victus!"

With that, he was gone. The strange blue light seemed to arc from the spot Timor was standing into a narrow line going straight toward Mr. Snickelfritz's heart. For a moment, the little folk's eyes shot open wide, and he arched his back as though in extreme pain. The light completely entered the little folk and resonated around his body for a few seconds before Mr. Snickelfritz fell back to the shelf with a small thud.

Then it was over. There was no blue light, no messenger, and only the original members of the company.

Everyone watched in anticipation for something to happen. Gruhit noticed the first thing was the feet. They were easier to see; they were less transparent. Then the effect began to go through the rest of the little folk's body so that everyone could more clearly see their dear friend. Before long, Mr. Snickelfritz's chest began to move up and down in a less labored way. He was beginning to breathe normally again. Finally, his eyes began to flutter open.

Mr. Snickelfritz began to slowly look around the room. "Mrs. Snickelfritz?" he asked. "Why is everyone staring at me? Who are these children? What is going on?"

Mrs. Snickelfritz smiled and hugged her husband deeply. Everyone in the room erupted into cheers and laughter. Amarie and Gripple (believe it or not) danced a little jig. Everything finally seemed to be well enough for celebration. Gruhit knew he had made the right decision.

Chapter 41
A Beautifully Cooked Turkey

Gruhit knelt backwards on the couch in the living room, staring out the window behind it. He saw many things which brought emotions to his mind.

He looked over to the left. The outdoor steps to the front door reminded him of the nervousness he had felt when he first came to live with the Wunders. Back then, it was odd to think he would ever feel comfortable here. Life had seemed dismal and bleak at that time. While it wasn't perfect now, he had learned to see through the bleakness to things that could be.

He looked at the factory across the street. It seemed lifeless and cold now. When Esna had occupied it, there was evil and darkness. Now it was just a building, rotting and decaying. Chardy wasn't scared of the factory but didn't want to look at it. The building brought up memories he wasn't proud of.

Gruhit felt the couch cushions sink a bit next to him.

"Are you alright, Master Gruhit?" Kieffer asked.

Gruhit turned sideways so he could face the guardling while still seeing out the window. It hadn't taken much time for Kieffer to recover from the ordeal. He was still learning to keep his balance and jump without the aid of his tail. Kieffer never complained or blamed Chardy. Instead, he seemed to wear the experience as a badge of honor.

"I'm good. I was just doing some thinking," Gruhit replied. "Kieffer, have you heard from the little folk?"

"They seem to be doing well. All of them have overcome so much. I don't think it's a surprise they are all enjoying Christmas Day at home by themselves," Kieffer explained.

"It's weird, isn't it?" Gruhit asked.

"What's that, Master Gruhit?" Kieffer wondered.

"They seem like such an important part of our community, yet I'd barely gotten to know them until the end of our adventure. I haven't even formally met the kids. What were their names? Tim and Lisa?"

"Lucy and Tad Schwartz," Kieffer responded with a small chuckle. "Now that you mention it, it does seem strange in a way. I imagine if our lives were merely a story, we would be wondering why the author didn't introduce us to them more often."

Gruhit gave a smile back at Kieffer.

"However, Master Gruhit, I have to also guess that there will be plenty of time to learn more about our friends in future adventures."

"Future adventures?" Samme asked, surprised, as he joined them on the couch. "Are you two plotting something? We just finished this adventure. Give us a little time to recover. It's Christmas Day after all."

Gruhit took his sketchbook out of his cargo pocket and flipped through the pages. "But we need a new adventure soon," he said. "I have so many more pages to fill, and I really want to be able to discover a new creature. How am I gonna do that if we aren't exploring?"

"You sound more like an Instinctual than a Timorine. Let's see that sketchbook,"

Samme said. "Look at all of these! They're very good, Gruhit. You can see how your sketches are improving as you keep practicing."

"I started writing about things I notice about the creatures too," Gruhit commented.

Suddenly, all three heard a commotion. Malda emerged from the kitchen with a large platter holding a beautifully cooked turkey. Her hair was done up in a cone which resembled a Christmas Tree. Blinking lights were woven throughout.

"All Wunders, let's get to the dining room! The food is ready!" Malda called out cheerfully. "Our guests should be here any minute."

Chapter 42
Tomorrow Is a New Day...

Gruhit jumped off of the couch and ran over to the dining room table. He admired the turkey along with the plethora of vegetables and other holiday goodies that were spread over it. Cups were filled with dwarf-made apple cider. Even though the little folk community were not with them, they had found time to decorate the table with intricate paper clippings of snowflakes, snowmen, and Christmas Trees.

Chardy walked into the dining room with Amarie bouncing along behind him. Everyone seemed so happy today. As Gruhit admired the whole scene, the door-bell interrupted his thoughts. Everyone looked at each other with anticipation, slightly guarding themselves against disappointment.

Samme walked to the front door and could be heard talking to a woman. All the residents in the house could hear the front door close. Footsteps approached the doorway of the living room.

"Candace!" Amarie squealed as she ran to greet the smiling caseworker. "Hello, Amarie. Merry Christmas!"

"I didn't know you were coming today," Gruhit said, a bit confused.

"I hope that's okay. We wouldn't have been able to do this get-together unless I was here to supervise," Candace said. "You three really have no idea how great this is. I didn't mind giving up my Christmas lunch plans at all. Most foster parents wouldn't allow this, and usually the foster agency wouldn't either."

Gruhit was now completely focused on the next person coming through the door.

"Momma!" Gruhit screamed as he ran to her.

Gruhit hugged her deeply. He was soon joined by Amarie and Chardy. Gruhit had learned to appreciate these moments. While the world was a great place, you never knew when a dark messenger, or Judy Credulent, would come from out of nowhere.

"We missed you so much, Momma," Amarie said, continuing to hug her mother.

"I missed you too," she said. "I have to apologize to all of you. I never should've missed that visit. Candace told me what that did to y'all. I'm so sorry, my dears. Everything was just getting so difficult and I just… well… I lost hope."

"I understand, Momma. We all lose hope sometimes and make mistakes," Chardy said lovingly.

"We'll all help each other stay hopeful from now on," Gruhit said, thinking that he never wanted to stop hugging her.

"Well, don't y'all sound so grown up," their mom said. "Y'all must be learning a lot from the Wunders."

"They're quick learners," Samme said. "But I think their mother instilled some great qualities in them that have helped them learn and grow so well."

"We are honored to have you here in our home for Christmas," Malda said. "Would you please do us the honor of sitting at the head of the table?"

Gruhit watched his momma take the seat usually reserved for Samme or Malda. Everyone else sat down. Even Kieffer sat in a chair. Malda quickly explained that the pet cat thought he was human and always ate meals with them. Gruhit chuckled under his breath as he saw Candace make a strange face at Kieffer, while

Kieffer looked slightly disgusted at being called a mere house cat.

As Gruhit looked around, he saw so many faces who cared about him. His life wasn't perfect by a long shot. He would soon have to go back to school and face the bullies there. Candace still had no idea if Momma was going to be able to have all three kids move back in with her anytime soon. Gruhit had no idea if he would be spending the summer with the Wunders or with his momma. He didn't know if he would be asked to move to a new foster home next week or stay with the Wunders. There was so much uncertainty. There was so much to be upset and anxious about.

But Gruhit had learned to hope. He had learned to rely on others and himself. If they stayed here, he would be glad to live with two of the most caring people he had ever met. If he could go with Momma, he would be grateful to be back with her.

Right now, though, he would choose to be thankful to be eating a good meal surrounded by his momma and the Wunders. Tomorrow was going to be a new day full of new adventures and most importantly… new hopes.